Beneath an Irish Sky

Beneath an Irish Sky

Isabella Connor

Published 2013 by Choc Lit Limited
Penrose House, Crawley Drive, Camberley, Surrey GU15 2AB, UK
www.choclitpublishing.com

ISBN: 978-1-78189-004-2

Printed and bound by CPI Group (UK) Ltd, Croydon, CR0 4YY

To Joe McFadden,
who started it all …

Acknowledgements

We jointly thank …

Di Baker for her never-ending bubbly enthusiasm, and for introducing us to Katie Fforde; **Katie Fforde** for introducing us to the RNA; **Richie Butler** – Traveller; **Joseph Cahill** – Pavee Point Information Service; **Claudia** – for her patient and efficient beta-reading and valued advice since Day One; **Sarah Holland** and **Sarah Lindsay** – for pointing us in the right direction; **Brigid Killen** for sharing her Cheshire knowledge; **Sue O'Reilly** for sharing her Irish knowledge; the **RNA readers** on the **RNA New Writers' Scheme** for the advice given in their constructive critiques; the **Choc Lit Tasting panel** who made it all possible; our fellow Choc Lit authors and everyone at **Choc Lit**; writers **Christina Courtenay, Linn Halton** and **Lesley Pearse** for their support and encouragement, and last, but by no means least, the wonderful, amazingly brave, **Jen Fishler**.

Valerie Olteanu thanks …

Gary McKeone, Jane O'Rourke, and **Carol Topalian** – for their support and friendship; all at the **Highgate Starbucks** in Burnaby for providing me with a home from home in which to write; **Liv,** for taking a leap of faith and choosing me as her writing partner; my mother, for teaching me the meaning of unconditional love and always believing in me; and my co-conspirators **Codin, Rafael** and **Darius** – for being the greatest support network a writer could have.

Liv Thomas thanks ...

Pat Starkey, for always believing in me; **my family** for putting up with me (most of the time), especially my mum, **Betty** from whom I inherited my passion for reading. And thanks **Val** for having exactly the same feelings as myself about this novel and the characters – that one shared brain. And last, but not least, the girls at **Cutting Edge,** without whom, I wouldn't venture outside the house!

Chapter One

'I'm here to identify the body of Annie Kiernan.' It was so long since Jack had spoken her name, the words almost stuck in his throat.

'And you are?'

The Guard was chewing a mouthful of sandwich. Jack caught the faint stink of onion through the gap in the security glass and his stomach turned. He shoved his passport into the tray and watched the police officer leaf through it.

'Are you next of kin?'

'Husband,' Jack replied, for want of a better word.

'Oh – sorry for your loss. Fill out this form, please.'

A paper and pen were pushed into the tray. The pen didn't work, so Jack took the Montblanc from his inside pocket. He pressed the words deep into the paper, a habit from years of signing contracts in triplicate, and passed back the completed paperwork. 'Where do I find the morgue?'

The man shook his head. 'It's in another building – only next door, but there needs to be a Guard with you to record the ID.'

Bloody bureaucracy. Jack would prefer to be alone when he saw Annie. He might do anything. Cry. Even slap her face. Better to have no witnesses to such loss of control.

'You came over from England?' the Guard asked.

'Yes.'

'Your wife lived in Ireland, though?'

'We were separated.'

Was that a flicker of interest? Or pity? That was worse. No one pitied Jack Stewart, least of all some desk sergeant in a crummy Dublin police station. He glanced at his Rolex. 'I'm booked on a return flight at two.'

'Right. Take a seat. Someone will be with you shortly.'

Jack wandered over to the decrepit waiting area with its rows of green plastic seats, where he joined the slouched bodies of the weary and the troubled.

'Shortly' was nearly thirty minutes.

'Jack Stewart?' A policeman scanned the waiting area.

'Yes.'

'I'm Sergeant Flynn.'

A handshake, as if Jack mattered. Christ, when did he become so cynical? But he knew the answer to that one. It was when she left him.

'Sorry for your loss.'

That platitude again. As if these people had any idea what he and Annie had shared, had lost. Of what he'd suffered because of her.

'If you'll come with me. We'll try to make it as quick as possible.'

Quick. Like her death. Alive one minute, driving her car, thinking of work or shopping or whatever she did these days, and then … gone. Wiped from the roll of the living. It was as much as he knew. As much as the police in Manchester knew. When they'd shown up in his office yesterday, telling him of an accident, he'd panicked and thought of his son, Matt, in Amsterdam on a stag night. That policewoman, oozing compassion, didn't know Jack had dropped down in his chair with relief, not grief. He'd refused to go to Dublin at first – Annie was firmly in the past – but then the police had pointed out he was still officially her next of kin. It wasn't until later the shock of having her reintroduced into his life hit him.

Flynn led Jack out of the police station and into the morgue next door. They were directed to a viewing room at the end of a corridor, but before they entered, Flynn said, 'The desk sergeant told me you and Mrs Stewart were separated. When did you last see her?'

Sod this. Weren't things bad enough without Jack having to announce his failure as a husband to everyone he met? 'I last saw her over twenty years ago,' he said, quietly enough, yet the words seemed to echo down the long empty corridor.

Flynn raised an eyebrow. 'So there's a chance you might not recognise her?'

Jack thought about that. Annie would have changed. No longer the young girl he'd married. Forty now. Maybe a few wrinkles, some grey hair. That could be a blessing. Like looking at a stranger. 'I'll know her,' he said, with more certainty than he felt. 'Let's get it over with.'

The fluorescent strip lighting in the viewing room was harsh, its relentless blue-white glare attacking every corner. A clock registered almost midday. The body lay in the centre of the room, covered with a sheet. The hairs on the back of Jack's neck prickled, although he'd seen a dead body before. Just once. An asthma attack had taken his first wife when she was only twenty-four. Jack had cradled Caroline in his arms as if he could will some of his own warmth back into her. His tears had soaked her face and hair, the grief like a knife in his gut. And now his second wife had left him behind, although she'd actually discarded him years before.

'Ready?' asked Flynn.

Jack nodded. He was as ready as he'd ever be. The sheet was folded back, and he was looking at a heart-shaped face, wounds prominent on skin the colour of chalk. Dark silky hair, maybe the only part of her alive now. He'd read once about people opening a coffin and finding the corpse's hair still growing. Annie would be in a coffin soon. In the dark earth. God, he wanted to throw up.

Flynn was at his elbow. 'Is it …?'

Jack swallowed hard, attempting to make his voice normal. 'It's her.'

'I'll give you a moment.'

The door closed and Jack was alone with Annie. At least, Annie's shell. He didn't touch her. She'd feel like ice, not warm the way he remembered her. Was she watching him? Her spirit floating around, looking down, wondering why he was there? No chance now to find out why she'd left him. The dead don't talk.

'Why?' His voice surprised him. Thinking out loud. 'Why, Annie?'

The lights hummed, the second hand on the clock moved. Nothing else. No miraculous revelation, no gift of closure. Nothing for him here. Jack pulled the sheet back over the face still as familiar to him as his own, and walked away.

In the next room, Flynn had organised tea. Jack gulped it down, feeling the hot, sweet liquid revive him a bit. Almost done now, then back to Baronsmere and normality.

'Just sign here. It says you've formally identified the body.'

Jack scribbled his name, not even bothering to read the form.

'Do you need the name of an undertaker?' Flynn asked.

'Sorry?'

'I have a list of local undertakers.'

'Why would I need that?'

'Well … for the funeral. We're releasing the body to you.'

'I can't take care of that! I only came here to identify her. I've got to get back to Manchester.'

'The body can't stay here, Mr Stewart.' Flynn spoke slowly, as if explaining something to a child.

'But what am I supposed to do with her?'

'The undertakers can move her to a funeral home.

There's one – McBride's – near the hospital, which would be practical. They'll help you arrange the burial.'

Arrangements. Paperwork. Phone calls. Red tape. This was ridiculous. And why was a location near the hospital 'practical'?

'She has other family,' Jack protested. 'What about them?' Was he the only relative here? That seemed more than a bit strange given Travellers' strong family connections.

Flynn consulted his paperwork but shook his head. 'The car was registered to Joseph Kiernan, but no one seems to know where he is. He and his brother work away a lot, apparently.'

Useless bastards her brothers were, anyway. No-hopers, who never forgave Annie for marrying an outsider. 'And there's no one else?' Jack asked, not really wanting the answer. Even now, he preferred not to think about Annie in another relationship.

'Her father's dead, according to neighbours. Your son might be able to tell you where other relatives are.'

How the hell would Matt know that? Just how incompetent were these people? 'What are you talking about? My son hasn't seen Annie since he was four.'

Flynn flicked back through his paperwork. 'Your son, Luke, was in the car with your wife when the accident happened. He's in St Aidan's Hospital.'

Jack shouldn't have been surprised, but it still rankled that Annie had found happiness with someone else – started a family, even used the name they'd planned for their own son. His hand curled into a fist in his lap. 'No one told me she had a son,' he said, his voice hard. 'So why haven't you contacted the father, her ... partner?' The Traveller. The one she'd shacked up with after leaving him and returning to her own people. 'He should be taking care of all this.'

'There is no partner, as far as we're aware,' Flynn told

him. 'The birth certificate identifies her son as Luke Stewart, although he appears to be using the name Kiernan now, and you're named as his father. I'm sorry, I thought the Manchester police explained this to you.'

'How old is he?' Jack asked.

'Twenty.'

The walls of the room seemed to close in. Not enough air. Jack closed his eyes. A son he never knew about! Not possible. Why would Annie do that? It was monstrous. Cruel. If she weren't already dead, he'd probably have killed her.

'You okay?' Flynn poured more tea, but Jack couldn't drink it.

'He's not my son.'

'But the birth certificate …'

'It's not true.'

Flynn nodded. 'Well, perhaps you should still go and see him. He might be able to tell you who to contact to take charge of the funeral. We'll have to interview him about the accident at some point, but he's been in Intensive Care.' He handed Jack a sheet of paper. 'Here's the list of undertakers. They'll know what to do.'

That was good, because Jack didn't. All he could think about was what he'd just been told. A twenty-year-old son he'd known nothing about …

'Will you be okay? Do you want me to drive you anywhere?'

That look of pity again. Jack felt a flash of anger. He was no helpless victim. He was New Business Director at Stewart Enterprises. A successful man, renowned for coping with anything. He'd get through this. Somehow. 'I'll find my own way – thanks.'

The taxi dropped Jack at the entrance to St Aidan's Hospital. He stood next to a few furtive smokers. Should he go inside or just walk away? He could pay some local undertaker a hefty sum to take care of everything. What else was money for if not to ease the rough patches in your life?

Someone thrust an open pack of cigarettes in front of him. He looked down at an elderly woman, bent under the weight of her widow's hump. 'No ... thanks.'

'Might take the edge off, son.'

So he looked like he felt. Gutted.

The old lady patted his arm. 'God'll take care of everything, y'know.'

'You don't happen to have his number, do you?'

The woman tutted and moved away. He was in one of the most Catholic countries in Europe. Insult God and it could be taken personally. Jack didn't believe in heavenly help or miracles, though. He was on his own. So he might as well talk to this young man who was supposed to be his son. Perhaps at last he was going to get answers.

'Good afternoon, Mr Kiernan.'

'My surname is Stewart. My wife and I were separated.' How many times would Jack have to repeat this?

The consultant, O'Meara, looked uncomfortable and glanced down at his notes. Probably preferred broken bodies to broken families. 'I'm sorry – my mistake. Luke's driving licence says Kiernan.'

'And his birth certificate says Stewart. Please just tell me about – my son.' This wasn't the place to voice doubts about Luke being his. The staff might get iffy if he wasn't a relative, and then he wouldn't be able to ask the kid any questions.

'Luke suffered concussion, bruised ribs and some torn knee ligaments.'

'But he's okay, yes?' That was all he needed to know. Why couldn't doctors just cut to the chase?

'Mr Stewart, Luke arrested at the scene. Luckily, a driver

7

who came to help was familiar with CPR – resuscitation. Luke still needs to be monitored in case of complications, but he's stable. We moved him from Intensive Care this morning.'

'Does he know? About his mother?'

To Jack's dismay, the doctor shook his head. 'He's been on morphine so in and out of awareness. Not a good time to talk to him.'

Great. Jack would have to book into a hotel. This thing could take days.

'His leg will take a few weeks to heal, same with his ribs. He'll need crutches for a while.'

Jack wasn't going to be hanging around for a few weeks. Hopefully the Kiernans would show up soon and take over. 'When can I see him?'

'A nurse can take you now.'

Jack stood up.

'One more thing, Mr Stewart ... Luke has bruises on his face and body that weren't caused by the crash. The colouring suggests he got them some days earlier.'

Why was Jack being told this? Were they afraid he'd sue them for malpractice?

'Do you know anything about those bruises?'

God, O'Meara thought he'd done it. Beaten the kid up. Obviously had him pegged as a bad father. 'I haven't been near Luke in years,' he said. The truth, although twisted.

'Well, I'd guess some time recently he's been badly beaten. He'll need peace and quiet – and support – to heal. The past couple of weeks have obviously been very traumatic for him.'

So Luke was the kind of person who got into fights. Not surprising, really, with uncles like Joe and Liam Kiernan. Some start in life. Things would have been very different if Luke had grown up in Baronsmere. *But he's not my son.* It disturbed Jack that he'd forgotten this. He didn't want to get emotionally involved.

Thankfully, Luke was in a single room. No nosy fellow patients or visitors to worry about. Jack watched from the doorway as the nurse checked the IV.

'Why don't you sit with him for a while?' she suggested. 'I'll fix you a cup of tea.'

'Thanks.'

Jack slumped down into a chair, hoping the boy wasn't going to wake up just yet because he didn't have a clue what to say. The hospital bed made him look small and young, about seventeen, maybe eighteen. Unfortunately, the birth certificate said otherwise. He focused on Luke's face with its cuts and bruises, and tried but failed to find any resemblance to the Stewarts. Luke was his mother's son. With his long dark eyelashes and black hair, the kid was so like Annie that it actually hurt. Jack had thought he was over the pain, but all this was bringing it back.

What exactly had Annie told her son? Luke had probably seen his birth certificate yet he'd never tried to make contact, which seemed strange, especially given the Stewart's wealth. And if Annie wanted nothing more to do with him, not even financial help, why did she put Jack on the birth certificate at all? It didn't make sense.

A monitor beeped, and he flicked his attention back to Luke, whose eyes were now open. He looked confused, and Jack wished he'd gone to a hotel for the rest of the day because now he'd have to say something reassuring, and probably identify himself. Standing up, he moved towards the bed. 'Luke? You're in hospital, but don't worry, you're going to be okay.' He sounded and felt awkward. 'You don't know me, but …'

'I know who you are. I've seen your picture. You're my bastard father.'

Jack froze, his mind replaying the words.

'You threw my mother out because – what was it? – you didn't want a *gypo* kid!'

Luke was staring daggers at him. Annie must have said Jack had rejected *her*, instead of the other way round. 'What the hell are you talking about? I never even knew you existed before today.'

'Liar!' Luke's voice was raised and cracking with the strain. He struggled to sit up, winced, and sank back against the pillows. He looked exhausted but somehow found the strength to sweep a jug of water from the locker beside him towards Jack. It missed by inches, clattering against the wall, its contents flooding the floor.

A nurse hurried into the room. She spoke gently to Luke but it had no effect. He was obviously distressed and in pain. A male nurse appeared and frowned at Jack. 'If you don't mind, sir. We need to settle the patient.'

A firm hand on his shoulder steered Jack towards the door. As if it were his fault. He flushed at the injustice. That was it. He was out of here, on a flight back to Manchester that afternoon.

'Where's my mother? I want to see my mother!'

Glancing back, the despair on Luke's face told Jack he already suspected the truth. Part of him was thankful he wouldn't have to be the one to tell the kid his mother was dead. The other part of him felt like a total shit, but what could he do? It wasn't his problem. It was all very sad but nothing to do with him. If he didn't go now, he'd miss the flight. Luke was not his son. But although his head said one thing, his heart said another. He couldn't walk out now and leave those terrible accusations unchallenged. 'I'll wait in the Relatives' Room,' he told the nurse.

Emer Sullivan sipped a strong black coffee and wished she

still smoked. Five years without a cigarette and she was still waiting for those occasional cravings to disappear. They came when her in-tray was overflowing. Being a hospital counsellor was great, but to get through all the paperwork, you'd have to give up talking to the patients. One of life's little ironies.

She opened the file on her desk. A new case had just developed into a crisis. The details were sketchy: a woman killed in a car crash, her son badly injured. The father had just appeared on the scene and there'd been an argument. Emer had been asked to tell the son, Luke Kiernan, his mother was dead. She glanced at her watch. An hour since the incident. His tranquilliser would be wearing off but he should still be calm enough for her to talk to him. Emer left her office and reached Luke's side room at the same time as a nurse finished taking his blood pressure. His eyes were fixed on the ceiling.

'Luke?' said Emer, after the nurse had gone.

There was no response.

'Luke, my name's Emer. I'm a trauma counsellor. I'm here to talk to you about your mother.'

'She's dead, isn't she?'

He must have guessed when nobody would give him a straight answer, which was what he needed now. 'Yes, Luke, I'm afraid she is. I'm so sorry.' No matter how many times Emer gave people bad news, it never got any easier.

Luke turned to her, pain evident in his sad eyes. 'What happened? I can't remember.'

He had a right to know the facts. Once he accepted them, he could start the grieving process. She pulled out the police report. 'An oncoming truck hit your car on the driver's side, making it roll over and hit a tree. Another driver got you out. The emergency services got your mother out later.' Cut her out from the tangled mess of metal, but he didn't need

11

to know that. 'A priest from the local village was with her during her last moments.' Maybe it would comfort him to know she'd received absolution and hadn't died alone.

'Thanks,' murmured Luke as he turned his head away.

It was a dismissal and Emer didn't blame him. He needed time alone to absorb what he'd been told and to start mourning his mother. She stood up. 'If you need to talk, just ask for me. I'll look in on you tomorrow.'

He didn't respond. There was nothing more she could do for him at that moment. Now she had to find the father.

Jack sat alone at a table in the Relatives' Room, nursing a cup of cold coffee, his mind focused on Luke's harsh, unjust words.

'Mr Stewart?'

Jack looked up to see a redhead, dressed in jeans and a Trinity College sweatshirt.

'My name's Emer Sullivan. I'm a counsellor. I've been talking with your son, Luke.'

Jack fixed his gaze on the coffee in front of him. He was in no mood to talk to anyone, least of all a counsellor. Perhaps if he was silent, the woman would take the hint and go away.

'That's pretty much the same treatment I got from Luke,' she said as she sat opposite him.

When Jack glanced at her, he was pinned by the intensity of her gaze. She had green-yellow eyes, like a cat.

'People react to grief in many different ways,' Emer continued. 'Some people keep busy. One widow I know cleans her entire house every day. The makers of bleach never had it so good. There are those who start a new life almost immediately, sell up and leave all the old ties, while others shut down, retreat into their grief, and let no one in.'

'And then there are those like Luke, who throw things,' said Jack. 'How should I deal with that?'

'You've both suffered a terrible shock. You've lost your wife. Luke's lost his mother. The next few days are going to be critical. You need to find a way to talk to each other. I can help you do that.'

She was well wide of the mark there. Thought she knew it all. 'Look here, Oprah ...'

'Emer.'

'Look here, Emer, I lost my wife over twenty years ago. She never told me I had a son. In fact, I'm not even sure he's mine.'

She didn't look shocked, just thoughtful. 'But you're still here,' she said. 'You could have washed your hands of it all, but you didn't. Why?'

'To make sure he's okay. To see if ... if he needs anything. I'm not the total bastard he thinks I am.' Although maybe he was. Because he wasn't on a mercy mission. He'd come for his own reasons – looking for closure. He felt a tiny trickle of guilt. Looking out of the window, he saw dusk approaching. He was losing track of time in this place. Losing track of himself.

'Luke is injured and grieving – and probably very frightened,' said Emer. 'Right now, he's hiding behind anger, but that anger won't last. And when it's gone, he'll have nothing left.'

That made sense, but all Jack could see was Luke's face. The hostility and the hatred. How could he fight that? He wouldn't know where to start. Wouldn't have the patience.

'I'm sure you have questions for each other,' said Emer. 'I'll talk to him tomorrow – try to persuade him to see you.'

'Good luck,' Jack murmured, unable to keep the bitterness from his voice.

'Mr Stewart, look at me.'

He looked at her determined face.

'I know how hard this is for you, but if you walk away now, you won't get answers and that will eat away at you for the rest of your life. I know – I've seen what regret does to people. Stay a while longer. Don't give up on Luke. He needs you, whether he knows it or not.'

Her expression was kind. She wasn't judging him, just trying to help. Perhaps she could work some kind of miracle. 'Do you know a good hotel?' he asked, and she smiled. That turned out to be quite a reward in itself.

Chapter Two

When Emer arrived to see Luke the next day, he was sitting up in bed, supported by a mound of pillows, and pushing pudding around a dish. She pointed at it. 'Don't touch that custard. It's lethal. You'll wish they'd left the drip in.'

He responded with a half-hearted smile.

'I'm Emer,' she said, pulling up a chair and sitting down. 'I came to see you yesterday. D'you remember?'

'Sure. You're the shrink. Come to see if I'm mad or not.'

He was mock cheerful. Raising barriers, just like his father. 'I've come to see how you're feeling,' she said.

'Me? I'm feelin' fine. Thanks for askin'.' Luke shifted his gaze to the window where a steady rain streaked across the glass. Emer watched it with him. Most people found extended silences uncomfortable, and the discomfort forced them to speak. It took a little longer than usual with Luke, but eventually he turned to face her. 'Aren't you goin' to show me ink blots?' he asked.

'Why would I do that?'

'Isn't that what psychiatrists do?'

'I'm not a psychiatrist. I'm a trauma counsellor. It's a little different. I try to help ...'

'I don't need any help,' he said, picking up his spoon and sloshing the custard around again.

'I think you might, Luke. Shall I tell you why?' The spoon slowed. He was listening. 'You've been badly injured. You've lost your mother. You could suffer sleeplessness, nightmares, flashbacks, guilt or panic attacks. And – last, but by no means least – your father shows up for the first time ever and you're angry about that.'

'Damn right I'm angry!' The spoon clattered onto the tray. 'Wouldn't you be?'

'I don't know. It's not me it happened to. Why are you angry?'

He threw up his hands in frustration. 'For Christ's sake, isn't it obvious? The bastard didn't want me when I was born so sure as hell won't now.'

'Then why is he here?'

Luke hesitated but then maintained his resistance. 'I don't know! Guilt? Maybe he wants to be seen doin' the right thing? Why don't you ask him?'

'Why don't *you* ask him?'

'Because I don't want to talk to him. I don't even want to look at him – ever.'

'That's a shame, because then you'll never know.'

'Know what?'

'Why he came all this way, why he sat by your bedside waiting for you to wake up. He didn't need to, so why did he?'

'I told you, I don't know, and I don't care.'

He sounded weary but she persevered. 'Luke, you have a chance to ask him why he wasn't around for you. Maybe you won't like his answer, and you won't want him in your life. That's your choice. But I think not to have at least one conversation with him is a mistake.'

Emer studied him. He seemed torn, maybe between curiosity and a desire for revenge. The latter might satisfy him for a while, but then he'd never have proper resolution or closure. She willed him to take a risk.

'I can't,' he said, rubbing his hand over his eyes. 'Just the thought of him makes me mad. I'd end up punchin' him, I know it.'

'Well, I can be here with you, if you like,' she offered. 'I used to referee girls' football teams. I know when to show the red card.'

He gave a wry smile. 'Girls can't play football. Too scared of breakin' their nails.'

'Cheeky bugger. Show me a bunch of men defending a free kick and I'll show you real fear.'

'I'm good at football.'

Evasion again, but she'd indulge him.

'I used to dream of playin' football for Manchester United. And Ireland. Earnin' millions. People chantin' my name and buyin' shirts with Kiernan on the back.'

She could identify with that. 'I dreamed of doing backing vocals for Take That. Used to mime to their songs using my hairbrush as a microphone. I was devastated they split up before they discovered me.'

He smiled and Emer was tempted to leave things there, but she remembered her promise to Jack. 'C'mon, Luke. What's there to lose? Just listen to what your father has to say.'

He was quiet for so long that Emer thought she'd lost the argument, but he surprised her.

'Okay – on condition you'll be there, like you said.'

That was a given. Luke and his father really did need a referee. 'I promise.'

He nodded. 'I owe it to Mam to make sure he doesn't get away with what he did.'

The edge in his voice left Emer in no doubt that Luke Kiernan was much tougher than he looked.

As Jack walked through the hotel lobby, the muscles in his neck were knotting again. So much for that massage in the hotel spa. He'd also managed twenty laps in the pool and some time on the treadmill. Trying to *exercise* his demons. He almost laughed aloud at that but dreadful puns didn't mask the fact the 'exorcism' hadn't worked. He couldn't block out Luke's words, or the memories of Annie.

Emer had arranged a three o'clock showdown. She'd be there as well, at Luke's request. Too scared to be alone with his wicked father? It was so bloody unfair.

He got to the hospital fifteen minutes early and went into the foyer shop to buy chocolate and fruit, not quite sure why he was bothering. Because it was the thing to do, he supposed.

'I hope the patient feels better soon,' smiled the assistant.

'Me too,' Jack said, and meant it. He had a job and a life to get back to. Now if he could just get some answers …

Seeing Luke again was a shock. Jack had tried to forget how much he looked like Annie. The long lashes, the hair colour – the far-too-discerning blue eyes. It was unnerving. Luke was scowling at him, chin jutting defiantly. Emer, seated on the other side of the bed, was smiling encouragement. It was like good cop, bad cop.

Jack put the fruit on the bedside locker. 'Vitamins,' he said. Then he held up the chocolate. 'This won't do any harm either.'

Luke said nothing. Probably guessed it was just for show.

Jack sat down, scooting the chair back slightly as he gauged the distance between himself and the water jug. He cleared his throat. 'First off, I'm sorry about your mother, Luke – truly sorry.'

'Sure you are.'

'What's that supposed to mean?' Jack was being sincere, and the little git was mocking him.

'Course you're sorry,' Luke replied. 'You're afraid you might be saddled with me.'

There was some truth to that. Deep down, Jack wanted to get away with giving the kid money, setting him up in a job somewhere. Not having to see him on any regular basis. Perhaps not having to see him at all because Luke's face was

Annie's face, and the similarity was too painful. 'Is that what you think?' he asked, stalling for time.

'It's what I know,' was the response. 'You didn't want me before, so don't pretend you do now.'

There was that accusation again. 'I already told you – until yesterday, I didn't know you existed.'

'That's a good one,' Luke retorted, 'but not what I heard.'

'Then you heard wrong!'

Luke's eyes flashed, and Jack was startled again by the hostility there. 'Don't call my mother a liar!'

Emer put her hand on Luke's arm to calm him, giving Jack a warning glance.

This was hopeless. He was only making things worse. 'I'm sorry, Luke. You obviously don't want me around. Do you know where your uncles are? I can call them.'

Luke shook his head, his eyes wide. 'No! I don't want them here!'

He seemed panic-stricken, his breathing rapid. Not just panic, though. Fear.

'Calm down,' said Jack. 'I won't call them. I don't even know where they are. Just relax, okay?'

'I think that's enough for today,' said Emer, but Jack wasn't finished. He'd been unjustly accused. He couldn't shrug that off. Perhaps now Luke had exhausted himself, he'd have a chance to speak.

'Luke, you have to believe me when I tell you I never knew Annie had a child.' Luke sighed and closed his eyes. But he couldn't close his ears. He would hear what Jack had to say. 'I don't know why your mother told you what she did. She must have had her reasons, but what do I do? Let you keep believing I threw her out? There was obviously a huge misunderstanding. I was working a lot – maybe too much. Perhaps she told me what was troubling her, and it didn't register.'

It was the best he could come up with, though it could

be true. He'd probably never know. There was no response from Luke. The meeting had been a waste of time. Jack left, feeling bitter disappointment.

I didn't know you existed until yesterday. Yeah, right. The man must think Luke an idiot. As if he wouldn't have been told what a scumbag his father was. He'd wanted to confront Jack Stewart ever since the day he learned his life had been a lie ....

Why didn't he stop? Even with his hands over his ears, Luke could still hear his uncle shouting. Annie was crying and that always made Joe even more mad. Only a matter of time till he slapped her. But Luke was eleven now. Time he did something to help her. 'Leave her alone, you bastard!' Annie wouldn't like him swearing, but it was what men did. 'If my da' was alive, he'd show you ...'

Joe turned his attention away from Annie and started to laugh. 'If your da' was alive ...'

'Joe, don't – please.' Annie was tugging her brother's arm, but he shrugged her off, still laughing.

What was so funny?

'Your da' is alive, you stupid little mongrel. And he isn't a Traveller. He isn't even Irish. You're half-Brit and your precious father didn't want you. Or her. Didn't want the embarrassment of a gypo in the family. And d'you know the best bit? He said she should have got rid of you.'

That was worse than the punch he'd expected. 'You're a liar! Mammy – he's a liar, isn't he?' But the look on Annie's face and the hesitation before she said 'Yes ... yes, of course he is,' told Luke his uncle wasn't lying. His heart was thumping and he couldn't breathe properly. He was vaguely aware of his mother's arm round his shoulder, and then Joe suddenly in front of him, waving a piece of paper. 'There you are. Read that, and see who's the liar.'

'Liam!' screamed Annie. 'How could you? I showed you that letter in confidence! I thought you'd destroyed it, not given it to Joe!'

Despite his mother's attempts to prevent it, Luke managed to see the words he'd never forget. Later, Annie talked about her husband, showed Luke his picture, said they'd been happy in the beginning. Had wanted a baby. The damage was done, though. One day Jack Stewart would pay.

'Why would she tell Luke I didn't want him?' Jack asked Emer as they talked over tea in her office. 'The Annie I knew was never cruel. Why would she let her own child think he'd been rejected?' He didn't usually discuss family business with outsiders, but there was no one else to talk to about this madness. As a counsellor, Emer would be discreet and her insight could prove useful.

'You might never know, because to answer that you'd need to know *why* she left you,' Emer replied.

Her words stung. *She left you.* 'I wish to God I did know!' Jack snapped. 'I came back from a meeting in Brussels and she just wasn't there. She'd packed her suitcases, cleared out her bank account and left. No note. Nothing. As if *I* were nothing. A mistake she just rubbed out. Do you know what that feels like?'

'I'm sure it must have been very hard to cope with. Did you look for her?'

'I had … a bit of a breakdown.' That was hard to admit, even to a sympathetic person like Emer. Jack hated to think of how he'd gone to pieces back then. Not working, not eating, not sleeping. Living on booze. He viewed his behaviour then as the worst kind of weakness. 'My mother hired a detective. He found Annie, but she said she didn't want to come back. And she was with a man. A fellow Traveller.'

Emer was Irish so would know about Travellers. Ireland's

outcasts. Some still on the road, following the nomadic lifestyle, some settled. Stereotyped and scorned. Annie had told him a lot about her people's problems.

'Did you never want to confront her in person?' asked Emer.

'When we got the news from the detective, I was devastated. Just couldn't face it.' Old guilt resurfaced. Had he let her go too easily? His mother had been furious about Annie leaving. Said how ungrateful she was, and how insulting that someone like her had rejected the Stewarts when they'd given her everything. Harped on constantly about how Jack had a duty to the business and the family name. Lady Grace Stewart had encouraged the anger and the hurt that hardened his heart, and she'd finally convinced him trying to bring Annie home would be a waste of time. That she'd just go again, and how unfair it would be on Matt. That had clinched it. 'I accepted it. Cleaned myself up and focused on taking care of my son Matt, who was only four. His mother, my first wife, died when he was two. Then suddenly his new mother wasn't there any more.'

'Were there any signs at all that Annie was troubled?' asked Emer.

Jack shook his head. 'And that's what bothers me. The suddenness of it. People have affairs and marriages break up. But this happened virtually overnight. We were so happy, then she was gone. It was all too quick, and that's what's never made sense.'

'Perhaps she just couldn't adjust to a settled life?' suggested Emer. 'Did Annie like the place where you live? Where is it?'

'Baronsmere – a village in Cheshire. About eight hundred people. It can be hard for newcomers, but Annie had friends. She worked in a bar in the village for a while. That's where I first met her. She'd only been in England a couple of weeks with her father and brothers and a few other Traveller families. Work was slow so they were trying their luck in England.'

'How long did you know Annie before you got married?'

Jack smiled. 'Three months. It was a whirlwind romance. There didn't seem much point in waiting. For me, it was love at first sight.'

He'd been on a pub crawl through the villages with his mates. They'd all flirted with the new barmaid at The Fox and Feathers, except Jack. Something about Annie had captivated him from the start. He'd wanted to be attentive, respectful. His mates had teased him, but he didn't care. For the first time since Caroline's death, there was a woman who made him feel something again.

'What did your parents think about you marrying Annie?'

It still hurt to think about it. His mother had actually screamed at him. Called him selfish. His father, Sir Nicholas Stewart, knight of the realm and prime bigot, had spent days trying to talk him out of it. *The shame of it* he'd said. *A gypsy in the family.* 'They weren't exactly overjoyed. They didn't come to the wedding.'

But it had been fine without them. Annie's delicate face framed by a white tulle veil. Matt, a charming little pageboy. Dave, his best man, calling him a lucky sod. Maggie, his housekeeper, crying for England. It had been a great day.

'And Annie's family? Did they come to the wedding?'

'No. They were back in Ireland by then.'

Annie had begged her father to come. She'd cried uncontrollably on the phone. No good, though. Jack always blamed her brother Joe for that. He'd likely persuaded the Kiernan family to cast her out because she refused to conform to their idea of how she should live – full-time housemaid for them until she married a fellow Traveller. But Annie was a free spirit – she wasn't afraid, like so many Traveller girls back then, of being on the shelf if she hadn't married by her eighteenth birthday. She wanted to earn a living and marry when the right man came along. In the end, Tony Hayes, owner of the pub where she'd worked, gave her away.

'Did Annie have much contact with your parents after you were married?'

'Not really,' said Jack. 'But there were times when they couldn't avoid each other.' He thought about the awkwardness of such occasions. The memories weren't pleasant. Like the elaborate cake his mother bought for Matt's birthday. Matt had preferred the one he'd helped Annie bake – Chocolate Mess they'd called it. You could have cut the atmosphere, never mind the cake, with a knife.

'But there were people who adored Annie,' he continued. 'My housekeeper considered her the daughter she never had. My sister, Claire, thought of her as family. And to Matt, she was simply his mother. *I* adored Annie. There was nothing I wouldn't have done for her. And, before you ask, we both wanted children. Even chose the name for our first child. Rebecca for a girl … and Luke for a boy. We had Matthew and would joke about eventually having Mark and John, too. I'd *never* have thrown Annie out. Or our child. *She* left *me*!' God, he felt like he was going to cry. All the memories. Things he hadn't thought about in years. It was too much. Emer must have guessed because she poured him more tea. The answer to everything.

'I believe you,' she said. 'And it must be terrible to be accused of something you haven't done.'

That was unexpected. He'd thought counsellors stayed neutral.

They did.

'I also believe Luke … well, I believe that *he* believes it. He's been told you rejected him and his mother. You never showed up to contradict that. So why should he trust you –

a stranger – over the people who've taken care of him all his life? Can you see that, Jack?'

He could, but there wasn't a damn thing he could do about it.

'In a strange way, the accident might help,' Emer said. 'Luke's not in a position to walk away right now, so you should have some time to try and convince him you care.'

'I don't know if … if I do care.' There, he'd said it aloud. Voiced the fears he'd held ever since Flynn told him of Luke's existence. He looked at Emer, expecting to see disgust.

'You've had a terrible shock,' was all she said. 'Not only learning your wife has died, but also finding out you have a grown-up son. And you don't know Luke. He's not like a child you've raised from birth. You can't be expected to feel instant love.'

'I don't even feel instant *like*. And if he isn't mine? That Traveller the detective said she was with, after she left England – he might be the real father.' He didn't tell her he wanted that to be true so he'd be off the hook.

Emer flicked through a form on her desk. 'Luke was born on the 28th of October. When did Annie leave?'

'Late February. So Annie was pregnant before leaving Baronsmere – unless Luke was premature. But …'

'But what?' prompted Emer.

'But maybe she met the Traveller in England. An affair would have been a reason for her to leave.' And what better time to do that than when Jack was abroad for a week? No arguments, no drama. But if that were true, then he'd completely misjudged Annie's character. And she'd given a performance worthy of an Oscar.

'A DNA test is the only way to find out for sure if you're the father.'

Jack nodded slowly, but he wasn't sure if he wanted hard proof that Annie had been unfaithful to him. Why put himself through all that? Luke hated him, and would want nothing more to do with the Stewarts when he got out of hospital.

'Luke might react very badly to a request for a DNA, though,' Emer commented. 'In his mind, it would be like another rejection. If he really is your son, you could lose him completely because of that. Perhaps you should wait until he's fully recovered from the accident.'

Jack frowned. 'He'll be back with his family then. He's not likely to want any more contact with me.'

Emer shook her head. 'I don't think so. Remember what happened when you asked about his uncles?'

True. Luke had seemed terrified. 'That would be any sane person's reaction.'

'Were they violent?'

'Liam Kiernan wasn't so bad. Annie told me they'd been quite close until he suffered a head injury on a construction site. After that, he had mental health issues and suffered bouts of aggression that were aggravated by booze. Joe Kiernan had a real temper. He got involved in more than one pub fight while he was in Baronsmere.' Jack gave a wry laugh. 'One of which was with me.'

'Do you think Joe was responsible for Luke's bruises?'

Jack shifted in his chair. He remembered the doctor's words: *He'll need peace and quiet … and support … to heal.* But Luke was an adult. He could make his own decisions. 'It's possible. Or a brawl … who knows? You'd have to ask Luke.'

'You know he and Annie were leaving Ireland,' said Emer. 'Luke told me they were going to Wales.'

'No, I didn't know that.'

'It's odd, though,' Emer said. 'There was just one suitcase between them. The hospital staff opened it, looking for information. There were a few personal items but little else.'

'So?'

'It seems they left in a hurry. Didn't even pack clothes. I wonder why.'

Jack sighed. 'You're asking me to guess the motives of a woman I haven't seen in more than twenty years. Well, I can't. Luke's the one who has all the answers, and he's not talking.'

'Not yet.'

Not ever, probably.

'There was no definite plan according to Luke. No job, nowhere to live.'

'I'll give him money,' said Jack. 'I'll make sure he's not homeless.'

'I see.' There was clear disapproval in Emer's voice.

'What's wrong with that?' he asked. 'It's probably more than anyone else would do for him.'

'Yes, I'm sure,' Emer agreed. 'But money isn't always the answer.'

In Jack's experience, it usually was. It bought comfort, security, opportunities. What more did people want? 'Emer, even if he is my son, he hates me. I'll do everything I can for him, but I'm not a miracle worker. I can't change the past.'

'You could take him home with you. At least for a few weeks until he's fully recovered. It'll be hard for him to manage on his own.'

He wished she hadn't suggested that. It was ridiculously out of touch with reality. Luke couldn't even bear to be in the same room as him. There was nothing to build on. No prospect of even liking each other, let alone the love a father and son should share. 'How would I explain to everyone back home who he is? Introduce him as my maybe-son?'

'I'm sure you could find a way to deal with that.'

Jack was silent, mulling it over.

'Are you ashamed of him?' asked Emer.

'No!' He was insulted she'd even asked. 'I'm not a bigot.

I married a Traveller, didn't I? It's just … Luke's so angry. And hard. I don't even know if I can feel anything for him. It wouldn't be fair to give him expectations.'

'I doubt very much he's hard. Give him the benefit of the doubt. Try to get to know him – and let him get to know you. Show you're making an effort. You still need answers. If you get closer to Luke, break down those barriers, he might tell you everything Annie told him.'

'Maybe …'

The phone rang, and Emer answered it. 'Okay, I'll be there soon.' She replaced the receiver. 'Sorry, Jack. I have to see a patient.'

'Are you free later for a drink?' Jack asked. 'Talking to you really helps.' The prospect of another evening spent alone in his hotel room was depressing. He'd only brood and rake over the past.

She held up the in-tray. 'Alas, I'll have to spend the evening with all this paperwork.'

'Lunch tomorrow?' God, he sounded desperate.

'I usually grab a sandwich in the hospital canteen around one o'clock.'

Jack smiled. 'I might see you then.'

At the door, he glanced back, appraising Emer this time as a woman rather than a counsellor. He liked what he saw, especially the long red curls. He noticed the light sprinkling of freckles on her nose, and her mouth had an enticingly full lower lip. She thankfully wasn't thin as a rake; the blue dress she wore showed curves in all the right places – and enough of her long legs to set a man's imagination alight. No 'might' about it. Jack would be in the hospital canteen tomorrow for sure.

Emer leaned against the kitchen counter and watched the tuna casserole begin its solo circular dance inside the microwave.

It was a godsend to have a sister living close by. Maeve kept Emer supplied with all her favourite home-cooked meals, believing a single woman who worked for the health service would have no time to shop or cook for herself.

She wasn't far wrong. The hours as a counsellor could be punishing and the irregularity made a personal life tricky. Emer glanced at the fridge, singling out the photo of her and Colm on holiday in Rome last year. She really should take the picture down. Their five years together were well and truly over. All through the autumn and winter she'd forced herself to look at it, and each day the pain eased just a fraction. Now she still felt sad at the sight of Colm but no longer had the urge to drown her sorrows in red wine. Emer had heard through the grapevine he was engaged to the woman he'd two-timed her with. Good luck to her. Once a cheater, always a cheater …

The food was ready and Emer served it up, brushing aside the guilt about not preparing a salad to go with it. Healthy eating took time and energy, and she was out of both this evening. Besides, she had a mission.

Moving through to the living room, Emer set the plate of bubbling food on the desk and settled down in front of her laptop. Once the search engine flicked up, she typed in *Jack Stewart, Baronsmere*.

She was spoiled for choice. The internet was teeming with information about the man Emer had met for the first time yesterday. Business magazine profiles jostled with short announcements in financial newspapers. Local Cheshire websites focused on Jack's charity work on literacy programmes and a scheme he'd set up to provide a taster of business work experience for older teens still at school.

There was a standard photo used in many of the articles and Emer enlarged it. Taken a few years ago, she reckoned, because there wasn't any grey in his hair at all. No hint of a smile but the eyes flashed an alertness, a power, that spoke of a man who knew how to get what he wanted.

And now he'd been blindsided by Annie and Luke. The Jack she'd seen in her office earlier was quite different from the man the internet articles portrayed as an astute and in-control businessman. Today, he'd been angry, confused and vulnerable. Was that why she'd refused his offer of a drink? Not because of any work conflict, certainly, because he wasn't her patient and she could have met him in the pub with a clear conscience. But Jack's life right now was complicated, and she wasn't sure if she could handle that.

Her mobile rang and she glanced at the caller information. Maeve.

'Don't tell me you got all the kids in bed,' Emer said, by way of a greeting. Her three nephews were proving to be night owls. 'That must be a record.'

'For sure,' laughed Maeve at the other end of the phone. 'Don't jinx it now. I'm sitting here, feet up, glass of wine in hand. Nothing good on the telly, of course. What are you up to?'

Emer clicked and saved Jack's photo to the computer. 'Oh, nothing much. Just a bit of research.'

'All work and no play ...'

... *makes Jack a dull boy*. Emer mentally finished the proverb and smiled. Perhaps it was a sign. Of what, though? Emer decided to give the analytical side of her brain the night off. And the warning bells could sod off, too.

After she'd finished talking to Maeve, Emer went into the kitchen, took the photo of Colm from the fridge, and relegated it to the bin.

'Goodbye to all that,' she murmured.

Jack woke with a start. Where the hell was he? The window was in the wrong place. And what was that wardrobe doing near the door? Then he remembered. This was the Beaumont Hotel in Dublin. He had a new son and a corpse to take care of. He glanced at the bedside clock. Past nine. Darkness had fallen outside. He'd slept for two hours, needing a break from the memories of Annie that kept flooding his mind.

He went into the bathroom and splashed water on his face. That woke him up a bit. Drying his hands, he assessed himself critically in the mirror. Forty-six but still looking good. Some grey flecks in his fair hair, but his mother said they made him look distinguished. Not balding at all, thank God. Some wrinkles on the forehead and round the eyes, but he could still pass for forty in the right light. He patted his stomach. No paunch. He exercised every day in the gym at work.

What age was Emer? Mid-thirties? No wedding ring. Admittedly, women didn't always wear them now. She was a looker. And sharp. The pillow talk would be great. He felt a stab of guilt. A dead wife and an injured son, and he was working out how to screw the bereavement counsellor.

Back in the bedroom, he stood by the window, watching worshippers leaving the church across the street. Sunday was almost over. How would he have spent the day in Baronsmere? A workout, the newspapers, lunch with the family at Edenbridge, an afternoon walk with the dogs, a drink or two in the evening with friends. No romance, although that flicker of hope he'd find someone special hadn't yet gone out. It had been his choice to end things with Sarah a couple of months ago, so he had no right to complain about being lonely. They'd broken up so many times over the years that the villagers were probably placing bets to see how long it was before they were back together. It was final this time, though. She hadn't made a big fuss when he'd broken things off, and had made no attempts to win him back, although she'd been a bit quiet of late – it was hard to know what she was really thinking.

He could guess what his parents would think, though, if he brought Luke back to Baronsmere. His would-be son, the thorn in his side. They'd think Jack had lost his mind. Emer had no idea what she was asking. Damn her. Damn Annie. And damn Luke. It had taken Jack so long to get over the shock of Annie leaving, but he'd survived and got his life back on track. The last thing he needed right now was a constant reminder of all that trauma in the form of a twenty-year-old with an attitude. And what the hell was all that about not being wanted because he was a *gypo*? Jack had never used that insult in his life, and he and Annie had wanted a child of their own, a brother or sister for Matt.

Matt! He'd have to tell him in case Luke got it into his head later to phone – or even worse, turn up on the doorstep. Then there would be some explaining to do. Jack took out his mobile and dialled his son's number.

'Dad!' It was good to hear Matt's voice. 'What's going on? Maggie said you're in Ireland.'

He hadn't given his housekeeper any details. Didn't want her weeping all over the place. 'Matt – I'm here because of Annie.'

'Annie? *Our* Annie?'

'There's been an accident …'

'Shit! Is she okay? Where's she been all this time?'

Jack had expected anger or indifference. How could Matt sound so concerned after Annie had abandoned him?

'Dad?'

'Matt, I'm sorry … she's dead. A car crash. I had to identify her.'

'Oh my God! Why didn't you tell me? I'd have come with you.'

'You had the stag night.'

'Fuck that! This is more important than some piss-up. Look, I'll come over …'

'No!' That was the last thing Jack wanted. Things were complicated enough.

'But what about the funeral? I should be there. And Maggie. We'll—'

'Stop! Just stop. There's something else. She had a son. He was with her in the car.'

'Is he dead too?'

'No, but he's injured. He's in hospital.'

'Poor sod,' said Matt. 'So his family are there, yeah? That must be tough for you.'

Jack was tempted to leave it there. Say Annie's family were taking care of things. But what if the truth came out later? Matt would know he'd lied. 'Well, that's the thing, Matt. Luke seems to think we're his family.'

'Come again.'

'Luke's twenty. His birth certificate says he's mine.' Jack hated doing this over the phone. He wished he could see Matt's reaction. 'Matt? You still there?'

'Yeah.'

'What are you thinking?'

'For starters – why the hell didn't Annie tell you?'

And now the questions would start. The last thing he needed. 'It's complicated. Too much to go into right now. I'm still trying to get my head round it.'

'I can imagine. So what's he like?'

Hostile, stubborn, unforgiving, throws things. That about summed it up. But he didn't have the energy for that now. 'He looks like Annie,' was all he said.

'I want to see him.'

Jack knew that tone of voice. Matt, determined to get his own way. 'It's not a good idea. He's not strong enough yet ...'

'All the more reason to see him, then. He's my brother, and it sounds like he needs us.'

Matt's anger sparked Jack's own temper. 'You don't know he's your brother! That could have been the reason Annie left.'

He hadn't meant to say that. Instantly regretted it. He'd never told Matt that Annie had found another man.

'You can't believe that, Dad! Not Annie! No way!'

Matt sounded really upset. Jack was botching this badly. 'I don't know what to believe. This whole thing has been a nightmare, and I'm shattered. Please – just give me a bit more time to talk to Luke, to see what he wants to do.'

'You'll be bringing him home, though?'

Now Matt was suggesting it! And any attempt by Jack to dismiss it as a bad idea could bring Matt over on the next flight. Would Luke want to come back to Baronsmere anyway? Maybe he'd refuse and Jack could offer him start-up money for his move to Wales. Matt could visit him if he wanted. Win-win.

'Okay, Matt, I'll ask him, but just don't get your hopes up.'

Chapter Three

Next morning rain had settled in, and Jack turned on all the lights in his suite to dispel the gloom. He spent an hour answering e-mails. They never stopped, not even for a family crisis. Then he phoned his secretary, saying he'd been detained in Ireland on business and she could leave messages on his mobile.

'And if Sir Nicholas needs to speak to you?' she'd asked.

'He can't. Not today, anyway. I'll be busy.' That would go down like the Titanic. He'd take the flak for it when he got home; right now he had different priorities.

After coffee and a Danish, Jack walked the short distance to the hospital. Dublin looked like any other big city with its shops and office buildings, a myriad of umbrellas adding colour to the grey streets. The traffic was bumper to bumper, as bad as Manchester's. He passed a building and recognised the name of the funeral home where Annie had been taken. He hadn't been there when they'd transferred her and he tried to ignore the guilt.

Pushing open the swing doors of the hospital, he was hit by the pungent smell of disinfectant. Why couldn't they use cleaning stuff that smelled of flowers? Might cheer people up a bit, and God knows everybody in St Aidan's looked like they needed that.

When he entered Luke's room, only a nurse was there, changing the sheets. 'Where's Luke? Has something happened?' Perhaps he'd discharged himself. Problem solved.

The nurse smiled. 'He's taking a walk to the day room to try out his crutches.'

Jack pushed aside a small kernel of disappointment and asked where he could find the day room.

Luke was heading slowly down the corridor, a nurse beside him. Jack was reminded of Matt's halting first steps all those years ago. He'd missed Luke's first steps. And so many other firsts. *But he's not my son.* Again, he'd forgotten this. Lulled into acceptance by the desire he and Annie had shared for a child, a desire he could still remember like it was yesterday.

They reached the day room at the same time and Jack held the door open. Luke glanced at him briefly before being helped into a chair by the nurse.

'Well done, Luke,' she said. 'You're making grand progress. You'll be dancing again in no time. Just rest here a bit. I'll get a wheelchair so I can take you for your scan.' She bustled out, leaving father and son alone, silent like strangers in a waiting room.

Jack sat in the chair next to Luke, staring at the wall as he spoke. 'Scan?'

'To check my head.'

A response at least. And bordering on polite. 'How are the crutches?'

'Okay. Not easy with the ribs, but at least I'll be able to get out of here soon.'

Another sentence without expletives. Definite progress. 'So where will you go when you get out?'

Luke sighed. 'What d'you care?'

'I'm guessing you won't be going back to your uncles. Is there someone else ...'

'Jesus!' Luke slammed his hands on the arms of the chair. 'What's it to you?'

That was more like the Luke he'd come to know. He'd have to choose his words carefully. 'Luke, whatever you think, I do care what happens to you. We should try to get to know each other a bit better.' He hesitated, knowing he was about to say something that could change his life and the lives of everyone dear to him. 'Come home with me.'

It was out now. No taking it back.

From the corner of his eye, he saw Luke's head turn towards him.

'Why would I want to do that?'

'I don't suppose you *would* want to,' Jack replied, avoiding eye contact. 'But what's your alternative? You need looking after. You can't manage on your own yet.' He'd made it sound like some kind of business proposal. Sign here. Agree to all terms and conditions.

'You don't want me.'

That was the truth, but Jack would never say it. He knew what rejection felt like and whatever the temptation, he wouldn't punish Annie through her son. 'Until you're fit,' he said. 'After that, do what you like.' Take it or leave it. The final offer.

'I don't think so.'

Well, he'd tried. Hadn't he?

He's my brother! Matt's voice was inside his head, like a reproach. He'd want to know everything Jack had said. Would probably criticise him for sounding too cold. He had to try again, for Matt. Jack took a photo from his wallet, holding it out to Luke.

'Matt,' he said. 'Your half-brother. He's twenty-five. Your mother took him everywhere with her – told him Irish stories, taught him Irish songs, which he'll still sing on drunken St Patrick's nights. He loved Annie. She was his mother for a year. The only one he remembers. He wants to meet you.'

Before Luke could respond, the nurse reappeared with a wheelchair. 'Time for your scan, Luke.'

Jack moved to help him get up. Luke's body stiffened, so Jack left it to the nurse. He held the door as she wheeled the chair out. 'Just think about it,' he said, but Luke left the room without looking at him.

* * *

37

Emer's phone alarm beeped at five minutes to one. Lunch time. And possibly Jack Stewart time. He might have forgotten her line to him yesterday about being in the hospital cafeteria, but she'd be there just in case. Last night, she'd admitted to herself she found Jack attractive. *Don't lie to your hormones.* One of Maeve's favourite sayings.

As usual, the lifts were packed to the gunnels with nurses, doctors and relatives. It was as bad as Grafton Street on a Saturday night. When the third lift arrived full, Emer gave up and took the stairs.

Clattering her way down to the first floor, she glanced at her watch. Almost ten after. In her experience, men didn't hang around long if they thought they'd been stood up. Still, she'd have a chance to see Jack another day, with Luke …

'Emer!'

She smiled when she spotted Jack, hovering outside the cafeteria. A brownie point to him for waiting. Now why hadn't she remembered to brush her hair? Even in a ponytail, her curls needed a lot of strict attention or they'd spring free, up and round her head like a wispy red halo. Still, perhaps the special-occasion amber drop earrings she'd spent five minutes looking for this morning would distract him.

She greeted him with a smile and said, 'Let's go in. I'm starving.' She could check the state of her hair in the glass of the food counter.

Jack hesitated, his expression uncertain. Emer felt a small stab of disappointment. Perhaps she'd jumped the gun and he wasn't staying for lunch after all. She should know better by now than to build castles in the air …

'It's really crowded in there. Is there somewhere quieter we can eat?' Jack asked, and the castle and clouds floated back into Emer's view.

They couldn't eat in her office. Never a minute's peace there. Outside was cold and damp, even if you wanted to combat the clouds of tobacco smoke from both visitors and patients who couldn't fight the nicotine cravings.

'There is a place,' she told him. 'You're not afraid of heights, are you?'

Jack blinked nervously. 'No, not really – why, what did you have in mind?'

'It'll be a surprise. C'mon, let's grab some sandwiches.'

He held up a carrier bag. 'Already got them.'

Another brownie point for him, only … 'I don't eat meat. Did you get a vegetarian option? Or fish is okay.'

'I bought one of everything,' he said solemnly, not seeming to think there was anything out of the ordinary in that.

'Oh.' Emer resisted the temptation to laugh, not wanting to hurt his feelings. 'Good for you, Jack. Right, onwards and upwards. Follow me.'

Some of the nurses cast appreciative glances at Jack as he stood chatting to Emer beside the lift. Even if it wasn't true, it still felt good to be thought of as part of a couple again.

Emer pushed open a door and Jack felt a cool breeze pluck at his hair and jacket. The rooftop lay ahead of them and now he understood her question about heights. He'd wanted more privacy and now he'd got it, because surely only the desperate and the bold would come out here. The clanking and echoes of the hospital behind him faded away and were replaced by the sounds of city traffic. Luckily, it had stopped raining.

'Well, thank you, Emer – I was hoping to see the sights …' he joked, peering over the edge. They were seven floors up and there was a reasonable view of Dublin. A park spread out on the left side, and the river glinted a steely grey through the heart of the city. In the distance, there seemed to be a giant knitting needle piercing the sky. 'What's that huge spike?' he asked Emer, who came over to stand beside him.

'That's the Millennium Spire,' she told him. 'The locals have given it ruder names than that, though. Four million euro to build and a million plus so far to keep it clean. Nobody knows what it's supposed to be, but it does make a grand meeting place.'

'Like this rooftop. Do you come here often?'

'I used to, when I still smoked, but I'm a clean-living girl now.' Emer winked and smiled, and the sight of her dimples made him smile back. 'C'mon over here, out of the wind.'

Jack followed her to a stone block sheltered by a large heating vent and they settled down side by side. He rummaged in the plastic bag and plucked out a sandwich. 'Cheese and pickle?'

'Grand,' she said, accepting the sandwich and a bottle of apple juice.

Perhaps he'd better not munch away at beef in her presence. He selected an avocado and prawn half baguette. About to unwrap it, he suddenly noticed Emer was shivering slightly. Standing up, he took his jacket off and draped it over her shoulders.

She looked surprised but murmured, 'Very gentlemanly of you.'

The sandwich had virtually no taste and Jack soon set it back in its plastic packet. Emer was gamely working her way through the cheese and pickle. Jack had been looking forward to seeing her again, but it was hard to get a conversation going when you were sitting side by side on a breezy rooftop, eating. Emer had less than an hour for lunch, though, so Jack would have to get things started. Best to begin with something she'd approve of.

'I saw Luke this morning. I asked him to come back with me.'

'Mmm.' Emer hurriedly swallowed her mouthful and half-turned towards him. 'What did he say?'

'He didn't seem to think it was a good idea.' Understatement of the year. Emer looked disappointed so he added, 'I showed him a photo of Matt, my son. Said he really wanted them to meet, which is true. I phoned Matt last night. Luke didn't say he'd come, but he didn't say no, either.'

Jack was painting his offer to Luke in a better light to get Emer's approval. If she'd been a fly on the wall in the day room, she'd likely have given him a low mark for effort.

'He'll need some time to think about it,' Emer concluded. 'But well done you for asking.'

Jack was surprised how much he needed that small sign of approval. He'd felt so very alone here in Dublin, not knowing what to do for the best.

They chatted on – about Luke, about Emer's job, about Ireland. She was close to finishing her sandwich. Time was ticking by so Jack risked a personal question. 'Do you have any children, Emer?' Hardly a subtle way to find out if someone was married or not, but it was the best he could come up with at short notice.

'No, I'm not married. I was nearly engaged once, but it didn't work out.'

She sounded sad and he wished he hadn't asked. Always putting his foot in it.

'What about you, Jack? Is there someone special in your life?'

He glanced at Emer and was sure he saw a spark of interest in her eyes. He could just imagine his mother telling him he'd fallen for one Irish woman and it hadn't worked out so it surely wasn't wise to risk it again. Pushing that thought aside, he surprised himself by answering Emer truthfully. 'I *was* in a relationship with the local hotelier, Sarah, but I ended it a few months ago. I hadn't been feeling any real emotion for some time, and I don't think she had either. I guess we both kept going because it was comfortable and convenient.' But empty. He'd never quite reached the level of emotion he'd had with both Caroline and Annie. And if Annie could leave their perfect relationship, what hope was there? Maybe that's why he'd never divorced her on the grounds of abandonment – because it was an excuse not to get married again, with all the risks that involved.

'Sarah and I have been friends since we were children.' Jack continued. 'I think maybe it was just easy because it didn't involve all the effort of getting to know each other – and it was without all that "first flush" stuff that can leave you drained when it goes wrong.'

He looked down at his hands, feeling a bit embarrassed and vulnerable at his revelation. Was he coming across as pathetic?

Emer spoke, quietly. 'My last relationship was a disaster. He was two-timing me. Seems like everyone else knew but me. Hard to hold your head up high after that. And it's made me a bit afraid of trying again.'

Jack had felt like that after Annie left. All the good memories soured and nothing left but a broken heart. 'He must be blind. Or stupid. Or both,' he said. 'You're well shot of him.'

Was there a hint of a blush on Emer's face? She pushed some escaped curls behind her ear and then yelped in pain. He could see her earring caught in a strand of hair. 'Let me …'

He carefully disentangled the earring and put it gently back in place, his fingers brushing her skin ever so slightly. She seemed to tremble, but perhaps she was still cold.

'Thank you, Jack. I'm such an eejit,' Emer said, folding and refolding the sandwich wrapper. 'I shouldn't wear dangly earrings with this hair. Who'd have thought curls could be so dangerous, eh?'

'I love curls.' The words were out before he could stop them. So uncool. He couldn't have been more embarrassingly obvious if he'd tried. Matt would be groaning if he could hear his father now. 'How was the sandwich?' he asked, grasping at any diverting topic.

'It filled the spot well. If you like, I can put those extra sandwiches in the Relatives' Room.'

'Good idea.' He passed her the carrier bag.

Spots of rain began to patter on the rooftop and they stood up.

'Well, that was at least twenty minutes without any rain,' said Emer. 'It's a miracle.'

As they headed to the door, Jack asked, 'Could we meet again tomorrow? If you don't have other plans, that is. You mentioned you had a half-day off.'

'Won't you be with Luke?'

That was a strong hint about where his duty lay. 'I'll see him in the morning, but I'm sure he'll be tired and want a rest in the afternoon.'

'Okay, then. We could meet up. What would you like to do?'

Leaving the rooftop behind, the noise of hospital life surged back again, but Jack was only dimly aware of his surroundings as he and Emer made plans for the next day.

One – pause ... two – pause. Luke hauled himself along the hospital corridor, crutches first, then his aching legs. A sharp pain from his ribs accompanied every movement. His heart was hammering. Half an hour to get this far. The afternoon would be over at this rate. He glanced at the signs on each of the doors he passed. Finally, the one he wanted. If she wasn't there, he'd have to collapse outside and wait. He managed an awkward knock.

'Come in.'

Could she not have come to the door and made his life a

bit easier? He fumbled with the handle, the crutches making it difficult to reach. He couldn't open it so knocked again.

'That's taking politeness too far …' Emer said, opening the door. 'Luke! Don't tell me you came all this way on your crutches?'

'It seemed a doddle when I started out – two days ago,' he joked.

'I do make house calls, y'know.'

'I needed the exercise.'

'Come in,' she said. 'Sit yourself down. I've just made some tea.'

Luke collapsed onto the sofa, the crutches falling untidily onto the floor. The pain in his ribs was a killer. Perhaps he wouldn't be up for this trip after all.

'I've broken out the ginger creams in your honour,' said Emer, a moment later, handing him a cup of tea with two biscuits on the saucer. She propped his crutches against the wall before sitting at her desk.

He liked her office. Toys in one corner. Books everywhere. Photos on the wall – her family maybe. Lots of plants.

'So, how's things?' she asked, sipping her tea.

Terrible. Traumatic. Sleepless nights filled with pain and memories. Best not to say any of that, though. He'd sound like a whiner. 'Jack Stewart asked me to go home with him.'

'And how do you feel about that?'

'He doesn't want me. He's just askin' out of guilt.' The man hadn't even looked at him when he'd suggested it. Going to Wales with his mam had been one thing. Going to England as good as alone was something else.

'I don't think you know Jack well enough to guess his motives.'

'I've heard plenty about him. I know what he is and what he's done.' Luke hated sounding so angry. So bitter and childish. But it wasn't his fault.

Emer set down her cup. 'That's just hearsay. Things other people have told you.'

'My mother's not "other people".'

'Of course not. I didn't mean that, but you should hear Jack's side before you decide what to do. Before you close any doors.'

She didn't understand. It was the Stewart family who'd closed doors. Years before. Slammed them in his mother's face. He'd seen the evidence with his own eyes.

'I just want to help, Luke. I don't want to push you.'

He wished she would. It would be easier if someone could make all his decisions for him. 'You *can* help me,' he said. 'It's why I came. Can you take me to see my mam?'

She was silent. He prayed she wouldn't let him down. He couldn't manage it alone.

'Don't you think Jack should be the one to take you?'

'No way! I wouldn't ask him for anythin'.' There he was, raising his voice again. Just the thought of Jack Stewart made him lose it.

'I'll have to clear it with your doctor first.'

He sat there while Emer made the necessary calls. This was going to be hard. Part of him wanted to remember his mother the way she was, but he'd regret it if he didn't see her. This was his only chance to say goodbye. It was the right thing to do, and he was glad Emer would be with him.

'If you'll come this way, Mr Kiernan.' It took a moment for Luke to realise the receptionist was talking to him. 'Mr Kiernan' meant his grand-da or his uncles, not him.

'I'll be right here, Luke,' Emer told him, settling in a chair at reception. 'Take your time.'

Now he was actually in the McBride Funeral Home, Luke felt less confident about his decision. What if it was really bad? What if the accident had wrecked his mother's face?

Joe's friend had crashed his motorbike into a tree and no one could recognise him at the wake. Imagine that being your last memory of a loved one.

'Just press the button by the door if you need anything, sir.'

The receptionist left Luke in a room with cream walls and high windows. The open casket was at the far side with imitation candles at both ends. Flowers banked the bier. Luke approached the coffin slowly, focusing on the crucifix on the wall. How had it come to this? Her life ended on a stupid country road. Such a waste. So unfair. He stopped by the coffin, took a deep breath, and looked down.

'Oh Mam!' She could have been sleeping, but for the cut down one side of her face. *Please God, let her open her eyes. Bring her back. Just bring her back. Don't make me go through life without her. Please.* The pain of loss was worse than all his injuries. And there was guilt, too. They'd had to leave Ennis because of him. He'd made a mistake and she'd paid for it. He had a lump in his throat, but no tears came. He hadn't cried in years. He'd learned not to.

Someone had twined a set of rosary beads through Annie's fingers. Not her rosary, the little silver one. That was still in the suitcase. He should be saying a prayer for her right now. Helping her soul to heaven. '*Eternal rest grant unto her, O Lord,*' he whispered. '*And let ... and let ...*' He couldn't finish. He knew the words, just couldn't get them out. What was wrong with him? He tried again, a different prayer.

'*Hail, holy Queen, Mother of Mercy,*
Our life, our sweetness, and our hope.
To thee do we cry, poor banished children of Eve ...'

Banished. His mother had been banished by the Stewarts. Rejected. Not good enough for them. A well of resentment was building inside. He tried to push it back down. This wasn't the time or the place. These were the last few precious moments with his mother. He needed to focus on her. Somehow he managed to lean down and kiss her cold cheek. 'Bye, Mam. I love you.'

He'd miss her all the days of his life, but she was finally at rest after years of suffering. That was some small consolation. Now he wanted revenge. He wanted chaos. Wreckage. And he wouldn't rest till the towers of the Stewart family came crashing down.

'Jack Stewart, please.'

Emer swirled the wine in her glass as she waited for the hotel receptionist to put her through to Jack's room. It was after nine – hopefully he wouldn't be sleeping. She wasn't even sure she should be calling him, but Luke's expression when he came out of the room at the funeral home had worried her. It was as if the trauma of the accident had hit him again with full force. His face was pale and his eyes hollow. Haunted.

'Hello?' Jack's voice came on the line.

'Hello, Jack – it's Emer.'

'Emer! I hope you're not going to cancel tomorrow.'

She couldn't help smiling to herself. It'd been a while since anybody had made her feel wanted. 'No, we're still on,' she told him. 'I just wanted to update you on Luke.'

'Oh.'

Emer wished he didn't sound so disappointed. His negativity towards Luke was, so far, the one thing about him she didn't like.

'I took him to the funeral home this afternoon. He asked me to go with him so he could say goodbye to his mother.'

There was silence at the end of the line.

'Jack – are you there?'

There was a long sigh. 'I wish he hadn't gone. Surely that's the last thing he needed. Couldn't you have stalled him until I had a chance to speak to him?'

She could have. Perhaps she should have, but Luke was an adult who had to be allowed to make his own decisions. 'I think he would have gone anyway. I preferred to be there in case he needed me.'

Silence again. Emer sipped at her wine, and waited.

'I suppose he was upset afterwards,' Jack finally said. 'Probably hated me afresh all over again.'

Emer bristled. 'It wasn't really about you, Jack. It was about Luke and his mother. And yes, he was upset. He was very pale when he came out. And very quiet. No tears, but he was shaken. I asked the nurses to keep a close eye on him.'

She'd spoken sharply and Jack might be offended. That would be unfortunate, but she was only doing her job. Luke was a young man in a world of pain and she'd do all she could to support him.

'Thank you,' said Jack, but there was still an undercurrent of frustration in his voice.

'You know,' Emer said, 'beneath that tough façade, I think Luke's crying out for affection – for someone who cares.'

Jack gave an ironic laugh. 'I must have missed that somehow. In between his throwing things and calling me a bastard.'

Emer wanted to shout *Get over yourself!* but held back. 'Luke's obviously built a defensive wall around himself. Can't you understand that? Every time you get into a confrontation with him, he builds the wall higher. Give him time to adjust. Support him whenever you can. And don't, for God's sake, criticise him for going to pay his respects to his mother. Promise me you won't do that tomorrow.'

'Of course not!' exclaimed Jack. 'What kind of a man do you think I am?'

It seemed father and son shared a bit of a temper. As did Emer – her father used to call her a spitfire when she'd give out about some perceived injustice. Time to take things down a notch now, though, or they'd all get nowhere fast. 'I think you're a generous man at heart. A kind man. And I'd like Luke to see that side of you. As I said, just be patient. You've both got a funeral to get through – you'll need all your strength for that.'

'The funeral.' All the fire had suddenly gone out of Jack's voice. 'I've put off thinking about that. I'll ask Luke tomorrow if he wants it to be in Ennis or here in Dublin.'

'Travellers like to be buried in a place they've known. You could ... no, I guess not ...' She stopped herself. It was a mad suggestion.

'What were you going to say? ... Emer?'

'Well, just that if Luke goes home with you to England, you could bury Annie there.'

There was silence. She'd probably overstepped the mark. It was none of her business really.

'Luke will likely veto that idea but I'll run it past him anyway,' conceded Jack.

He was making an effort, Emer could see that. Jack's life had also been turned upside down when the past had come back to haunt him in a shocking way. Perhaps she should cut him some slack.

'So, do you still want to meet tomorrow?' she asked. 'Or have you had enough of my bossiness?'

'I'll be there,' he promised. 'But I might be wearing a bulletproof vest.'

Emer laughed, relieved she hadn't scared him off. It wasn't everyone who would take on a straight-talking woman. She'd tone it down a bit tomorrow, though.

Chapter Four

Tuesday morning. Three days since Jack had arrived in Dublin. It seemed longer. He was eating breakfast when his mobile rang: Emer.

'Jack – can you come to the hospital?'

He caught the urgency in her voice. 'Has something happened to Luke?'

'No, he's okay,' she reassured him. 'But the Guards have just turned up to interview him. They're in the waiting room while he's having some tests. I told you how upset he was yesterday. I think he needs some support, a family member in his corner … This is important, Jack.'

God, they'd be raking over the accident. All the details about the car crash. Could Jack cope with that? 'Can't you …'

Emer hung up without saying goodbye. Obviously pissed off with him. Great.

Jack pushed his breakfast aside and grabbed his coat. He'd only been about to say *Can't you put them off for today?* Emer, though, probably thought he was suggesting she take Jack's place during the police interview. Now their afternoon could be spoiled because of this.

Not for the first time, he cursed Luke Kiernan.

Luke assessed the two Guards standing in his hospital room. The usual double act. Introduced themselves as though that made them individuals, but they seemed like all the other Guards he'd met. They generally despised Travellers. Assumed they were all crooks and troublemakers. Didn't give a damn about the decent ones. Only regular folk got respect and protection.

Like that night, some ten years ago, when his Uncle Joe was knocking Annie about … again. Luke had quietly called the police from the hall phone. The Guards didn't turn up till the next day, and when they did, they brought a search warrant and ransacked the house, looking for stolen goods. Any excuse. They eventually looked at his mother's bruises, asking if she wanted to press charges, but of course she'd said no. They made a comment about her child being worried, which landed Luke in it good and proper. Joe had gone mental because the police had been called and later he bashed Luke's head so hard against a wall that blood ran from his ear. He couldn't stand up for a week without feeling dizzy.

It was a lesson. The authorities were added to Luke's growing list of people not to trust. No one was going to help him or his mother. They were on their own, and it was down to him to look after her. Fine job he'd made of that.

The older of the Guards, Sergeant Connolly, spoke. 'We have a few questions about the accident, Luke.'

'Mr Kiernan,' he muttered. Typical. Not even asking if they could call him by his first name. No words of sympathy about his mother, either. His jaw clenched.

'If you're up to it, that is,' said Byrne, the second policeman. He pulled up a chair and took out a notebook and pen.

Luke almost laughed aloud. Like they cared if he was up to it.

Byrne flipped some pages, found the one he wanted, and read out the details. 'Luke Kiernan from Ennis? Aged twenty, born 28 October …?'

Luke stayed silent. Let the bastard work for it.

'Is that correct?' prompted Connolly.

'Yeah. I'll expect a card then, will I?' No response. They'd clearly had a sense of humour bypass.

'Address?' Byrne asked.

'No, just a card'll be fine. I'm not into women's clothes.' His uncle always said his smart mouth would get him into trouble, but these condescending gobshites deserved it. Oh well, if they hit him, he was in the right place.

'Confirm your address for us, son,' said Connolly slowly, as if he thought Luke might be simple.

'I'm between places right now.'

'Really?' said Byrne. 'According to our records, your address is 42 Carnlough Street, Ennis.'

'So why ask me? But like I said, I'm between places. I left Ennis.'

'No fixed abode, then.' Byrne was obviously happy to have something to write down. 'So where were you and your mother headed?'

'None of your business!' snapped Luke. 'We were in a crash. My mother's dead. End of story.'

'Not quite,' said Connolly. 'We need to establish the cause of the accident. What do you remember?'

'Nothin'.' And that was true. Dr O'Meara had told him he might never remember those last few minutes of his mother's life. Something about trauma affecting memory. Maybe it was for the best. Remembering might be worse.

Byrne came to life again, reading from his little black book. 'The driver of the truck you collided with said your mother was driving too fast.'

Maybe. Luke recalled the journey. Darkness. Silence in the car, apart from the swish of faulty windscreen wipers. Had it been Annie's fault? The rain *was* interfering with her vision, and she *was* driving fast because a traffic jam had held them up. They had to catch the last ferry to Wales. Waiting hours for the next one was too risky. If Joe and Liam had followed them …

'Had she been drinking?'

'She fuckin' had not! She never drank. Don't you dare say that about my mother or …'

'Luke! Don't get yourself upset.'

That was all he needed. Jack Stewart poking his nose in. Mind, he'd wanted to punch that policeman which wouldn't have been the best move.

'Good advice,' said Connolly, 'because that temper got you in trouble once before, didn't it, Luke?'

That hadn't taken long, then. Jack seemed to be ignoring the comment, though, and came to stand by his chair. Probably expected it.

'My wife's blood tests revealed no traces of alcohol. As I'm sure you already know.'

'Your wife?' said Connolly.

The look of surprise on the Guard's face was a treat.

'Yes. I'm Jack Stewart. Annie was my wife, and Luke is my son.'

Jack's hand on his shoulder made Luke cringe, but it was a great performance so he'd put up with it.

'We're both deeply distressed by what's happened, as I'm sure you'll appreciate. Luke has told you all he knows. He needs to rest now.'

Jack moved to the door and held it open. The policemen glanced at each other then headed out, but Connolly fired a parting shot. 'One other thing. The car your mother was driving was registered to Joseph Kiernan of the same address. A relative, I presume?'

'Not much gets past you, does it?' Luke hoped his sarcastic tone masked his growing panic.

Connolly scowled. 'We've left a message for him to get in touch. He's got several outstanding parking fines. Why don't you jog his memory about them?'

It wasn't the smug look of satisfaction on the man's face that made Luke feel sick, but the knowledge the police had been trying to track down Joe. It was unlikely the Guards would find out his uncle's whereabouts from any Travellers, but if word somehow got back to them about the accident, Joe might well turn up here at St Aidan's. Mad as hell, and swinging his fists. Then Luke would have a lot more than a damaged knee and bruised ribs to worry about.

After the door swung shut behind the Guards, Luke turned to Jack. 'When can we leave? Tomorrow?' It hurt his pride to have to go along with Jack's idea but he needed an escape route.

'You want to come to England?' Jack looked surprised. 'Are you sure?'

'Tryin' to talk me out of it already? Don't worry, it'll only be till I can manage by myself.'

'I'll have to check with the doctor to make sure you're fit to travel,' said Jack.

'If you don't get me out of here soon, I'll discharge myself.' Luke meant it, even though trying to make it on his own wouldn't be easy. But he'd do it if he had to.

Jack nodded. 'I'll arrange the earliest flight home I can.'

Home. Where was home now? It had only been Ennis because his mother was there and she needed him. Most of the time it felt like prison. Now he belonged nowhere. He'd go with Jack Stewart to England, but he wouldn't belong there either, among people who'd made his mother feel worthless. Still, part of him wanted to meet the rest of the Stewarts. To see the shock on their faces, the panic in their eyes when they thought he'd be staying around. It would be worth going just to see that.

'Luke?'

What now? Couldn't the man just leave him in peace?

'We need to discuss the funeral.'

He'd wondered about that. Supposed Annie would have to be buried in Dublin since nothing on God's earth would drag him back to Ennis. Travellers preferred to be buried in earth that had known them and Annie hadn't known Dublin that well, but there was nothing he could do about that. She should have had the full works, surrounded by friends and relatives, not a quick ceremony in some unfamiliar church, mourned only by her son, with her no-good husband there for show.

'I have a suggestion,' said Jack. 'We take Annie back – bury her in the family plot.'

Jesus, he surely wasn't serious. 'England? Where she was treated like dirt.'

'Maybe she was – by some. But what's the alternative?' asked Jack. 'Bury her here and then leave her? I know Matt will want to pay his respects, and so will Maggie, my housekeeper. It would give Annie a decent send-off – a proper goodbye.'

Luke was out of his depth. He'd never organised a funeral. Wouldn't know where to start.

'Your mother used to attend our local Catholic church,' said Jack. 'We could hold it there.'

Luke considered it for a moment. At least there would be more than two mourners. It was probably the best that could be done. Reluctantly, he nodded.

'What about the rest of your family, friends?' Jack asked. 'Do you want to contact anyone?'

'No. There's no one who matters.' Actually, there were plenty who mattered, especially Jessie. But he couldn't risk it because of the two who didn't.

All this talk about funerals was too much. It reminded Luke his mother was really gone. He felt tired in both body and spirit, and no longer independent but lonely and needy. 'I said goodbye to her yesterday,' he whispered. 'To Mam.'

'I know. I can understand you wanting to, but I'm not sure you're strong enough yet to cope with something like that.'

Was that concern? No matter how hard Luke tried to fight it, he craved comfort and protection. If Jack had hugged him then, offering safe, fatherly arms, he wouldn't have resisted. But it didn't happen. Jack was glancing at his watch.

Luke bit his lip. He hadn't given him any encouragement, so maybe Jack didn't want further rejection. More likely though, he just didn't care. In a moment of weakness, Luke had let down his defences. It wouldn't happen again. The bitter reality was that as far as the Stewarts were concerned, he was unwanted. He looked at his father, trying to glean some resolve from reawakening the resentment he had always felt for him. He knew where he was with that. It gave him back some normality. He'd always hated his mother's husband, but it had been easier before he became real. 'We'll bury her in England,' he told Jack, 'but in the churchyard, not your family's plot. I don't want her pushin' up the daisies on Stewart land.'

He looked away and turned on his television. The conversation was over. He stared unseeing at the screen as he listened for the closing of the door.

Emer had chosen La Mer Wine Barge and Bistro for her lunch with Jack. The boat was moored on the Grand Canal, close to the city centre, and it gave office workers the chance to sit somewhere away from the bustle for a while and gaze at the water.

The interior was cosy, with plush blue cushions, varnished wood and quaint portholes. A smooth background jazz was playing as Emer and Jack settled at their table. Hopefully, the mellow atmosphere would have a relaxing effect on him. He'd been tense ever since they met up and left the hospital together. The first thing he'd done was explain their misunderstanding on the phone that morning, and Emer had apologised for jumping to conclusions. It couldn't have been easy for him to deal with both Luke and the Guards, not to mention hearing about Annie and the accident again. It was no surprise to hear him say he wasn't very hungry. Stress played havoc with the digestive system.

When the waiter came by to take their order, Emer chose baked mussels for an appetiser, and Jack ordered the minestrone soup, without much enthusiasm. He also ordered a beer.

'Jack, you don't have to pass up on meat just because I don't eat it,' Emer said, when the waiter had left. 'It doesn't bother me – really.'

He smiled. 'Okay.'

They made small talk about the weather and the restaurant until the drinks arrived. Jack gulped down half his beer in one go, like a man who'd been lost for weeks in a desert.

He set down the glass, looking a bit shamefaced. 'Sorry – I really needed that.'

'Was it bad – Luke and the Guards, I mean?'

Jack cast a swift glance at the diners close by. They were all absorbed in their own conversations, but Jack lowered his voice anyway. 'They were implying Annie had been drinking. Luke almost lost it. Lucky I was there.'

'Perhaps he needs a solicitor,' Emer fretted.

Jack shook his head. 'They were just fishing. Hopefully they don't need Luke any longer. They don't know he's leaving Ireland.'

'Is he going home with you?' Emer mentally crossed her fingers.

'Yes, for a few weeks at least, but I think that's more from lack of options than any great desire to be with me.'

'Doesn't matter, Jack. The important thing is you'll have some time together. You can find out a bit more about him …'

'And maybe why Annie left.'

Emer nodded. That was his main reason for inviting Luke home, she knew that. Jack was coming at this thing from the wrong angle but at least it was a start.

'Luke also agreed to let me organise the funeral. It'll be at the local Catholic church Annie attended.'

Clearly Jack could be very persuasive when necessary. He'd not have been the successful businessman she'd read about otherwise. 'That's a lot of arrangements to make. If you have to get straight back to the hotel after lunch …'

'No.' He shook his head vigorously. 'I need some time away from it all. I want to hear all about *you* – your family, your career, why you don't eat meat, what you think about the ozone layer – the works.'

Emer laughed. 'In that case, it'll be a short lunch. I'm really very uninteresting.'

'Oh, I doubt that.'

The compliment and his direct gaze made Emer blush, not something that had happened much since school days. She silently blessed the waiter who turned up at that moment with their food.

The tension was slowly draining out of Jack's neck and shoulders. This leisurely lunch in a nice venue with a good-looking woman was exactly what he needed. Emer had been telling him all about her childhood in a small town in County Mayo, on the west coast of Ireland, where her father was still the local doctor. The memories she shared of a convent education, Irish dancing lessons and long carefree summers on Achill Island were soothing in their remoteness. So completely unlike Jack's early years, split between a grim boarding school and the family estate at Edenbridge, where fun was never on the agenda.

'How many brothers and sisters do you have?' asked Jack,

grinding pepper onto a plate of pan-fried Toulouse sausages with mash. His appetite was coming back.

'Three,' said Emer. 'My older sister, Maeve, lives here in Dublin – she's married with three sons. My other sister lives in America, and my brother's working as an accountant in England. So we've all scattered, but we try to get the Sullivan clan together – including aunts, uncles and cousins – at least every other year.'

'The Sullivans,' mused Jack. 'Wasn't that a TV soap?'

'So it was! But I'm sure it consisted of more than an hour of boisterous redheads talking over one another. The real Sullivans wouldn't get great ratings.'

A scatter of raindrops rattled against the porthole window. For once Jack welcomed the dreary weather. It was a good reason for them to prolong the meal, snug and dry indoors, and he'd get the chance to hear more about Emer's life. 'So what made you choose counselling as a career?' he asked.

Emer's knife and fork slowed, and she frowned. Perhaps he should have let her choose the topics, although career was usually a safe one. Jack poured them both more water, giving her time if she needed it to prepare an answer.

'Actually, it's a bit of a sad story. Maybe best save it for another day. I don't want to drag the afternoon down.'

'I'd like to hear it,' Jack said gently. 'If you feel up to it.'

Emer nodded, took a sip of her drink, and began the story. 'I met Michael at university. We were both studying psychology. It was like we'd known each other forever. We were going to get engaged when we graduated ...'

'Were?' prompted Jack.

'We buried him instead. Such a waste. Party on the beach in Kerry, too much to drink – went and got himself drowned, the poor eejit.'

'Emer, I'm so sorry.'

'Me too,' she murmured, looking out at the rain. 'A light definitely went out for me with his passing.'

Jack knew exactly what she meant. He'd felt that way after losing Caroline, and then Annie. The world made no sense and nothing mattered any more. When he next spoke, it was as one survivor to another. 'How did you get through it?'

'Threw myself into my work,' admitted Emer, triggering another jolt of recognition. The success of Stewart Enterprises had become almost an obsession for Jack back then. 'Seems like I spent every waking hour studying,' she continued. 'Classic displacement behaviour – bury the grief in order to survive. My friends and family were so worried. They persuaded me to see a counsellor. I wasn't the easiest of patients but something kept me going back, and it worked. I pulled through.'

'So that's why you chose a career in counselling?'

'I actually started my PhD researching stress in emergency personnel, but the more time I spent in hospitals, the more I was drawn to the patients. I switched my PhD focus, then did an internship in trauma counselling.'

Brains, beauty *and* compassion. One powerful combination.

'Have I got food on my face?' Emer asked, brushing at her chin.

He'd been staring. 'No, you're just perfect,' he said, and meant it.

She smiled and grabbed her glass, holding it to her cheek. 'So, what's your line of business?'

Jack didn't really want to talk about himself but he'd humour her. 'It's a family business. Stewart Enterprises. Leisure and property development. My father built it up from nothing. He started on a shoestring, saved hard, made some lucky investments, expanded, and earned his first million by the age of twenty-five.'

'A real rags-to-riches story.'

It did sound impressive. Jack had grown up in awe of his father. The man who could do anything. And a knighthood at sixty-five to boot. He doubted he'd ever be able to top that.

'And what about your mother? Did she work?'

His mother. Lady Grace. Not many people in Baronsmere could claim such an impeccable ancestry. 'No, she never worked. All she wanted was to make a good marriage,' he said. 'She was the daughter of a respected Cheshire family, but the family fortune dipped during the Depression. She had the right connections, my father had serious money, so they got married.'

'Sounds like they were made for each other,' said Emer.

'Hardly,' muttered Jack, but he didn't want to get into all of that. His parents already seemed to control so much of his life. He wanted to be free of them today.

There was an awkward silence after his comment and Jack tried to think how to get the conversation going again on an even keel.

Emer did it for him. The dessert trolley was wheeled past and she pointed. 'Look at those profiteroles. Let's have some for dessert. Pure decadence but I think we deserve it, don't you?'

The possibility of being able to wipe a smudge of chocolate from the corner of Emer's mouth cheered Jack immensely.

'So did you kiss him?' Maeve's chopsticks were poised over the takeaway carton of king prawn mushrooms.

'Maeve!' Emer produced her best scandalised expression. 'I hardly know Jack!'

'You've had lunch with him twice. And both times he paid. Nowadays that's virtually a proposal of marriage.'

Emer smiled and wrapped some noodles round her fork. She'd never been able to get the hang of chopsticks even though a Chinese takeaway at her flat had been the sisters' monthly ritual for years. 'After lunch, we went for a walk on the Green and then up to Trinity.'

Maeve waggled a chopstick in Emer's direction. 'You're out with a hot man and you show him round your old university. Did you never watch *Blind Date*? You clearly need some tips.'

Emer laughed. 'He wanted to see the sights. We had a really nice afternoon.'

'I don't think men like him are looking for "nice", to be honest.'

Emer frowned. 'Men like what?'

Maeve grabbed the computer printout about Jack that Emer had shared with her earlier. 'By all accounts, he's a rich man. He could have any woman he wants. He'll not be one you can keep on hold for long.'

'So what should I have done, Maeve? Lunged at him in the hallowed cloisters of Trinity College?'

'Well, it would have given him some kind of sign at least.'

'A sign of what – that I'm a willing whore?'

Her sister dropped the takeaway carton and gave a mock shriek. 'Emer Sullivan, wash your mouth out with soap!'

As usual, Maeve did an expert impression of their mother and both women burst out laughing. Emer looked at her sister with affection. It had been a big decision to tell Maeve about Jack – it made him and the beginnings of what they might have together seem more real.

'Are you seeing him again?' asked Maeve, wiping the tears of laughter from her eyes.

'Tomorrow. He's taking me to dinner at the Beaumont.'

'Ooh – swanky. That'll give you a chance to dress up a bit. Now, let's see if you've still got anything suitable in your wardrobe to entice a man. Or did you get rid of it all after that idiot Colm made the biggest mistake of his life?'

They went into the bedroom and Maeve critically swished through the hangers of clothes in the wardrobe. Emer was in two minds about Jack. She *was* attracted to him but there were still so many unknowns. And whether he realised it or not, he was grieving for his dead wife. Not only that, but all the trauma of her leaving him had also been resurrected. It wasn't the best time for him to get involved with a new woman. If it all went wrong, Emer would be left the wrong side of thirty holding the pieces of another failed relationship. That was a sobering thought and Maeve's excitement as she pulled out what she called The Seduction Dress couldn't make it go away.

The campfire was strong, the wood crackling and snapping. It gave everyone's face a golden glow. Luke watched them all, parents and children, huddled together, delaying the dead of night with their laughter. Potatoes were cooking on the fire and his friend, Padraig, was flipping a coin through his fingers, trying to make it disappear. It had been their favourite game all summer since they'd seen a street magician do it. In the background, one of the men was singing a lullaby to his baby daughter.

These were his people. This was his life. And it was good. He pitied folk stuck in their houses. They missed the sun creeping slowly up of a morning, and they never fell asleep under the stars or stood in the woods during a rain shower to catch that earthy growing smell as the plants drank their fill. They missed out on so much.

'Now then, young Luke, let's see what the future's storin' up.'

Jessie had taken hold of his hand, smoothed the palm out flat, and she was peering hard at it in the dim light. No one really believed she had the gift of sight. It was just a bit of fun. Some of the men laughed at her and said certain

*things happened to everyone so it was easy to guess them.
Luke only knew he loved Jessie with her mop of grey-white
hair and easy smile, and he'd do nothing to offend her. He
listened carefully as she spoke.*

'Ye'll grow into a handsome man ...' Jessie began.

*There was a hoot of laughter and Padraig's da said, 'Sure,
and you've only to look at Annie to know that!'*

*'Your first love'll be your last love,' Jessie continued. 'And
there's choices ahead. Money's there for the askin' but the
price is high.'*

*His mother shifted position beside him. 'That's enough
for tonight, Jessie,' she said. There was something in her
voice he couldn't quite place.*

'How 'bout a song, Annie?' someone asked.

'The babies'll wake,' said Annie.

*'Now wouldn't the angels themselves want to be awake
to listen to your voice? Luke needs a song on his birthday.'*

*The evening ended in music, his mother's voice ringing
out sweet and clear in the Galway darkness. The words of
the song burned themselves into Luke's memory, along with
the scent of woodsmoke and the gleam of fire in the eyes of
those he loved ...*

That memory of his eighth birthday was so clear, Luke felt
he could reach out and touch it. But those people and that
feeling of safety vanished once he and Annie moved out of
Jessie's cramped but homely caravan to live with his grand-
da. His uncles were always around then, and the good times
ended, the days all running bleakly together like endless
rain. And now he would never see his mother again, never
hear her laugh or sing.

There was no one Luke wasn't angry with at that moment.
Himself for feeling so vulnerable. Annie for leaving him. Joe
for treating Annie like a maid and knocking her about when

the mood took him, and Liam for letting him. His grand-da, a good man but weak. And Luke was angry with Jack just for being Jack. A father who hadn't cared for twenty years and was now taking over. Trying to make Luke question everything he'd been told. Well, if his mother had lied, she'd had good reason. Jack Stewart wasn't going to insult her memory. Luke had managed fine without the man who fathered him, and although it rankled to accept his help now, it was only for a few weeks, thank God.

God was someone else he was mad at, and Luke said so to Father Brennan, the elderly priest from the hospital chapel who'd turned up earlier. The man's benevolent smile had irritated Luke right away. The last thing he'd wanted was to hear about God's will.

'At least your mother is with God now,' the priest had said, after telling Luke how normal his reaction was.

'Is bein' killed at forty somethin' to be grateful for, then?' Luke had snapped. 'Well, I hope she tells Him what she thinks of his reward for being a good Catholic. All her life she had nothin'.'

'She had you.'

The priest meant well, but Annie had actually stopped living the moment Luke was born, and then he'd finally killed her.

'I'll pray for you, Luke,' Father Brennan had said as he left. Christ, priests were on a different planet.

Jack woke from a nightmare about Annie. They were trying to bury her but he knew she wasn't dead. No one would listen to his protests.

He slowly freed himself from the bedsheets he'd thrashed into a tangled mess during the dream. The clock told him it was three in the morning, but he had to get up and move around, to try to clear the residual horror from his mind.

The fluorescent light in the suite's kitchen hummed into stark brightness and Jack reached into the fridge for a beer. He slumped at the kitchen counter, holding the cool can against his cheek. He missed Matt. And Maggie. And Claire, the sister who was always on his side, no matter what. He'd phoned her the day after speaking to Matt. Told her about Annie and Luke but asked her to keep it to herself until he got back. The last thing he needed was his father flying over and asking a million questions.

So long as he was here in Dublin, Jack felt oddly safe. As if time had temporarily stopped, which in a way it had. The real nightmare would begin once he got back to Baronsmere. Then there would be arguments and tension and confusion, none of which he could easily resolve because of his uncertainty that Luke was his son. He was being forced to go out on a limb.

Jack opened the can and took a long swallow in the hopes the alcohol would shut down his monkey mind. Seeing the mobile on the counter, he flicked it on and scrolled through the gallery of photos to find the one taken today by a stranger on St Stephen's Green. There it was: Jack and Emer, arm in arm, smiling in the watery sunshine. He tapped his finger and zoomed in on Emer. She wasn't Hollywood beautiful, but she had a pretty face. Good skin, even features. And those big green eyes – so lively, so mischievous.

What he liked most about Emer, though, was that she spoke her mind. Not in the way his father did, with the intention of bludgeoning someone into submission; not even in the way Maggie did, which sprang from an irritation at everyone else's inefficiency. When Emer told you the truth, however painful it was, you somehow knew that you needed to hear it. That she had your best interests at heart.

He'd be leaving Dublin soon. Leaving Emer. And he was suddenly sad about that. He had to find out if she felt something for him, if there was anything here to build on. And he had to do that soon. Tomorrow's dinner might be his last chance alone with her. He'd pull out all the stops. Impress her. Woo her. Let her see the Jack Stewart he used to be before Annie Kiernan broke his heart.

Luke's anger lasted well into the night. He woke from dreams filled with violent memories. Fists and boots hurting his body. Annie screaming. She'd warned him enough times not to react, but he knew best. As always. And where were his uncles now? Maybe returning to an empty house and a missing car. Going to England was the right decision. Joe and Liam would never expect him to go to Jack's house because, in their minds, that would be like supping with the devil. He wasn't safe here, though, in Dublin. He *had* to get out of this hospital. That feeling of desperation made Luke beg the doctor next morning to discharge him.

'If your test results are good, Luke, then we'll let you go tomorrow, but you'll need to follow up with your family doctor. Head trauma needs careful monitoring.'

The doctor had no idea Luke's health was more at risk if he stayed.

Chapter Five

Luke forced himself to keep going on his crutches. He was walking a slow circuit of the first floor, trying to build his strength up. Six days since the accident and the pain was no better. Bruised ribs weren't as bad as broken ones, the doctor had said. Luke would have to take his word for that. He'd rested as best he could, but today he felt closed in. He hated being cooped up. When they'd moved to the house in Ennis, it was like being put in a cage.

'Ten to one, I'd say.'

Luke glanced up to see a smiling Emer, standing at the entrance to the cafeteria. 'Are you takin' bets on me?' he asked, resting on his crutches.

'Well, you're getting speedier there ... I thought you might be in training.'

He laughed despite the pain from his ribs. 'If I was a horse, I'd be a rank outsider. You wouldn't want to bet on me.'

'Oh, I think I'd take a risk. Outsiders can surprise you. So ... are you a betting man, Luke?'

'No,' he said. 'A horses man. Often helped prepare them for fairs.'

'I'd like to hear about that. Have you time in your training schedule for a drink?'

'That'd be grand,' Luke replied, and she held the door open and told him to find a seat. He chose a spot near the window, away from the groups of chattering visitors, and watched Emer as she queued at the till. Her red hair was loose and it curled round her face. She looked lovely. He wanted to tell her that, but he was too shy. It would come out all wrong, as if he fancied her. Well, he did a bit, but his chances there were zero. He was just a little Traveller, not that experienced with women. He'd never get a backward glance from someone like Emer. No point in making an eejit of himself by trying. It was enough that she seemed to like his company. When she came to the table, she brought two bottles of apple juice and an iced doughnut. 'They were out of oats, so I got you this instead.'

He accepted it gratefully. His walk had given him an appetite.

'So, tell me about you and horses,' said Emer.

'Horses are a big part of Traveller life,' he told her. 'Never owned one myself, though I did get to ride a thoroughbred once that eventually sold for a packet. Windtalker, his name was. Rode him along the beach at Doolin, just as the tide was comin' in. No one around but us. I wanted it to last forever ...' He stopped, lost in the memory of a time when he'd been truly content. It didn't seem to happen that often.

'It sounds magical,' said Emer. 'Would you like to work with horses?'

Luke sighed. 'Sure, but no owner would let a Traveller near their stables. When I was a kid, some who weren't too bigoted would let me help out, but it changed as I got older. Probably scared I'd do a moonlight flit with the horses. Suppose you couldn't blame them. I wouldn't steal, but those who do give us a bad name.'

'I saw Jack. He told me you're going back with him. Maybe you could find something with horses when you get there.'

It was a nice thought, but he'd learned not to hope for too much. It saved disappointment later. 'Yeah ... well, we'll see.'

'How are you feeling about England, Luke?'

'It's somewhere to go. For now.'

'It could be a lot more than that,' said Emer. 'A chance to meet your brother, and other family too. Might be a good thing.'

And it might be a disaster, but he didn't say that. Emer was trying to be optimistic, so he wouldn't spoil it. He swallowed the last of his juice and started to pick at the label. 'Well anyway, I'm not goin' with any expectations.'

'Maybe that's best – not to have any preconceived ideas.'

'It'll be strange, though. I've never been out of Ireland. Had a passport for over two years since me and some other lads decided we'd take off and see the world. Mam was all for it, but when it came to it, I couldn't leave her to fend for herself.'

'You and your mother were leaving, though. Why was that?'

He didn't answer for a moment. Didn't want to talk about it. Didn't want to think about it. 'Just a fresh start. It's hard to get work when people find out you're a Traveller. Thought it might be better in Wales.'

'Did you never want to go to England? To find your father and confront him?'

'Sometimes, but if I suggested it, Mam would get stressed.' Actually, he'd often dreamed about going to England and shoving that letter down Jack Stewart's throat. Pity he'd left it behind. With everything else. He would get round to confronting Jack about it, though. Once he felt stronger and his stay in England was near an end.

'What happened to her, Luke – to both of you – after she left England?'

A lot he didn't want to talk about. He'd not lie to Emer, though – just not mention it. 'We lived with a group of Travellers. My grand-da and my uncles were on the road too, but not always with us. We shared a van with an old woman called Jessie who took Mam in when I was two. We saw Grand-da every so often, then he had his first stroke. Mam and I moved in with him to take care of him. He refused to go into hospital since my Gran died in one. Somethin' went wrong when she had my Mam. Eventually, the Settled Housing Scheme got us a house in Ennis. Jessie stayed close by us – in a haltin' site. She thought of my mam as her daughter.'

'You don't talk much about your uncles or want them to know where you are. Why is that, Luke? Do you not think they should be at the funeral?'

'They wouldn't give a damn!' He was annoyed with himself for raising his voice, and the lull in the chatter around them made him flush with embarrassment. 'They're workin' away somewhere, anyway. Probably couldn't make it. Besides, Mam's goin' to be buried in England. Her devoted husband's idea.'

If Emer noticed the contempt in his voice when he spoke about Jack, she ignored it. She reached into her pocket and handed him a card. 'My mobile number. Call if you need help or advice, okay? Or even just someone to talk to. Your mother's funeral is a huge deal. Don't feel you have to be strong. You can call me and let it all out if you need to.'

'Thanks.' He picked up the card and stared at it. Did she always give this out? Maybe she just felt sorry for him.

'Are you okay, Luke?'

'Yeah,' he lied. 'Just thinkin'. I'd like to say somethin' at the funeral, but I don't know what. I've never talked in public before. How can you really sum up a person – a whole life – with a few words and some bits of music?' He shook his head. 'Mam was a really special person, but the Stewarts couldn't see that. Not good enough for them. They made her feel like nothin'.'

'Just say what's in your heart, Luke, and you won't go wrong. Let them know how special she was.'

He nodded. 'I wish you could have known Mam,' he said. 'I think you'd have liked each other.'

Emer smiled. 'I'm sure we would. And thank you. I take that as a great compliment … You know, after the funeral, I hope you'll finally be able to do the things you want. Maybe use that passport to travel. Right now, you can't think of enjoying yourself, but eventually you will. You shouldn't feel guilty. You need to know that.'

'Maybe. Mam would probably agree with you. She used to worry I wasn't doin' the same as other lads, havin' a girlfriend and all.' Why had he said that? Too much information. Now he was blushing. Emer would think he was a freak. Maybe that was for the best. The facts about his limited experience with the opposite sex weren't something he wanted to remember. Or share.

'So there's no one special in your life?'

'No, it wasn't exactly easy. No Traveller girls around my age where we lived. And settled people weren't acceptable.' He didn't mention that he would never have wanted to take a girl home in case she witnessed his uncles being abusive.

'Don't worry,' said Emer, with a smile. 'The girls in England love an Irish accent, and eyelashes like yours will have them queuing up.'

He grinned. 'Sounds like I'll need my own confessional.'

She smiled back, and Luke wished she could be there, in England. She made him feel special. 'Will you see me off tomorrow, Emer?'

'You bet,' she replied, and he felt the unfamiliar glow of an inner satisfaction. The list of people he trusted was very short. It would be good to add another name to it.

'Your drink, sir.' The waiter in the hotel restaurant served a glass of twenty-one-year-old single malt, which was Jack's reward to himself for a day spent battling bureaucracy. The paperwork required to transport a body from one country to another was unbelievable. Taking Annie back to Ennis would have been much simpler.

'Would you like to order, sir?'

'Not yet. I'll wait for my guest.'

Jack had gone all out to impress Emer, like he'd resolved to do during last night's post-nightmare drinking session. He'd taken the time today to buy a charcoal-grey Armani suit and some silver and onyx cufflinks. He'd given the *maître d'* a hefty tip to get a window table at such short notice. The view of Dublin by night was breathtaking.

A vaulted ceiling rose above him, and a live quartet playing Mozart added to the genteel ambience. This was Jack's turf. He felt comfortable surrounded by the luxury and good taste money could buy. In his experience, women usually appreciated men who could provide them with the finer things in life. That certainly seemed to be the case with the blonde at a nearby table who'd been coyly making eye contact with him since he sat down.

'I think she's spoken for. That man at the bar is looking daggers at you.'

Emer slipped into the seat opposite and Jack almost spilled his drink. She'd caught him making eyes at another woman … a great start to the evening. He'd have to be extra attentive to atone.

And being attentive wasn't a problem because Emer looked stunning. Her silver and black dress showed an enticing amount of cleavage, but the *pièce de résistance* was her auburn curls caught up in a number of diamanté combs. Some tendrils had escaped – any second now, he'd have to reach out and twine them back in.

'Are you thinking that I clean up nicely?' she asked.

He'd been staring too much, but her tone was playful. 'It's certainly a change from jeans,' Jack said, pouring her a glass of water.

'It is that. Hospitals and high heels just don't go together, but I enjoy dressing up when I can. Thanks for inviting me. It's the first time I've been in here.'

73

'No, thank *you*, Emer. I don't know how I'd have got through this week without you.' He basked in the glow of her smile. 'You've been so supportive – a dinner doesn't really seem to cover it.'

'It's more than enough, believe me, especially given these prices. I'd have been happy with a pub meal.'

It felt like she'd thrown his wealth back in his face. 'Well, there's still time,' he said, an edge to his voice. 'We could change back into our jeans and go to the pub on the corner.'

'What are you talking about?' Emer was clearly startled. 'I'm staying right here. I might never get this chance again.'

Jack had overreacted and she didn't deserve his heavy sarcasm. 'Sorry – it's just I wanted this evening to be special.'

'It *is* special,' she said, her eyes kind. 'And I love all this. I'm not used to it, that's all. Sorry if I put my foot in it.'

Jack shook his head. 'You didn't. It's my fault. I was oversensitive. If you have a bit of money, you're often criticised, whatever you do with it. My family's company provides jobs and donates a lot to charity but some people just can't forgive a nice car or an overseas vacation or a meal in a good restaurant.'

Emer was listening but she stayed quiet. He was just making things worse. 'I'm coming across as a privileged whiner,' he said. 'I need to shut up, don't I?'

She smiled. 'Jack, I don't judge people by their money or lack of it. Money can do a lot of good in this world, but I'm more interested in who a person is and what they believe in, rather than what they have.'

She looked deep into his eyes and her expression showed him this was her truth. She'd accept his financial generosity but not compromise herself for it. The difference between Emer and Sarah was startling. Sarah knew the price of everything and had to have the very best that money could buy. Annie had been the opposite – nervous around too much wealth. Emer, though, could dine in a fancy restaurant or share a sandwich on a rooftop, and she'd be okay with both.

The waiter suddenly swooped over, notebook in hand. 'Are you ready to order?'

'Have you got any humble pie?' asked Jack.

'Er ...'

Emer's laughter was a welcome sound. The evening was back on track.

'I think I've just died and gone to heaven,' said Emer, after savouring the last mouthful of her white and dark chocolate raspberry tart. 'A-ma-zing.'

Jack was grinning. He'd finished his lemon tart first so had watched as she communed with her dessert. 'And I thought that was a myth,' he said. 'About women and chocolate.'

'No myth. Women and chocolate are the best of pals. Mr Cadbury has never let me down yet.'

'Perhaps I should have had this gift-wrapped in chocolate.' Jack took something out of his pocket and set it down on the table near Emer's glass.

It was a Tiffany blue box tied up with a white ribbon. Something she'd only seen before in movies. Her heart skipped a beat.

'Open it,' encouraged Jack. 'It's the second part of my thank you.'

Speechless, she did as he asked, gently pulling at the ribbon and lifting the lid of the box. Inside was an amber drop pendant – an exact match for the earrings she'd been wearing the other day. This was a man who paid attention to details. Her fingers gently stroked the smooth gem. 'Oh, Jack ... it's beautiful. Thank you so much.'

His smile of pleasure was genuine, not smug. 'Amber's called the lucky stone, you know.' He cleared his throat. 'I'd really like to see you again, Emer … I mean, after I'm back in England … Is that something you'd want, too?'

It was the hesitation and uncertainty in his voice more than the expensive gift that decided Emer. 'When the funeral's over and Luke's feeling stronger, I'd like to see you again. Very much.'

Lord knows how they'd manage to get a relationship going when they lived on different islands. Maeve would be pleased, though. No doubt she'd put the success of the evening down to her words of wisdom and choice of dress.

So it seemed a new chapter had started in Emer's life. And that was a good thing. Except the desire to celebrate couldn't quite overcome her heart's reluctance to expose itself to hurt again.

Thursday lunchtime. Rain again. Luke stood propped against the window of his room, watching people getting drenched. At least they could run. He'd never take that for granted again. He'd been here a week, although it seemed much longer, but finally this morning the doctor told him he could leave. Luke had asked a nurse to call Jack and let him know. He couldn't face having to ask a favour from a man he'd grown up despising.

'Luke?'

God, here he was now. Jack Stewart, hair plastered to his head and looking a right eejit. All that money and he couldn't fork out for an umbrella.

'I heard the good news,' said Jack. 'They're doing the paperwork now.'

Maybe Luke could still change his mind. Go to Wales. Hole up in a bed-and-breakfast somewhere for a few weeks till he was fit again. It'd be bleak but at least he'd be his own man.

Jack dumped some bags on the bed. 'Got you some

clothes. I'm sure you don't want to arrive in England wearing a hospital-issue tracksuit.'

'I don't want charity.' Jack looked pissed off, but Luke had lived off handouts most of his life, and the last thing he wanted was to feel obliged to a Stewart.

'You can pay me back later, then. But I know you've got no clothes. They had to cut off the ones you were wearing when you were brought in. And there were none in your suitcase.'

Luke's heart jumped. 'How do you know that? Why were you goin' through my things?'

'I never touched your things. The medical staff did when they needed to identify you. I hope these'll fit you.' Jack laid out the clothes on the bed: an Ireland rugby shirt, jeans, tracksuit bottoms, T-shirts, a roll-neck sweater, socks, underwear and a pair of trainers. There was also a simple, but stylish, black leather jacket.

Most of Luke's gear had been second-hand from charities like St Vincent de Paul. Or Dunnes if he was lucky. This was like several Christmases and birthdays all rolled into one. Judging from the labels, Jack had spent a small fortune. But then, he could afford it. Probably spent nearly as much in a posh restaurant. This was just guilt money. Or maybe he didn't want to be embarrassed by his *gypo* son. 'It'll take me forever to pay you back,' Luke mumbled, ignoring that small nagging voice which told him he was being unreasonable.

'Take as long as you like. Just don't make an issue out of it. You needed clothes, I bought them.'

'What time's our flight?' Luke asked, relieved to be changing the subject. He could give as good as he got in an argument, but right now he was tired and anxious. There would be plenty of time later to tell Jack what he could do with his money.

'Our flight's tomorrow,' answered Jack. 'It's the earliest

one that could accommodate a ... a coffin. We'll go back to my hotel for the night.'

More delays. And even worse, stuck in a hotel room with Father of the Year.

'There's TV and a computer there ... you won't be bored. Luke – is something wrong?'

'What could be wrong? My mother's dead, I can't walk without crutches, and I'm leavin' my country to stay with strangers. Can't wait.'

Jack stared at him. Luke jutted out his chin, ready for the inevitable angry response. It never came. 'You get ready, Luke. I'm just going to make a few business calls.'

That look in Jack's eyes. Luke had seen it before from social workers, teachers, doctors. Pity, that's what it was. Usually it made him angry. Now he just felt small and insignificant, and he didn't want to go to England, where he knew no one and would stick out like a sore thumb.

Jack and Luke were seated side by side in the hospital cafeteria, not talking or looking at each other. Emer watched them for a moment, father and son embarking on a journey far greater than the one across the Irish Sea. Physically, they looked nothing alike. Jack was taller and more muscular, and Luke was dark while his father was fair. Jack's confident manner and his impeccable clothes also contrasted sharply with his son's bewildered look and the leather jacket that seemed a size too big for him. Emer's heart went out to Luke. He had so much to offer, and she hoped Jack and his family would help him realise his potential.

She'd never felt so emotionally involved with a patient – or a relative. She'd spent a lot of last night reliving her dinner date with Jack. The gorgeous restaurant, the delicious food – and their goodnight kiss outside the hotel. Soft and gentle at first, tipping over into passionate, until they'd pulled away from each other as though both sensing a line neither was yet prepared to cross.

And perhaps for Emer that line had something to do with Luke. How would he feel about her getting involved with his father? He assumed she was on his side against the Stewarts – the only ally he felt he had. There was no point in depriving him of that illusion when he had the nightmare of his mother's funeral to get through. That would be cruel. Plus it was important to see how Jack dealt with his new son. Of course he was upset about Annie, but the kind of man Emer wanted to be with needed to have a big heart and to put family first.

Jack spotted her in the doorway and smiled. Emer moved forward. It was time to say goodbye.

As he stepped through the entrance of the Beaumont Hotel, Luke wanted to turn around and walk back out again. This wasn't a hotel, it was a palace. Marble columns, a huge staircase and a bloody chandelier. How the other half lived. Jack's suite was the same. Plush carpet, tapestries on the walls, marble everywhere. Luke wasn't impressed. 'The starvin' millions would love this.'

'Meaning?' asked Jack.

'Well there's only you in it. Do you spend money just for the sake of it?'

'Maybe I should have checked into the YMCA and made a donation to Oxfam.'

Jack's sarcasm was irritating. The man didn't have a clue how insensitive it was to flaunt his wealth. To show Luke what he'd been missing. 'Why not?' he countered.

'Luke, I've got money!' Jack snapped. 'Just deal with it – okay?'

How could his mother ever have loved this insufferable bastard? While he was living the high life, Annie would think she was well off when her jam jar was full of small coins. 'Did you *ever* give a thought to how we struggled?'

Jack threw up his hands and moved forward. 'For God's sake … I *never* knew about you. How many more times?'

Luke stumbled back, waiting for the blow. He hit the corner of the table and a sharp pain in his chest made him cry out. Then Jack was there, helping him into an armchair, ignoring the weakened attempt to shrug him aside.

'Bastard!' hissed Luke, when he'd caught his breath.

Jack was watching him, frowning. 'You thought I was going to hit you, didn't you?'

Luke didn't answer but held Jack's gaze.

'I would never do that!' Jack said, shaking his head.

'*Course* not,' said Luke. Jack was probably no different to Joe. Just wore better clothes.

Jack sat down on the end of the bed and stared at his hands as he spoke. 'Luke, you make me angry and frustrated – but I would never hit you.' He looked up. 'Who gave you those bruises? The ones on your face, your arms – all over your body.'

'I was in a car crash!' snapped Luke. 'Did you miss that bit?'

'No, you got those bruises before. Someone beat you up.'

'What do you care?' He was not about to spill out his life story to Jack Stewart. Sitting there so self-righteous, like all the problems hadn't been caused by him. His thoughts were interrupted by a knock at the door. 'Who's that?' he whispered. Who knew they were here? Would the hospital have told anyone?

'Room service, probably,' said Jack. He had the door open before Luke could hide in the other room. A waiter walked in with a trolley of covered dishes and bottled drinks. Jack tipped him and then they were alone again. 'I thought it best to eat here.'

'Are you ashamed of me?' demanded Luke. 'I *can* use a knife and fork.'

Jack leaned forward and, with an exaggerated gesture, flicked at Luke's shoulder. 'That chip is getting tiresome. Lose it. I just thought it better for you to rest your leg instead of struggling down to the restaurant.'

'Why don't you let me make my own decisions?' Luke saw the corners of Jack's mouth twitching. The scumbag was laughing at him. 'What's so funny?'

'I thought you were only your mother's son,' said Jack, 'but I was wrong. You're stubborn and you're bolshie. You could be more like me than I thought.'

'Great,' muttered Luke. Just what he needed.

'Anything else I should know, Mr Stewart?'

Jack sipped at his coffee. Freshly ground Colombian beans. Nothing better to start the day. He spoke into the phone. 'Yes. Watch out for the Kiernans, especially Joe. He's a hard bastard. Quick with his fists.'

'Don't worry, I can handle myself.' And the man probably could. Doyle, ex-Guard turned private detective. Recommended by Flynn. 'How should I contact you?'

'Call this number – my mobile,' Jack told him. 'Don't ever ring my office. And put nothing on paper.'

'Understood. I'll get to Ennis on Monday. Then give me a while to nose around, see what I can find.'

Replacing the receiver, Jack felt a twinge of guilt. Should he be prying into Luke's life? But surely he had a right – and a responsibility – to know what he was taking on. There were those bruises for a start. And the police at the hospital had mentioned some trouble. Luke had been acting very suspiciously about his suitcase. There was Matt's safety to think about. And Maggie's. Luke, of course, must never find out that a detective had been hired.

Jack buttered a croissant and glanced at the flight details. This was it. Back to Baronsmere with Luke, and Annie's body. The shit would really hit the fan then. A few weeks of hell ahead. And this week had been bloody torture, too. Well, apart from Emer. She'd been the one highlight.

He couldn't believe he hadn't asked her to spend the night with him, but something had held him back, maybe fear of rejection. She wasn't like the usual women he met, who often fell at his feet. Would she just forget him now? Out of sight, out of mind? There was one way to fix that. He picked up the phone and called the front desk. 'I'd like to send thirty long-stemmed red roses to Emer Sullivan at St Aidan's Hospital ...'

'Would you like more orange juice, sir?'

Luke had never been called 'sir' so much in his life. He politely refused and the flight attendant moved away. Jack had his head stuck in the *Financial Times*. They'd hardly spoken at all, which suited Luke just fine. He wanted to be left alone. Watching them load Annie's coffin into the hold had drained any fighting spirit, and right now he didn't feel he'd ever get it back. Why hadn't they let him die at the roadside, along with his mother? How very different it could have been if they'd been on that road just a few minutes later, or earlier – they'd be in Wales now, starting a new life.

Luke glanced out of the window at the green fields below. It looked like Ireland. Except it wasn't. It was a foreign land, and he felt pangs of homesickness. Would he ever be able to return? Had he made the right decision? He wasn't guaranteed safety in England. Joe was a thug, but he wasn't stupid. If Connolly or Byrne ever did get hold of Joe, would they mention having met Luke's father? If they did, Joe would put two and two together and turn up on Jack's doorstep. Luke's only hope was that his uncles would dodge the police, like they always did.

'Sir, please put your seat into the upright position and fasten your seatbelt. We'll be landing soon.'

He did as he was asked, wincing from the pain in his ribs. Everything was such an effort.

'Are you okay?' asked Jack.

Luke nodded.

'We should be home in an hour once we clear the terminal,' Jack told him.

Home. That was a laugh. The Stewart family would choke on their caviar when they saw him. He wouldn't fit in with them, nor did he want to. They meant nothing to him, but he wished it was different. He hated feeling so alone.

As the plane began its descent, Luke closed his eyes and wondered when he'd next sleep beneath an Irish sky.

Chapter Six

'Honey, I'm home!'

Jack was in his study when he heard Matt arrive home, calling out what was now a standing family joke, immediately followed by the sound of claws slithering along the wooden floor as Honey the Golden Labrador raced to greet her master. It was comforting. Jack needed such moments of familiarity now more than ever.

'There's someone trying to sleep,' scolded Maggie. Their voices receded, Matt doubtless following the housekeeper into her domain, the kitchen. The smell of roasting beef wafted along the passageway into Jack's study, but he had little appetite.

When they'd got home from the airport a few hours ago, Maggie was all over Luke, hugging him and saying how sorry she was about Annie. Luke, probably shell-shocked by this outpouring of affection, had soon retreated to his bedroom in the downstairs guest suite, which was really a self-contained flat, useful when entertaining potential business clients – and useful now for a fiery invalid. He'd said he was tired and would prefer to eat dinner in his room and then sleep.

'He's so like his poor mother,' Maggie had said. 'Same dark hair, and those blue eyes. I'd have known him anywhere.' And that was the problem. Luke was too much like Annie and seeing him here in this house brought it all back – the pain her leaving had caused.

It would be so helpful to hear Emer's calm voice right now. Jack had tried phoning her earlier but the call had gone straight to voicemail. No point in hiding away here in the study – best go and see Matt and make sure he was on side.

Maybe enjoy a final father–son chat before the duo became a trio.

In the kitchen, Matt was helping himself to the strawberries set aside for pudding. 'Ow!' he yelped, as Maggie rapped his knuckles with a wooden spoon. 'That's child abuse, that is.'

Jack smiled. It was good to be back home with Matt and Maggie.

'Hey, Dad, good to see you,' said Matt, sneaking another strawberry when Maggie's back was turned. 'Sorry I wasn't here when you got back. Had a meeting about the designs for the nightclub. I can't wait to meet Luke. Maggie says I can't go in and say hello because he's sleeping.'

The ability of the young to adapt to radically altered circumstances never ceased to amaze Jack. Here was Matt, full of enthusiasm at the thought of meeting his newfound brother. Not a cloud on his horizon.

'Don't expect too much,' Jack advised. 'He's still grieving. Probably still in shock, too. Maggie – my parents have decided to come over for dinner. Sorry for the short notice.'

'Shit! Talk about bad timing!'

'Don't bring that pub talk home, Matthew,' warned Maggie, hands on hips. 'You weren't raised to be a foul-mouth.'

'You know, Maggie, I'm twenty-five. I can do whatever I want.'

'Not in my kitchen, you can't.'

'And what are you planning for dinner, Maggie? A fatted calf?' joked Matt.

'You'd better get changed,' she said, brandishing the wooden spoon in his direction. 'No doubt your gran'll be done up to the nines. We'll never hear the end of it if you're in jeans. I'm glad Luke decided to have dinner in his room. At least he won't have to listen to her going on about cocktail parties and hats for Ascot.'

Jack grinned at Matt. Maggie and Grace Stewart had been at war for years. Their spats were village legend. It was good that some things never changed.

Jack drew on a Cohiba cigar as he sat in the drawing room, waiting for his parents to arrive. He didn't smoke often – just when he was stressed. He made a mental note to get in a good supply. How was he going to tell his parents about Luke? Should he come right out with it or lead up to it gradually? It would be so much easier if he was enthusiastic himself but he was far from sure he'd done the right thing bringing Luke home. Matt and Maggie were pleased but Nicholas and Grace were going to react very differently. Jack could handle confrontations in the business world with ease; it was a different matter, though, when it happened in his own home.

'Aunt Claire called when you were in the shower.' Matt entered the drawing room, dressed now in grey flannels and white shirt. 'She wants to meet Luke. We might all take a trip to Manchester on Monday.'

'Okay.' Claire and Annie had always got on well. His sister would be in Maggie and Matt's camp.

Matt sat down on the sofa near the fireplace. He took up a magazine from the coffee table, flicked through it, then tossed it aside. His foot was tapping impatiently. He glanced at Jack. 'Are you really up for this, Dad? You look done in. I could call and cancel, if you like?'

Surely that would be better all round. A quite dinner and bed, then the grand revelation tomorrow. It would only delay the inevitable, though. 'Thanks, Matt, but it's too late for that. Anyway, there's never going to be a right time. They'll be very shocked.'

Matt frowned. 'Well, yeah, at first – but Luke is their grandson. A Stewart. It'll all be fine.'

If only it could be that easy. 'I don't think so, Matt. There's a lot about the past you don't know.'

Matt waved a dismissive hand. 'I know Gran and Annie didn't get on but that's got nothing to do with Luke. He's family, and families stick together. Isn't that what you've always told me?'

Nothing was worse than children quoting back your words of wisdom, especially when those words were going to prove to be untrue. 'It's not going to be that easy, Matt. Luke doesn't want to be here and I think he holds me responsible for everything, including Annie's death. He hardly talked to me at all in the hospital. And he's been even more withdrawn since we left Dublin. Of course, it didn't help when he saw his mother's coffin being loaded on the plane.'

'Coffin?' Matt looked shocked.

Jack rubbed his forehead. 'I can't believe I forgot to mention it. Must be more tired than I thought. Luke and I decided to have Annie buried here at St John's.'

Matt's expression was approving. Jack silently thanked Emer for her suggestion about the burial. He needed all the bonus points he could get right now.

The doorbell rang.

'I'll go smooth the way,' Matt offered, getting up and going into the hallway to join Maggie who was already clicking her way to the front door.

Matt was the apple of his grandmother's eye. Just seeing him would spark off her happy daydreams of a big wedding for him to the daughter of some royal. And she'd be more likely to behave when he was present. Keep up the façade of *noblesse oblige*.

'Matt! Where have you been hiding this past month? Too busy for Sunday lunch now, eh?'

And Sir Nicholas Stewart had entered the building.

People said his voice could be heard two fields away. He'd spent his early years booming out commands across noisy construction sites and he'd never really toned it down. From his vantage point in the drawing room, Jack saw his father check his watch against the grandfather clock in the hallway. Probably worried that minutes might be trying to escape. Time is money was his philosophy.

Grace swept into view, holding out her coat to Maggie without so much as a glance at the servant she considered bold and disrespectful, and Jack smiled as Maggie dropped an exaggerated curtsey behind her back.

'Matt, darling!' Grace kissed Matt's cheek and rearranged his collar. 'We were talking about you today, Victoria McLean and I. Her niece, The Honourable Rosalind Delaney, finishes at Marlborough this summer.'

That was even quicker than Jack had expected. Grace was never going to be happy till she'd married Matt off. As long as it was to someone of her choosing. Someone who knew which sauce to serve with duck but probably not much else.

'She has plans to study at the Courtauld,' Grace persevered. 'Very bright girl. Rides extremely well, too.'

Thankfully Matt managed to resist making a comment on that one. 'Good for her,' he said. 'I'm sure she'll make someone else a lovely wife. Now – how about an aperitif before dinner? Let's join Dad in the drawing room.'

That was Jack's cue. He stood up to greet his parents. Grace moved so smoothly across the Turkish carpet that she could have been on casters. She kissed his cheek, enveloping him in her cloying floral scent, and then draped herself elegantly on the Louis Quinze sofa.

'So, Jack – what was this secret mission all about?' Nicholas found his favourite armchair. 'Lots of links golf courses in Ireland. Or some hotel development, perhaps?'

Jack hadn't phoned his father once from Ireland, despite

Nicholas having left several messages demanding an update. He'd e-mailed to say he'd explain everything on his return. Luke's arrival was news that should be broken face to face. Right now, though, Jack wished he could postpone it indefinitely.

Matt handed round the drinks. Jack got his usual whisky, which he downed it in one gulp, hoping it would steady him for what was to come. As he lowered the glass, he saw them all watching him. He felt acutely self-conscious and wished they would all vanish and leave him in peace. Including Luke. Especially Luke.

'Are you all right, Jack?' asked his mother.

'I'm tired,' he said.

Grace's expression was disapproving. 'In that case, darling, we won't stay long.'

As polite as ever, but the word 'darling' could drip from her mouth as easily as water from a tap, and just as transparent.

'So, tell us about Ireland,' said Nicholas. 'I'm rather hoping it's connected to the Macallan Consortium.'

Jack took a deep breath. 'I wasn't in Ireland on business.'

For once, Nicholas seemed confused. 'Why didn't you tell me you'd scheduled a holiday? The deal with Canalside Leisure is at a fairly critical stage. Not good to keep them waiting ...'

Jack held up his hand to stop the flow of criticism. He focused on the French Empire ormolu and marble clock on the mantelpiece, its loud and irritating tick the only sound in the room for several seconds. Best get it over with. 'I've just discovered I have a son. I brought him back with me.'

He watched his parents as the shock registered. He sympathised. His world had tilted, too, when he'd heard the news.

'What are you saying?' asked Grace. 'That you've been having an affair, which has resulted in a child?'

'No, no, he's—'

'For heaven's sake, Jack!' interrupted Nicholas. 'What kind of fool are you? A man in your position has to ensure precautions are taken or you could be a prime target for some gold-digger looking for a very nice little income – not to mention landing you with a millstone around your neck for eighteen years!'

They'd got it all wrong. Assumed he was talking about a baby, a new child. Instead, they'd have to meet a belligerent and resentful young man who was the image of the woman they'd rejected.

'So who is this woman?' asked Grace. 'Not another – *diddakoi* – I trust?'

'No, the same one,' came a quiet voice behind them.

Shit! Luke was in the doorway, balanced uncomfortably on his crutches. The door to the drawing room was old oak, heavy, and generally left open. Jack could have kicked himself for not thinking to close it.

It was Matt who finally broke the awkward silence. 'Hi, Luke. I'm Matt. It's good to meet you.' His words of welcome got no response from Luke who was staring – no, glaring – at Grace.

Jack was acutely aware how out of place Luke was in these formal surroundings – casually dressed, hair tangled from sleep, cuts and bruising prominent on his pale face. *Are you ashamed of him?* Emer's words echoed, uncomfortably.

'Come and sit down, Luke.' Matt was the only one making an effort, but there was still no response. Jack saw Grace glance at Nicholas. He felt sorry for his parents. He'd had some time to adjust to the revelation; they were learning about it in the very presence of their 'new' grandson, who had overheard their harsh words. Why hadn't Luke just stayed in his room? Why did he always make everything so difficult?

'He's … Annie's son?' asked Grace.

Jack nodded.

Nicholas got up and stood in front of the fireplace, arms crossed, looking every inch the lord of the manor. 'Well, I'm sorry, but I'm finding this a bit hard to swallow. We hear nothing for years and then a stranger shows up claiming a family connection. Let's be realistic here – we can't just simply take his word for things. We are wealthy, we have prestige. We are a target – for the media, for blackmail, for confidence tricksters …'

'And that's what you think I am?' Luke interrupted.

'Is it money you want?'

Nice one, Dad. Jack closed his eyes, waiting for the eruption from Luke, which surprisingly never came. It came from Matt instead.

'Luke's here because Dad and I want him here.' Matt's tone was sharp, his expression angry. 'He's my brother. Your grandson. And right now I'm ashamed to be a Stewart.'

Nicholas ignored him, continuing to interrogate Luke. 'Why now? After so long? How old are you, anyway? Eighteen? Nineteen?'

'Sorry to disappoint you. I'm twenty.'

'Still a long time to have made no contact,' said Nicholas.

'Not long enough.'

Luke's temper appeared to be surfacing. Jack cast a wary eye at nearby breakables.

'How long have you known about this, Jack?' Grace's tone was pure steel.

'I had no idea about Luke's existence until a week ago.'

'And is *she* here, too? Did she come with him?'

Such contempt wasn't pleasant to hear but maybe understandable. Annie had deserted Jack and his mother had witnessed his near breakdown.

'My mother's dead!' spat Luke. 'Killed in a car crash.

Sorry I couldn't have been more obligin', but this was the best I could manage.' He indicated his crutches. There was a brief pause before he continued. 'Thank you for not bein' hypocrites and sayin' you're sorry. She told me how you wanted rid of her.'

Luke turned and left the room. Nobody spoke. Jack looked at Matt who looked at Grace who looked at Nicholas. It was like a stage farce. And the damned clock still dominated the room with its ticking.

'Excuse me,' Matt said, as he followed Luke.

Eventually, Jack spoke. 'Dad, how could you say that – about Luke probably being a confidence trickster and wanting money?' He wasn't going to let him get away with that. It had been cruel and unnecessary. A nagging voice told him he should have taken Nicholas to task when Luke was still in the room.

Before Nicholas could answer, Grace stood up, bright spots of anger in her cheeks. 'Because it's the oldest trick in the book and you're falling for it! Annie left you for another man, who probably *is* the father, and now the boy is out to make some money. How can you be so naïve?'

Now Jack was grateful Luke had left the room. Grace's insensitive outburst was embarrassing. Made him feel ashamed. 'He hasn't asked me for a penny,' he said.

'Not yet.'

Keeping his temper wasn't easy. 'Annie left in February. Luke was born in late October. He *could* be my son, so I can't just turn my back. I have a responsibility. Surely you can see that?'

'Will you be doing a DNA?' his father asked.

'I doubt Luke would agree to it,' said Jack. 'It'd make him feel even more rejected than he does already. I don't want to do anything I might regret.'

'Well, perhaps that's for the best.'

That was a surprise. Jack would have expected Nicholas to demand proof.

'We don't want to risk a scandal,' Nicholas continued. 'We have quite a few deals where negotiations are delicately poised. A DNA test could lead to unpleasant publicity. The media would have a field day with the whole gypsy thing. If, as you seem to expect, he's proved to be your son, there would be accusations of the Stewarts abandoning their own because of his culture – we'd be associated with bigotry, racism and God knows what. Hardly worth the risk.'

Ah, that explained it. Business first, as usual.

'Please tell me you're not planning to keep him here, Jack,' said Grace.

'He's staying till he's well. Then he might be moving on. Matt wants the chance to get to know him better. I can't block that. They could be brothers.'

'And just how are we going to explain his presence?' demanded Grace. 'Will you tell everyone he's your son? We'll be a laughing stock. They'll think you've been tricked a second time by your tinker wife.'

The insult burned its way into Jack's mind. How many times had Annie endured it? She'd talked about how hard it had been to ignore such name-calling when she was growing up. 'She wasn't a tinker!' he snapped. 'Nor a gypsy. She was a Traveller. And that's what you'll call Luke from now on.'

'Don't be pedantic,' said Grace.

Jack met his mother's eyes and didn't flinch. Maybe Luke wasn't his – but maybe he was. And what kind of a father would he be if he allowed such scorn to pass unchallenged? 'So long as Luke is living under this roof, I don't want to hear him insulted again. He's just lost his mother, for God's sake. Can't you both try to show a bit of compassion?'

'Your mother only has your best interests at heart, Jack,'

said Nicholas. 'You were crushed when Annie left. We don't ever want to see that again.'

'The past is over. What does it really matter now?'

'The past is never over,' his father said. 'If today has proved anything, it's proved that.'

'Then try to make up for the past, and the fact you were never exactly welcoming to Luke's mother.'

'You know Annie was totally unacceptable,' Grace snapped. 'You were just blinded by a pretty face ... and the novelty. I understand. You were grieving for Caroline and it impaired your judgement. But if Annie hadn't left you, do you seriously believe it would have lasted? You were from totally different worlds and Luke will realise that eventually. Whether he's your son or not is irrelevant. He doesn't belong here and it was wrong of you to make him believe he ever could.'

His parents clearly weren't going to buy the family connection. Wouldn't accept Luke even if a DNA proved it. How could Jack ever have thought otherwise? Oh well, in for a penny ... 'I'm having Annie buried here. I brought her back, too.'

Grace stood up, smoothing the creases from her silk dress. She refused to look at Jack when she spoke. 'I hope you're not planning to use the family plot because that will be over *my* dead body!'

'You're a snob, Mother, through and through.' There. He'd finally said it and it was a relief, even though his accusation now hung between them, souring the atmosphere even more.

'We won't be staying for dinner. Nicholas – take me home.'

In a rare show of what might have been fatherly concern, Nicholas stood up and came over to Jack, putting a hand on his shoulder. 'I suggest you come to some financial arrangement with the boy and let him go somewhere we'll all be happier with – himself included. I'm sure a substantial cheque will solve the matter to everyone's satisfaction.'

Jack refused to stand up to see his parents off. Things had been said that couldn't be unsaid. And nothing had been resolved.

When all was finally quiet, Jack went to the kitchen. Matt was alone at the table, the sports pages of the newspaper spread out in front of him. He was shovelling down a portion of Beef Wellington.

Glancing up at Jack, he said, 'Better eat some of this. Maggie's livid that she cooked all this extra food for nothing.'

Jack carefully closed the door. He didn't want a repeat performance of what had happened earlier. 'Where's Luke?' he asked as he sat down.

Matt jerked his fork in the direction of the door. 'Went to his room. Can't say I blame him. I apologised on your behalf.'

So Jack was being reproached for not making a dramatic exit from the drawing room to check on Luke like Matt did. Best tread carefully now. Get him back on side. 'Matt, I'm sorry about all that was said in there tonight.'

'Me too,' said Matt, frowning. 'What a welcome.'

'Well, it was never going to be easy.'

'Easy! Dad, it was unforgivable!'

Maybe it was – but was it also inevitable? Matt wanted Luke here but had no idea what the repercussions would be. 'Perhaps it was a mistake to bring him back.'

'Why?' asked Matt. 'What happened years ago isn't his fault.'

'I told you. It's complicated …' Matt was setting himself up for one big disappointment. Jack would have to warn him. 'Be careful about getting too attached.'

Matt clattered his knife and fork onto the plate. 'What d'you mean? How can I *not* get attached? Luke's my brother and I'm going to tell him he can depend on *me* at least.'

Great. Matt had cast himself in the role of hero-protector. Jack glanced behind him at the door. Still closed, but he lowered his voice anyway. 'Luke agreed to stay here until he's fit enough but hinted that he'd be moving on after that.'

Matt wasn't having it. 'Course he did. Because he doesn't feel welcome. It's up to us to persuade him to stay. Look, I'll talk to him tomorrow. I tried tonight, but he wasn't in the mood.'

Jack sighed. 'Luke's like that all the time. What makes you think he'll be any different tomorrow?'

'Maybe he won't be – but *I'm* not giving up on him.'

Had Jack given up on Luke? But he'd brought him back – what more could people reasonably expect? 'Okay, you talk to him then,' he said. 'But perhaps I'd better make myself scarce tomorrow. I'm not exactly his favourite person.'

Matt pushed his plate aside. 'We'll need to sort out a date for the funeral.'

Jack nodded. 'I'll ring Father Quinn over in Baronswood. Find out what we have to do.' Another nightmare looming. The funeral.

'Hey,' grinned Matt. 'If things get sticky with Father Quinn, tell him this joke. The devil proposed a football match between Heaven and Hell. God said, "But don't you know we've got all the good players?" And the devil said …'

'"Yeah, but we've got all the refs."'

Matt smiled. 'See, Dad – we're still a team.'

He was back on Jack's side. For now, at least.

Chapter Seven

Luke leaned, exhausted, against the frame of the open bathroom door. Clouds of steam escaped around him into the bedroom. He looked at the clock. He'd been struggling with the shower for almost an hour, trying to stand on his injured leg. Wars had been fought and won in less time. Maybe he should have skipped the whole thing, but he kept remembering the way his so-called grandparents had looked at him. Like he was scum. Then as good as calling him a beggar. *Is it money you want?* He'd not feed their prejudice by looking the part.

After making it to the bed, Luke sat down and pulled on his clothes, slowly because the pain from his ribs was bad. He saw his reflection in the mirror on the wardrobe door. The rugby shirt was a good choice. He'd probably never have worn one back home, but he was proud of being Irish. It was weird to think he was half-Brit.

Maggie had brought him a cup of tea earlier, but he'd pretended to be asleep, not up to conversation. He liked the housekeeper. Annie had told him about the friendly woman who'd been like a mother to her. Maggie had seemed pleased to see him yesterday, saying how sorry she was about Annie.

There was a loud knock and Luke held his breath. Don't let it be Jack. Better all round if they kept out of each other's way.

It was Matt. 'Hey, good morning! Come and get some breakfast. There's just us. Dad's gone out. Maggie's cooked for an army – bacon, eggs, the works.'

His brother. It was strange to think of him that way. Matt was a puzzle. He'd openly defended Luke last night, even following him to apologise for his family's behaviour.

He seemed genuinely friendly. Luke desperately wanted to believe he was one of the good guys, but Matt was a Stewart. He'd surely stick with them if push came to shove. Best trust no one, although Emer had said he should take things as they come and stop dividing the world into friends and enemies.

'I'm not really hungry, thanks,' he mumbled.

Matt tutted, shook his head, and wagged a finger. 'Luke, there are only two rules in this house. Eat everything Maggie makes, and do everything Maggie says.'

'And if I don't?'

'Don't even go there, bro,' laughed Matt. 'Come on. I'm starving, even if you're not.'

Luke's spirits lifted a little. It felt good to be called 'bro'. He grabbed his crutches and followed Matt to the kitchen.

After breakfast, Matt suggested a tour of the downstairs. So far they'd seen the drawing room with its fancy ornaments, and Jack's study, all done in wood and smelling of cigar smoke.

'This is the dining room,' said Matt, pushing open a heavy wooden door. All the doors in this house seemed to creak. Luke would buy them a can of oil when he left. Something to remember him by. The dining room, with cabinets full of silver and china, was even more pretentious than the other rooms. The table in the centre was a massive, gleaming monster, almost as big as Luke's bedroom back home. Passing the salt must take forever.

'We only eat dinner in here on special occasions,' Matt told him. 'Maggie likes to keep it spotless. A crumb on the Persian rug and you're for it.'

Matt was trying to put him at ease with jokes, but it wasn't really working. Just being in this house seemed like a betrayal. How had Annie felt when she'd had to trade in all this luxury for struggle and hardship? Like catching sight of Paradise then having the door slammed in your face and being dispatched to Hell.

'Great Aunt Rose,' said Matt, pointing to a dingy oil painting of a plain woman in tweeds. 'She left Dad this house in her will, though he'll be expected to decamp to Edenbridge when Gran and Granddad pop their clogs.'

'Edenbridge?'

'The family estate. A few miles from here. A reward from Charles II for loyalty to the Crown during the Civil War.'

The family estate? The Crown? What the hell was he doing here in this posh house with its paintings and silver teapots? This wasn't his world and he didn't want it to be.

'You okay?'

Luke had sighed before he could stop it. Better cover up his frustration or he might offend Matt. 'I'm just a bit tired.' He slumped slightly over the crutches to make the point.

'Okay, let's go to the living room and you can rest up.'

The living room was another revelation. Huge, cream leather sofas and armchairs, and a wall-mounted TV with the biggest screen Luke had ever seen. By the patio windows was a full-size pool table. Joe and Liam would spit chips if they could see that. He might send them a photo of it when he was well clear.

Matt settled down on the sofa, stretching his long legs out on the coffee table, and Luke took the armchair opposite. They sat in silence for a few moments, and Luke assessed his brother. Matt was like a young Jack. Similar build and height with light brown hair. Luke wondered what Matt's mother had been like. Jack's first wife, the one who'd died young. Pity that – if she'd lived, Annie would have been spared the Stewarts. Of course, he'd never have been born then, but that might have been better for her too. Was he staring too much? Matt was looking a bit uncomfortable.

Better break the silence. 'Do you like football?' was all he could think of to say.

'Too right,' Matt replied. 'I support United – Manchester United, that is.'

'There's only one United,' Luke said with a grin, feeling pleased he and his brother had something in common.

'No way!' Matt slapped his hands on his knees. 'You too? That's great. We've got an Executive Box at Old Trafford. Dad uses it a lot for business – says the best deals are made there. I prefer the stands, though. Tell you what, I'll take you to see a match before the end of the season.'

Luke had often dreamed about that when kicking a ball around. He'd hoped to take a trip to see United once he and Annie had settled in Wales. Now it was being offered to him with bells on. It was tempting, but Luke couldn't afford to start believing in all the home and family stuff. Best not to encourage Matt – or himself – so he changed the subject. 'What exactly *is* the business?'

'Stewart Enterprises.' Matt swung his legs down and rifled through a stack of magazines on the table. Plucking one out, he tossed it to Luke. It was a glossy brochure, showing a tall, modern building with glass windows and 'Stewart Enterprises' in huge silver letters above the wide entrance. 'We do property development,' Matt explained. 'Residential housing, business parks, leisure centres. You name the pie, we've got a finger in it. The offices are in Manchester.'

'Do you work there?' asked Luke. Hard to imagine Matt in a suit, making deals behind a desk.

'God, no! That kind of stuff doesn't interest me. I work in the local pub.'

'What! Behind the bar?'

'Well, I manage the bar, so I get to boss others around. And hire the barmaids.' Matt winked. 'We're planning to open a nightclub soon.'

'But why do that when you could have an easy life workin' for your da'?' He couldn't bring himself to say 'our' da'.

'Ha!' said Matt, leaning back into the sofa, hands clasped behind his head. 'Dad wouldn't let me have an easy life, believe you me … and, like I said, I'm just not interested in it. I'd be bored stupid.'

Another thing they had in common, then.

'Soon as I sat my A levels,' Matt continued, 'I took a year out and went travelling. Hong Kong, Australia, New Zealand, Fiji. Worked in hotels and bars, and really enjoyed it. When I came back, I went to college, got a diploma in business management and marketing, then started working at the Foresters Arms – the pub and hotel down in the village.'

How easy it was for the rich. At twenty, this was Luke's first time abroad, yet Matt had already lived and worked on the other side of the world. People said money didn't matter, but it must have been the rich who came up with that one.

'What about you? What did you do in Ireland?'

In a word, nothing. It was embarrassing. 'Odd jobs here and there,' he said, not looking at Matt. 'Nothin' special.'

'I was gutted to hear about Annie.'

Luke lowered his eyes.

'Sorry, mate. D'you mind me talking about her?'

They might as well discuss it, get it out into the open. 'No, it's okay. D'you remember her then?' It was weird to think she'd been Matt's mother before she was his.

'A bit, yeah, but I was only four when she left, so it's hazy. I remember her singing me to sleep, though. She had a cracking voice.'

'She did that,' agreed Luke, with pride.

'Luke, is it true … that Annie said Dad didn't want the two of you?'

So it had started. The disbelief, the doubt. 'Yeah, it's true. Why – don't you believe me?'

'I just wanted to be sure I had it straight. I don't know what to believe, but I do know Dad. He can be a hard man, sure, but he's not cruel. And he's not a bigot. He'd hardly have married Annie if he was, would he?'

'Maybe he just wasn't man enough to deal with all that disapproval,' said Luke, unable to keep the bitterness from his voice.

'When he phoned from Dublin, he was in shock. I don't think he was faking it.'

Shocked? Afraid the truth would come out, more like.

Luke was resolute. 'My mam never lied to me.'

Matt's eyes narrowed, but Luke wasn't going to back down on this one, even if it meant their relationship was over almost as soon as it had begun.

'Luke,' said Matt, 'whatever happened in the past, I think Annie would have liked us to get to know each other, don't you?'

Surely that wouldn't be a betrayal. After all, none of this was Matt's fault. 'I always wanted a brother,' Luke said. That was true, but saying it made him feel shy and a bit nervous. He was still scared of feeling emotions that could be shattered so easily if – when – things went wrong.

'The Stewart brothers!' declared Matt, stomping his feet. 'Double trouble. Baronsmere had better watch out.'

He preferred to think of himself as a Kiernan not a Stewart, but Matt was trying to be kind. Luke would play along – for now, at least.

Luke left the living room, not wanting to sit there brooding by himself. Matt had gone out after a friend phoned. He'd offered to take Luke with him but Luke hadn't wanted to go. He hadn't wanted Matt to go either. His brother's energy and enthusiasm had helped him cope with this difficult first morning, making him feel less like a stranger, an intruder.

But he hadn't told Matt this. Didn't want to spoil his plans. Some of his friends had younger brothers who'd been a pain in the neck. He didn't want to be one of those.

Using his crutch, Luke pushed open the kitchen door and went in. Maggie was stirring and shaking pots on the stove while a dog sat close to the range, watching the cooking process intently.

'Hello, love.' Maggie's homely face lit up with a smile when she saw him. 'Can I get you something?'

'I was wonderin' if you needed a hand?'

'Well, that's kind of you. How do you feel about peeling potatoes?'

He smiled. 'I'm Irish, Maggie. There's nothin' I can't do with a potato.'

Once Luke had settled at the huge scrubbed wooden table, Maggie placed a bowl of potatoes in front of him and handed him the peeler. The dog came over and sniffed around his feet. 'What's his name?' Luke asked.

'Ollie. He's obviously having a good day. He's got a touch of arthritis which sometimes makes him cranky with people.'

'What breed is he?'

'Chesapeake Bay Retriever. Used to be Jack's gun dog.'

'Gun dog? As in hunting?' Luke couldn't keep the disapproval out of his voice. Typical of the Stewarts to be into callous blood sports.

'Yes. A hunting dog. One of the best he was, so they say. Though why grown men should feel the need to go around blasting God's own creatures out of the sky is beyond me. I blame it on too much red meat. Feeds the aggression.'

Luke grinned. 'You could be on to somethin' there.'

They continued chatting and Luke felt some of his tension release. He was comfortable in this kitchen, probably because it was the least formal place in the house. It was full of light from three big windows, and the copper pans hanging from the ceiling cast gleams of gold around the room. A rocking chair with patchwork cushions stood in the corner, and there was a cluster of large framed photos on the wall. Luke's stomach lurched as his eye was caught by the central photo. Annie. Covered with streamers, holding on to Jack Stewart. The sight of his mother brought the pain of loss sharply back again. He stopped peeling. 'When was that taken?' he asked.

'Your father doesn't like that being there,' said Maggie, as she came to stand beside him. 'Doesn't like reminders. He'll never look in this direction. But this is my kitchen so I insisted. The picture was taken at New Year. Lord Leighton threw a big party. Annie looked beautiful that night. Her hair was done by a top Manchester stylist. Jack paid for him to come to the house.' Maggie pointed to another photo, which Luke hadn't noticed. Jack, Maggie, Annie and a small boy – obviously Matt. 'And that one was taken in Spain,' she continued. 'We all went.'

Spain? Luke never knew his mother had been to Spain. He wondered what else he didn't know. He looked at Jack and Annie, happy together, but the man had caused her so much heartache, and Luke dismissed the idea Jack had cared. It was easier that way.

'Why did she leave, Luke?' Maggie asked, sitting down at the table next to him. 'Was it some trouble back in Ireland? Or was she homesick?'

Jack had covered his tracks well. Not even those he shared a house with could see through his lies. Eventually, he'd tackle Jack about that letter but would wait until he felt better, not just physically but emotionally. Jack would just deny it, and Luke wasn't up to more arguments with him just yet, especially as he needed a safe refuge right now.

Is it money you want? Nicholas's words were still there at the back of his mind. He couldn't let such an insult go unchallenged. 'She left because she wasn't wanted. Made to feel she didn't belong.'

'Is that what she told you?' Maggie looked shocked. It was hard to have to burst her bubble. Annie had shared some memories with him over the years, and Joe and Liam had relished giving him the rest of the details, things that were too painful for her to talk about.

'It's what I *know*. And what I saw last night.' That ugly scene in the drawing room had confirmed the prejudice his mother said she'd experienced in Baronsmere.

'I know Grace and Nicholas never accepted your mother. That was their loss. But she had Jack and Matt and me. We loved her. I hoped that would right the balance.'

'Jack rejected her, too,' Luke insisted.

'No, I can't believe that.' Her expression was a combination of confusion and hurt, and Luke felt guilty. Why hadn't he just kept his mouth shut? 'Annie and Jack were happy together. Believe me. I saw them every day. When you live with people, know them well, you can sense their moods, see if things are wrong. There was never a hint of problems. Annie and Jack were soulmates. They belonged together. And they wanted a baby – they *both* wanted *you*.'

Her voice held such sadness that Luke knew without any doubt Maggie had loved his mother, and it was comforting but he shook his head. People saw what they wanted to see. They chose the good things to remember and ignored the bad because it was easier.

'Matt had a part in a Sunday School play the week after Annie left,' Maggie continued. 'He was so excited. Only had a few lines but Annie rehearsed them with him over and over. She made his costume and was looking forward to watching him. And they were going to France for Easter, to stay with Matt's grandparents – Caroline's mum and dad.

Annie was planning for a future *here*. There were no signs she was unhappy.'

Despite himself, Luke remembered the confusion in Jack's eyes when he heard the accusation that he'd driven Annie away. Maybe the man had been as insensitive back then as he was now. Wrapped up in his wealth and precious status, blind to Annie's suffering and his own parents' insults. Or, Jack could just be a very good actor. Hadn't he played the part of a loving father in front of the Guards? But even if there was some truth to Maggie's version of events, nothing excused Jack's later rejection of Annie when she'd begged him for help. That took cold, ruthless calculation.

'Jack wasn't even here the week Annie left,' said Maggie. 'He was in Brussels on business. So it's not like they had a row or anything. I'd have known. I'd have seen it in her face.'

It was true Annie could never hide what she was feeling. She was too honest for that. 'What did she say to you on her last day?' he asked. Perhaps the clues were there. Maggie just needed some help to remember.

'I wasn't here,' she said, her voice little more than a whisper. 'My sister had been ill. I used to go over to her place on Saturdays to clean up and cook. Matt was staying with a school-friend.'

So Annie had been alone. She could have had a nasty phone call from Jack and no one would have known. 'Did she leave a note?'

'No, nothing,' said Maggie. 'When I came back, she was gone, but I didn't know until next day. I thought she'd gone to bed early. When I realised she was missing, I called everyone I could think of. Jack took the next flight home. He talked to the police, but they couldn't do much. She'd withdrawn money from her bank account and taken her things. There was no reason to think she was in trouble.'

'And he never tried to find her?'

'They hired a detective,' Maggie told him. 'I never heard all the details but after he reported back, Jack changed. Became harder. Bitter. When I asked, he just said Annie didn't want to come back and he wouldn't talk about it. Jack was shattered, Luke. Didn't eat, didn't speak for days. And then your grandmother got to work on him, persuaded him to accept the rejection and move on. It was a mistake – I told him so – but he wouldn't listen.'

Maggie seemed close to tears. No good was coming of raking over the past like this. She had to go on living here. Why spoil things for her? His real target was Jack – and Jack's parents. He should leave the innocent alone. 'I'm sorry, Maggie. It's over and done. Perhaps it's best to move on.' He was doling out advice he himself had no intention of following.

She gave him a weak smile. 'You're right. The most important thing is that you're here now, with us. Where you belong.'

When she leaned over and switched the radio on, music and chatter filled the room and Luke was thankful for it. He didn't feel like talking any more.

Jack felt that familiar ache in his legs as he reached the summit of Hartswood Hill. Over thirty years of climbing it most weekends, yet it never got any easier. Still, it kept him fit. Plus it was a kind of active meditation. He was usually so focused on not stumbling over a rock and breaking his leg that worries slipped to the back of his mind.

But that wasn't happening today. Because of Luke. Who could be here even longer than planned since Matt might not let go of him easily. Already lines were being drawn. Grace and Nicholas on one side, Matt and Maggie on the other. Just like before, when he'd tried to keep everybody happy, making sure Annie and his parents never had to spend much time together. He'd thought it was working out back then – he must have been blind.

He stared out at the view in front of him as if there might be an answer there. Baronsmere's houses and cottages huddled close to the lake, the ancient mere. Trees hid his own house, but he could see Edenbridge set off grandly in its own grounds. Growing up in that place, more mausoleum than family home, had been depressing. Annie hadn't taken to it either. She'd shivered in the draughty corridors and perched on the drawing room sofa like a bird about to take flight.

Jack had brought her up here on their second date. He'd told her the history of the Hartswood Hill area – how Henry VIII had hunted deer in the days when the hill was covered with trees. He'd shown her the villages, spread out around them like the four points of a compass: Baronsmere; Baronswood with St John's Church, famous for its murals; Hadleigh dotted with farms and sheep; and Marsham, the former mill town with its ramshackle houses.

He'd shown Annie his world that day, the place where his roots ran deep. All human life – farm and factory, rich and poor – was here. He could think of nowhere better to raise a family, and he'd hoped she would fall in love with the view, with the place – with him.

A light rain was falling, but Jack stayed there in the open, feeling the droplets run down his face like tears. It had rained the last time he and Annie had been together on the Hill. Their first wedding anniversary. They'd waited under the weathered oak for the shower to pass, and Jack had carved JS & AS into the bark, surrounding the letters with a heart. It was still visible, and Jack gently traced it with his fingers, remembering how Annie had kissed him, her lips wet with the rain. A month later, she'd abandoned him. Had he missed a vital clue? Was the writing on the wall even then?

The beginnings of a March wind whispered around Jack like voices from the past …

'Sarah told me she's going to Brussels as well,' said Annie.

The rain had stopped and they were sitting on a blanket on the Hill, watching the storm clouds roll away to the west.

'She is. Sarah's got big plans. She's thinking of expanding the B&B into a hotel. She's worked hard and she's making a good profit now. She deserves one of those EU tourism grants.' He'd written the application for her and now she'd get the chance to present her case in Brussels. It felt good to help someone out. There was no profit in it for him, just the satisfaction of seeing a childhood friend do well.

'Why don't I come with you?' Annie suggested. *'I'd like to see Brussels. And I'd be company for you.'*

And a major distraction. Jack couldn't focus on anything for long when Annie was around. *'Sweetheart, I'd really prefer it if you stayed here with Matt. I don't like us both being away from him, especially not when we wouldn't even get to see each other much.'*

Annie picked at the fringes of the blanket. *'Sarah said there's dinner and dancin' in the evenings.'*

Jack snorted. *'It's her first trip to Brussels. She's going to be in for quite a surprise if she's hoping for a lively nightlife. It's not a vacation. EU meetings can go on forever.'*

'You've helped Sarah a lot.'

'Well, Martin certainly hasn't. God knows why she married someone so clueless about business.'

'Maybe she loves him.'

That was Annie all over. Love was the answer to everything. Sometimes he wished he shared her uncomplicated view of the world. *'She could have done better. I've told her so, too.'*

Annie tutted. *'That's not nice.'*

Jack kissed her hand. 'Probably not. At least Martin's better than that git my sister married. He never spends any time with her.'

'At least your sister has Gavin although I think she's a bit lonely now he's at school.'

'Speaking of children, Mrs Stewart ... we need to think about making our own. Let's go home and practise some more.'

'Such a chore,' said Annie, and laughed. 'But you'll have to catch me first.'

And she'd run back down the hill, sure-footed and nimble, stopping halfway, and calling back, mischievously, 'Hurry up. I can't run any slower.'

Was that it? Was Annie angry Jack wouldn't take her to Brussels? Was she jealous of Sarah? Did she think perhaps they were having an affair? She'd seemed fine when he left, though. One of the many things he'd loved about her was she didn't brood. But had it been an act? He took out his mobile phone and dialled Sarah's number. No harm in checking if she remembered anything. Just to be sure. He'd suggest they meet at the flat above the pub instead of her cottage. She might be less forthcoming if her daughter was around.

Sarah Walker dabbed some miracle cream on the fine lines around her eyes. Three hundred pounds for a tiny jar, but it worked. For a while at least. Ageing gracefully was damned expensive. And hard work. Some days Sarah just wanted to shut the door in her trainer's face and have an extra hour in bed. It would be so easy to let it all go, but she was the wrong side of forty to stop taking care of herself. Fifty was looming ...

She checked the fridge: two bottles of Chablis, some foie gras, a jar of Beluga caviar and peaches soaked in honey.

Jack's favourites. Usually eaten after sex, they'd christened it PCF – post-coital food. She'd kept the fridge stocked these past two months just in case they got back together, but so far Jack had resisted every subtle attempt she'd made at reconciliation.

The reason Jack had broken up with her was just petty in Sarah's opinion. He'd asked her to attend a dinner for the staff of one of his charities, expecting her to come along and listen to endless speeches and make small talk with some of the most boring people on the planet. That charity got thousands from Stewart Enterprises every year. Surely that was enough. Did they really need to be wined and dined as well? When she'd said that, Jack had gone ballistic and called her spoiled and thoughtless. So unjust.

He knew nothing about the sacrifices she'd made for him. He didn't know she forced herself to read the dull property sections of the newspapers to be able to converse with him about his work. She faked an interest in rugby, had gone on many a tedious shooting weekend, and even pretended to like Jack's bad-tempered old dog, Ollie. She had transformed this flat above the pub – now in many ways more luxurious than the cottage she shared with her daughter – into a safe haven for Jack, a place he could come to relax, be waited upon, and never talk about things he didn't want to. How could he possibly criticise her for being thoughtless?

Perhaps it was just the male midlife crisis. He'd date a few bimbos, buy a fast car or two, and then return to Sarah's net of comfort and harmony. He might even mention love again, a word that seemed to have vanished from his vocabulary in the past year or so. All it took was patience. She had plenty of that. And here he was now, coming round to see her. He'd been quite pleasant on the phone, asking after the nightclub, and Kate. Sarah would be kind and witty and attentive – show him what he'd been missing.

She was pouring two glasses of wine in the living room when she heard his key in the lock. 'Through here, Jack!' she called, and smiled as he walked in. He wasn't smiling, though, and his green eyes were without their usual spark. She held out a glass. 'Welcome back, stranger. Matt said you were on a business trip. How was it?'

'Exhausting.'

His fingers brushed hers as he accepted the wine, and she felt a jolt of desire. Not so Jack, apparently. He took his drink and went over to the sofa.

'You shouldn't work so hard, Jack,' she purred, sitting down next to him as close as possible. She could smell his cologne – the one she'd bought for him.

He took a big gulp of wine before he spoke. 'It wasn't work, Sarah. That's why I came round. I need to talk to you …'

'What is it? You can tell me anything, you know that.' The seconds dragged by.

'I was in Ireland. About Annie …' Jack blurted out.

'Annie? Your ex?' The shock of his words hit Sarah like an actual body blow. 'So she contacted you – after all these years? The cheek …'

'No, no, that's not it.' Jack stood up, paced the floor. 'Annie's dead. She died in a car crash just over a week ago. The police asked me to go and identify her.'

'Oh …' Sarah felt relief drain through her, then guilt. What kind of person was happy someone had died? Only it did finally free Jack for marriage. He could have gotten a divorce easily after Annie had been gone for seven years, but he'd always resisted, for no satisfactory reason he'd ever given Sarah.

'I brought her back here,' Jack was saying. 'Didn't know what else to do. None of her relatives were around to organise a funeral.'

He looked gutted. Sarah couldn't help a twinge of jealousy. Twenty years gone, now dead, and Annie Kiernan's power still held sway.

'The funeral will be at St John's. Next Wednesday. I wondered ... would you maybe come to the service? I know it's a lot to ask.'

'Of course I'll come. And I could sort out the catering if you'd like?'

He nodded and smiled appreciatively.

Just one question to get out of the way. 'So – you're not going to track down her family then?'

Jack shook his head and Sarah allowed herself to breathe again. 'I'm still her next of kin, so the funeral's up to me. At least I can give her a decent send-off. Her brothers probably couldn't afford to do that. Wish Luke would see it that way – cut me some slack ...'

'Luke?' Sarah jerked back on the sofa.

'Turns out Annie had a son. Mine, apparently. An angry young man – mad at me, mad at the world. Twenty years and I never knew about Luke. Matt's made up about it, though – he finally got that younger brother he always wanted.'

'He's here? In Baronsmere?'

'I couldn't just leave him over there,' said Jack, frowning at her. 'He was with Annie in the car. He nearly died, too. Needs looking after for a bit.'

'Do your parents know?'

'Oh yes.' Jack grimaced. 'They met yesterday. It was a nightmare. Not a civil word to each other.'

Sarah gulped down some wine. 'Did he tell you why Annie left?'

Jack looked at Sarah but his mind was elsewhere. The strain of all this was clear to see on his face. 'He claims I threw Annie out.'

'Threw her out ...' Sarah could only manage a hoarse whisper.

'As if I would do that. He's obviously been told a pack of lies.'

'Obviously ...' She'd have to stop parroting everything he said.

'I was thinking back to the weeks before Annie left. Did she ever say anything that would make you think she was ...'

'Was what?' Sarah's drifting mind suddenly locked back into sharp focus.

'Well, jealous of you. Do you think she got the wrong idea about us going to Brussels together? It was strictly business. But I wonder ...'

'Don't do this, Jack,' urged Sarah. 'It's not fair on yourself. You worked so hard to pick up the pieces and get your life back on track. I'm sorry Annie's dead but she chose to leave you ... to abandon you. Short of a medium, we're probably never going to know why she left, why she lied to her son. Just let it go.' And she prayed he would.

'Hard to do that while Luke's around.' He put his glass on the coffee table. 'Thanks for listening, Sarah. I'd better go.'

Any other time she'd have tried to persuade him to stay, but right now she needed to be alone. 'Call me to discuss the funeral arrangements, okay?'

As the front door closed behind Jack, Sarah curled up on the sofa, overwhelmed by memories. And guilt.

Jack's words kept playing over in her head. *I never knew about Luke.*

No, Jack didn't. But she did.

Chapter Eight

Sunday mornings in Baronsmere irritated the hell out of Jack. Five years ago, the new vicar had shifted the church service from eleven to nine o'clock. Now no one could have a lie-in because of the bloody bells. Last year, Sarah had finally forked out on double glazing for her cottage, sacrificing the special-feature mullioned windows in the process. She'd sent the bill to the vicar claiming noise harassment, but he'd returned it with a box of jellied fruits and a note suggesting she might enjoy the bells more if she attended church.

So, as usual, Jack was up at eight, relaxing in the living room where he could read the papers in peace. Matt wouldn't show till noon. Nothing but a full-scale earthquake would rouse him. Luke hadn't appeared yet. He'd eaten dinner in his room last night, claiming tiredness. Avoidance, more like, but at least Jack didn't have to sit in an unpleasant atmosphere.

The door opened and Maggie came in with a pot of fresh coffee. 'Sun's coming out,' she told him.

How did she do it? Sixty-six, and though she had a touch of arthritis, she still ran the house like clockwork, bossing everyone around into the bargain.

'Maggie, can I ask you a favour?'

She stopped plumping the cushions and stood there, hand on hip. 'What is it? I need to get ready for church.'

Jack cleared his throat. 'Luke needs to see Father Quinn about the funeral, and he might want to go to Mass as well. Could you take him? You can have lunch out. My treat.'

'You want *me* to go with Luke to sort out his mother's funeral?'

'You're Catholic and going to St John's this morning. Isn't it logical that Luke goes with you?'

'Don't you think the lad might want his father to go with him?' It wasn't a question but an accusation. Maggie had assumed the role of Luke's protector, just as Matt had.

'Don't look at me like that, Maggie. I know it's not ideal but I have to see a few people – Dave and Evie, Tony and Barbara – to tell them about Annie. Hopefully they'll come to the funeral. After that, I'm going to Edenbridge to settle things with the family. For Luke's sake.' Fat chance of that, but he'd have to give it a try.

'For your sake, you mean!'

'Don't give me grief. I can't leave things as they are. Luke'll probably prefer to go with you anyway. Where is he now? Still asleep?'

'*I'll* go and check on him, shall I? God forbid he might see you taking an interest.'

Jack banged his cup down on the saucer. 'Sometimes, Maggie, you go too far!'

They glared at each other.

'You'd better sack me, then. I speak my mind, Jack – always have, always will.'

God knows, he'd been tempted more than once to send her packing, but they both knew he'd never do it because they shared a history. Right back to when Maggie had been Caroline's nanny, and she and Jack's nanny were friends who often helped each other out in times of need. Maggie had been there at every stage of Jack's life, through good times and challenges.

Maggie finally broke the charged silence. 'I *will* take Luke to Baronswood, but will *you* go and get him up for breakfast, please. He needs to eat more.'

'Thanks, Maggie.' He left the room before she could change her mind. One confrontation over, another looming. He knocked on Luke's door and heard a muted, 'Come in.'

Luke was stretched out on the bed, fully clothed, reading

116

a book. 'So you're awake,' said Jack. 'Why haven't you come through for breakfast?'

Luke stayed focused on his book. 'Not hungry.'

'Well, Maggie wants you to eat something. You need to build your strength up, hungry or not.'

'Okay,' said Luke, still reading.

Jack resisted the urge to shake him for his rudeness. 'What are you reading?' he asked.

'*The Dead*.' said Luke. He turned back to the front cover of the book. 'Short stories by James Joyce. Found it in the bookcase in the livin' room.'

'It was your mother's,' murmured Jack. 'I gave it to her on her twentieth birthday.'

Luke breathed in deeply and laid the book down on the bed. Jack regretted blurting it out like that, but at least he now had Luke's attention. 'Maggie's going to take you to see Father Quinn, the priest at Baronswood, to discuss the funeral.'

Luke frowned. 'Maggie is?'

'I need to smooth things over with the family.'

'And that's more important …'

'It *is* important, Luke, yes, for everyone's sake.' There was silence from the direction of the bed. 'Anyway, Maggie will take you. Matt's still asleep, and probably won't surface much before the afternoon.'

'So Maggie drew the short straw?'

Jack sighed. 'It's not like that.'

'Whatever.' Luke picked up the book again and started flicking through the pages.

'I'll see you later, then.' Jack was determined to keep things civil. 'Make sure you get some breakfast.'

He turned to leave, but Luke brought him up short. 'What about the funeral? Think you'll manage to make that?'

'Father Quinn was very helpful,' said Maggie as they drove

away from St John's. 'Younger priests like him sometimes don't mind breaking with Catholic tradition a bit. It's good that you can have things the way you want them, isn't it?'

'Yes,' Luke agreed. He'd been surprised to get approval for modern music and a eulogy before the Mass rather than at the interment. Maybe Father Quinn was a bit of a rebel, or maybe he was concerned about Luke having to stand too long on crutches at the graveside on what could be a damp day. At least it wasn't going to be a full Mass, so he wouldn't need to take communion. He had no plans to make confession. Maybe he never would again. He took no comfort in the church now.

'Tell you what – why don't we drive back via the scenic route,' suggested Maggie. 'Make the most of the sunshine. Then we can stop somewhere for lunch.'

'Okay.' Luke knew Maggie was trying to distract him and he appreciated her concern. He'd been upset when Jack said he wasn't coming. One minute he claimed he'd loved Annie, the next he couldn't even be bothered to help plan her funeral. At least Annie wasn't being buried on Stewart land. He couldn't have stomached that. Thinking about burying his mother gave him a pain in his heart that was almost physical. 'Y'know, Maggie, Mam was devout all her life but it didn't get her anywhere.'

'Good people get their reward in heaven, lad.'

'She'll be livin' it up now then, but she deserved it when she was here.' A moment later, he regretted dismissing Maggie's attempts at comfort. None of this was her fault. 'I'm sorry, I just miss her.'

Maggie squeezed his hand. 'Of course you do, love, she was your mum. Life can be very cruel.'

'I keep thinkin,' if only we hadn't been on the road at that time – even just a few minutes earlier or later, and things might have been different. If only …'

He paused. If only he'd kept his temper, if only he hadn't borrowed Joe's car on St Patrick's Day. Remembering made him feel light-headed and hot as his mind filled with unpleasant memories. He reached out for the dashboard, using it to prevent himself falling forward. He was finding it hard to breathe.

Cool gusts of air filled the car as Maggie pulled off the road and the windows were automatically opened. 'Take slow deep breaths, Luke,' she commanded, and he gasped in lungfuls of air until he felt better.

They were quiet for some time, staring out at the view of green fields and trees that were just beginning to sprout leaves. A river wound its way gently into the distance. The peaceful scene calmed Luke. It wasn't unlike Ireland. Suddenly, a red deer stepped out from between the trees. It glanced briefly at the car, then picked its way delicately over the gravel before disappearing.

'Did you see that?' said Maggie, in a hushed voice. 'He must have come from Tatton Deer Park.'

'She,' corrected Luke. 'It was a hind.' Maggie looked at him in amazement. 'Animals I know, Maggie,' he said. 'It's people I have problems with.'

'Speaking of animals, I'll let you into a secret. I call your Grandmother the Cheshire Cat.'

Luke couldn't help it. He started to laugh. It was a relief, even though it hurt his ribs. And seeing the deer had been magical. An omen of love, some believed. Maybe Annie had sent it.

Lunch at the Foresters Arms was in full swing when Luke and Maggie arrived. They squeezed into a corner table with just enough room for Luke to stretch out his injured leg. He was aware of people giving him sidelong glances, probably wondering who the hell he was. Unless they'd heard and just wanted to stare at the Traveller.

'Don't mind them, Luke,' said Maggie. 'They're just curious. Not much happens here, so anyone new is the centre of attention. Next week, they'll be talking about someone else.'

He hoped so. He wanted to keep a low profile. Quick in and out, as they'd often had to do in Ireland.

'Nice to see you here, Maggie.' A waitress appeared at their table, and Luke was now the one staring. The girl had light brown hair with blonde highlights, big green eyes, and a friendly smile.

'Hello, Kate,' said Maggie. 'We thought we'd have a spot of lunch. This is Luke – Matt's brother.'

The green eyes turned on him. 'Hello, Luke. Matt told me all about you – he was on the phone the minute he knew. He's made up. It's lovely to meet you. I'm Kate – Kate Walker.'

She held out her hand. It was cool and dry. His wasn't. 'Good to meet you, too.'

'Kate's mum – Sarah – is the owner,' said Maggie. 'That's her behind the bar.'

Sarah was blonde. Bleached by the look of it. Not as subtle as Kate's. Her clothes weren't subtle either – looked like she was going to a film première. And she must have bought some shop's entire supply of make-up. Not an original piece of skin in sight. She'd been one of those staring when he came in, or scowling more like. Did she know who he was? Didn't want a Traveller in her pub?

'I'm afraid there's not much on offer,' said Kate. 'Chef's sick today, so it's fish and chips or spaghetti bolognese.'

Luke and Maggie decided on fish and chips, with the promise of chocolate cheesecake for dessert.

'Come over and have a chat, Kate, if you get a minute,' suggested Maggie. 'You can give Luke the low-down on Baronsmere.'

'Will do.'

Kate flashed her glorious smile at Luke as she walked away. She looked as good from the back as she did from the front. 'She seems nice,' said Luke. Serious understatement.

'Yes, she is. She only works here sometimes.'

Definitely his lucky day, then.

'She's at university,' continued Maggie. 'Studying journalism.'

Out of his league. She'd be going places, and in the opposite direction to him. Christ, he had to stop this self-pity.

'Sarah used to be your dad's girlfriend,' Maggie told him. 'They split up a few months ago. Not the first time that's happened, though. They could be back together again soon.'

That would be why she was giving him the evil eye then – Jack had dumped her so she thought of any family members as guilty by association.

'Afternoon, Maggie.'

One of the customers came to their table, probably to gossip and gawp. Luke plastered a smile on his face for Maggie's sake.

Jack was seated opposite the scowling Sir Hugh Vernon, who had been hanged for supporting the Royalist cause at the Battle of Rowton Moor but who continued to haunt the Stewarts through his depressing portrait. Sunday lunch at Edenbridge was always a stuffy, formal affair. The Sèvres porcelain, Sheffield plate and expensive damask tablecloth embroidered by Belgian nuns put in an appearance every week without fail. All for show. Was it any wonder he preferred the simplicity of his own plain wooden kitchen table?

'Where's Matt today, Jack?' Nicholas asked, selecting a choice piece of salmon from the platter the butler had presented. 'We don't see as much of him as we used to.'

'He's busy.'

'Hah! Pulling pints? Very demanding.' Gavin, Jack's

obnoxious nephew, was always shoving his opinions down people's throats. He was the main reason Matt missed so many Sunday lunches, worried he'd lose it and break a family heirloom over Gavin's thick skull.

'He's supervising the planning of the new nightclub,' said Jack, through gritted teeth.

'I really don't see the need for a nightclub,' said Grace, frowning. 'Loud music and late-night drinking, and cars revving at all hours. It's so out of keeping with Baronsmere. I must say, I'm surprised at Sarah.'

'The new nightclub?' said Richard Morland, walking into the dining room. Jack wondered where his brother-in-law had been skulking. It wasn't like him to be late for Sunday lunch, especially since he was on site, living with Claire and Gavin in the east wing at Edenbridge. Richard never missed a chance to ingratiate himself with the in-laws. Now the despicable crawler was grovelling an apology to Grace. Jack should have seen him off years ago when he'd first started sniffing around Claire. No apology or kiss for her, Jack noted. She might as well have been invisible.

'Whilst socially it might be a bit of a nightmare,' said Richard, sitting down and unfolding his napkin, 'it does make good business sense. Lots of young people in Baronsmere and the surrounding villages now. A nightclub will be a draw.'

Richard was just repeating what he'd heard Sarah say. The idiot had zero intuition when it came to business, and absolutely no ethics. Jack wanted to say as much but wouldn't upset Claire by starting an argument. Richard wasn't worth it.

'How's Luke doing, Jack?' asked Claire. Her voice was little more than a whisper, her eyes wide and nervous.

'Thank you, Henderson,' Grace told the butler before Jack could answer. 'We can manage from here.'

Jack knew exactly what she was doing and resented it. 'What's wrong, Mother? Don't want the servants to hear?' he asked as the door closed.

'Servants do gossip, Jack – as you know.' This was obviously a reference to Maggie, who Grace believed shared her knowledge of the Stewart family with her equally inquisitive sister.

'Everyone will know about Luke soon enough,' said Jack, setting down his cutlery – he'd lost his appetite. 'It's Annie's funeral on Wednesday, at St John's. I spoke to Dave and Evie this morning – they're coming. And Tony said he and Barbara will be there.' Silence. Everybody suddenly seemed intent on their food. 'So, who else is going to come to represent the family?' he asked. 'Apart from myself and Matt.'

Jack saw his mother throw a warning glance at Nicholas. He turned to his father. 'Dad?'

Nicholas sipped his wine, then set the glass down carefully. 'Well, under the circumstances, I don't think it would be appropriate for us to attend.'

There it was. *Appropriate*. The word Jack had heard far too often throughout his life. A word that was supposed to govern every action, every emotion, including grief apparently. 'I'd hoped you might have reconsidered,' he said. 'If only for show. The Stewart family united in grief ...' His words carried more than a hint of sarcasm.

'After Annie walking out on you all those years ago?'

Jack frowned at his father's words. 'It was me she walked out on. If I can put that aside, why can't you?'

'I'll come to the funeral.'

Jack smiled his gratitude at Claire's offer. She hated conflict, so it must have been difficult to speak out.

'There you are. Claire to the rescue.' Richard was smirking. 'She'll cry up a storm, I'm sure.'

'I *liked* Annie!' Claire's voice was so loud everyone turned

123

to look at her. She blushed but stared her husband down. Jack wanted to hug her.

'I'll go, too,' said Gavin. 'Get a look at my pikey cousin.'

How Jack would love to rearrange Gavin's smug features, but he'd have to find another way to prevent his nephew from attending. For Matt's sake, as well as Luke's. Matt didn't always have his father's self-control, and he'd become very protective of Luke. Any rude comments from Gavin could easily spark trouble. 'I think it best if it's just people who actually knew Annie,' Jack said, grasping at the only reasonable excuse he could think of.

'First you want to swell the numbers, then you don't,' said Richard. 'Make your mind up. None of her own relatives coming then? Or can we expect an influx of caravans …?'

'Will you be having a meal afterwards, Jack? At the house?' asked Claire, interrupting Richard, who looked surprised and annoyed. Claire was always on Jack's side but was usually too overwhelmed by Richard's personality to speak her mind. Today though, she had proved a real ally.

'Sarah's doing the catering,' he said. 'Afternoon tea at the house.'

'Speaking of catering,' said Grace, 'you won't believe what they served for pudding at the Conservative Women's Club luncheon last week. Tinned peaches with synthetic cream. I simply couldn't eat it. Something should be done about their chef …'

And polite conversation was restored, all *inappropriate* topics brushed under the carpet, Annie and Luke dismissed as irrelevant. Jack looked at Grace, chattering away about nothing of any consequence, and failed to see a mother, just an insufferable snob. Now he was glad his parents wouldn't be at the funeral.

Lunch was over and the crowd in the pub was starting to

thin out. Maggie was talking to someone, and Kate had just sat down opposite Luke. He told her the cheesecake was great. What to talk about next?

'So you're Irish,' said Kate. 'I've been to a few horse shows there.'

'You like horses?' said Luke, clutching at this straw of a common interest. 'Me too.'

'I love them. We own the local stables. Maybe you'd like to visit?'

'Sure.' God, that sounded offhand. 'I'd like that,' he added quickly. 'It's just, well, I can't see past the funeral right now.'

Kate reached across the table to touch Luke's hand, and he almost jumped. 'Of course. I'm sorry. I wasn't thinking. It's Wednesday, isn't it?'

'How d'you know that?'

'My mum's doing the catering. She's asked me to help out.'

Luke hoped Jack and Sarah had parted on good terms. He'd seen a movie once where a woman had served her ex-boyfriend's family beef that had passed its sell-by date.

They smiled at each other, but the moment didn't last. A group of people banged through the pub door and came over to the table. A red-haired girl wearing a low-cut top and blinding pink lipstick took the chair next to Luke. Kate introduced him as Matt's brother. The redhead gazed at him. 'Are those eyelashes for real?' she drawled. 'I'm Abbie.'

'I saw him first,' Luke heard Kate whisper, and he blushed.

'Welcome, Matt's little brother!' A male voice suddenly boomed above Luke's head, its owner tall and thin with dark hair flopping over one eye. He was wearing a T-shirt that declared *Looking good is a curse*. 'Welcome to Baronsmere – England's most boring backwater, a rathole teeming with turgid Tories who'll be first against the wall come the revolution.'

This outburst, accompanied by flamboyant arm gestures, left Luke too stunned to reply. The speaker was hustled aside.

'So speaks The Honourable Timothy Leighton who forgets he'll also be against that wall when the revolution comes. Allister – Al. Abbie's twin. Nice to meet you, Luke.'

'Thanks,' Luke said, wishing he had something more original to say, but Al and Tim were already wandering off to the snooker table.

As Abbie headed off to the bar for crisps, Maggie came over. 'Ready to go, Luke?' she asked. He nodded, feeling disappointed. He wanted to stay longer.

'I'll see you Wednesday, Luke,' said Kate, helping him to settle onto his crutches. 'And if you feel up to it, maybe we can sort out the visit to the stables.'

He smiled at her. At last a bright spark on a very bleak horizon.

'Pop your eyes back in, darling. It's not at all attractive.'

Sarah joined Kate at a table near the window. Her daughter had been deep in conversation with Luke Kiernan. Now she was watching him as he left the Foresters and Sarah was not happy with that look in her eye. Whatever plans Kate might have in that direction would have to be nipped in the bud.

'Don't know what you mean, Mum,' said Kate, with a dreamy smile that confirmed Sarah's suspicions. Her fears.

'Looks like your friend has the same idea.' Sarah nodded towards Abbie, leaning on a snooker cue and also watching Luke through the pub window as Maggie helped him into the car. It wouldn't be ideal but rather Abbie than Kate. Abbie's family owned the largest farm in the area. Wealthy enough, though with little class. Abbie's father was happier drinking in The Fox and Feathers, and that suited Sarah just fine.

It would be far better all round, though, if Luke Kiernan were completely out of the picture. Out of Cheshire, out of England. Out of Sarah's head.

Seeing Luke had given her quite a jolt. Made her remember what it was like back then when a naïve, unsophisticated Traveller girl had made her feel so insignificant. Turned Jack's head just as Sarah had decided he was *the one*. And now, here was Annie's son, raised in Ireland as a Traveller instead of one of Jack's heirs – though that might change if he were to stay around. Perish the thought. His kind didn't belong in Baronsmere – and certainly not with Kate, who had a bright future ahead of her. A university degree, a career and eventually a good marriage. Not living in a trailer, constantly on the move, giving birth every other year until she was old before her time. Sarah shuddered. No, there would be no *Big Fat Gypsy Wedding* for her daughter. Not if she had any say in it.

'Are you listening, Mum? I said I've already warned Abbie off.' Kate's expression was mischievous. 'Come on, lighten up. I've only known Luke an hour or so. But I think I'll go to the funeral on Wednesday.'

'Don't be ridiculous, Kate. I need you at the Stewarts to oversee the food delivery – to make sure everything is there and laid out correctly. What on earth do you want to go to a funeral for? They aren't enjoyable, you know.'

Kate widened her eyes. 'Are they not? There go my plans for a fun day out. Anyway, you don't need me to organise the buffet – you've got very reliable staff you can trust. Matt said there probably won't be many at the funeral. Very few family and friends. I think that's sad, don't you? And Matt will be upset – she was his stepmother, after all.'

'Ah, so you're going to support Matt.'

'I won't buy you a fishing rod for your birthday,' Kate said. 'You don't need one! Okay, I'm going to support Luke as well. It will be horrible for him to see such a low turnout for someone he loved.'

'As you said yourself, you've only known him for an hour.'

Kate gave an impatient sigh. 'He's Matt's brother and Matt's my friend. If it comes to it … why are *you* going? To support Jack even though you've broken up?'

'Jack invited me to the funeral. He wants me there. And I knew Annie.'

'So what's the big deal?' Kate asked. 'You, Jack, Matt – you'll all be there. Is it so strange that I want to go? Anyway, I've made up my mind.' With that, she stood up, downed the remains of her drink, and went to join Abbie and the boys at the snooker table.

Sarah's mind worked overtime. How could she ever welcome Luke Kiernan into her home? She couldn't stand his mother and had always rejected Annie's attempts to socialise, preferring to stay on the right side of Nicholas and Grace. She'd done it subtly, of course, so there was nothing Annie could say to Jack that wouldn't seem like her imagination. It wasn't as if she and Annie had anything in common, after all. Except Jack …

Luke Kiernan had to go. Wrong class, wrong nationality, wrong religion.

And another reason which only Sarah knew about …

Jack glanced at his watch. Almost four o'clock. Time to go home. He'd spent a peaceful hour nursing a pint and reading the paper in a nondescript pub in Chester where nobody knew him. Anonymity could be a blessing. Those who waxed lyrical about rural idylls had usually never experienced the relentless scrutiny that often accompanied village life. The whole of Baronsmere would soon be gossiping about Luke and interrogating Jack at every opportunity. Perhaps he could just claim sickness and take to his bed. How tempting was that?

Heading homewards, Jack thought about Annie. When was the last time he'd actually seen her, spoken to her? She'd left in February, a couple of days before he was due back from Brussels. The night before his departure, she'd been too tired to make love. He'd joked he shouldn't leave her alone too much or she might lose interest in him. Did she take that as a criticism? Or, worse, had she not wanted to make love because she'd already met the other man? These thoughts had plagued him for years after she left, and he resented them starting up again. Jack turned the car into his long driveway. Only forty-eight hours had passed and he'd already argued with his parents, and Matt seemed to resent him for not joyfully embracing Luke as one of the family. The sooner the kid left the better. Jack wanted his old life back again …

A figure loomed up unexpectedly at the bend in the drive. Jack jammed his foot on the brake and pumped the horn, then sprang out of the car. Luke was standing there, startled, balanced on his crutches, and Ollie was with him. Ollie, who was always wary of strangers! Jack couldn't believe it. The dog was barking furiously, obviously set off by the screech of brakes. When he saw it was Jack, he calmed down and ambled towards him, tail wagging. 'What the fuck do you think you're doing!' Jack yelled at Luke. 'I nearly ran you over!'

'What does it look like I'm doin'?' snapped Luke. 'I was takin' a walk. Sorry if I came round the corner too fast.'

Jack had overreacted, but his heart still pounded with shock. A shock that was coming out as anger. 'I wasn't expecting you to be there, especially with my dog off his lead.'

'No excuse for drivin' like an idiot,' Luke answered. 'And

I can hardly hold a lead, can I? I assumed the driveway would be safe.'

'What are you doing with him, anyway? He's temperamental. He can turn vicious with strangers.' They both looked down at Ollie, who sat between them staring sleepily into the middle of a hedge. Jack felt more than a little foolish.

'I guess he thought I was part of the family. His mistake.' Luke turned abruptly and headed back up the drive, and Jack watched in disbelief as Ollie followed. He got back into the car and arrived at the entrance just ahead of them, leaving the front door open behind him.

'Maggie!' Jack shouted, waiting in the hallway, his arms folded across his chest. She appeared from the kitchen, drying her hands just as Luke and Ollie walked in.

'Hello, love,' she said, smiling at Luke. 'Ready for some tea and a slice of my walnut cake?'

Unbelievable. It was as if Jack didn't exist. 'Maggie, I must say, I'm more than a little surprised at you.'

Maggie helped Luke remove his jacket. 'And why would that be? What am I supposed to have done?'

'Letting Luke go wandering on his own. He's only just out of hospital. He should be taking it easy.'

'I've got a damaged knee and sore ribs. I'm not on life support,' Luke muttered.

'He needed some fresh air,' said Maggie. 'If you'd been back earlier, you could have gone out with him.'

'I had a lot of things to sort out,' said Jack, his voice raised. Maggie tutted as he brushed impatiently past her, heading for the study.

'Well, we've had a nice afternoon,' she said. 'Just because *you've* had a bad day, you don't have to take it out on me – or Luke.'

Jack stopped. Maggie was right. He was being totally

unreasonable. He turned back, and moved forward to give her an apologetic kiss on the cheek, but Luke stepped between them, jaw set and head raised defiantly. 'What the …?' Jack began.

Maggie touched Luke's arm. 'Thank you, Luke – but it's okay, really.'

Jack glared at Luke as the penny dropped. 'Did you seriously think I was going to hit Maggie? For Christ's sake, that might be how it is where you come from, but you're in civilisation now!'

Without speaking, Luke limped off on his crutches to his room.

'Well done, Jack. Well done,' said Maggie.

Jack raised his hands in frustration. 'How do you expect me to react? After what I was just accused of?'

'Oh, wake up!' Maggie lowered her voice. 'He didn't accuse you of anything – he reacted instinctively. Doesn't that tell you something?'

'I know he's been around violence, but …'

'But what? Can't you see? He thought you were going to hit me – men hitting women is something he expects. Do you see what I'm getting at?'

Suddenly he did. And it was sickening. Had Luke seen that happening to Annie? But she'd chosen to leave him. Ultimately, she was responsible for her own fate. And her son's. It wasn't Jack's fault.

So why was he the one who felt so guilty?

Chapter Nine

Luke stood at the bedroom window, staring out at the hearse. The coffin was covered with sprays of flowers and wreaths. All show. Annie had lived and died unappreciated by the Stewarts. It still didn't seem right she was to be buried here, in their world. He took a deep breath. It hurt, the pain in his ribs made worse by what felt like a tight band around his chest. Fear? Or was this what was meant by heartache?

It was finally here, the day he'd dreaded. Burying his mother would mean burying part of himself. He'd stayed awake all night, keeping his own silent vigil – remembering her and wishing he could wake up in his own home, in his own bed, with her calling him for breakfast. If he closed his eyes and prayed hard enough, the past two weeks might just have been the worst kind of nightmare. Maybe he was still unconscious in Limerick's A&E after the beating, and the fatal trip to Dublin was all in his head.

He looked at the mirrored wardrobe and a stranger looked back. A stranger wearing a black suit from Next, which Matt and his aunt Claire had taken him to buy on Monday. It had cost four times as much as his suit back home. It hurt that his mam would never see him in it. She'd loved seeing him dressed smart for special occasions.

There was a knock at the door and Matt walked in. He too was wearing a dark suit, and he looked tense. He'd cut himself shaving. Sometimes Luke forgot that Annie had been Matt's mother too. The only one he'd ever known.

'Ready?'

Luke would never be ready, but he had no choice.

* * *

On the journey to Baronswood, Luke kept his eyes fixed on the back of the hearse moving slowly in front of them. The coffin was now draped with the Irish tricolour, which he'd bought from a backstreet sports shop in Manchester. His mother was being buried on foreign soil, but this gave her some identity.

Jack was in the front of the car, Matt sitting next to Luke. He might as well have been alone, though. He felt alone. He wished the journey could last forever so he wouldn't have to watch Annie being lowered into the ground, but all too soon the car reached the church.

Father Quinn was standing in the doorway, hands clasped in front of him. Maggie was there too, holding down her black hat against gusts of wind. Matt helped Luke out before moving to the back of the hearse to take up his position as one of the pallbearers. Jack was another, along with his friend Dave and the guy Annie had worked for. Luke was gutted he couldn't share the responsibility. Not wanting to see the coffin unloaded or the flag removed for the entry into the church, he turned away and moved towards the church door. A single bell was tolling, the lonely sound deepening his misery.

'God give you strength, Luke,' he heard Father Quinn say, but he was too numb to respond. With Maggie at his side, he entered the church to the smell of incense and sandalwood, and the ominous sound of the organ's slow, dramatic chords. From habit, he stopped by the holy water stoup and crossed himself. Genuflection was impossible, but who cared? Certainly not the sad-faced statue of the Virgin Mary, hands outstretched, as if to try and ease his pain. She knew all about grief and loss. How had she found a way through it?

The walk up the centre aisle seemed endless. The statue of Christ on the cross behind the altar never seemed to get any closer. It had been the right decision not to walk behind the coffin. Limping on crutches, he'd just have been a pitiful reminder of the accident. It was his mother who deserved the sympathy today, not him.

Finally, he and Maggie reached the front. She helped him sit down, resting his crutches close by, then slipped into the pew behind. 'I'm right here,' she whispered, putting her hand on his shoulder. She was already crying and he wished the tears would come for him too, his grief walled up uncomfortably inside, demanding release.

He turned round to thank Maggie and noticed with sadness the small number of mourners. By rights, the church should have been overflowing for such a special person. His fists clenched with a desire to punch the world until he saw the woman a few rows back, across the aisle, elegantly dressed in a black suit and grey scarf, red hair hanging loose around her shoulders. Suddenly, he didn't feel quite so alone.

Emer's shoes were too tight. She'd bought them during a lunch hour, grabbing the first black pair she could find, not bothering to try them on. Now she was paying the price, and church wasn't exactly an appropriate place to slip them off.

Luke had just spotted her and his genuine smile showed he was pleased she'd made it. He'd phoned her on Sunday evening for advice about the eulogy and to ask if she would come to the funeral. She hadn't wanted him to feel alone on such a day, so she'd arranged cover at work, booked a flight, and here she was. Jack had wanted her to come to the house and leave for the church with them, but her flight landed too late to allow that.

It had been the right decision to come. Luke, sitting at the front of the church, head bowed, needed all the support he could get. Emer's heart went out to him. The woman who had been the rock at the centre of his world was gone, and he was faced with building a new life – a daunting prospect.

Emer had been through it herself, with Michael. Her grief, confusion, despair and fear of the future were still more than just a memory. She wished she could spare Luke that, but death was part of life, one of the hardest lessons to learn. At least she could be here for him today, to show her support, her friendship, and to listen if he needed to talk.

The organist stopped, and a man went to the microphone at the side of the altar. There was movement at the back of the church and glancing round, Emer saw the priest ready to lead the cortège. Luke had stood up, holding on to the back of the pew for support, his eyes fixed on the coffin. He looked resolute and dignified, head held high, but he was pale and had dark circles under his eyes. He seemed slighter than she remembered, but he looked smart in his suit. Annie would surely have been proud.

The rich baritone of a male soloist singing 'You Raise me Up' suddenly filled the church and, as the singer ended the first verse, Emer watched Annie's coffin borne down the aisle to the sound of uilleann pipes. The haunting sound, so unmistakeably Irish, made her think of the rolling green of her homeland and of a young woman with a dark-haired, blue-eyed toddler, battling against the odds. Emer was glad the music brought Luke's world into this small English church.

As the coffin neared, she made the sign of the cross and saw Jack was one of the pallbearers. Staring straight ahead, his face was strained. The young man sharing the load on the other side could only be his son, Matt. Same-shaped face, same eyes. He looked tearful, and Emer remembered that at just four years of age, he'd lost two mothers.

As the sound of the pipes built to a crescendo, the soloist and the choir resumed the poignant vocals of the modern hymn. Although she hadn't known Annie, Emer was feeling her loss and Luke's pain. He was more than just a patient to her now, and Jack was more than just a relative. The longer she spent with them, the harder it would be to pull back. And truth was, she didn't really want to.

The coffin was set down in front of the altar, the wreaths of beautiful white lilies and yellow roses placed nearby. As the music stopped, Jack and Matt moved to the front pew next to Luke, and the priest sprinkled holy water, intoning solemnly, 'The grace of our Lord Jesus Christ and the love of God and the fellowship of the Holy Spirit be with you all.'

Because of the sparse gathering, Emer was relieved there was a choir, and following their beautiful rendition of the *Ave Maria*, the priest moved on to the prayer. Although an order of service sheet had been provided, most of the congregation was clearly not Catholic because the responses were few and fumbled.

Jack's jaw was set, his focus on the coffin, his feelings probably a confusing mix, part love, part anger. Luke sat rigid in the pew, maybe waiting for the sign from the priest, which eventually came when the sermon was over, in the form of a nod and a reassuring smile.

Emer clenched her hands, nails digging into the palms as Luke, unsteady on his crutches, went to the lectern, clutching a piece of paper, which he placed in front of him. He took a deep breath and lifted his head. Proudly. She could read his feelings as easily as if they were written down in front of her. It was all there – love, anger, defiance and stubborn resolve. Every emotion needed to survive this ordeal. She was glad to be here for this remarkable young man who was rising above his grief to pay tribute to his mother. Tears pricked her eyes. She hadn't felt able to give a eulogy for Michael, yet here was Luke, younger and comparatively uneducated, standing there bravely in front of strangers.

'I could read before I was five,' Luke began, his voice

quiet and wavering slightly. 'My mother taught me because she wanted me to share her love of books and she wanted me to be educated so's I could make a decent future. She was a realist, my mam, and she knew bein' at school wasn't always easy for Travellers.'

Emer was mentally willing him on and his confidence appeared to be increasing, his voice growing stronger as he continued. 'She didn't own much. Books from car boot sales, second-hand clothes and music from an old radio I found in a skip. There was nothin' wrong with the radio. Easy come, easy go for some folk. But my mam was rich in other ways – in the things that matter. People loved her because she cared.

'She'd help anyone. Would share whatever she had, even if it wasn't much. She encouraged Traveller kids to learn as much as they could. She cared for my grand-da when he got sick. She'd sit up all night, puttin' cool cloths on his head or readin' to him, but she still found time to take whatever jobs she could to help us live. She cleaned offices, delivered leaflets, picked fruit. Society doesn't give many options to Travellers, but she never complained, just made the best of it. When she felt down, she'd sing. She loved to sing.

'She always wanted me to have the best things in life, but to her, those were things money couldn't buy. If I felt sorry for myself because I didn't have a PlayStation or decent football boots, she'd tell me we were rich compared to people who had nothin' and were starvin'. She'd say a lot of people had a better deal than us – but even more had a worse one.'

At this point, Luke turned slightly to look at Jack. 'She didn't have a privileged life, but she had more principles than most. Things weren't easy, but *she* made me feel loved and wanted – the most important thing for any kid.'

Luke's eyes had remained on his father, and Jack would

surely have registered the emphasis on the word *she*, for it seemed a deliberate slight.

'Bein' rich doesn't mean someone's honest and bein' poor doesn't mean they're dishonest,' Luke continued, before pausing once more, and turning to look at Annie's coffin. 'When life got difficult, she gave me strength. I hope I did the same for her. I'm not ashamed of what I am because the finest person I'm ever likely to know was a Traveller. They say no one's perfect, but my mam came close, and anyone should have been proud to know her.'

He folded up the paper and put it into his pocket, then moved slowly away from the lectern and back to his seat for the rest of the service. When it was over, he made his way to the coffin. As he placed his hand on it, the closest he could get to touching his mother for the last time, Emer heard him say, 'Go well, Mam. I love you.' Then the pall-bearers took up their positions to carry Annie Kiernan to her final resting place.

Emer's vision blurred and her throat constricted painfully as she tried not to cry. Luke had succeeded in painting a vivid picture of a woman who'd struggled against the odds but never given up on life, or on her son, and it was patently obvious how much he'd loved her. Whether her tears were for Annie or for Luke, or maybe just the whole sadness of the occasion, Emer wasn't sure. What she did know was that Luke had arranged this funeral with the intention of squeezing as much emotion as possible from those who attended. He'd admitted that on Sunday night when he'd said bitterly, 'They'll remember my mother's death, even if they didn't remember her life.'

His eyes downcast, Luke followed the coffin out of the church. There were no tears, but he must surely be feeling more than he was showing. Emer was humbled by the way this young man had honoured his mother with a dignified, untutored eloquence. If that didn't soften Jack's heart, nothing would.

Kate tried to stop her teeth chattering as she stood at the graveside. The freezing wind was cutting right through. Father Quinn was still going strong after ten minutes, raising his voice at times to compete with the noisy rooks. Every time Kate thought he was about to close, the priest just took a breath and kept going. How many more saints could there be left to name?

Kate distracted herself by discreetly looking around at the mourners. Not many for a woman's lifetime. She wondered who the pretty redhead was. A woman standing alone, at some distance, as though she felt she didn't belong. Maybe one of those serial funeral attenders Kate had read about.

Matt's godparents, Dave and Evie Mitchell, had come. Dave was Baronsmere's policeman – as a young teen, Kate had been on the receiving end of more than one fatherly warning for silly things, like that incident with the vodka ... The joy of living in a small, rural community – even the police were your friends. Would Luke have been a tearaway if he'd grown up here? Would he have become almost a brother to her, as Matt had ... or would they have been childhood sweethearts? Yes, she had definite plans for him and they weren't sisterly ones.

Tony and Barbara Hayes were there, too – before she married Jack, Annie had worked in their pub, the Fox and Feathers, which Sarah disparagingly called 'the plebs' local'. Tony looked gutted. So did Claire, Jack's sister. She was unaccompanied – no one else from the Stewarts had shown up. Claire's husband, Richard, had dropped her off and quickly disappeared. He was a vile human being. Claire was lovely, and Kate could only assume Richard had changed drastically after he married her, because by all accounts, he was a lousy husband. Matt said he and Luke had met up with Claire on Monday, and she'd bonded instantly with Luke. That wouldn't have gone down well with Richard.

Kate turned to her left and glanced at Jack. There was no sign of emotion. In the church, he'd stared straight ahead at the altar. Maybe he felt nothing. It had been twenty-odd years since he'd been with Annie. In contrast, Maggie was weeping, as she had been since the service began. Matt said she'd loved Annie like a daughter. Matt had cried, too. He said he'd cried for Annie after she left, but Jack would get angry if she was mentioned so Matt got used to not talking about her, mourning her in private, missing his bedtime stories, missing her cuddles.

Luke, like Jack, hadn't cried once during the funeral service. Funny that – the two people closest to Annie hadn't shed any tears. When she'd told Matt she was going to the funeral, he'd laughingly accused her of only doing it because she fancied Luke, but she really did want to support him. He was a stranger to the village and must surely feel overwhelmed. Kate didn't need to support her mother, that was for sure. Sarah was tough as nails and didn't need anybody's shoulder to cry on. Her head was bowed, but not in grief – she was discreetly looking at a valuable bracelet one of her men friends had given her. Rose-gold moonstone, she said it was. All week she'd been twisting her wrist to see it shine in the light.

Finally Kate heard the words 'ashes to ashes, dust to dust' that signalled the end. The priest sprinkled holy water over the coffin then Jack knelt down, picked up some earth, and threw it into the grave. Matt did the same, murmuring, 'Rest in peace, Annie.'

Kate watched as Matt picked up some more earth and pressed it discreetly into Luke's hand, but there was no response at first. Luke seemed dazed, which wasn't surprising.

'Goodbye, Mam,' he said finally, his voice almost a whisper, as he crumbled the soil over the tricolour now replaced on top of the coffin, its coloured stripes of green, white and orange streaked with mud and earth. Kate wanted to cry. She wanted to hold Luke's hand, give him a hug, and tell him it would all be okay, except it wouldn't. Not for a long time.

And that was it. Father Quinn closed his Bible and people started to walk away. The funeral was over.

'Let's go,' Matt urged Luke, who hadn't moved. Then he just crumpled, falling against Matt who caught him before he hit the ground.

'Dad!' Matt sounded panic-stricken.

Jack was quickly at the other side, supporting Luke who seemed barely conscious. 'Okay, okay – I've got him,' he said.

'Mum?' Sarah was a certified first-aider, but Kate noticed she offered no assistance.

'They're doing fine,' said Sarah, but her voice was cold. 'He doesn't need to be crowded.'

Maggie hurried over. 'I was afraid of this,' she said. 'He's hardly eaten in days.'

Luke's eyes fluttered open and between them Jack and Matt settled him back onto his crutches. Matt pulled out his hip flask, forcing Luke to take a sip of the brandy. He gagged but at least regained some colour and nodded weakly when Jack asked if he could make it to the car.

They set off slowly toward the cemetery gates, passing the unknown redhead, who was gazing at Luke with concern. 'Are you okay?' the woman asked as she moved forward and touched his arm. He smiled, obviously pleased to see her.

She looked nice, and Kate was grateful Luke had a familiar face there for him today.

'Looks like you're not needed after all,' Sarah commented, linking her arm through Kate's.

God, her mother could be a bitch at times.

Jack scanned the drawing room from the doorway but couldn't see Emer. There'd been no chance to talk to her since arriving back from the church.

'She's in the dining room,' said Matt, handing him a glass of wine.

'Thanks,' said Jack, taking a sip. A nice flinty Chablis. Sarah always chose well. 'Sorry – who's in the dining room?'

'The redhead. Who is she?'

Jack tried to sound casual. 'Emer Sullivan. Luke's bereavement counsellor.' He sensed he was under scrutiny but stared straight ahead at the portrait of Great-Uncle George in his regimental uniform.

'She's a long way from home, isn't she?'

An innocent remark? Probably not. Matt could read him like a book.

'A sad business, Jack, a sad business,' said Tony Hayes, joining them in the doorway. 'Can't believe that sweet lass is gone.' Jack gave a non-committal murmur and gulped down some wine. 'Where's her ladyship then?'

Could Tony talk any louder? Draw any more attention to the fact his parents had boycotted the funeral? 'She's a bit under the weather, Tony,' said Jack, through gritted teeth. Having to cover for his parents was a nightmare.

'Coming through, coming through.'

They moved aside as Kate came into the drawing room with Luke in tow. He still looked pale. After the incident at the graveside, Jack had arranged for the family doctor to call.

'Hey, bro – come and meet Tony,' said Matt.

Jack excused himself and went into the hall. Now, where was Emer?

'Jack ...'

Sarah pulled him into the nook next to the grandfather clock. 'How are you? This must have been so traumatic. I can only imagine ...'

She was standing very close to him. Too close for people who were no longer in a relationship. Jack hoped Sarah wasn't going to suggest they get back together. 'I have to get back to the guests,' he said, trying to sidle around her.

Then two things happened at once. Richard walked in through the front door and Emer came out of the dining room.

'Well, well,' smirked Richard, eyeing Jack and Sarah. 'Look at you two lovebirds. There are six bedrooms in this house – couldn't you find one of them?' He caught sight of Emer and smiled. 'Hello. I don't believe we've been introduced. I'm Richard. Shall we go through? It's a little crowded out here.'

Emer glanced at Jack before being propelled by Richard into the drawing room.

'Who's *she*?' asked Sarah.

'Emer,' said Jack. 'She counselled Luke after the accident.'

'Isn't this a bit above and beyond the call of duty?'

'I think it's more personal now. She became quite attached to Luke – and he to her.'

'Judging from the look on her face just now, I don't think it was only Luke she became attached to.' There was a hard edge to Sarah's voice and she brushed past him, heading for the dining room.

Suddenly, it was all too much. Jack needed to get away from everyone, to clear his head of the memories threatening to engulf him. If he allowed that to happen, he'd be back where he was twenty years ago. Flailing, unable to cope. Overwhelmed by grief, shock, bitterness. He went to his study and closed the door. It was the wrong decision. Alone, the memories flooded back. Memories of Annie, and his love for her. Hers for him. If it had been bad when she first left, it was ten times worse now. At least then he hadn't known that she had a child whose head she'd filled with lies. A son she'd kept from him. A son who was out there now, sick and bereft.

Jack wanted to make more effort with Luke. He wasn't so hard he didn't feel compassion, but it had taken him a long time to get over Annie. He wasn't even sure he ever had. Embracing her son might reopen the wounds that had been all but fatal emotionally, but would he regret it if he didn't try? Jack left the study, knowing what he should do but still not knowing if he could.

Emer and Richard were standing by the dining-room window, just behind the sofa where Tony was seated next to Luke. 'Your mother was one of the best barmaids I ever had,' Jack heard Tony say. 'So if you're in the market for a job, just give me a shout.'

Dear God, Matt *and* Luke working behind a bar. Well, he'd always championed the working man – no one could say Jack Stewart was a snob.

'There you are,' said Richard, exuding fake bonhomie, as Jack took a glass of wine from a tray carried by a waitress. 'Nice "do" you've put on.'

Jack wanted to strangle him. If insensitivity could be bottled, the man would be the main supplier. 'For God's sake, Richard, have a bit of respect – it's not a bloody party.'

'I was a bit alarmed when I dropped Claire off at the church,' Richard continued. 'Thought I'd stumbled on some militant funeral with that flag on the coffin. I was waiting for the gunfire volley.'

From the corner of his eye, Jack saw Luke ease himself up from the nearby sofa and move in their direction, his expression worryingly familiar. 'I'm Luke,' he said to Richard. 'Would you like a drink?'

'That's very hospit—' Richard began, but got no further. Despite the awkwardness of his crutches, Luke managed to take Jack's wine glass and throw the contents into Richard's face. It was the hospital all over again, but Jack felt no sympathy for his brother-in-law. Luke was already on his way out of the room, leaving Tony Hayes chortling away on the sofa and the other guests trying to hide their smiles. Richard had never been popular.

'Little animal!' he ranted, as Claire dabbed his face with some serviettes. 'Deserves a good hiding!'

'Let's go home,' said Claire. Richard followed her out of the room, shoving his way through the guests, and Jack heard the front door slam moments later. He turned to talk to Emer but she'd disappeared. Great. The feuding Stewart family had probably scared her off.

'Like mother, like son,' he heard Tony say.

'Sorry?'

'His mother did the same thing.'

'What – threw a drink over Richard?' This was the first Jack had heard of it.

'Aye,' confirmed Tony, with a satisfied smile. 'She hadn't been working for me long. Richard had a few too many and kept hassling Annie, which she laughed off till he grabbed hold of her – then he got a full pint over him. He was often in – it was obvious he fancied her.'

'She never told me that.' And Richard had been married to Claire then. Was there no limit to how low the bastard could sink?

'No,' Tony was saying, 'I don't suppose she would have mentioned it. She weren't that kind of a lass – not a troublemaker. Looks like she raised a good 'un there, eh?'

Jack half-heartedly nodded. He didn't blame Luke for

throwing the drink – he'd like to have done it himself, glass and all. He wanted to tell Luke that, for them to share a laugh over it as most fathers and sons would do.

Father and son. Jack didn't think of Luke in that way often. It was easier not to. But now he should go after him, make his peace. It was what he'd planned to do earlier, but his feet wouldn't move. Just like at the funeral, when he should have put his arm around Luke. He'd actually wanted to but couldn't do it. Holding Annie's son, who looked so much like her, would be torture. There would have been conflicting emotions that he couldn't deal with right now – wondering if Luke was his, or whether he was holding the result of Annie's betrayal.

So instead, he stood there, pretending to listen to Tony although the conversation was lost on him. Jack was too busy hating himself.

Chapter Ten

When Emer went to the garden to find Luke, she stopped for a moment to drink in the scene. Giant oaks and beech trees, a summerhouse, seemingly endless stretches of lawn and a lake. Beauty, space and privacy. Jack Stewart was a lucky man.

Luke was settled on an ornamental ironwork seat facing the lake. The dog at his feet wagged its tail as she approached.

'Hello, you,' Emer said to Luke, who gave a weary smile. He didn't look well. She sat down and the dog nuzzled her hand. 'Who's this then?'

'Matt's dog, Honey. She's very friendly.'

'Unlike your man inside, eh?'

'Why did I do that?' Luke shook his head. 'Why do I never think? I'm an eejit.'

'I'd say he's the one who's the eejit,' Emer reassured him. She hadn't liked Richard. Within minutes he'd informed her of his lofty position in Stewart Enterprises and how he would one day inherit a large part of the family fortune. She'd mentally filed him under *P* for Prat.

'I don't even know who he is.'

'I can help you there. He's married to Jack's sister, which I guess makes him your uncle.'

Luke groaned. 'Great! Another reason for Jack to bawl me out.'

'Are the two of you not getting on still?' she asked. She liked Jack. She liked Luke. Mediating between them would be tricky.

'We clash all the time. It was a mistake to come here. It's never goin' to work. Jack doesn't want me, and his parents said to my face they don't believe I'm a Stewart.'

Emer wondered what kind of people could be so unkind to someone recently bereaved. 'It's their loss, Luke. What about Matt, though? You said on the phone he seemed glad you're here.'

'Yeah, but he's not around much. He's got his own life.'

'You'll make your own life too, I know you will. Right now, you've got too much time on your hands and you're brooding. You need to get out. Meet people.'

'With these?' Luke indicated his crutches.

'Yes, with those. The housekeeper here looks like she'd do anything for you. She may have a car. And what about that pretty girl you were talking to?'

'Kate. She's really nice. Her mam owns some stables.'

Emer saw the hint of a blush. She'd told him back in Dublin that the girls would be on the scene for him soon enough. 'Don't lock yourself away, Luke. You'll miss out on so much.'

He nodded, but would he take her advice? Guilt could play a big part in a person's not being able to move on after bereavement. She put her arm round him and gave him a hug. He seemed to welcome the contact, leaning against her slightly. 'Do you ever forget?' he asked. 'Seein' someone put into the ground?'

'No, you don't – but eventually you learn to live with it.'

'I still can't believe she's gone,' he whispered. 'Every mornin' I wake up and think things are how they used to be. Then it hits me.'

'That's normal,' she told him, and he nodded slowly as though he accepted it, but what was he really thinking and feeling? There had been no tears at all at the funeral. Did he cry in private, or did he fear his grief too much to let go? 'You held it together very well today. It can't have been easy.'

'I know what you're thinkin'. I'm not ashamed to cry. It's just not somethin' I do.'

That was worrying. Did the reason lie in his past? She thought again about the bruises. Were they from a fight – or something more sinister? She wanted to help him but there just wasn't time, and her professionalism wouldn't allow her to begin an exploration of buried emotions when she wouldn't be around to monitor the consequences.

'Luke!'

Emer turned to see the housekeeper approaching.

'Dr Freeman's here,' Maggie said. 'He wants to check you over.'

'I'm fine. I don't need a doctor.'

Luke was so stubborn. 'Best be on the safe side,' said Emer, handing him the crutches. He hauled himself up from the seat and the three of them started walking towards the house.

'Maybe we could go out somewhere tomorrow,' Emer suggested. 'I don't need to be at the airport till four.'

'I'd like that,' he replied, then with that gentle smile she found so endearing, he looked up at the sky. 'Hope the weather'll be better than this.'

'C'mon, Luke. We're Irish,' teased Emer. 'First thing they do when we're born is give us an umbrella. Now you see that doctor or I'll change my mind.'

Sarah gulped more wine and held the cool glass to her cheek. She felt hot, a little dizzy. This whole day had been too much. Luke was so like Annie – same eyes, same shape of face. Like she'd come back to haunt them. Sarah had tried to block it all out, to keep focused only on Jack, but now he was avoiding her. Someone turned the dining-room door handle. If it was Tony Hayes, she'd have to be rude and walk out. Mindless chatter was the last thing she needed.

The redhead walked in. The counsellor, who'd apparently trekked all the way from Ireland just for little Luke. As if.

Jack Stewart was probably the best catch she'd ever seen in whatever backwater she came from.

'Hello. I'm Emer Sullivan. Luke's counsellor.'

'Sarah Walker. Jack's partner.' He helped her out from time to time with the pub's financial matters so it wasn't exactly a lie. Hopefully this woman would interpret it to mean Sarah was Jack's girlfriend.

Emer moved forward and shook Sarah's hand. That was an off-the-peg dress and jacket for sure. But it was Emer's hair that would catch a man's eye. Jack loved curls. Sarah's hair was poker straight.

'Just getting some food for Maggie,' said Emer, starting to fill a plate. 'She hasn't eaten anything yet. Too worried about Luke. He's had such a rough time.'

'So has Jack,' said Sarah, irritated at Emer's over-familiarity with Maggie, with the house.

'Yes, but I think Jack can take care of himself, don't you?'

Sarah frowned. This little upstart needed putting in her place. 'Can he? He's a complicated man. Not many know him well. It takes years. It was a long time before he got over Annie deserting him, and I think her death has upset him more than he lets on. It's brought it all back.'

'Yes, I'm sure.'

'At least he has family and friends around him here,' Sarah continued. 'People who can help him adjust. He really needs stability in his life right now.' There. If the woman had any sense, she'd see that as a warning shot across her bow.

'I'm sure Jack knows exactly what he needs,' said Emer.

'Let's hope so.' Sarah couldn't read Emer's expression. Hard to know if her warning had had any impact.

'Well, nice to meet you,' said Emer. 'I'll just take this to Maggie.'

A thought suddenly occurred to Sarah. 'If you need somewhere to stay, I run the local hotel.'

Emer smiled. 'Thanks, but I'm staying here tonight. Jack invited me earlier. I was planning to stay in Manchester, but I think Luke needs support right now.'

If this was a poker game, that was the trump card. Sarah couldn't beat that. Jack was supremely vulnerable today, and Emer and her curls would be there to comfort him. She'd bet her last dollar both of them were using Luke as an excuse. All those years she'd devoted to Jack, and now he was finally free of Annie Kiernan but drifting away from her. It was so unfair. Still, Emer would be back in Ireland soon enough. Out of sight and hopefully out of mind. And when Jack needed a shoulder to cry on, Sarah fully intended to be there.

The doctor had just left when there was a knock on the door. Luke prayed it wasn't Jack. He was still waiting to be read the riot act for dowsing Richard.

It was Kate. 'Are you okay?' she asked.

He struggled upright, propping himself against the pillows. 'Fine, thanks. Just tired.'

'What did the doctor say?'

'*Get some food down you, boy. I've seen more meat on a butcher's pencil.*' Luke did his best to imitate Dr Freeman's no-nonsense voice. 'I thought it was Maggie, dressed up.'

Kate laughed, and Luke's initial shyness disappeared. She moved over to the armchair by the window, where she sat sideways, draping her legs over the arm. 'It's good to see you smile. This is such a difficult day for you. I can't imagine how I'd cope if I lost my mum. I've only ever had her. Like you, really.'

'What happened to your da'?'

'He left, not long after I was born.'

'Do you not see him?'

'No, never. Last Mum heard, he was in America.'

Luke couldn't understand any man abandoning his own child. 'Does that upset you?'

'I don't really care,' said Kate. 'Don't think I've missed much. Jack's been great. When I was little, I'd pretend he was my dad. Matt's like my brother. We had holidays together and days out – me and Mum, Jack and Matt.'

So, while Luke had been living with poverty and violence, Jack was playing happy families with another man's child. Kate was still talking, not realising how her words had cut Luke like a knife. She would, of course, believe Annie was the guilty one, that she'd abandoned Jack and kept his son from him. He could set her straight, but what would it achieve? She'd lost her real father – who was Luke to take away her substitute?

He listened to her talk – about an article she'd written for the student newspaper, her hopes for the future, the May Day riding competition – and it soothed him. It was disappointing when Maggie knocked on the door and said Sarah was probably over the limit and Kate would have to drive her home. He didn't want her to go.

Kate walked over to the bed, took a pen from her bag and wrote a number on his hand. 'There – now you won't lose it, but copy it before you wash,' she said. 'We'll go to the stables on Saturday, but call me if you need anything. Well, call me anyway.' She leaned over and kissed his cheek. 'Bye.'

'Bye,' he responded, and as soon as she was gone, he put his hand to his cheek, where the touch of her lips lingered.

Emer was resting on the bed in Jack's guest room. The mourners had left over an hour ago and the house was now quiet. The family had needed a time-out after the stress of the funeral so everyone had retired to their rooms, agreeing with Maggie's suggestion to use the leftovers in the fridge when they were hungry. Jack had suggested Emer come down to the drawing room around seven for a drink. So formal. She wondered, not for the first time, if a small-town girl like her could fit into his world. Perhaps Annie had wondered the same thing …

The phone shrilled. The display light flashed 'internal call'. 'Hello?' she answered.

'Emer.' Jack's voice. 'How does a slap-up meal sound?'

She looked in the mirror. Not a 'slap-up meal' look. 'It'll take me a while to get ready.'

'No, come as you are. I'll give you two minutes,' Jack said before hanging up.

He was waiting for her at the foot of the stairs, a tea towel draped over his arm. 'Can I escort you to your table, Madam?'

The slap-up meal was on the kitchen table in takeaway containers. 'Reheated leftovers didn't sound very appetising, so I ordered a takeaway,' said Jack. 'I remembered you said you and your sister always had a Chinese once a month.'

'Thank you. That was very thoughtful.' He looked so eager to please and it was touching.

After he'd shared out the food, Emer said, 'You look tired, Jack. How are you feeling?'

'Exhausted,' he admitted. 'Having to talk and think about the past so much was … difficult.'

Emer remembered watching in admiration as he worked the room, spending time with every mourner there. She'd overheard people telling him their memories of Annie and he'd listened politely, only the slight set of his jaw revealing the strain of guarding his emotions. 'I think you did Annie proud today, Jack.'

'I'm so glad you could make it, Emer,' he said. 'It meant a lot to me – and to Luke as well, I'm sure … What time are you leaving tomorrow?'.

'My flight's at six.'

'And what are your plans for the day?'

'I thought I'd take Luke for a drive. He's always wanted to see Old Trafford.'

'I see,' said Jack, clearly disappointed. 'That sounds like a good idea. I have to be at the office, anyway.'

Poor Jack. He was probably used to getting what he wanted when he wanted it, and being thwarted didn't come easily.

'Is this okay?' Jack indicated the takeaway cartons. 'Given that last time you told me cheap food doesn't matter if the company's good.'

She was flattered he'd remembered her words and glad he was relaxed enough to let his sense of humour come through. 'It's lovely,' she told him. 'Going out for a meal wouldn't have seemed right, somehow.' She took a bite from a spring roll. 'And these are the best I've ever tasted.'

'Are you warm enough?' Jack swivelled the portable heater and the warm air embraced Emer's feet. She snuggled deeper into the coat Jack had loaned her, smelling faint traces of cologne. They were alone together on the patio sharing a nightcap. It had been a nice evening – considering the circumstances – but she was feeling confused about Sarah Walker. Emer had stayed in the kitchen with Maggie for the rest of the afternoon, wary of another run-in with Jack's 'partner'.

'Penny for them?' asked Jack.

He'd just cut a cigar, and the rich, sweet smoke reminded her of her grandfather's favourite indulgence. Jack had had a rough day. Perhaps she should go easy on him. But that elephant on the patio table between them was annoying. Emer took a quick gulp of brandy. 'I remember what you said in Dublin – about Sarah ...'

'Yes?'

'I met her earlier in the dining room. She introduced herself as your partner.'

'What!' Jack sounded angry. 'I don't know what she's playing at. We split up over two months ago. We did, Emer, I swear.'

There was no guile about him, she could see that. He was being truthful. 'I'm guessing she's changed her mind,' Emer told him. 'She definitely warned me off.'

'Then she's too late. I'm not going to lose you.'

He looked directly into her eyes and she felt a jolt of strong connection. Desire, curiosity, excitement, hope – all those emotions a potential new relationship brings. 'You don't exactly have me, Jack,' she whispered.

'I can wait,' he told her. 'I know we've only just met but I really want to get to know you better. And for you to get to know me. You've seen me at my worst – I'd like you to have a chance to see me at my best.' He paused. 'You're beautiful, Emer, but it's not only about that. Being with you feels right. The way you see things, what you talk about – it's new for me. Makes me realise what I've been missing.'

This was a man declaring feelings on the day of his wife's funeral. A desire to reaffirm life in the face of death. She had to be careful. No emotion could be trusted here.

'What about your parents?'

He frowned. 'What about them?'

'They didn't exactly welcome Annie, you said. Didn't come to the wedding, didn't even come to the funeral today. They might think your getting involved with another Irish woman is a mistake.'

'I don't think Annie being Irish was the problem. It was because she was a Traveller. You'd be far more respectable in their eyes.' Jack made a dismissive gesture. 'Anyway, I don't care what they think. I'm a grown man. I can do what I like.'

155

He sounded more like a defiant teenager than an adult, but he'd likely blow up if she said that. 'I don't want to come between you and your family, Jack. I know my family's very important to me. I couldn't be without them.'

Jack shifted in his chair, rubbed his hand along the back of his neck. Emer waited, hoping he'd give what she said careful consideration.

'When I was young, Emer,' he said, 'my parents were always telling me to behave appropriately. To do the things they considered best. They had my whole future mapped out for me while I was still at school.'

He drew on his cigar and watched the smoke rising into the night air. 'At university, I rebelled. Lived away from home. Shared a cramped flat in Manchester with friends I chose on my own. Raised hell at weekends on my motorbike. Got involved in all kinds of student protests and was even arrested on one. That was reported in Baronsmere's local paper. My mother turned up at the flat to chew me out. I shut the door in her face and we didn't speak for nearly a year.'

It was hard to reconcile the conventional Jack she knew with the young rebel he was describing. 'What changed all that?' she asked.

Jack looked out toward the lake as if he could see the past there. 'The summer before I graduated, I got a really bad dose of glandular fever. I came home to Edenbridge, the family estate, to get better. I met Caroline again, a girl I'd known since childhood but suddenly all grown up. And so beautiful. I fell in love – hard and fast. The first time for me. I proposed out there by the lake at summer's end. Before I knew it, we were married, and had a baby on the way. Once I graduated, I started working in the family firm. One summer – and my whole life changed.'

'Do you regret it?'

Jack switched his focus back to her. 'God, no! I loved Caro and I wanted to make her happy. But Baronsmere was stifling me then. The gossip, the snobbery, the closed minds. I thought about moving us all to London but Caro begged me not to. And then … she died of an asthma attack.'

'That must have been terrible for you.' Jack had suffered two big losses in his life – Caroline and Annie. It was a wonder the man had the courage left to love again at all. He was silent for a while and she could see in his eyes the pain the memories brought. 'Jack, you don't have to tell me about Annie, you know. Not today.'

'It's okay,' he said. 'I've been thinking about her all day anyway.' He gulped down some brandy. 'Being with Annie reminded me of the freedom I'd had in those university days. She was open and honest and didn't care about doing the conventional things. She brought me back to life. You know, when we were together, I was thinking again about leaving Baronsmere. Going down south, setting up in business for myself. I'd talked to Annie about it – she was supportive. My father was opposed … of course …'

'And then Annie left.'

'And then Annie left.' He repeated her words and she heard the disbelief in them. 'All the fight went out of me. I stayed here, raised Matt, and never rocked the boat again.'

Emer sat there, absorbing everything she'd told him, trying to see it through a counsellor's eyes. There was one nagging doubt. 'Jack – I'm Irish and I'm not from your social class. Do you see me as your last chance to break free? As a way to rock the boat again?'

Jack's face flushed, his jaw tightened, his eyes narrowed. 'Is that what you think of me, Emer? That I'm a calculating, fucked-up son-of-a-bitch?'

'Jack!'

'A hopeless case that no self-respecting woman should touch with a barge pole ...'

'Stop right there!' Emer interrupted, her voice sharp. 'I never said that! You're totally overreacting. So – you've got issues – who doesn't? We're all human.'

Jack said nothing, just stared moodily into his brandy.

'Okay, let's analyse me. Let's take a good hard look at Emer Sullivan and her issues.'

'No, don't,' Jack protested, looking up. 'I'm just tired and half-cut. That's when I usually fly off the handle.'

'I insist.' Emer leaned forward. 'You were honest with me, and you deserve the same. So – people assume Emer's got all her ducks in a row – she must have, she's a counsellor, isn't she? And, to an extent, it's true. She tries not to play games with people, she shoots from the hip when necessary, and she's a loyal friend.'

'So far so good,' commented Jack.

'But there are times when Emer doesn't know all the answers. When she fails to help a patient, her professional pride is hurt and she feels bad. Her job, you see, is ninety percent of her life so whenever that doesn't go well, she's left with nothing to fall back on. And that's not healthy.' She gulped down the last of her brandy. 'Also, five years in a failed relationship has left her worried she doesn't have the emotional energy necessary to invest in another. Even though she actually wants love more than anything.'

'God,' breathed Jack. 'It's like looking in a mirror.'

In many ways it was. Loss, grief, regret, avoidance – they had all those emotions in common. But wasn't that a reason *not* to start a relationship? Wasn't it better when partners had different weaknesses, could compensate for each other, make one whole healthy unit?

'Is there more?' asked Jack.

Emer bit her lip. The hard bit was coming up. 'Emer

came to Baronsmere to support Luke, but also because she's attracted to Jack. And she's nervous about that because it might turn her safe little world upside down.' There. It was all out now. The patio table was littered with their emotional baggage. Not exactly romantic, but they'd covered more ground in one evening than some couples did in years. Would Jack feel the mystery had gone out of things, though? She pushed her glass across to Jack. 'I think I need another brandy.'

'Me too,' he said, reaching for the bottle.

When the drinks were ready, they lifted their glasses to each other in a silent toast and drank in tandem. Jack shook his head, and Emer looked at him, quizzically. 'Sorry,' he told her. 'I'm finding it hard to get past the best part of what you said.'

'There was a best part?'

'Yes. The part about Emer being attracted to Jack.'

She smiled. 'I think the odds might be against us but I'd like to give it a try. Give us a try.' Risky perhaps, but she'd not close the door on this relationship unless she really had to.

'What about this weekend? Can we meet up?'

Now that was keen. It was hard to disappoint him but she'd have to. 'I'm afraid I'm fully booked this weekend. And you have a new son to bond with.'

Jack turned his head slightly, but she saw him grimace at the mention of Luke. It seemed like he had no intention of getting closer to his son. Perhaps she could influence him and change that.

'A fortnight on Saturday then?' Jack persisted. 'It's my birthday. There's a party for me. You could be my plus one. Wear your hair up again – blow everyone away. And you might get to meet my terrible parents – if they turn up after all that's happened. Maybe they've disowned me by now.

But if they come, you could do a quick counselling job on them.'

Emer laughed. 'What an offer!'

'What do you think – could you make it? Please say yes. Give me something to look forward to.'

Jack could be very persuasive. 'I'll be there.' And where else did she have to go? A singles bar with some of her lost and lonely friends? This was a much better offer.

'Great!' Jack's excitement made him look ten years younger.

The rain had started up again, and a sudden gust of wind dusted them with fine droplets. 'Time to go in, I think,' she said.

They stood up, and as she moved round the table he caught her up into his arms and kissed her before she knew what was happening. It felt like the most natural thing in the world. When they broke apart, Jack still held her close. 'I don't suppose you'd consider ... a change of bedroom?' he whispered.

It took all her strength to deny him. 'It's not the right time. There's Luke to consider ...'

'Well, it's not really his business, is it?'

'Yes, it is, Jack,' she insisted. 'Luke's my friend. I don't want him to think I used his mother's funeral as a way of getting closer to you.'

Jack rolled his eyes. 'Luke has to learn the world doesn't revolve round him.'

Emer shook her head. 'No. He has to learn that sometimes it *does*. At the moment he has no such confidence in his own importance.'

'I never have this kind of trouble with Matt.'

'Matt's had a security Luke's never had. Cut him some slack. He buried his mother today.'

'And I buried a wife.'

'If this was a competition to see who's suffering the most grief, Luke would win hands down! He spent nearly every day of his life with his mother. You may have loved her once – maybe you still do – but it's different for him.'

Anger flashed across his face but it quickly changed into a wry smile. 'I never get away with anything with you, do I?'

'But you know it's good for you.'

'Hmm.' He looked down at her like she was a naughty child.

She played along. 'I'm worth it – honest.'

'Oh, I know that,' he said, and kissed her again.

The wind blew and the rain spattered against them, but Emer cared only about the intensity of Jack's embrace.

Chapter Eleven

Early morning was Emer's favourite time of day. She liked the hush and the muted quality of the dawn light. Back home she'd eat breakfast looking out at her scrap of garden, enjoying the solitude before the city came to life. Those snatched tranquil moments helped her cope with the raw emotions of her patients.

This morning, Emer kept to her routine, rising at six and showering. Everyone else was still asleep, so she pocketed an apple from the fruit bowl in the kitchen and went for a drive around early-morning Baronsmere. Yesterday's clouds had gone, although a low-lying mist was still clearing. It gradually revealed the village, which had a cosy, intimate feel, reminding her of remote places tucked away in corners of Ireland. She parked in the public car park opposite the Foresters Arms and took a leisurely stroll around the streets.

The cottages were well-tended: fresh paint, tasteful curtains, rockeries beginning to flower. She read the signs on the small shops as she passed: Wilson & Sons, Grocers & Provisioners; The Misses Ellsworth's Tea Shop, est. 1883; Buckley's Saddler's Shop, serving Baronsmere since 1786. Tradition was probably everything here, and the quality of your ancestry was important. Richard had boasted his mother-in-law's family had been here since the Norman Conquest. No wonder Jack's unconventional marriage to a Traveller had been considered a scandal.

Emer turned at the sound of clopping hooves. Kate, Luke's new-found friend, was approaching on a feisty-looking horse. Barbour, hard hat, gleaming riding boots – this girl was no occasional rider. They'd met briefly at the funeral, and Emer had liked her immediately.

'You're an early bird,' Kate said, stopping beside her.

'So are you.' Emer held out her hand for the horse to get her scent. 'He's a beauty. What's his name?'

'Petruchio.'

Emer smiled. 'As in *Taming of the Shrew*?'

'With a name like Kate, it seemed appropriate.'

Emer stroked the horse's neck. He tossed his head, obviously impatient to be on his way.

'How's Luke?' asked Kate.

'I haven't seen him yet, but I'm taking him to the Manchester United stadium. He's a big fan. There's a museum there and they do daily tours. My flight leaves at six, and I have to check in at four, so Maggie's going to pick Luke up and bring him back here.'

'I could bring him back.' Kate's face had lit up. 'I'm at uni in Manchester, so I'm really close. My last lecture's done by three.'

Who was Emer to stand in the way of a budding romance? 'Okay – I'll let Maggie know.'

'Luke's got my mobile number if there's any problem.'

So, all sorted except … Kate seemed a nice girl, but surely more worldly than Luke. Emer wanted to tell her to be kind to him, to take good care of him, and never to hurt him because he'd suffered so much, but that was ridiculous because they'd only just met and perhaps nothing would develop. Emer shouldn't be attempting to shield Luke from the world, but the urge to protect him was strong. He needed a good experience to boost his self-esteem enough to cope with any future disappointments. 'Thanks for being so kind and spending time with Luke yesterday, Kate,' she said.

'I've offered to show him our stables.'

'He'll enjoy that. Just doing something normal. His emotions have taken a beating these last couple of weeks.

He needs time to recover. I'm not sure he can cope with any more drama.'

Kate nodded. 'Don't worry. I know that. I'll look after him.'

Although she didn't want to cause offence, Emer had to be sure the message got across. 'It's just … well … Luke is vulnerable and might read more into a kindness than is actually there, if you see what I mean.'

'Sure,' said Kate, 'but I like Luke – a lot. I genuinely enjoy his company and want to get to know him better.'

'I think the feeling's mutual.'

Kate beamed her dazzling smile again, though she was fighting to control Petruchio, who was tearing up the nearby grass. 'I'd best be off. This one's playing up.'

'Enjoy your ride,' said Emer.

'Enjoy your day, and safe trip home.'

As the horse eagerly moved off along the street, Kate looked back over her shoulder. 'Hey, Emer,' she called. 'You know the other reason I like spending time with Luke? He's *hot!*'

They grinned at each other and then Kate was gone, her horse breaking into a trot and turning up a side lane. At least Luke wasn't chasing rainbows. Maybe nothing would come of it, but he had to start somewhere.

Emer took the apple from her pocket and bit into it, savouring the sweetness and catching the juice as it dribbled down her chin. As she headed back to the car, a silver BMW swerved into The Foresters car park. A pair of legs swung out first, sporting killer stilettos, and then the rest of Sarah emerged just as elegantly. Emer was impressed – she could only ever manage an undignified scramble from a vehicle since deportment wasn't high on the list at the school she'd attended. Sarah must have seen her but offered no greeting, just pushed her sunglasses to the top of her head and slammed the car door before striding into the hotel. She'd looked immaculate in a navy suit, apricot scarf at her throat, and Emer felt spectacularly underdressed in her simple black jacket, half-eaten apple in hand. If Jack could see them both now, would he still choose her?

There hadn't been many mourners at Annie's funeral but those who came had done her proud, with an impressive display of wreaths and flowers. Luke bent forward awkwardly to read some of the attached cards.

> *God bless you. Taken*
> *too soon.*
> Tony and Barbara Hayes

> *I never forgot you.*
> *I never will.*
> Love, Maggie

> *Rest in peace, Annie.*
> Your loving sister-in-law,
> Claire

Of course, the biggest wreath – white lilies and roses – was from Jack. Why did he have to be so showy, although a small wreath would have pissed Luke off, too. Jack had written '*Why?*' on the card. Still pushing the lie? Or proof he really didn't force Annie to leave? Luke was tired of trying to figure it all out, yet until he did, he wouldn't know what to believe, who to trust.

'It's what I want to know too, Mam,' he whispered.

'Why? I don't understand – but I know whatever you did, you thought it was right. I miss you. This is all my fault and I'm so sorry.'

A small bunch of shamrock tied with a dark green ribbon caught his eye. The message said simply *'Rest in Peace, Annie.* Emer Sullivan' and it meant as much to Luke as any of the other tributes. Emer had helped him more than she could know, encouraging him with the eulogy and coming all this way to support him.

She was waiting in the car. She'd known, without him saying, that he'd wanted some time alone with his mother. He felt he should stay longer, but Emer had planned a special day for him. He'd not be rude and spoil it, but he might not be great company. The last few sleepless nights had taken it out of him. A thought suddenly occurred to him about another way to honour Annie. He'd need a quiet place to do it, though. And no one around. He turned and walked back to Emer's car, feeling a little more ready for the day ahead.

Luke couldn't remember when he'd ever enjoyed a day so much. A trip to Old Trafford, home of his Manchester United heroes, had been a welcome break from his grief. A few children had looked at him on his crutches, maybe thinking he was an injured player, and he'd allowed himself a moment of fantasy.

When Emer had told him Kate would be driving him home, Luke's heart literally jumped. A perfect end to the day.

'Will I see you again, Emer?' he asked as they waited outside the stadium. He felt anxious again. Lost.

'Haven't we just shared a great day together? The first of many, I hope,' she said as she hugged him. That gave him a lift. Sounded like she was committed to the friendship. It was something to hold on to. Emer had become very special to him.

Jack swung open the door to Richard's office. His bastard brother-in-law was sipping coffee and reading the newspaper as if he hadn't a care in the world.

'Jack! A knock would be nice ...'

'Oh, I'll knock you, Richard – into the middle of next week. What the fuck is this?' He slapped down the contract he'd found buried within the pile of papers on his desk.

Richard glanced at the document. 'It's a contract with Redgate. They're going to build us market housing units in the riverfront section of the Woodlands development. We can sell them for a song to all those city types who want to swap the smell of car fumes for the smell of manure. The profits will be huge and ...'

'There are people living on part of that land, Richard, as you are well aware. Low-income families, some who've been there for generations. And you also knew I was looking into retaining their houses for them. We'd have got great press. Now all we'll get is the media denouncing us as greedy property developers, destroying a long-established community for the sake of profit ... Richard, are you listening to me?' The git had just taken another sip of coffee and glanced back at his newspaper.

'Jack,' sighed Richard. 'I did the figures. Market housing units, particularly in that location by the river, will generate considerable profit. Anyway, do you really think the well-off will want to mingle with society's lowlifes? Get real!' He laughed, and Jack felt the urge to smash his fist into the man's arrogant face.

'Woodlands will be valuable precisely because there'll be no riff-raff,' Richard continued. 'We're a business, not a charity. We exist to make profits.'

With that, Jack swept Richard's coffee cup off the desk. Petulant, but worth it. Richard jumped up, his suit and desk splattered. 'Don't lecture me, you jumped-up pen-pusher!' Jack snapped. 'My father and I built this business. You just hitched a ride. Those "lowlifes" as you call them have rights and could take us to court. That kind of publicity we don't need.'

'Calm down, Jack. The existing homeowners have been offered compensation. More money than they could ever see from a lifetime of dole scrounging. They'll all sign.'

Jack couldn't believe what he was hearing. *'They'll. All. Sign!'* he repeated, dwelling on each word. Perhaps slow talking would get through to Richard.

'What's your problem, Jack?'

Where to start? Richard treated Claire like a nobody, he'd been made Planning Director last year despite Jack's protests, and his son Gavin was an obnoxious git. 'My problem is, you appear to have committed us to a contract with Redgate before getting agreement from all the interested parties – only an idiot would do that.'

Richard's expression closed down at the insult, and he jutted his jaw defiantly. 'There are a few signatures still to come in, yes, but it's not a problem. People know a good deal when they see one.'

Jack splayed his hands on the desk, leaning over to stare at his brother-in-law. 'I hope you're right because if anything goes wrong, you'll be the one to burn for it.'

'Well, Sir Nicholas didn't seem to have reservations,' said Richard. 'He was more than happy to put his signature to it. I did try to get in touch with you, but you obviously had your hands full with Traveller boy. Now – was there anything else?'

'Yes, but it would involve you having a brain transplant.'

As Jack headed to the door, Richard's voice followed him. 'Tell Rebecca to come and clear this up.'

Jack half-turned in the doorway. 'There won't always be someone around to clean up your mess, Richard.'

Despite his anger, Jack allowed himself a satisfied smile at the sight of Richard trying to salvage something from the soggy paperwork. His smile faded when he remembered the water-jug incident back in Dublin. Did Luke hate him as much as Jack hated Richard? It was a sobering thought.

'This reminds me of home,' Luke said, as he and Kate drove through the Cheshire countryside. 'Funny to think I could have grown up here.'

'Do you miss it? Travelling?'

'In a way. But some things I don't miss.'

'Such as?'

Luke hesitated. Telling a virtual stranger about the humiliations of your life wasn't easy, especially if it was a girl you really liked, but he'd been raised to be truthful. Annie had always told him to never tell a lie and never fear the truth. 'Sometimes you're not welcome in places because you're a Traveller – pubs, shops and the like,' Luke told Kate. 'People throw rubbish at you when you're parked at the side of the road. You get hassle from the Guards who always assume you're a thief. The Council are forever tryin' to move you on. The settled kids in schools call you names like "dirty knacker" ...' Luke glanced down at his hands, which had clenched into fists. 'Once, a few Traveller women, includin' my mam, tried to take us kids to see the Santa in a department store in Cork. The security guards ran us out. They didn't trust us to be in their store. Season of goodwill, except for Travellers.'

'That's terrible!' Kate exclaimed. 'How can people behave like that?'

'Because Travellers are considered a problem,' Luke told her. 'Sure, there are those who deserve the reputation we have, but a lot don't. There's good and bad, same as there is everywhere. The authorities want to stop us livin' the way we've always lived so they make it hard for us to travel round. They won't provide facilities, and eventually it wears you down. So you give in, and accept a place in a settled housing scheme. We did that when my grand-da got sick, but it was somethin' we'd have felt pushed into eventually.'

'God, I'm so sorry, Luke,' said Kate. 'I had no idea. That's blown my stupid romantic notions right out of the window, hasn't it? I pictured campfires and lots of singing and pretty painted caravans.'

He smiled. She was probably thinking of Romanies, but her honesty was refreshing. 'There can be all that too, though caravans aren't pretty these days – just your regular sort. I didn't tell you all that to make you feel sorry for me, Kate. I'm proud of who I am.'

'Still, I'm glad you're away from all that hassle now,' she said.

'Am I?' Luke thought about his grandparents. 'Somehow I think it's the same everywhere.'

'Not if I have anything to do with it,' said Kate. Her tone told him she meant it, but she was connected to the people who had turned a cold shoulder on his mother. Faced with their disapproval, Kate might not be strong enough to stand up to them.

'Let's have some music,' she suggested, switching on the CD player. 'I bought this today – specially for you.' The strains of 'The Fields of Athenry' filled the car and it touched Luke that Kate had gone to such trouble to make him feel at home. He leaned his head back against the seat and closed his eyes. Almost without being aware, he started to sing softly. After a few bars, his voice tailed off.

'What's wrong?' Kate asked.

'My mother was buried yesterday – and I'm singin'.'

'Luke, give yourself a break,' she said, and squeezed his hand.

'That was one of Mam's favourites. I guess she'd not mind me singin' it ... or enjoyin' myself a bit.'

'I'm sure she wouldn't,' Kate agreed. 'And I don't think she'd want you to feel guilty for having a good day.'

Luke leaned his head back against the rest. 'It's not bein' happy that bothers me. It's that she'll never *see* me happy.'

Kate slowed down behind a tractor, and looked at him. 'Are you okay?'

He nodded. And really he should be. He was in a Peugeot convertible, being driven through a posh area of Cheshire by the girl of his dreams. He'd spent so much of his life being treated like an undesirable, it was hard to take in.

'You look really pale,' she told him. 'Good job we're nearly there.'

Luke actually didn't feel so well, but he had something very important to do later. Matt would be working, and Jack was going to some charity dinner. Hopefully, they'd stick to their plans and leave the coast clear.

Luke poked at the firepit in the garden and sparks and flames flew out, bringing with them a strong smell of paraffin that made his eyes water. Hampered by his crutches, it had taken him half an hour to get everything set up. Maybe he'd overdone the fuel. Setting that nearby shed alight would go down really well. Jack would think he'd done it deliberately, for sure.

Jessie had told Luke about seeing her dead grandmother's wagon set on fire, with all the old woman's possessions still inside. That way nothing tied her to this world. Luke wanted to help free his mother's spirit in the same way. It was hard, doing this alone. Back in Ireland, there'd have been other Travellers there to help him.

Annie's battered old suitcase was light enough for Luke to lift into the pit, although the movement made it feel like his ribs were being busted all over again. The case was half in, half out of the fire, though. He leaned against the edge of the pit wall, reaching out his hand to try and push it further into the blaze …

'Jesus!' Matt suddenly appeared from nowhere, scaring the life out of Luke. 'Move back, you idiot – I'll get it!'

He started pulling at the case with a garden spade to bring it out of the flames. Matt had got it all wrong. Thought it had fallen in by accident. He was spoiling everything.

'Leave it, Matt!' shouted Luke, trying to pull his brother away, but Matt shouldered him and he fell to the ground, crying out in pain. Moments later, the burning suitcase was on the ground and Matt was stamping down the flames with his heavy boots. Luke watched, trying to catch his breath as his brother flipped the case over.

'What the …?' Matt had seen the bank notes stuffed into the lining. Now there'd be all kinds of explaining to do, but he had to get the case back in the fire first …

Desperate, Luke kicked out at Matt's ankle. Caught off balance, his brother went down but was back up on his feet before Luke could get the case. He gave up and flopped back on the ground. He was in too much pain to do any more. At least he'd tried.

Matt towered over him, his eyes flashing with anger. 'Did you start this deliberately – using paraffin? You idiot! With this wind, you could have set light to the shed or the trees – or yourself!'

'I was burnin' Mam's things,' Luke told him. 'Old Traveller ritual.'

'Oh.' Matt looked surprised. And a bit guilty.

'Get me up, will you,' asked Luke. 'My ribs are killin'

me.' Perhaps he could play on Matt's guilt and steer him away from the subject of what was in the case.

No chance. Once Matt had helped Luke away from the firepit and seated him against the nearest tree, he sat down close by and asked about the money. Whose it was. Where Luke had got it.

'We had some saved,' said Luke, as casually as he could.

'Don't piss about!' snapped Matt. 'In church, you talked about how you never had any money, yet now you've got a suitcase full of it. How much is there anyway?'

'About thirty thousand euro.' And it had brought Annie and him nothing but bad luck. He'd have been glad to see it all go up in flames.

'Fuck! What did you do – rob a bank?'

'No, I didn't! Why is it everyone thinks a Traveller with money must have stolen it? You're as bad as your fuckin' grandparents. I'm goin' in ...' Luke scrabbled for his crutches. He'd not be able to get up on his own, though. It was terrible to feel so helpless.

'Hey – I was only kidding,' said Matt. 'Christ! Stay where you are. If you do more damage to yourself, I'll have Maggie to answer to.'

Luke leaned back against the tree trunk. He was done in. 'I hope she doesn't come out and find us here. She said she had a headache and was goin' to bed early. Not before she made me dinner, though.' He chuckled softly. 'Nothin' will stop her from tryin' to feed me up.'

Matt grinned. 'The house was all quiet when I came in. I didn't see Maggie.'

'You were supposed to be at work, Matt.'

'Told Sarah I wasn't feeling well. Wanted to get back here and see how you were.'

Was that true? Matt *had* come out searching for Luke. He seemed to care. It would be good to have someone watching out for him. His brother was an outsider, though. Luke didn't even trust people he'd known for years. Hard to change the habits of a lifetime.

'I can put the case back on the fire, Luke, and leave you alone for a bit so you can finish what you started. But could we keep the money aside? I can put it in the safe in my room for now. I'll give you the combination – you can take it any time you want. But if you don't want it, think about giving it to some charity.'

Luke nodded. Matt wasn't going to force him to explain about the money. And he understood the burning ritual was important. That counted for a lot.

His brother got a bin bag from the shed and used gloves to handle the smouldering suitcase. Only a few of the bank notes were ruined.

'Right,' said Matt. 'I'll take this dosh inside. You do what you have to do. I'll bring some coffee. It's getting cold out here.'

He picked up the suitcase and threw it back on the fire. He was about to leave when Luke said, 'Matt ... stay with me. She was your mam, too.'

Matt nodded, looking pleased. They could stand together and remember Annie. Maybe Luke really had found a brother.

It was getting dark. The fire had roared its way through the cheap suitcase, spitting out angry sparks. Now it was down to a warm glow, making Luke think of campfires and his days on the road.

Matt had just come back from putting the money in his safe. He'd brought out two patio chairs and a thermos of coffee as well.

'Do you think her spirit is free now, Luke?' asked Matt. He'd said a few kind words about Annie during the ritual and Luke had been grateful.

'Hope so. Unless keepin' that money was a mistake. She might be worryin' still about it.'

'Did you find the money?' asked Matt. 'Or win the lottery?'

Luke was silent. Stared at the flames. It was so hard to bring himself to trust anyone.

Matt spoke again. 'Luke, I've always wanted a brother and now I've got one. Even if you're a git at times and look like a chimney sweep right now—'

Luke choked down a laugh and showed Matt the finger.

'—I need to know you're okay. If something bothers you, it bothers me. I can keep a secret, I promise, and I'll help you any way I can. Course if you don't tell me where that money came from, then it'll have to be torture. I'll do things with that garden spade that'll make your eyes water.'

Luke grinned and sipped his coffee. Matt had been more than decent up to now. And it would be good to talk about the money, lift the burden of it all from his shoulders a bit. He'd take the risk and tell Matt everything.

'Back in Ireland, we lived with my uncles, Joe and Liam. My Uncle Joe had the money. Stashed in a holdall in a wardrobe, buried under towels and stuff.'

'Hiding it? Why?'

'To keep it to himself, I suppose.' Joe's face flashed up in Luke's mind and his free hand clenched into a fist. 'He's a right bastard. Never gave a fuck about anyone but himself. Treated Mam like an unpaid servant and I was just an inconvenient expense. He and Liam had regular work, but there never seemed to be enough money for Mam and me. We always had to scrape by while they went out drinkin'. They bought a new caravan, one of those motorised ones, and a car, but Mam had to drive round in the old one that she could never afford to get fixed up. The one she died in.'

That night on the rainy road and the blaring truck horn

filled his mind, but thankfully Matt's next question helped him push it aside.

'Did you ever ask them how they had the money for all that?'

'I asked them once,' Luke told him. 'After Joe beat the shit out of me, he said Liam was winnin' bare-knuckle contests and if I ever mentioned it again, he'd rip my head off. I preferred the idea of livin' a bit longer, so I never asked again.'

'Fuck!'

Matt sounded really shocked. Jack had probably never laid a finger on him. Matt had always been sheltered, protected. Violence would be just some sad thing that happened to other people.

'Joe and Liam had gone off somewhere in their motor-caravan. They were always comin' and goin' on jobs – we never knew when to expect them back. Mam lost her purse and we needed some cash so I looked in Joe's room. Thought I might find a few euro. When I opened that holdall … well, it was a real shock. I showed Mam, and she was so scared. Thought we were goin' to get raided or somethin'. I got to thinkin' that this would be our chance to leave. I persuaded Mam we should go to Wales for a fresh start. We'd talked about doin' that for ages but could never afford it. I told her we should take Joe's stash. She didn't want to, but I said I wasn't hangin' round to get another beatin' and I'd take it and go by myself. I wouldn't have, but she couldn't be sure of that, so she hid the money by stitchin' it into the linin' of the case, protected by cardboard. We left all our stuff behind so's whenever they came back they wouldn't realise straight away we'd gone.'

Matt pulled a hip flask from his jacket pocket and drank straight from it. He offered it to Luke, who shook his head although he was tempted. Best not go down that road, turning to alcohol to solve his problems. Matt sighed. 'Why did you do that, Luke? Take the money? We're not talking small change here. Your uncles'll want that money back. They could go to the police.'

Luke shook his head. 'Travellers don't go to the police. We sort things out ourselves. I learned that the hard way, a long time ago.'

'So we wait for Joe and Liam to come knocking, is that it?' Matt sounded angry.

'They won't come knockin'. They'll never think to look for me here. They know I hate Jack. I've been raised to hate him.' Luke said the bitter words with more confidence than he felt.

Matt got up to check the fire. It gave his face a weird orange glow. He turned and stared at Luke, his expression full of worry. 'And if the money *doesn't* belong to your uncles, what then?'

'It's theirs,' Luke insisted. 'Joe's a thug, but he doesn't steal.' He believed that. Even though his uncle was a bully, Luke had never known him to be dishonest. But now Matt had put doubts about his safety into Luke's mind. 'You know, comin' here was wrong. I should just go. It's not fair to drag you all into this.'

'Don't you even think about doing a runner,' warned Matt. 'We're family. I don't want to lose you, bro. We'll figure this out together, yeah, and I'll support you, whatever happens.'

'Thanks.' Luke hoped Matt really meant those words. He felt so shaky right now that a betrayal would break him. A thought suddenly occurred to him. 'Matt, promise me you won't say anythin' about this to Jack. He can't stand me as it is. This would just about finish things.'

It was asking a lot, putting Matt in the position of keeping information from Jack, but Luke had just taken the huge risk of trusting his brother, who was still an unknown quantity. He felt he had a right to ask something in return.

Matt nodded. 'I'll keep this between us, I promise. Now, let's go in. You don't look so good.'

Matt helped Luke up from the chair and settled him on the crutches, patting his shoulder reassuringly. Luke remembered his brother's supportive arms when he'd collapsed at the funeral. It had felt good. 'Matt ... thanks for everythin'.'

Matt smiled. 'No worries.'

Luke wished that was the case, but he was worried. And scared.

Chapter Twelve

Kate knocked at Luke's bedroom door and put her head round before he'd had time to answer. He looked startled but, luckily, was decent. She'd have to curb her enthusiasm. He was sitting against the headboard, cushioned by several pillows, with a book in his lap. He gave her a big smile. Although still a bit pale, he looked a lot better than when she'd driven him home from Manchester last week. He'd been struck down after that with a chest infection. Standing around in that damp churchyard at the funeral when his resistance was already low had probably started it.

'Are you feeling a bit better, Luke?' Kate asked, sitting down beside him on the bed. She'd wanted to visit before now, but Maggie wouldn't allow it.

'Maggie's in charge,' he said. 'I wouldn't dare not get better, although she's nearly killed me with kindness and chicken soup.'

The affection in his voice told her he'd become very fond of the housekeeper.

'I've got us chocolate,' said Kate, delving into her bag. 'And some DVDs. You can choose what to watch. If you want to, that is.'

She looked at him anxiously. Was she being too pushy? She wanted him to know how much she liked him, but didn't want to scare him off. Maybe Traveller men were old-fashioned about women, and wanted to be the ones doing the chasing.

'Sure,' he said. 'It's grand to have company.'

He really had such a gorgeous smile. The most beautiful face. 'I'd love to paint you,' she blurted out before she could stop herself.

179

'What colour?'

Kate laughed. He looked amused, but not shocked at her forwardness. 'Seriously, Luke – I used to paint as a hobby. Neglected it a bit since I've been at uni, but you'd be a great model.'

'Well as long as you don't expect me to get my kit off, I'll think about it.'

It was on the tip of her tongue to say she had other activities in mind that would involve getting his clothes off, but she resisted. God, the effect this guy was having on her – just being in close proximity to him made her feel like jelly. Kate was used to being chased, and although she was sure Luke liked her, it wasn't going to hurt to give him a bit of encouragement.

'I love listening to you talk,' she told him. 'You have such a lovely accent.'

He smiled again. 'I haven't got an accent. You have, though.'

'I suppose you're right,' she laughed. 'Anyway – tell me about yourself, Luke. What would you like to be doing ten years from now?'

'I'd like to work with animals,' he said. 'I'm goin' to make somethin' of my life, for my mam, as well as for me. I'd have to go back to school, though. It can be humiliatin' when you go for jobs you know you can do but have to admit to having no actual qualifications and don't even get considered.'

Had she said the wrong thing? 'I hope I haven't embarrassed you.'

'No. I don't feel embarrassed around you at all,' he said with a smile.

If Luke had been on the Titanic, he could have melted the iceberg, let alone Kate's heart, which was currently doing a jig.

'Why are you botherin' with me, Kate?' he asked suddenly.

'Don't get me wrong. I like you bein' here. I just don't know why you are.'

'Because you have to ask,' she replied.

He looked confused, so she explained. 'You don't appreciate yourself, Luke. So many guys I know are just full of themselves – but you're … you're gorgeous, frankly, and you don't even realise it. And anyway, you're interesting to talk to, nice to be with.'

'Maybe that's down to the company.'

On impulse, Kate leaned over and kissed his cheek. He turned to face her, and his lips brushed against hers. A chaste kiss, but with the promise of so much more.

Once she'd set up his choice of DVD to play, Kate stretched out next to Luke on the big double bed. As they watched the film, she laughed when he did, but she couldn't concentrate much on what was happening onscreen. Being physically so close to Luke was a huge distraction, and her mind kept drifting off into romantic fantasies.

'Will you come visit me again?' asked Luke later, as she was preparing to leave.

'Oh yes,' she said, with a smile that she hoped left Luke in no doubt about her feelings for him.

Luke coughed, then gasped as the movement hurt his chest.

'You okay?' asked Matt.

'Better than I was, that's for sure,' Luke assured him. Matt was driving him home from Chester, where he'd had had some painful physio, but the good news was he'd been told he could walk without his crutches when he felt able. 'It's grand to get out.'

Luke had been ill and cooped up inside for a week. It hadn't been all bad, though. Kate's visit had almost made being ill worthwhile. They'd watched some films together and it was enough to have her there, to watch her as she watched the TV screen. God, he had it bad. He still found it hard to believe he could attract a girl like Kate, but she definitely seemed keen. Sometimes he wondered if she was just being nice because he was Matt's brother, but then he'd remembered her words to Abbie – 'I saw him first.' That and the brief kiss they'd shared in the bedroom. He wondered what Matt would make of it.

'Kate's takin' me to see her mam's stables tomorrow,' said Luke.

'She's horse-mad,' commented Matt. 'Not my scene, though.'

'Does she have a boyfriend?' Luke asked, trying to sound casual. 'Girls like her aren't usually single.'

'Well she's never short of offers. But there's no one serious.'

'Not you?'

Matt snorted. 'Christ, no! We've been virtually raised together. It would be like incest.'

Luke had to be sure. 'What about Tim or Al?'

'Al has a girlfriend at uni in Leeds. And Tim – well, let's just say Tim would be more interested in you than in Kate.'

Luke was quiet for a moment, digesting that information. To his knowledge, he'd never met anyone who was gay. It was kind of taboo among Travellers. At least, the ones he knew. His uncles had often made their bigoted feelings known with crude or aggressive remarks, but they were out of the picture now and had no say in who Luke chose to spend time with. He was free to live his own life. Tim had seemed a fun person and he was Kate and Matt's friend. That was all that mattered.

'So, go for it,' said Matt, 'With *Katie*, I mean.' He winked.

'Matt, I don't even know if she's interested in me so don't go blabbin', okay?'

'My lips are sealed,' promised Matt. 'Girls are serious business.'

They certainly were. Especially when you'd never had a proper girlfriend. It was uncharted territory for Luke. He'd been left behind by other Traveller lads, who all seemed confident with girls.

'Don't know about you, bro, but a beer would go down well,' said Matt, as he pulled into a flower-decked country pub on the outskirts of Marsham.

'Sounds good,' Luke agreed, enjoying the feeling of freedom, of family. He and his brother having a drink together. And tomorrow to look forward to.

Jack had been reading the same page of a property survey for ten minutes. It was Emer's fault he couldn't concentrate. Since the funeral, they'd spoken every morning without fail, but today – Friday – she hadn't called and it was nearly midday. He'd just tried her mobile again with no luck and left another message. He hoped he wasn't coming across as a stalker. He'd known her only a short time yet already he was attuning himself to the rhythms of her daily life. He thought back to that kiss they'd shared before she left. It seemed a welcome promise of what the future could hold. Jack had loved two women in his life and been so shattered by their loss that he'd assumed there was no more passion left to give …

His mobile rang. An unknown landline – must be Emer calling from the hospital. He smiled as he pressed the *talk* button. 'That was quick.'

'I wouldn't say that. It's been a fortnight. This is Doyle.'

Damn, it was the private detective from Ireland, not Emer. Just as well he hadn't launched into sweet nothings. 'Sorry, I was expecting another call. So – what about the Kiernans? Did you find them?'

'No. They've been gone for nearly a month. Took their motor-caravan. Rumour is they might be working on a construction job abroad, but I wasn't able to confirm that. I did find something strange, though, when I checked into their finances. Their income doesn't match their outgoings. This year, Joe treated himself to a brand new Renault Espace. Paid cash. Last year, they bought that motor-caravan. Also, brother Liam has a weakness for the races – he's well-known at the local bookie's. Bets hundreds at a time and is never too gutted when he loses. Also plays the big man in the pub, buying rounds for everyone.'

None of this seemed to tally with what Luke had said about growing up poor. He'd sounded sincere – was he that good a liar?

'When Pat Kiernan, the father, had a stroke, they were offered accommodation under the Settled Housing Scheme,' Doyle continued. 'Government-run programme designed to persuade Travellers to give up life on the road.'

'Did you get a look at their house?'

'Your average rabbit hutch. Nothing special. I looked in the windows – saw what looked like a new TV, but no luxury furnishings. Clean enough but basic.'

'But if they've got all that money to throw around, why not buy something decent?'

'Who knows?' said Doyle. 'Not a priority for them, maybe.'

'So where's the money coming from? Are they involved in drugs?'

'No sign of it. And I know where to look. I wondered – did your wife take any cash with her when she left England?'

Jack flinched at the mention of Annie. She was cold in the ground now, but her betrayal could still hurt. 'She took about five grand that was in her bank account. Nothing more.'

'I can keep looking,' Doyle told him, 'but it seems the

brothers have covered their tracks pretty well. What about the boy, Luke – has he told you anything useful?'

'No.' And Jack didn't plan to ask. They were barely on speaking terms as it was, and Luke was very closed about his life. 'So, if they're abroad, they probably don't know about Annie's death yet?'

'Who knows?' replied Doyle. 'The accident was reported in the Dublin papers, but only a few lines. Depends on whether they're in touch with someone back here. Incidentally, did you know Luke's had some trouble with the law?'

That must have been what the Guard in the hospital had been referring to. Great. His parents would have a field day with that. 'Tell me.'

'Assault charge. Punched a man in the face – hard enough to knock his bridge out. Claims the man was hassling Annie. Big businessman from Dublin – supposedly Joe Kiernan had promised him Annie would do him sexual favours. She obviously didn't agree. Luke got probation and community service. First and only offence.'

It could have been worse. Violence was never the answer, but it sounded like Luke had had a valid reason. Jack would probably have done the same.

'That record made it hard for Luke to find a job,' Doyle continued. 'He regularly volunteered at an Animal Rescue Centre and helped out at a Traveller halting site, but mostly he lived on unemployment.'

If Luke had been on benefits, Joe and Liam probably weren't sharing their wealth. So what Luke had said at the funeral could have been true. 'And what about Annie?'

'Not a lot to tell about recent years,' admitted Doyle. 'Her Traveller friends wouldn't say much. Most didn't know about the accident so were pretty shocked and as much as told me to let the dead rest in peace. But I struck lucky in Kerry. Went to the hospital where Luke was born and managed to find the address he'd been registered at – confidentiality doesn't mean much if you offer the right incentive. Anyway, it was a bedsit in a house she shared with other women who were on their own with kids. No one there now who knew her, but I did find a neighbour who remembered her well. She often had Luke while Annie worked – cleaning offices until she got sick. Having a job and a kid wore her down. She ended up in hospital with bronchial pneumonia. Luke was taken into care ...'

'Care!' repeated Jack. That was a surprise. 'So Annie was on her own by this time?'

'I got the idea she'd always been on her own,' said Doyle. 'Anyway, she lost her job and then struggled to pay the rent so was evicted. She stayed with the neighbour for a few weeks and tried to get Luke back, but she was basically homeless so the authorities wouldn't permit it. Eventually, she hooked up with a Traveller woman and took to the road again. It was a home of sorts and Luke was returned to her. She stayed on the road until her father became ill and she went to nurse him.'

I got the idea she'd always been on her own. Jack's mind replayed Doyle's words. Something wasn't adding up. 'When did you say she moved into this bedsit?' he asked.

'According to her friend, it would have been the March before Luke was born,' said the detective. 'She remembers it because she was in her last month of pregnancy herself. Annie did shopping for her and helped with her other kids.'

Jack remembered the last private detective's report, some twenty years ago, which told of Annie's return to life as a Traveller. That she was with another man. Now Doyle was telling him that in March, only a month after she left Baronsmere, Annie had been living in a bedsit. Alone. Had the detective got it wrong? Perhaps the man had just been a friend, not a lover. Or maybe, as he'd suspected, Annie started an affair before she left Baronsmere, and the other man was only interested in the fact she was married to a millionaire. She'd fallen for him and left Jack, only to be dumped for that very reason.

Jack thought a detective would clarify things, not raise even more questions. Still, at least Jack had learned something about Annie and Luke's life in Ireland.

'Mr Stewart? Do you want me to do anything else?'

Jack stopped his speculation and refocused on the conversation. 'No, not for the moment. I'll be in touch if I need you for anything else. Thanks, Doyle. Good work.'

Jack sat at his desk, thinking about what he'd just heard. Luke had claimed poverty but it seemed his uncles had money to play with. That didn't make any sense, but if he pressed Luke for more information, he'd get a mouthful of abuse. And did any of it really matter anyway? Annie was gone. Revelations from the past wouldn't do her any good. Or him. Perhaps he should just look to the future …

His phone rang again, but thankfully it was Emer this time. They talked about ordinary things – a movie they'd both seen, the unexpected sunny weather, Emer's nephew with the measles, Ollie's worsening arthritis. Every day, their knowledge about each other increased. Slender threads of connection pulled them closer and closer together and went some way to offsetting Jack's frustration at being apart from her.

Kate held up two jumpers in front of the mirror. The black chenille was sophisticated, but the blue lambswool went well with her fair hair. Which one would Luke like? She guessed the blue. Decision made.

She plugged in her hair straighteners then sat at the dressing table to apply some mascara. Pity she didn't have

Luke's ridiculously long lashes. They fascinated her. *He* fascinated her, more so than any other man she'd met. Of course he was different – Irish, and with a very contrasting background to her own – which made him interesting. She didn't know a lot about Travellers, but she was learning a little more each day.

Luke wasn't just easy on the eye, he was so easy to talk to. Even more importantly, he treated her with respect, something idiots like Gavin Morland would never understand. She'd been on a date with Gavin once – a pity date because he'd just been dumped – and now he seemed to think he had a claim on her.

Kate wasn't blind. Luke clearly fancied her. He seemed quite an innocent, but that was part of his charm. Kate was prepared to take things slowly. The best things in life were worth waiting for.

'So what's on the agenda today?' Sarah asked, suddenly appearing in the doorway to the bedroom.

Kate continued applying her mascara without looking at her mother. 'I'm taking Luke to the stables – he loves horses – then lunch, and maybe a drive through the villages. He's been sick all week so he needs some fresh air.'

Sarah walked in and sat on the bed. 'What about breakfast? We always have that together on a Saturday.'

Kate could smell fresh coffee wafting up from the kitchen and it was tempting. 'Sorry, Mum – I should have woken you when I had mine. But I'm running late as it is.'

'Kate … I'm not sure it's a good idea for you to get involved with Luke.'

'Shit!' Kate swore under her breath as her hand brushed against the hot straighteners. Lack of concentration – her mother's fault. 'We're going to the stables,' she said, sucking at her index finger. 'Not announcing our engagement.'

'I just don't want you hurt,' said Sarah. 'Matt's worried

that Luke might move on soon – he's not getting on with Jack.'

Luke might be leaving? She'd have to try and change his mind. 'Don't worry so much, Mum. I'm a big girl – I can take care of myself.'

And she could. Unlike Luke, Kate was no innocent. She'd always been popular with boys, but most of her previous boyfriends were the strong, silent type. For some reason, she attracted men who felt it was their duty to protect her. Too often, though, strong and silent really meant all brawn, no brain or just plain dull.

Luke seemed nothing like them. He wasn't much taller than her, but though there might not be a lot of him, he was very nicely put together. She'd always laughed at the sappy love stories where the woman's heart would flip when she first saw the hero, but her heart really did flip when she saw Luke's beautiful face. Served her right for being so cynical in the past. Now she'd been caught completely off guard by her runaway emotions. Although it was obvious Sarah already suspected this, Kate wasn't yet ready to share her true feelings with anyone but him.

'Just be careful, Kate,' said her mum. 'Luke is a Traveller.'

Kate tugged on her hair, harder than she'd intended, and her eyes watered. Sarah never interfered in Kate's relationships, only giving advice when asked. What on earth was the matter with her? It was winding Kate up. 'What does Luke being a Traveller have to do with anything?'

Sarah was quiet for a moment before saying 'He's not our class. I don't want you tarnished by association.'

For a moment, Kate was too shocked to respond. 'I wish you hadn't said that, Mum. I never had you down as a bigot.'

Sarah shook her head. 'I'm not a bigot, Kate,' she said. 'I'm a realist.' She stood up and left the room without saying anything else, and Kate had to fight the urge to kick the door closed. It was obvious that any relationship she might have with Luke was not going to have her mother's blessing.

The sun had come out, transforming the landscape from dull olive to a more vivid green, though there was still a slight chill in the air. Kate was sitting on the slope overlooking the stables and the paddocks, Luke sprawled on his back beside her on the blanket she'd brought from the car. Two riders were in action below, and in the third paddock, a small boy was perched uncertainly on the back of a Shetland pony, being guided around on a lunge rope by the stable hand. How could anyone not enjoy the woods, the open spaces, the freedom of the countryside? Kate had to commute to university in Manchester during the week, but this place was her weekend haven. 'Have you read *The Hobbit*, Luke?'

'Ages ago,' he replied. 'Why?'

'When I was young, I used to think Baronsmere was in The Shire. It's always been peaceful and beautiful, virtually unchanged for generations.' She stopped. Luke was staring at her. Probably thought she was nuts. 'What?' she asked.

Luke smiled. 'I'm just tryin' to picture you as a little girl.'

'Oh God, don't! I was skinny, with braces and pigtails.'

'Sounds like we were a good pair. I was so puny I needed weighted boots to stop the wind blowin' me away.'

They smiled at each other and Kate shivered slightly, but not from the cold. Whenever Luke was focused on her, she felt a thrill, a sensation of deep pleasure. She imagined his gorgeous blue eyes widening appreciatively as she undressed for him.

'You're lucky to own all this – and a horse of your own, too,' said Luke. 'How long have you had him?'

'Jack bought him for my fifteenth birthday. It was a wonderful surprise. Jack always chooses the best pres …' Her voice tailed off and she bit her lip. Luke had never had a birthday present from Jack in his life. Time to change the subject. She didn't want to upset him, especially after what her mother had said. *He might not stay around for long.* Luke wouldn't leave if he really liked her, would he? 'Do you think you'll stay in Baronsmere, Luke?'

'Why d'you ask that?'

Best not to lie. 'It's just … my mum said things aren't great between you and Jack.'

'Did she now?' Luke's tone was angry, and he sat up. 'And what business is that of hers?'

'It wasn't said as gossip, honestly. She's just concerned that … that I'll get hurt. Because, well, I like you.'

'You do?'

She looked up, and was caught again by the intensity of his eyes. There was something in his expression – hope, longing, fear, doubt – that tugged at her heart. 'You know I do,' she murmured. 'I want you to stay, Luke.'

'Kate,' he said, 'I know you're close to Jack, so I'm sorry if it upsets you that I can't get along with him. I don't like bein' so angry all the time. It's not the kind of person I want to be.'

The Jack Kate knew was kind and generous, not a man who would abandon his wife and child. But whatever the truth of it, Luke had obviously been told a completely different story, so Kate couldn't blame him for his attitude. She certainly wasn't going to fight Jack's corner for him. Letting Luke know what he'd missed wasn't going to be helpful.

'You've just lost your mum, Luke. Your emotions must be all over the place. Just take things a day at a time.'

Luke reached out a hand, brushed a lock of hair away from her face and caressed her cheek. She moved towards him. He was shy so it was down to her, and she wasn't going to waste the opportunity. Her lips brushed briefly against his, enough to let him know it was what she wanted, and he responded. Their first kiss was hesitant, exploring unfamiliar territory, before becoming more assured, more passionate. It felt right. Not just right – perfect. He obviously had a natural talent for it.

A few minutes later, a clatter from the paddock below broke the spell. A horse had misjudged its jump, sending the poles flying. Kate turned her attention back to Luke. His face was flushed, and she knew hers was, too.

'You're the most beautiful girl I've ever seen, Kate Walker,' Luke told her. 'Not even Niamh of the Golden Hair could hold a candle to you.'

'Niamh,' she breathed. 'Who's she?'

'A goddess from an Irish folk tale. She falls in love with Oisin, a young poet and hero, and takes him to Tír na nÓg, the Land of Eternal Youth.'

'Will you tell me the story?' Kate asked.

He lay back, staring at the sky. She settled down on her side next to him, fingers curled in his, head on his shoulder, as she listened to the magic of his voice telling her the ancient tale of love from his homeland. 'Long ago in Ireland lived a man called Oisin ...'

The Foresters seemed to cater for all ages and was very different from the spit and sawdust pub Luke's uncles drank in. Kate asked the barman for two orange juices before leading Luke to an alcoved table. She waved across at Al and Tim, playing at the pool table. Her face was flushed from the cold air and she touched a hand to Luke's cheek. 'It's so cold out there! More like winter than spring. I don't think global warming's ever going to reach Cheshire.'

Before he had time to think, Luke caught hold of her hand and rubbed it between his own to generate some warmth. Jesus, what was he doing? Kissing at the stables was one thing, but here everyone could see. He took Kate's hand and laid it down on the table, palm facing upwards. He needed to cover his embarrassment. 'Tell your fortune, Miss?' he said, with a smile.

Kate laughed, but not unkindly. 'Okay, but only tell me the good things.'

Luke had watched Jessie do this many times but couldn't remember much. Not that it mattered. It was clear from Kate's sceptical smile she was thinking of it as nothing more than a game. 'You'll have a long life, Kate Walker, to be sure,' he said, exaggerating his accent, which made her giggle. He had to try to stop his own hands trembling as he delicately traced the lines on hers. 'Hmm. Looks like you'll move away – maybe abroad.'

'Oh, yes?' Kate raised an eyebrow. 'Hollywood beckoning no doubt!'

'Your heart and your head line are well-balanced,' Luke continued, 'which means you'll keep your wits about you, and no tragic love affairs.'

'Well, that sounds a bit dull.' Kate gave a mock pout. 'Every woman should have at least one passionate romance.'

'I didn't say there wouldn't be passion,' said Luke, unable to meet her eyes. He gently stroked the skin at the base of her thumb. What was he on? Flirting with a gorgeous girl like he was an expert. That kiss at the stables had been very inspiring. Kate was silent, and the air between them grew charged, the din around them distant background noise.

Luke forced himself to keep going, turning her palm to the side. 'Marriage for sure, and two children – maybe three. Daughters as beautiful as their mother.' He couldn't believe he'd just said that. He held his breath and continued staring at her palm.

'You can't tell that from the lines, surely,' Kate whispered.

'No,' Luke admitted, 'but beauty is usually passed on in the genes.'

He stopped, wondering if he'd gone too far. Thankfully, she smiled and curled her fingers upwards to touch his hand. She'd registered the compliment and not been offended by it. *Ah, Kate Walker,* he thought, remembering some lines from Yeats: *Had I the heavens' embroidered cloths ... I would spread the cloths under your feet ...*

'Well, well, what have we here.' A loud voice interrupted them. A tall, dark-haired man was sneering down at Luke. He seemed familiar. Two other young men lurked just behind the newcomer, who continued talking. 'Still picking up waifs and strays, Katie? This the latest lost cause then? Why are you such a soft touch?'

Kate's expression hardened. 'And why are you such a prick? Get lost.'

With a glance at Luke, the stranger said, 'Our pleasure – we're fussy about who we keep company with, anyway.' As he turned to go, he called over his shoulder to his friends, 'Keep hold of your wallets, guys.'

The remark was obviously aimed at Luke, and he felt uncomfortable.

'Don't mind him.' Kate's hand touched his. 'As they say, you can't choose your relatives.'

'You're related to him?' asked Luke.

'No, you are,' Kate told him. 'He's your cousin – that's Claire's son, Gavin.'

Sarah rang the doorbell. She needed to talk to Jack urgently. The sight of Luke Kiernan pawing Kate in the Foresters was more than she could bear. Nightmare visions of Kate pregnant and tied to this Traveller for the rest of her life were stronger than ever. Annie had snared Jack all those years ago. Sarah would be damned if she'd see history repeat itself.

'Hello, Sarah.' Maggie opened the door, looking a bit

surprised to see her. Since the break up, Sarah hadn't been to the house at all. Well, apart from the funeral but that didn't count.

'Hello, Maggie. Is Jack in? I really need to speak to him.'

She was shown into the drawing room while Maggie went to find Jack. Sarah moved around the room, taking in once again the expensive porcelain pieces, the French clock, the family portraits. She loved this room and imagined elegant Victorian ladies taking their tea here in days gone by. Of course, Edenbridge was the big prize for anyone married to Jack. He didn't like the place much, but Sarah had always dreamed of living there. She might not have the impeccable bloodline of Lady Grace Stewart but she knew how to do things right, the upper-class way. Emer Sullivan wouldn't have a clue.

'Sarah – what brings you away from The Foresters on a busy Saturday night?'

Jack didn't exactly look overjoyed to see her as he offered and poured her a gin and tonic.

'I needed to talk to you about Kate,' she said, taking her usual place on the Louis Quinze sofa. She crossed her legs and hitched her skirt up slightly. Jack was a leg man. No harm in reminding him what he was missing.

'Is she okay?' asked Jack, hovering in front of the fireplace.

The concern in his voice for her daughter was gratifying. If she could get him onside about Luke, the looming problem with Kate might never materialise.

'She's in the Foresters right now – with Luke. When I left, he was holding her hand. And she seemed to be enjoying it.'

Jack stared at her. He was probably whirring through the unpleasant potential consequences, just as she'd done earlier. 'Perhaps it was only a friendly gesture?'

'No, it wasn't. Kate went to the funeral to support Luke. She took him to the stables this morning – God knows what

195

they got up to there. And now this cosy little drink together. You know Kate – anyone a little bit different always catches her attention.'

Jack sat down. He looked worried, but he said 'Kate's an adult, Sarah. I don't want to interfere.'

'I don't want her hurt, Jack. What if Luke doesn't stay around? Leaves without a word.' She hesitated before adding 'Like his mother did.'

There was a brief flare of anger in Jack's expression – talk of Annie was usually forbidden. 'What is it you want me to do, Sarah?'

'Have a word with her. Discreetly. Find out what's going on. She respects you, Jack. She'll listen to you. But go easy – she's headstrong these days. Forbid something and she might want it more.'

Jack frowned. 'I can't forbid her to do anything, but I'll warn her not to get too involved.'

Sarah sighed with relief. 'Thank you.' She wondered if Jack would ask her to stay a bit longer this evening. They could share a late supper, watch some TV. Get closer and closer on the sofa until …

'I need to ask you something,' said Jack, swirling his drink.

Sarah couldn't help it. She imagined him taking her in his arms, saying how much he loved her and what a fool he'd been to let her go. They'd go up to the bedroom and everything would be back to how it was.

'At the funeral, you told Emer you were my partner.'

'What?' Her mind raced back to that meeting with the redhead. She must have told Jack about their conversation. What a bitch. Now how to get out of this? 'I don't really remember saying that. I'd had a bit to drink. I probably meant that you help me out with the business from time to time.'

She watched his face to see if he'd accept that. This was so humiliating, having to cover her tracks because of that upstart.

Jack nodded. 'Right. It was a hard day for us all. Thank you again for being there, and for doing the catering.'

'You know I'd do anything for you, Jack.' Her words were full of subtext. She had to give it one last try.

He looked uncomfortable, not the desired effect. 'Sarah, I've invited Emer to my birthday party next weekend. If she comes, we'll be there as a couple. I hope you'll be okay with that.'

A terrifying rage blinded Sarah for a few moments. She wanted to throw her glass in Jack's face and leave him wounded and bleeding. All those years she'd put into their relationship, wiped out and forgotten when someone younger flashed a smile. It was enough to drive her to despair.

She assembled the last remnants of her dignity. 'I care for you, Jack. I can't switch it off so easily, but I won't stand in the way of your happiness. Just know that I'll always be here for you if you need me.'

She deserved an Oscar for that, for covering up her murderous thoughts. Tears were dangerously close. It was time to go.

As she stood up, Jack came over and kissed her cheek. 'Thank you, Sarah. We'll always be friends – yes?'

Friendship. The consolation prize for the older woman. Not good enough. Sarah hadn't got where she was today by giving up when the going got tough. She and Jack had a long history. When the chips were down, surely that would count for something. She'd watch and wait for this Irish redhead to slip up.

'Shove up,' said Tim, as he and Al appeared with more drinks. Sitting there talking to Kate and her friends in the Foresters,

Luke felt a warm sense of belonging. It was reassuring after the incident with his unfriendly cousin. Perhaps Gavin had heard about Luke throwing beer in his father's face and had, understandably, taken against him. Hopefully, their paths wouldn't cross too much.

'Let's go get some pizza,' suggested Kate. 'Wait here a couple of minutes. I'll bring the car up to the entrance.'

After she'd left, a man approached the table, handing out leaflets.

'What's this then?' Tim stopped juggling beer mats.

'Protest meeting,' the man informed him. 'Got to stop the Woodlands development forcing people out of their homes so the property developers can line their pockets.'

'A protest!' shrieked Tim, scanning the leaflet. 'Policemen with truncheons grappling our bodies to the ground! Revolution! What fun!'

'No, this isn't for us, Tim,' said Al, also reading a leaflet. 'Stewart Enterprises are involved in the Woodlands development. Best not shit on our own doorstep.'

'Guess not,' agreed Tim, ripping up the paper and stuffing the pieces into an empty beer glass. Luke quickly pocketed one of the leaflets. He planned to find out more. If there was one thing he didn't like, it was people getting pushed around.

Chapter Thirteen

Sunday morning. Jack's head was splitting and this time it wasn't the church bells. He hadn't slept well. Broken sleep had been the norm since he'd got the news about Annie. Last night, his dream had been about Emer: he'd been kissing her on the patio when Luke appeared and said, 'The coffin's here.'

At times Jack felt guilty about the lack of effort he put into forging a relationship with Luke, but it was hard to know where to start. Luke probably felt the same. He generally avoided Jack and didn't have much to say for himself when their paths did cross. It had been a relief in some ways that he'd had that chest infection and had rested in his room for much of the past week. Admittedly, he hadn't looked well. Maybe Jack should have made an attempt to communicate then, when Luke was a bit less feisty. He hadn't, though. He'd barely looked in on him, even just to ask how he was. He'd made do with asking Maggie and Matt.

Wondering whether Luke was his son tormented Jack. The thought of caring for Luke and then finding out he wasn't his was more than he could handle. If Luke was the result of Annie's betrayal ... well, Jack just wasn't saintly enough to say it wouldn't matter. He was angry with Annie, jealous of her lover, and he knew he punished Luke for it. Exactly what Emer had warned him not to do. One more thing for him to feel guilty about, which wasn't helping his headache.

And he was worried about Kate. Sarah was right to be concerned. Jack had been like a father to Kate, and he didn't want her hurt if Luke upped and left. He'd have to talk to her. Find out what was what. But he just wasn't feeling up to it today.

He'd missed his walk yesterday to Hartswood Hill. His father had been inundating Jack with work recently – Nicholas's equivalent of a hundred lines for Jack's bad behaviour: having the audacity to leave the business for a week. Perhaps he'd feel better after some fresh air. More ready to cope with the cold comfort that was Sunday lunch at Edenbridge.

Jack arrived home still tired. The walk and the fresh air had done nothing to alleviate the tension, still a tight band around his head. He wasn't surprised. The headache was unlikely to go while the cause remained. Turning into his driveway, he tried to alleviate some of his frustration by flooring the accelerator and racing up to the house before swerving across the gravel and grinding to a sudden halt. He got out of the car, slamming the door shut.

'Mr Stewart ...'

Jack turned to see Rob, the gardener, walking towards him. Within moments, his headache was a lot worse.

In the living room, Matt and Luke were hunched over a chessboard. Chatting away like best friends. The cuckoo in the nest now had Kate, Maggie and Matt well and truly onside while Jack was being marginalised. His resentment surged.

Matt glanced up. 'Hi, Dad. I'm teaching Luke how to play chess.'

Jack ignored Matt. 'My study, Luke – now!' he snapped.

'What the –?' began Matt, but Jack cut him off.

'Stay here, Matt. I need to talk to Luke in private.'

Jack marched out of the living room, banged open his study door, and sat down on the edge of the desk, arms folded.

Luke appeared in the doorway, scowling. 'What's wrong? Is playin' chess above my status?'

'I want to know what the fuck is going on.' Jack held up the charred remains of *The Dead*.

'I burned Mam's things,' said Luke, his tone defiant. 'It's Traveller tradition. You said the book was hers.'

Annie *had* once told Jack about that ritual, but he wasn't about to let Luke off the hook. 'Yes, it was her book, but you could have consulted me first instead of just going ahead and destroying it. It was a rare illustrated edition, worth several hundred pounds.'

Luke shrugged, a habit that irritated Jack intensely. 'It's always about money.'

'It's not always about money!' snapped Jack. 'But you need to learn respect for people's property.'

Luke bristled. 'What does that mean? I didn't do it out of a lack of respect …'

'No,' agreed Jack. 'You did it out of spite. To get at me. Your mother left the book, so it was hardly necessary to include it in an obvious attempt to flaunt your background in my face.'

'Is that what you think?'

'Why not? Your mother left the Travelling life. By all accounts she only went back to it because she had no choice. You think she'd have wanted this?'

'You don't know anythin'!' spat Luke. 'My mother wanted a better life, but that didn't mean she didn't have respect for Traveller culture … and it was *her* book.'

'Annie loved books. I don't think she'd have wanted it destroyed. But, anyway, it's not really about the book. It's about this.' He held up a tangled mass of chain and dusty gemstones, found that morning by the gardener. 'Where did you get this?'

Luke clenched his jaw. He looked angry but not guilty. 'What do you mean – where did I get it? It was with Mam's things.'

'Don't lie to me, Luke. Your mother didn't take this with her.'

'Why don't you just come right out and call me a fuckin' thief?'

'Watch your mouth,' Jack demanded.

'Like you did when I walked in here,' argued Luke. 'Jesus, but you're a hypocrite.'

Jack focused his attention back on the necklace, determined to get the truth. 'I'll ask you again, Luke. Where did you get it?'

Luke looked as if he was fighting the urge to punch Jack. 'Ask as many times as you like. You'll get the same answer. If you don't believe me, ring the hospital. They probably saw it when they poked their noses in.'

'I think they'd have mentioned it, don't you? Offered to put it in a safe, perhaps.'

'Maybe they didn't think it was worth anythin',' Luke retorted. 'I don't suppose they're experts.'

Suddenly Jack was unsure. It was impossible for Annie to have had the necklace, but there was something in Luke's expression that seemed sincere, and in hospital he'd been very anxious that his suitcase was safe. 'But she left it behind!' he said, and slammed the necklace onto the desk in frustration. 'I gave it to her on our wedding day and I was gutted she didn't think enough of me, or our marriage, to take it with her. It *couldn't* have been in the case.'

Luke's voice rose in anger. 'So I'm a liar as well as a thief!'

Their raised voices brought both Maggie and Matt to the study.

'What the hell's going on?' asked Matt.

Matt was doubtless going to take his brother's side, no matter what. But just how solid was the evidence? Maybe Jack had been wrong to go after Luke so aggressively. It had achieved nothing. 'I asked Luke to explain something he couldn't – at least, not to my satisfaction.' He indicated the necklace. 'Rob found this. Luke apparently tried to burn Annie's things out in the firepit.'

'Did you, love?' Maggie looked worried. 'That sounds very dangerous.'

'It's a Traveller tradition,' said Matt. 'I was with him. Made sure he was okay.' He exchanged a glance and small smile with Luke.

So Matt had known. Again Jack felt like an outsider. 'I want to know where he got it because Annie didn't take it with her.'

'Are you sure?' asked Matt. 'Do you actually remember seeing it after she'd gone?'

'Yes.' It was there in Annie's jewel case with all the other pieces he'd given her. Jack had got drunk after seeing such a blatant rejection of his affection for her.

'Annie's jewellery was sent to auction,' said Maggie. 'That was your mother's idea.'

Jack frowned. 'I don't remember that.'

'I'm not surprised – you were drunk as a skunk most of the time.'

Jack glared at Maggie for her insolence, but she was right. He'd been fit for nothing for months.

'You agreed with Grace. Said you wanted all of Annie's things out of the house.'

Thinking about it, he could vaguely remember that happening, which meant that Luke couldn't have found the necklace. Jack so didn't want a mystery. He wanted Luke to have discovered the necklace somewhere in the house, and to have used it as part of the funeral ritual. It was easier that way.

'So how did Mam get it then?' asked Luke.

'Someone could have bought it at the auction and sent it to her,' suggested Maggie.

'But who would know where she was?' asked Matt, voicing Jack's own question.

'Your mother hired that detective ...' Maggie's voice trailed off, but she looked pointedly at Jack.

He knew what she was implying but her theory made no sense. Grace would never have sent an expensive necklace to Annie. He wondered about Claire – she'd been close to Annie, but she was also very loyal to Jack. She'd not go behind his back.

'Ask Gran what she knows,' said Matt. 'Maybe she remembers who bought the necklace at auction. You're going there for lunch anyway.'

How to ask his mother without it seeming like an accusation? She was very touchy about anything connected to Annie. Matt's presence would put her in a good mood. 'Okay, I'll ask her. Will you come with me for lunch, Matt?'

'Nope. If Luke's not invited, I'm certainly not going. And I think you owe Luke an apology for calling him a thief.'

'I didn't call him a thief,' snapped Jack, although indirectly he knew he had. 'Have the decency to phone your grandmother and give your apologies. You've missed Sunday lunches for weeks now. It's just plain rude.'

Jack knew he was being unreasonable, lashing out at Matt because of his own assumptions about the necklace, but the way everyone seemed to automatically side with Luke and cast Jack as the villain was irritating. Matt was scowling at him now, and Maggie was wearing her indignant expression. 'I'm better go and change into something decent before I go,' he said, and turned on his heel.

'A human bein' maybe,' he heard Luke mutter behind him.

At Edenbridge, the dining room was empty, apart from the maid, who was clearing away the china. She gave Jack a pitying look. 'Her Ladyship's in the morning room, sir.'

He'd stopped off at The Feathers for a pint, mulling over what had happened that morning. Before he knew it, an hour had passed, meaning lunch at Edenbridge was over. His subconscious had probably done that deliberately because he was unsure how to broach such a sensitive issue with his mother. Eventually, though, he'd decided to ask her about the necklace because he wanted to solve the mystery.

He knocked on the door of the morning room and entered when he heard his mother's sharp 'Come in'.

She was bent over her writing desk, signing a card, and didn't look up. This was Grace's domain where she co-ordinated and consolidated her pre-eminent role in Baronsmere society. Here she wrote her invitations, planned her dinner parties, and telephoned her network of cronies. It was a beautiful room, all carefully chosen chintz and china, but Jack had never felt at ease here. Once, as a boy, he'd accidentally knocked over a Dresden shepherdess and watched in dismay as it smashed into hundreds of tiny pieces, beyond repair. His mother had shouted at him and he'd been banished from her presence for days. At the time, as a child, that had upset him. Now, as an adult, he could see it made little difference. She'd never been a warm, loving mother.

'So, you're here at last. Lunch is finished, I'm afraid. I'm far too busy to delay meals for thoughtless people. The May Day celebration is coming up – I've got the seating arrangements to approve and the marquees aren't big enough.'

She put the signed card into an envelope, which she then started to address in her small, neat handwriting. She still hadn't looked at him. She was obviously waiting for an apology. If there was going to be any opportunity for discussion, Jack would have to give her what she wanted. 'I'm sorry I missed lunch, Mother.'

Grace put the cap on her fountain pen and sighed deeply,

finally turning to look at him. 'May I ask why you didn't turn up?'

Where to start? Probably best to come right out with it. He took the necklace from his jacket pocket. 'We've got something of a mystery. I gave this necklace to Annie on our wedding day. You remember? I bought it from Cartier.'

A look of distaste had crossed Grace's face at the mention of Annie. She peered at the necklace. 'Yes, I remember. Sapphires and diamonds. A beautiful piece. Very extravagant of you, I thought. What on earth has happened to it?'

'It got burned, never mind how.' The last thing Jack wanted to mention was Traveller funeral rituals. 'The strange thing is, Luke had it.'

'So?' He could sense Grace losing interest, which irritated him.

'Annie didn't take it with her. So … either she came back to get it, which I think is unlikely, or …' He paused. 'Or … someone sent it to her.'

He watched his mother's face closely for any signs of guilt, but found none.

'Why would anyone do that?' she asked.

'That's the million dollar question, isn't it?'

'Perhaps she asked for it,' suggested Grace. 'Your own servant might have sent it to her. Lord knows, they were thick as thieves, those two.'

Jack had heard Annie slyly denigrated in this way many times over the years, but today he didn't want to hear it. 'Maggie has given me her word she knew nothing about it.'

'You're too trusting, Jack.'

That barb rankled, but he let it pass. Tried to keep focused on the issue. 'Apparently Annie's jewellery was auctioned. Your idea.'

'So?'

'Do you remember who bought the necklace?'

Grace rolled her eyes. 'It was twenty years ago. I can't remember that. I don't think I even attended. Why would I have?'

'Which auction house handled the sale?'

'I don't remember that either.'

He'd reached a dead end. The suspicion had been there at the back of his mind that his mother had sent Annie the necklace, but it seemed so unlikely. And she hadn't flinched when he'd brought the topic of the auction up. There was another possibility, though ...

'The market value of that necklace would have paid the rent for quite a few years. Kept a roof over the head of a mother – and her child. Made sure Annie didn't need to come back here.'

The atmosphere in the room changed perceptibly. Grace stood up. Her tone was steely. 'Are you going somewhere with all this, Jack?'

Jack hesitated, but he needed answers. 'Do you think Dad sent the necklace to Annie?'

Grace stared at him. 'He most certainly did not! He was glad to see the back of her!'

Jack's stomach churned. 'Yes, I know. And neither of you wanted her to come back, did you?'

His mother's cheeks were flushed with anger. 'I know what's sparked this! It's because your father and I wouldn't go to the funeral. And we wouldn't blithely accept that boy as our own. Well, whatever mess you've gotten yourself into, don't involve me. Or your father. He'd be incensed if he knew what you're suggesting.'

'Where is he? Maybe I should talk to him.'

Grace banged the desk with her fist. 'Will you stop, Jack! Just stop!' She shook her finger in his face. 'That boy is doing what he came to do. Causing trouble. How you can keep him under your roof, I don't know ...'

Jack couldn't disguise his disgust any longer. Further discussion was pointless. 'I'll see myself out. You've got marquees to attend to. What could be more important than that?'

As he closed the door, his mother called him, demanding he return. Grace always liked to have the last word and there was some small satisfaction in depriving her of that, but he was still left wondering about the necklace.

Jack stood at the huge window in his father's office at Stewart Enterprises. The damp grey roofs of Manchester stared back. Two cups of coffee had finally woken him up, but Jack still wasn't feeling that usual buzz about a brand new business day. The weekend from hell had drained him. And depressed him. He could have done without this Monday morning meeting, but Nicholas always insisted on a catch-up session first thing. Said it was best to 'grab the week by the balls.'

'Morning. Sorry for the delay – couple of urgent calls from clients.' Richard had joined them. The man with no balls. Who didn't know one end of a levelling rod from another. Who never set foot on a messy construction site if he could help it. Who was called Thick Dick – and not as a compliment – by site managers. Jack often dreamed of firing him when Nicholas handed over the business, but he never would, because of Claire. He loved his sister more than he hated Richard.

Richard smirked at Jack, and said 'Pity you missed luncheon yesterday – there was some excellent salmon.'

Pity the prat hadn't choked on a fish bone. Richard had probably stoked Grace's anger all through the meal. He never missed a chance to make himself look good at the expense of others.

'Was your absence from lunch something to do with

Traveller Boy? We all know things are difficult at present, Jack. If there's anything you feel you can't handle here, just pass it on to me.'

'Okay. Try handling this, then.' Jack thrust the protest meeting leaflet into Richard's hands. 'These have been circulated all round the village.'

Richard scanned the leaflet. 'Oh dear.' His tone indicated a total lack of interest.

'Is that all you can say?'

Richard tutted. 'Well, the grammar is atrocious.' He looked back at the leaflet, reading aloud. '"Many people will *loose* their homes." I don't know what they're teaching them in schools these days.'

'It's not a bloody spelling test, Richard! This is serious!'

'Come on, Jack. Who's going to show up? Some Marxist deadbeats whining about capitalism? A lot of talk, a few placards, and then it'll all blow over. It's happened before.'

'Not to us, it hasn't.' Nicholas set aside a pile of papers he'd been reading, and frowned. 'I don't like it. I thought you said everyone had signed, Richard.'

'Almost everyone. They all agreed to the compensation in principle.' Richard was looking uncomfortable.

'Obviously not,' Jack pointed out.

Richard directed his appeal to Nicholas. 'Look – the troublemakers behind this are probably testing us to see if we'll raise the already generous compensation offer. They'll lose interest in a week or so if we ignore them.'

Jack shook his head. 'I don't think we should just sit here and do nothing.'

Nicholas nodded. 'Nor do I, Jack. It's too risky. Redgate are twitchy about adverse media exposure since they got burned a few years ago over that holiday-home scam.'

Burned by association when bent property developers disappeared with nearly a million in deposits, leaving

Redgate Construction with half-built apartments and no money to finish them. If anything went wrong with the Woodlands deal, the Stewart name would be mud.

'I don't want them to get cold feet,' continued Nicholas. 'Someone should go to this meeting. We need to know what – and who – we're dealing with.'

'Why don't you go, Richard?' suggested Jack. 'It's your project, as you keep reminding me.' There was silence. 'Or are you afraid of a few Marxist deadbeats?'

Richard glared. 'Of course not. I just don't think it's a good idea. They'll probably clam up if they see me …'

'Or heckle you out of the place.' Jack would love to see that.

'We need to send someone they won't know,' said Nicholas. 'Someone junior – low-profile and discreet. Who do you suggest, Richard?'

'Um …' he stalled, looking out of the window as if searching for inspiration. Jack almost laughed aloud. Richard knew none of the junior staff. If someone wasn't at least on the Board of Directors, he couldn't be bothered to speak to them. Jack, on the other hand, made it his business to know everyone by name. Had asked HR to advise him of every new employee so that he could personally welcome them to the company.

'Lynda Thomas,' he suggested, while Richard was still trying to think of someone. 'Legal assistant. She's done good work on the Sterne contract.'

'I'm not sure a woman can handle this …' Richard began, but Nicholas cut his protestations short with a wave of his hand.

'It's a good idea. A woman will seem less of a threat. Not local, is she?'

'No,' said Jack. 'She's from Chester.'

'Okay, Jack, you brief her – and bring the PR department

up to speed. Richard, get over to Woodlands right now. If you can get those outstanding signatures, there'll be nothing to protest about.'

'I'll try,' said Richard sulkily, and left.

Jack stayed where he was. Nicholas pulled the pile of papers back in front of him. Clearly Grace hadn't told him about the necklace and Jack's accusations, or it would have been mentioned by now.

'Was there anything else, Jack?' Nicholas asked, steepling his fingers. 'Time is money.'

'Keep an eye on Richard with this Redgate deal, Dad. I think he might be in over his head. In my opinion, we should have left the riverfront houses alone. Breaking up that community doesn't feel right.'

Nicholas raised an eyebrow. 'We are a business, not a charity. It's not like you to be so puritanical.'

'Just trying to protect our reputation.'

Nicholas smiled. 'Don't worry. You know there's nothing I wouldn't do to protect the family name.'

Jack left the office with those words ringing in his ears, and they haunted him for the rest of the morning, as he wondered to what lengths Nicholas would go to – and perhaps *had* gone to – to protect the Stewart name.

Chapter Fourteen

Luke switched the TV off. The day was dragging. He wanted to stretch out on the sofa and sleep, but lately he'd been having nightmares about the crash. The truck's lights, the car swerving. Images had started to come back in dribs and drabs, like he'd been told might happen. It made him want to stay awake permanently. He had more control over his thoughts then.

He pulled the necklace from his pocket, counting the stones through his fingers like rosary beads. Jack had given it back to him, claiming Grace knew nothing about it. Maybe he hadn't even asked her. Anything for an easy life. Finding justice for Annie was going to be tough, but he'd get to the truth somehow.

His mobile rang, startling him. He'd never had his own phone until Matt presented it to him yesterday, all wrapped up, saying it was something he should keep with him at all times, for protection in case his uncles showed up. For a moment, Luke had expected to see a gun.

The call display showed Kate's number. He'd called her yesterday, but she was the first call he'd received on this new phone. How sweet was that. He pressed the talk button. 'Baronsmere Fortune Tellin'. What can we predict for you today?' A squeal of laughter at the other end of the phone and the bleak day suddenly seemed more bearable.

'I'd like a reading in person, please,' said Kate. 'Tonight. Seven o'clock. My place. Dinner. Can you tell me if a certain Irishman with the bluest eyes and the longest eyelashes in the world can make it?'

A beautiful girl wanted to spend the evening with him – surely any minute now he'd wake up. 'Let me check my engagement diary. It'll mean disappointin' Ollie – no excitin' walk down the drive for him later. Still, for you, Kate, anythin'.'

'Great! I'll cook, and play you my new CD.'

'Nothin' you expect me to dance to, I hope.'

'No, don't worry. It's soul ballads.'

'That's a relief,' said Luke. 'I'm not up to Riverdance.' A thought occurred to him. 'What about your mam – will she be there?' Luke had met Sarah briefly at the funeral. She hadn't seemed especially friendly, and her look had been downright frosty when he'd been in The Foresters.

'No,' Kate replied. 'She's at some party in Manchester. Won't be back until after midnight.'

'I'll see if Maggie or Matt can give me a lift. You'll have your hands full.'

'Hmm. I certainly hope so. Later then, handsome.'

Luke was going to be alone with Kate. He'd want to kiss her again for sure. They'd practised a lot on Saturday, so he was quite confident about that bit, but maybe there'd be more. Twenty, and he'd never had a proper girlfriend. Pathetic. He'd had sex before, but he'd never made love. He wanted it to be special, not some meaningless grope in the dark, but he found it hard to trust. He and Kate had talked about it a bit on Saturday. She'd told him she was experienced, and he'd told her he wasn't. She didn't seem to mind that, and he hadn't minded telling her. He hated thinking about that first experience, though. A brief relationship with someone who should have been off limits. Like a lot of things in his life, it ended with humiliation and violence. He hadn't bothered since.

Sinead. He hadn't loved her. She hadn't loved him either. Just fancied the idea of being his first. He was seventeen and she was twelve years older. She helped run the Animal Centre where Luke volunteered. She'd definitely given him the come-on, and she was attractive. He wasn't ashamed of being a virgin at seventeen, but he did get fed up with Joe and Liam making coarse comments about it. Sinead wasn't a Traveller, but she seemed to like Luke well enough.

She'd told Luke she was separated, but one night her husband had come round to the house and nearly hammered the door down. Joe had given Luke a bollocking, going on about shaming the family. He'd chased Luke upstairs, given him a battering, then kicked him back down. Luke's back had given him grief ever since. He never saw Sinead again – he heard she'd gone to Holland with her husband who worked on the oil rigs and had obviously forgiven her. Annie had been great. Told Luke she understood, and believed he hadn't known about the husband, but her being there when the man came round shouting filth and accusations had been so humiliating.

He'd given it up after that. It was expected he'd marry within the culture, and Traveller girls had to be wedded before bedded. So he'd resigned himself to waiting for the right one to come along. Never thought it would be an outsider, though. A girl like Kate wouldn't be acceptable back home, but she was lovely. Kind and caring. He'd have preferred it if she wasn't experienced, but he couldn't just switch off his feelings. Didn't want to.

He closed his eyes and stretched out on the sofa, thinking about Kate, and dozed into dreams of Ireland – singing along with Annie to the radio, him beating time with a spoon on the kitchen table …

He jerked awake, sick with disappointment to find himself in England and alone. The dream had been so real. For a brief moment, he'd had his mother back, but that happiness wasn't worth the loss he felt now. There were no tears, but inside he was crying.

Excitement at spending the evening with Kate was

gone. Annie would never be able to share the happiness of this, his first love. If he was lucky enough to get married, she'd never know the joy of grandchildren. His children would never know the joy of her. It was wrong to be finding pleasure in life when the earth around his mother's grave was still soft. Perhaps he should call Kate and tell her he couldn't make it. Just stay in his room this evening and grieve for his mam.

The crash of the front door opening interrupted his thoughts. He heard Matt's familiar 'Honey! I'm home!' There was a brief conversation with Maggie, then the living room door opened.

'Hey, bro!' Matt ruffled Luke's hair before he threw himself onto the sofa. 'Whatcha doing?'

'Oh, just restin'. Thinkin'. How was work?'

'Bloody awful. Getting things ready for the nightclub renovation. God, I hate paperwork. Pulling pints and chatting to the punters, that's what I'm best at.'

It was good to have Matt there. Luke felt less depressed when he was around. Unfortunately his brother always seemed to be working, sleeping, or enjoying a social life well into the early hours, which meant he had little free time. Not as much as Luke would have liked, anyway. He didn't want to complain, but he did get lonely sometimes.

'Maggie's planning steak pie for dinner,' said Matt, patting his stomach. 'That's what makes the idea of marriage so hard. None of the girlfriends to date could cook like our Maggie.'

The mention of dinner reminded Luke of his dilemma. 'I'm supposed to be seein' Kate tonight.'

Matt sat upright, giving Luke his full attention. 'So you finally asked her out?'

'Not exactly. She phoned earlier. She's cookin' for me. Wants me to listen to her new CD.'

Matt laughed. 'Yeah, right. Some excuse. She'll be all over you before the first track ends.'

Luke's imagination ran with that idea for a few moments before guilt closed it down. 'Matt – is it okay for me to be doin' this – seein' a girl when my mam ... you know?'

Matt's smile faded. 'I think she'd want you to be making friends, Luke. It doesn't mean you're grieving any less.'

Luke nodded. There was truth in that. The voice of reproach in his head was Luke's own, not Annie's. He'd take things a step at a time, a day at a time. Start doing normal things again.

Matt grabbed the remote and switched on the TV, flicking from channel to channel. 'You'll need some protection. I'll get you something later from my stash. Best not let Maggie see, though.'

'Best not let Maggie see what?'

Luke literally jumped in his chair as the housekeeper came into the room carrying a huge chocolate cake. He hoped Maggie couldn't see that he was blushing a bit. He hadn't even thought about protection.

'You don't want to know, Maggie,' said Matt. 'Choccie cake. Sweet! Two slices for me, please.'

'Dirty boots off the sofa, please, Matthew. Let's at least pretend we're civilised.'

'Yes, Ma'am!' Matt saluted and shifted his feet. 'By the way, Luke's out for dinner tonight. Kate's cooking for him.'

'I hope you know what you're getting into, Luke,' she said, exchanging a quick look with Matt.

Luke hadn't expected that from Maggie. His voice, when he spoke, was tense. 'Is there a problem?'

Maggie shook her head, a worried expression on her face. 'Well, I don't know – I hope not – but that young lady's been waited on hand, foot and finger. I'm not sure she even knows how to turn the oven on.'

216

Maggie's face broke into a smile, and Luke's heartbeat returned to normal. They were just teasing. 'Will I have two slices of cake then?' he asked, with a grin. 'Just in case.'

'Good idea,' said Matt. 'And with any luck, Kate'll see sense and get a takeaway.'

Luke felt an unfamiliar glow of contentment. At that moment, it felt like family.

'Have a nice time,' said Maggie, pulling up outside Kate's house. Luke sat there in the car, staring out unseeing at the street ahead till she asked, 'Something wrong, love?'

'Maggie – how do you go on? When you lose someone?' He still felt guilty for even thinking of enjoying himself.

Sadness clouded Maggie's face. 'It will ease in time, lad – the grief.'

'Earlier, I dreamed Mam wasn't dead. Wakin' up was like goin' through it all over again.'

'That's normal, Luke,' Maggie told him, and her words were of some comfort. At least he wasn't cracking up. Maggie squeezed his hand. 'I'll save some steak pie for you – just in case.' Then she drove away leaving him in front of the Walkers' cottage.

Some cottage. He'd imagined somewhere small and quaint with a thatched roof. This house seemed to spill out in all directions. What would Kate make of his poky home in Ennis? He dodged the plant pots near the entrance and rang the bell. He waited a moment before pressing it again. He couldn't stand there all night ringing the doorbell like an eejit, and he couldn't phone because he'd forgotten his mobile. He decided to try round the back but just as he got there a frying pan flew out of the door and landed in one of the flowerbeds. The pan was on fire.

'Bugger!' he heard Kate shout.

As Luke came in view of the window, he could see Kate inside. She was jumping up and down, trying to switch off the smoke alarm with a broom handle. No wonder she hadn't heard the doorbell. He stepped into the kitchen at the same time as the alarm stopped.

'Bugger!' Kate said again, dropping the broom and turning back towards the cooker.

'I've been called worse,' quipped Luke, his eyes watering in the smoky kitchen.

'Oh, Luke! It's all gone wrong!'

'So I see,' he said. A tea towel smouldered in the sink next to him. 'Are we eatin' outside?'

'What?'

'Well, is that the main course in the garden?'

Kate burst out laughing. 'No, those are – were – the sautéed potatoes. I used too much oil and the stupid things caught fire so I panicked. The main course is lamb – it must be ready by now.' Putting on oven gloves, she hauled a roasting dish out of the oven. The smell was deadly. The joint of meat lay there, defeated. Maggie and Matt had known what they were talking about.

'That's okay,' joked Luke. 'I like mine well done.'

'Oh God!' wailed Kate, prodding at the meat with a fork. 'I turned the heat up to make sure it was really cooked. What a disaster! I wanted everything to be special and now it's all spoiled. And look at me – I must be a real sight, and my clothes smell smoky.'

Tears seemed close. Luke did some quick thinking. 'Have you got eggs, milk, butter – maybe some bacon?'

Kate peered into the fridge. 'Yes, we've got all that. Why?'

'Is there another fryin' pan? I'll make us an omelette, while you go and change.'

Kate stared at him. 'Oh no, that's not fair. I invited *you* for dinner. Look, we could order a takeaway …'

'I can manage, Kate. I like cookin', really. Just pull that stool over for me. My leg aches a bit.'

She took the ingredients from the fridge and Luke settled himself at the counter. 'Now, go. This'll be ready in twenty minutes.' He started cracking the eggs into the bowl.

'Bless you,' Kate said, and kissed his cheek, making his hand waver. 'I'll put some oven chips in, shall I?'

She put a tray of frozen chips into the oven and Luke determined to check the temperature as soon as she left. 'Kate …'

She stopped in the doorway. 'Yes?'

He looked appreciatively at the sexy black jumper she wore, its wide neck pulled down to reveal her shoulders. 'That top really suits you. Do you have to change?'

'I've got another one just like it,' she murmured.

The omelettes were nearly done. Not half bad either. He'd often made them for his mother when she looked like she needed a rest. Music drifted down from upstairs. Kate wasn't ready yet so he turned the heat down under the frying pan. The door opposite the kitchen was open and Luke glimpsed a table and chairs. That must be where they'd eat. He'd see if anything needed doing in there. It was a posh dining room, like the one in Jack's house, but half the size. Fancy china plates, crystal glasses, and tall candles in silver candlesticks, waiting to be lit. Kate had gone to a lot of trouble.

Smiling, Luke turned to leave, and was confronted by Jack Stewart. Or many Jacks, to be precise. One wall of the Walkers' dining room was decorated with a myriad of framed family photos, and Jack and Matt were in most of them. Luke bit his lip. He knew Matt considered Kate almost as a sister, but seeing evidence of Jack playing happy families was like a punch in the gut.

'Luke?' Kate called from the direction of the kitchen, and

he numbly answered 'In here', unable to tear his eyes away from Jack's face. He smelled Kate's perfume as she came to stand beside him and he felt his heart ache. She was all he wanted, but what did he have to offer?

'Luke,' she said, touching his arm. 'What's wrong?'

'Me. I'm what's wrong.'

'What do you mean?'

He couldn't answer. She moved in front of him, blocking his view of the photos. He looked into her lovely green eyes.

'I know what you're thinking, Luke. That we shouldn't get involved because I'm close to Jack and you're not – at least, not yet.' She took hold of his arm. 'We think differently about Jack, it's true, but we're idiots if we let that come between us.'

'Kate,' he said, willing her to understand him. 'I wish it was that easy, but it's hard to see Jack pretendin' to be a family man when he didn't give a shit about me and my mam.'

She was silent, and he waited for the inevitable. This was it – the end. He'd screwed up, but then he felt Kate's hand in his, her palm soft and warm in his cold one. Finally, she spoke. 'All I know, Luke Kiernan, is I want to be with you.' She smiled. 'Who knows, I might even learn to cook for you.'

'Don't bother,' he said, stroking her hand with his fingertips. 'I like you just the way you are.'

'Right answer! Now, let's get out of here – we'll eat in the living room. Where's that omelette? I'm starving.'

They moved towards the door and Kate flicked off the light. Luke exhaled in relief as the photos and their powerful memories were left in darkness.

They'd eaten in the living room, trays on their laps. The omelettes had gone down well. Even the chips had been good.

Kate brought in dessert. 'Here we go. Chocolate-covered strawberries and amaretto ice cream. At least I couldn't spoil that.'

Luke was still hungry and grateful for more food. 'This is grand,' he told Kate, as he savoured the almond flavour.

'Mmm-mmm,' was all she said, licking some chocolate from her lips. He wanted to volunteer to finish the job. He was glad Kate couldn't read his mind. Although, she'd dimmed the lights when she came back into the living room, so maybe she was thinking about more than just food, too.

'Penny for them?' Kate asked, her spoon poised above her bowl.

Why not say what he was thinking? Might as well take the plunge. 'Honestly? I was thinkin' how gorgeous you are.' Now the words were out, they sounded pathetic. Insincere. She'd either laugh or change the subject. And he'd need to learn to keep his mouth shut. He glanced up at her and their eyes locked. Luke swallowed hard. The room around him receded and the music was edged out by the pounding of his heart, which she must be able to hear.

She was still looking at him, a smile playing about her lips. She pointed to his bowl. 'Finished?'

Mutely, he offered it up and she set it down, quickly returning her attention to him. Sliding along the sofa, she curled her body in close to his. She was so pretty, so delicate. She made him feel masculine and protective, and he kissed the top of her head. Kate changed position slightly and looked up at him. All doubts vanished then. It was clear she was exactly where she wanted to be. Luke gently tilted her chin and kissed her. His tongue found hers, and he could taste the sweetness of strawberries. He slid his fingers underneath her hair, which felt like silk and smelled of summer flowers.

Kate was now half on top of him, her thigh against his. She must surely notice he was ready for more. His body seemed to have an instinct of its own. Hopefully, he wouldn't get carried away too soon. He tried to take his mind off his own pleasure and concentrate on hers. As he slid his free hand around Kate's shoulder, her jumper slipped, revealing the tops of her breasts. She moaned softly and entwined her hands in his hair, pulling it firmly but gently, as their kiss became more intense. Despite his efforts not to, he felt dangerously close to losing control …

A car horn blared outside in the street and Luke broke away from Kate. A dog was barking noisily somewhere close.

'What's wrong?' murmured Kate, trying to pull him close again.

'Is that your mam comin' home?' What would Sarah say if she found him virtually making love to her daughter? A Traveller girl's mother would have smacked his face and the father would have brained him. And then her brothers would have come round later with sticks.

'No – I told you. She won't be back until late,' Kate said, and he could hear the frustration in her voice.

She took his hand and placed it on her breast. Luke kissed her again for a while but it was no good. The mood was broken.

'I'm sorry, Kate,' he said, stroking her hair. 'I can't get the image of your mam walkin' in on us out of my head.'

Kate sighed and got up. Straightening her jumper and smoothing her hair, she sat down in the armchair. Her cheeks were flushed, whether from anger or desire, he couldn't tell. She watched and waited for him to speak.

'I feel like a right eejit, Kate,' he said, moving slowly upright. 'You're the girl of my dreams. And I want you – so much. It's just … in Traveller culture, you wouldn't kiss or touch a girl in her parents' home. There'd be hell to pay. I guess it's just ingrained in me. So sorry.'

'There's always the garden,' suggested Kate, and he was relieved to see humour in her eyes. 'Love among the burnt potatoes.'

'Kate – don't you know what the cold air does to a man?'

She laughed and it felt like things were okay again. When she was driving him home later, Kate asked if he was planning to go to Jack's birthday party that coming Saturday.

Jack hadn't even mentioned the party, likely not wanting Luke to attend. It was Matt who'd told told him about it, said it would be a blast and that he wanted Luke to go. A hundred guests, tons of food and drink, a DJ. Not wanting confrontation, Luke had told Matt he might not be up to it physically. Truth was, spending an evening watching the hypocrites of Baronsmere fawning over a Stewart was not his idea of fun. And there was another reason, which he shared now with Kate. 'Travellers don't usually go to parties or celebrations for a year after the death of a family member.'

'Oh.'

He could hear disappointment in her voice.

'I was hoping we could go together,' she said, 'but I totally understand if you feel it's not appropriate.'

'Not everybody follows that tradition now, though,' he told her. 'Some just don't drink or dance at a party.'

'That sounds like a good compromise. And you know, there's a big raffle at the party and all the proceeds go to charity. We could buy tickets – help out a good cause.'

Kate was working hard to convince him. It was flattering that she really wanted him to be there. By the time she dropped him off at Jack's house, Luke had as good as said he'd go, trying to ignore the nagging voice of his conscience that said it wasn't right and no good would come of it.

It had been a hectic Thursday morning at St Aidan's Hospital. A bus had skidded out of control in Pearse Street and the A&E had been flooded with everything from cuts and abrasions to serious head injuries. The bus driver was dead – a suspected coronary, the likely cause of the crash – and Emer had spent the morning consoling his widow. She was immersed in paperwork in her office when the phone rang. She answered it, putting the call on speakerphone so she could continue writing. 'Emer Sullivan.'

'Emer, it's Mary at reception. There's a gentleman here who needs some information about a patient. When I looked at the patient's records, it said all enquiries should be directed to you.'

'Who's the patient?'

'Luke Kiernan. He was discharged three weeks ago.'

Emer stopped writing. 'And who's asking?'

'A Mr Joseph Kiernan – the patient's uncle.'

'I'll be right down, Mary.' So, here it was. Emer had been half expecting a visit. Jack had told her Luke's uncles were abroad, but once they came back to an empty house and news that Annie was dead, it was logical that they might follow the route their sister and nephew had taken.

In the reception area, Emer caught sight of Joe Kiernan before he saw her: mid- to late-forties, black hair with traces of grey, fleshy but still quite handsome. His suit was well-cut and of good quality wool, but the flash of an assortment of gold rings on his hand resting on the counter marked him out as new money. 'Mr Kiernan?'

He flicked his attention to Emer and she was startled by his eyes – same shape as Luke's, though a lighter shade of blue. The similarity was unnerving but her years of experience helped Emer keep a poker face. She shook his hand and introduced himself. 'I'm Emer Sullivan – hospital counsellor.'

He appraised her, flicking his eyes quickly over her body, then he smiled in return – a slightly lopsided grin, which he probably used to try to charm women.

224

'How can I help you?'

'Well, as I explained to Mary here, my sister Annie was killed a few weeks ago. Car crash. I've only just found out about it 'cause I've been abroad. I'm a businessman, see – I travel a lot.'

'She wasn't a patient here,' Mary chipped in, tapping away at her computer.

'I'm so sorry for your loss,' said Emer. She used those words every day and sometimes they came out sounding more automatic than she would have liked: now, however, she meant them, having been to Annie's funeral.

'Thank you.' Joe didn't show any spark of emotion about Annie's death but then some people could be very closed with their feelings, especially in a public place. 'Thing is, Emer, her son Luke – my nephew – was with her when the accident happened. The Guards told me he'd been brought to this hospital. And now he's gone missing. I need to find him.'

'Does he live with you?' Emer wanted to make this man talk – the more he did, the better she could assess his motives and sincerity.

Joe rubbed the bridge of his nose: covering a lie? His gaze, though, stayed steady. 'Yeah, he does. But, like I said, I've been away – there'd have been no one at home for him, see. He probably didn't want to be alone.'

'Have you contacted friends, other family members?'

'Course. No one's seen him. I'm very worried.'

'Well, all I can suggest is you wait for Luke to get in touch.'

He wasn't going to be put off so easily. 'Look, Emer, could we go somewhere a bit more private? It's like a zoo out here.'

'Room two's free,' said Mary, still typing.

'This way, Mr Kiernan.'

Emer held the door open for Joe, then followed him in,

making sure she left the door ajar. The room held a few battered chairs and a coffee table. There were toys in the corner and someone had tried to cheer up the place by taping a poster of the Wicklow hills on the wall. 'Have a seat.' She angled a chair sideways to him so she could see his face. 'Can I get you a tea or coffee?'

'No … but thanks, love.' The lopsided grin was back in place. 'Look, Emer, I don't want to involve the Guards. It'd scare Luke, see. He's had a bit of trouble with them before.'

That was news to Emer but maybe it wasn't true. Just a way for Joe to get her to do what he wanted. 'I see. I understand, I really do, but it's hospital policy not to give out personal information about patients.'

'Not even to a relative?'

'If the patient's over eighteen, then no,' Emer confirmed. 'I'm sure Luke will be in touch when he's ready. He's been through a lot, what with the accident and his mother's death. Just give him some time.'

Joe frowned and rubbed his forehead. 'I don't want to do that. See, Luke – well'—he leaned forward in his chair and lowered his voice confidentially—'just between you and me, he's a bit unstable. Always has been. Not the brightest card in the deck, unfortunately. He needs people around to take care of him.'

'Really? He seemed balanced enough when I spoke to him.' Too late, Emer realised she'd revealed more information than she should have. Now the door was wide open for Joe to ask more probing questions. Which he did.

'So you spoke to him then? Why? What about? Don't you deal with headcases and weirdos?'

His tone had subtly shifted and there was suspicion in his eyes. The charming façade was slipping.

'I'm a trauma counsellor not a psychiatrist. It's my job to counsel the bereaved.'

Joe cut to the chase. 'Where did he say he was goin'?'

'I've told you, even if I knew, I'm not allowed to reveal information of that kind.'

'Look, if you knew where he went, you'd better tell me cause if he's lyin' dead in a ditch somewhere it'll be this hospital's fault.'

'The doctor assessed Luke's physical *and* mental condition and decided he was fit to leave. I'm sorry I can't give you the answers you want, but this is not a prison – we can't keep patients here if they want to leave.'

Joe snorted. 'Sounds like a case of gettin' the filthy knacker on his way as soon as you can.'

Emer bristled at the accusation of discrimination. 'That's not the way it was, I can assure you. All patients are treated equally in this hospital.' She stood up. 'I'm sorry we can't help you.'

Joe stood up abruptly, kicking the chair out behind him in a temper. His bulk was between her and the door and Emer felt very uncomfortable, the hairs on the back of her neck prickling a warning.

'What is it with you people?' he hissed. 'You get a little bit of power and you think you can abuse the rest of us. You make me sick!'

'This conversation is over. Please let me pass.'

He held position, looming over her, a slight smile twisting his lips. This man was a bully, someone who enjoyed using his power over others. Emer could sense the violence in him, and her hands clenched involuntarily into fists. Fight or flight – he'd activated her adrenalin response, and he knew it. She was about to push past him – shout for help, if necessary – when he swung away to the side, mockingly gesturing for her to pass. As she reached the door, he fired a final question at her. 'Where's the body?'

'The body?'

'My sister's body. Where's she buried?'

The beautiful old church in Baronswood sprang to mind but there was no way she was telling this bastard about that. 'I'm afraid I have no idea,' she lied.

'Well, where do they put the soddin' dead bodies after an accident, for Christ's sake?' Joe asked, as if she were simple.

'She was killed at the scene of the accident and was never brought to the hospital. They would have taken her straight to the morgue and then released her body to a relative.'

'To Luke, you mean?'

'I don't know anything about that,' she said coldly.

'You don't know much, do you, darlin'?' sneered Joe. 'Or so you claim. In fact, you've been pretty useless all round.'

'Time to go, Mr Kiernan.' She felt safer now with the bustle of hospital life visible and within reach.

He swaggered towards the door and stopped just in front of her. 'Be a good girl and pass a message on to Luke for me. Tell him I'm lookin' for him and he can't run away forever.' He leaned in closer and she could feel his breath warm against her cheek. His voice was a whisper but she heard the words clearly enough. 'And if I find out you've been lyin' to me, Emer, I won't forget it.'

Then he was gone, winding his way calmly through the nurses and patients, past the reception desk and out the sliding front doors. Emer exhaled a long, slow breath but her relief was short-lived because she started to think about Luke. She'd seen fear in his eyes when he talked about his uncles. Joe was almost twice Luke's build. He could have given Luke those bruises. And now it seemed his uncle was determined to find him. Joe wouldn't discover Annie had been taken to England for burial – Jack had told her he'd given the funeral home explicit instructions about that. But what if Joe decided to contact Jack or worse, turn up in Baronsmere?

Emer took out her mobile and dialled Jack's number with shaky hands.

Jack was pacing the office as he spoke to Doyle. He'd called the detective immediately after speaking to Emer. She was a woman who spent her working hours assessing people and she had sounded worried about Joe Kiernan's attitude and motives. That was enough for Jack.

'Pick up Emer from the hospital this evening and take her home,' he instructed Doyle. 'I need someone outside her flat all night. She's to be taken to work in the morning and accompanied home again, then to the airport on Saturday morning. Keep a check on her flat over the weekend. Can you arrange that?'

'Of course.' Doyle's gravelly voice was reassuringly matter-of-fact. 'If Kiernan shows up, I'll scare him off. I take it you don't want the police involved?'

'No police,' confirmed Jack. 'Although you can let him think *you're* the police. He would just assume Emer was scared and had reported him as a threat.'

Jack was still wild with anger at the thought of Joe Kiernan threatening Emer. If the man were in the room with him now, he'd choke the life out of him.

'What will you do if he turns up in Baronsmere?' asked Doyle.

If only. He'd break both the man's legs. 'I doubt he will. It's the last place he'd expect Luke to go. But have someone keep an eye on Joe when he gets back to Ennis.'

'How long for? Surveillance is expensive.'

What was money compared to Emer's safety? 'A week. Hopefully after that, they'll give up.'

'What's he running from?'

'Who?'

'Luke. Joe said he couldn't run away forever. What's he done?'

Jack was suddenly tired of all this mystery surrounding Annie and Luke. 'God knows. See if you can find that out as well.'

There was a long pause. 'It'd be easier just to ask Luke.'

'Only if I have to,' decided Jack. 'He's touchy as hell and doesn't trust anyone.'

Once the phone call was over, Jack sat back down at his desk. The adrenalin surge was wearing off, leaving him with an uncomfortable residue of worry. Should he tell Luke that Joe was trying to track him down? Probably not. He might take off. For the first time, Jack felt a glimmer of genuine pity. He'd been quick to be concerned about Emer's safety, but what about Luke's? What had he endured in the past? Was it any wonder the kid was so difficult when the odds had been stacked against him from the start?

Emer wanted Jack to cut Luke some slack. Surely it wouldn't kill him to do that. He'd make sure he invited Luke to his birthday on Saturday – it would be cruel and insensitive not to. Matt and Kate would be making sure he was there anyway, but maybe a personal invite from Jack himself could start the thaw.

Chapter Fifteen

'Happy birthday, Jack!'

As Jack entered, the room erupted with cheers and blasts from horns and streamers flying out of party poppers. This year's party was in Tim's house, the very grand Leighton Hall. The huge conservatory had been decorated in blue and silver and looked like a giant spaceship. Glitter balls dangling from the ceiling cast patches of silver light over the guests, and trays of blue drinks were being served by waiters with silvered faces, wearing what looked like tin foil. Tim certainly knew how to put on a show.

Usually Jack dreaded his birthday. One year closer to the grave yet he was supposed to eat, drink and be merry. This evening, though, he felt like he could take on the world and the reason for that was Emer on his arm.

He glanced at her and she smiled. The tight-fitting green dress she was wearing shimmered in the glitterball light and her curls were a work of art. He'd loaned her his grandmother's emerald necklace, an heirloom that by tradition always skipped a generation. Jack would one day give it to Matt's firstborn.

'Look, Jack!' Emer swivelled him round and they saw themselves distorted long and lanky in a funfair joke mirror.

Jack exploded with laughter at the ridiculous sight. As he did so, he felt some long-held burden of sorrow and disappointment lift from his shoulders. It was like he was looking at the world through fresh eyes.

'Come and meet my friends, you gorgeous woman,' he said, hugging Emer close to him like the treasure she was.

Kate was snuggled up close to Luke on a space-age puffy

silver sofa. The party was in full swing. Jack was drifting around the dance floor with Emer in his arms, looking like he was in seventh heaven. In fact he looked like a completely different man tonight – all lit-up inside, and happier than she'd ever seen him. She'd thought he seemed happy with her mother, but he'd never had this glow. She silently wished him well with his new romance.

Kate had danced with Tim and Matt because Luke didn't want her to miss out on any of the fun. He needn't have worried about cramping her style. There was no one Kate would rather be with than Luke. The party could have vanished around them and she wouldn't have cared. His arm around her shoulder reminded her of their recent tumble on the sofa. It hadn't gone anywhere, but it had still been good. Luke claimed inexperience, but he'd seemed to know what he was doing.

'What you thinkin' about?' asked Luke, and she raised her head from his shoulder.

Rubbing his nose with hers, she whispered 'Being alone with you …'

He pulled her closer and they melted into a kiss, more sensual than anything Kate had ever experienced because her feelings for this man were stronger than anything she'd ever known.

Sarah was sitting by herself at the bar, nursing a Blue Martini. She had a clear view of Kate making a spectacle of herself with Luke. She wanted to scream.

Richard slipped onto the barstool beside her and followed her gaze. 'Ah – love's young dream. Shame about the reality. I'm surprised you've let it go this far, Sarah. I know this is the twenty-first century and all that …'

She looked around, hoping no one had heard. The last thing she needed was for all that to be brought out into the open.

'I'm dealing with it, Richard,' she said, wishing he would disappear.

'Doesn't look like it.' He nodded his head in the direction of Luke and Kate, still locked together in a kiss.

'I've already spoken to Jack about it. He doesn't think the relationship's a good idea either. Said he'd talk to Kate.'

Richard's eyes lit up. 'And we know how close she is to him. Your disapproval and Jack's disapproval might just swing it. Otherwise, you're going to have to come clean.'

'Not unless I have to,' Sarah said. She'd woven such a tangled web over all this that she'd likely be the one snared and hurt. 'And please don't go saying anything, Richard. It would be my secret to tell.'

'Just don't wait too long,' Richard advised. 'Grace did that all those years ago, and before she knew it there was a pikey in her drawing room. She wants Traveller Boy gone. So does Nicholas. They've asked me to sort it out. No one will blame you for doing what's right to protect your daughter. Why don't you play hardball? Tell Kate she has to choose – you or Luke.'

'But then she'll blame me for breaking it up.' Or what if she chose Luke? Losing Kate was unthinkable. Sarah hadn't been the greatest mother in the world but she did love her daughter.

Richard lowered his voice. 'We saw his mother off, didn't we? And she had a wedding ring and Jack curled round her little finger. This should be a piece of cake. It's best that he goes, Sarah. Sort it out. If you need my help, let me know.' He stood up and patted her shoulder in an attempt at reassurance. 'I see Grace and Nicholas have arrived ... I must go and say hello.'

Sarah watched Jack's parents as they entered the conservatory and looked around at the décor with thinly veiled disapproval. By rights they should have been her in-laws. Now little Emer Sullivan would have that honour.

Sarah glanced again at Kate, laughing at something Luke had said. She drained her martini and ordered another.

'I've got three chins.' Emer giggled at her reflection in another of the funfair distortion mirrors. 'Maybe that's how many I'll have when I'm sixty.'

'I look like Henry the Eighth,' said Jack, checking out the sideways view. 'That's what too much port and venison does for you. Still'—he winked at Emer in the mirror—'six wives might not be so bad.'

'Good evening, Jack.'

A figure loomed up behind them. The mirror's distortion showed a woman with bulging eyes and hair as big as those towering wigs they used to wear at the French court. Luckily Emer stifled her giggle because the next thing she heard was Jack saying 'Hello, Mother'. They turned round together.

Grace accepted a peck on the cheek from Jack and asked if he was enjoying the party, giving Emer a chance to assess his mother while he replied. In her late sixties, slim, cheekbones that could cut you, impeccably dressed, adorned with discreet but obviously expensive pieces of jewellery. An air of absolute self-possession, like royalty.

'Mother, this is Emer Sullivan, my guest this evening. Emer, this is my mother, Lady Grace Stewart.'

Emer stopped herself from curtseying just in time. She held out her hand instead. 'Nice to meet you.'

'Pleased to meet you, my dear,' said Grace, allowing her white-gloved hand to briefly make contact. She was eyeing the emeralds around Emer's neck like the witch coveting Dorothy's ruby slippers.

'Emer's a trauma counsellor in a hospital,' said Jack.

'Goodness – that sounds like a challenging job. Where did you say you were from, my dear?'

'I didn't. I'm from Ireland.'

'Ireland.' Grace made it sound like The Black Hole of Calcutta.

'Emer and I met in Dublin,' Jack informed her. 'She was Luke's counsellor after the accident.'

'I see.'

The mention of Luke killed the conversation stone dead. Emer wondered if she should leave Grace and Jack alone to talk, but perhaps that would be a breach of etiquette. She was all at sea here.

A waiter with a silver face and a silver wig stopped next to them and presented a tray of champagne flutes. Grace accepted one and then said loudly, 'It's kind of Timothy to give us such a lovely venue but he has some very strange ideas about décor. And I must say, it's most disappointing that Lord and Lady Leighton haven't returned.'

'Extended their holiday, I believe,' Jack explained. 'Trusted Tim with the arrangements. He's in his element. And I think it's great fun.'

Grace's eyebrows shot up. 'Indeed?'

Just then, someone bumped into Emer and her wine sloshed right down the front of her dress. A widening circle of dark red stained the green silk.

'Gavin, you idiot!' snapped Jack. 'Why don't you look where you're going?'

'I'm *so* sorry.'

Gavin was a tall young man of dark good looks. Despite his words of apology, Emer could have sworn she saw a glimmer of satisfaction in what he'd done.

'My dear, I'm sure that will sponge off ...' murmured Grace.

Probably not, so she'd be left with an unsightly stain on her dress for the rest of the evening. Emer could have cried.

'Make way for the fashion police!' A tall thin man with hair flopping over one eye joined the group. He was wearing a spacesuit minus the helmet. 'Gavin blunders again, I see.'

'It wasn't *my* fault. That stupid robot banged into me,' commented Gavin, pointing at someone dressed up like C-3PO from *Star Wars*. 'Idiot must have thought this was a fancy dress party.'

'No, no, he's one of my sci-fi entertainers. They're all going to sing and dance the *Time Warp* later.'

'I'll look forward to that, Tim,' said Jack, with a smile. 'You've outdone yourself this time.'

The young man with the flopping hair bowed. He had to be Timothy Leighton, the host. Jack had told Emer he was a bit off the wall but had a heart of gold. Tim offered her his arm. 'Come with me, gorgeous. We'll raid my mother's wardrobe. Get you glammed up in cloth of gold.'

His smile was kind. 'Thank you,' she said.

'Or something from Tim's wardrobe,' said Gavin, who proceeded to have hysterics at his own 'joke', but Tim just grinned, and said 'That's a possibility too.'

As they moved off, Emer heard Grace behind her say, 'A word, please, Jack …'

'Were those your grandmother's emeralds?' asked Grace, in a frosty tone.

'Yes.' They were Jack's to do with as he pleased. 'And still are.'

'So – is it serious – with this woman?'

'Her name is Emer, Mother. And yes, it could be very serious.'

Jack waited, wondering what she would say. She'd no doubt try to warn him off. After his split with Sarah, she'd casually mentioned a few available women, who 'would fit in well'.

'She's obviously intelligent. A career woman.'

'She is,' said Jack, proudly.

'She probably wouldn't want to give all that up.'

If this were a game of chess, Grace had just moved her Bishop out for attack but he could defend himself easily enough. 'I wouldn't want her to give it up. She loves her job. And she's good at it.'

'Mmm.'

Jack could almost hear his mother's brain working overtime, flicking through the remaining options.

'Exterminate! Exterminate!' A model Dalek whizzed up to them, pointing its sucker at Grace.

She waved it away, impatiently. 'This is too much! Your father and I have been seriously misinformed about this … event.'

Jack smothered a grin. Seeing his mother so flustered robbed her of some of her power.

She made one last attempt, though. 'Emer lives in Ireland, Jack. The Irish do love their country so, and Baronsmere would seem very small compared to Dublin …'

He was ready for her. Moved his Queen out to take her Bishop. 'Who knows – I might just relocate to Dublin. Excuse me – I've just seen Dave and Evie arrive.'

He left his mother standing there open-mouthed, the Dalek circling her like a shark. When she saw Luke, her evening would be complete. Jack smiled at the thought.

Kate had gone to talk to Abbie, so Luke went to the buffet table to get her some more of those salmon roll-ups she loved. After heaping the plate, he looked in amazement at Jack's fancy birthday cake – it was a replica in miniature of his house and garden, all done in chocolate and coloured icing. Luke could see his own bedroom window, and there was even the firepit and the lake. Must have cost a small fortune.

'Jack will cut that later. Don't touch it.'

He spun round to see Nicholas scowling at him. Did he seriously think Luke was going to help himself to a slice? He peered over his left shoulder, then his right. 'I'm sorry – I thought you were talkin' to one of the waiters, not another guest. Left your manners at home?'

Heart pounding, Luke turned away from the buffet table. He'd quite enjoyed that. Nothing his grandparents could say or do would upset him because he expected only the worst from them. Nicholas must be really annoyed that he was still around in Baronsmere, let alone been invited here tonight. And it was Jack who'd invited him. That had been a surprise. Maybe under pressure from Matt, but he'd seemed genuine enough. Luke had been tempted to say no, but Kate had talked him into it. Said she wanted him there. The clincher, though, was when she said how much it would piss Nicholas and Grace off.

'Quite right, too, Luke.' It was Emer, who had obviously just witnessed his confrontation with Nicholas. She was smiling, both in greeting and amusement, and she walked over and gave him a hug. 'Let's sit down and chat for a bit.'

They found a table that was free. Luke had been hoping for a chance to chat privately with Emer at some point. She'd arrived just after lunch and Jack had monopolised her all afternoon.

'You've changed your dress,' he noted. She'd started the evening flying Ireland's colours in a beautiful emerald green; now she was wearing a breathtaking silver beaded dress. 'You look amazin'.'

'Thank you. Someone called Gavin spilled wine on me so Tim loaned me something from his mother's wardrobe. One of her twelve wardrobes, I should say.'

Luke couldn't help scowling at the mention of his cousin. 'Gavin's Richard's son. Turns out he's as big an eejit as his dad ... but Tim's grand, isn't he?'

'A lovely fella,' she agreed. 'So – I saw you with Kate earlier. The pair of you were completely wrapped up in each other. Remember I said the girls would find you irresistible?'

Luke blushed at the compliment. It was good that at least one person was happy for them. 'I don't think Kate's mam approves of me, though. She's been glarin' at me all night.'

Emer clucked in sympathy. 'I know how you feel. I met Lady Grace earlier and she could hardly bring herself to speak to me. I'm sure she was having palpitations beneath that frosty exterior at the thought of me with her son.'

'The Cheshire Cat – that's what Maggie calls her,' said Luke, and they both shared a laugh.

'Do you mind that, Luke? Me and Jack ... being together?'

Luke *had* minded at first when Jack told him Emer would be his guest, but wanting her to be his exclusive friend was selfish – and childish. Kate had helped him see that. Better of course if Emer had chosen anyone other than Jack Stewart, but at least Luke knew she'd fight his corner if need be. 'I was surprised,' he admitted. 'But then I realised I might get to see more of you, which would be grand. And maybe you'll be a good influence on him. Did you tell him to invite me to this party?'

'No, I didn't.'

She wouldn't lie to him, he knew that. Maybe Jack had done it just to impress her, but whatever the reason, his attitude to Luke seemed a bit improved. Luke couldn't really respond in kind because the letter still stood between them, though people here had put doubts in his mind about that. It was too confusing. He'd seen it with his own eyes, and yet now he was questioning it. As much as he wanted answers, he didn't want to risk alienating Matt or Kate. It had waited ten years. A bit longer wouldn't hurt.

* * *

Sarah finished her drink and scanned the crowds for Kate. It was getting late and she'd had more than enough of this party. The oblivion of sleep was all she craved now. She'd find Kate, try to persuade her to come home, too. Away from Luke's influence.

Not seeing Kate in the conservatory, Sarah wandered out into the Leighton's massive hallway. A number of rooms led off from this main area, and she searched them one by one.

Kate and Luke were in the third room she checked, stretched out on the sofa, mouths locked together. Sarah felt a surge of rage. Finding the dimmer switch, she turned it on full, flooding the room with light. 'Well, this is cosy.'

Kate scrambled to her feet. 'Mum, could you give us some privacy here?'

'Sorry …' Luke mumbled, struggling to sit up on the sofa.

'Don't, Luke!' Kate sounded angry. 'You have nothing to apologise for.'

'I told you I didn't want you involved with him,' Sarah said.

Luke flushed and glanced at Kate. She obviously hadn't told him that. He'd been kept in the dark like the outsider he was.

'Same old story, is it?' Luke's eyes were flashing fire. 'A Traveller not being acceptable …'

'Well, your mother realised that eventually – you should do the same.'

'Mum!' cried Kate. 'That's an awful thing to say! What's wrong with you?'

Sarah glared at Luke. She had to finish this. 'I don't want you involved with my daughter.'

'How dare you talk to Luke like that! He's my friend!' Kate was shouting now.

'Really? *Friends* don't usually grope each other, do they?'

'Mum!'

'Kate!' Sarah's voice was hard. 'So long as you live under my roof, you will *not* see him. I forbid it.'

Kate glared back at her mother. 'You're sounding ridiculous! Like a Victorian. But it's easily solved. I won't live under your roof.'

That took Sarah by surprise. Luke had won the day, although to his credit, he didn't look happy about it. 'Don't go with him, Kate. Please. You'll only get hurt.'

Her appeal fell on deaf ears. Kate gently pushed Luke ahead of her out of the room and slammed the door shut behind her. The laughter and music drifting through from the conservatory seemed to mock Sarah's misery.

Kate drank the coffee Luke had made, hoping its strength would revive her. The scene with her mother had been appalling. She'd never felt so ashamed of Sarah.

'I'm really sorry about what happened, Kate.'

Luke was sitting opposite her at the kitchen table in Jack's house, his face pale with worry. The house was quiet. Everyone else was still at the party. She hadn't felt able to stay at the Leighton's, worried in case her mother tracked her down again. 'Me too,' she said. 'You should *never* have been put through that. I think she was drunk but that's still no excuse.'

'You won't really leave home, though, will you? Not because of me.'

'I'm not giving you up, Luke. Not for anybody.' She reached out her hand and he twined his fingers through hers.

'Will you stay here?'

'For tonight only.' He looked disappointed. 'It'll cause problems for Jack if I'm here. I'll stay at Tim's house. He's my friend; he'll help me out. His parents are away, but they're lovely. They won't mind. We'll be able to meet in peace there.'

And then maybe she'd get her own flat. Become independent. It was time for that. 'Hey, it's not so bad,' she told him. 'At Tim's, I'll get all my meals made, my laundry done. There's a swimming pool and tennis courts and a beautiful garden. Just like a hotel, really. I'll be living in the lap of luxury.'

Luke showed the glimmer of a smile but then he said, 'Don't cut yourself off completely from your mam, Kate. She's your flesh and blood. She thinks she's protectin' you, that's all. But she's wrong – I'd never hurt you. You know that, don't you?'

Luke's generosity towards Sarah in the wake of her ugly words was humbling. Kate felt like she might cry.

The taxi rumbled off down the drive, and Jack grabbed Emer by the hand, guiding her upstairs. When she gave a small stumble on one of the landings, he decided to sweep her up in his arms and carry her the rest of the way. He'd been waiting for this moment all evening, and it couldn't come fast enough.

Emer giggled, her head resting on his shoulder. Her face was a little flushed, but Jack knew she wasn't drunk. Nor was he. He'd been careful not to down too much alcohol, knowing he'd kick himself later if he was unable to take advantage of Emer staying overnight.

He flicked at the door handle of his bedroom and carried her inside, lowering her gently to her feet but not letting go, wrapping his arms around her waist. 'You're the best birthday present I've ever had, Emer,' he told her, stroking her face.

'Surely I can't compete with Thomas the Tank Engine – or Action Man,' she said, and it was his turn to laugh.

The moon was almost full and it spilled its glittering light over the bed. There was no need to switch the light on. They lay down and slowly undressed each other, and he adored how the moonlight bathed her body in a silvery glow. Their kisses were tender yet passionate. Jack's hands traced the lines and curves of Emer's body, wanting to know every inch of her.

They'd been building up to this moment all day, every dance and conversation pulling them closer. Of course Jack wanted the sex – what man wouldn't? – but more than that, he wanted a strong emotional bond with this woman, the kind he'd only known once before. He'd loved Caroline very much, but it had been a childhood sweetheart kind of a romance. Annie had been the true love of his life. Until now.

'Jack …' Emer murmured, pulling him out of the past and anchoring him firmly in the present.

He'd been more than ready for some time, but he let her set the pace. He'd been selfish with past girlfriends. This time it would be different. That was the wonderful thing about Emer – she made him want to be a better man.

Emer was still sleeping when Jack woke from a fitful sleep. Last night had been wonderful, and he'd been unable to stop thinking about it. Even when he did doze off, he thought about Emer and how good she made him feel – about himself, and about life. He was tired but felt he could tackle anything today. He got out of bed quietly, pulled on a T-shirt and some tracksuit bottoms, and went downstairs. He'd catch the news on TV, read the morning paper, and then cook everyone breakfast – and if Maggie came home from her sister's in time, he'd cook her one as well.

With the TV on low, Jack settled in the armchair in the living room and opened up his Sunday newspaper. A movement caught his eye, and as he lowered the paper, he saw a mound on the sofa opposite, covered in a duvet. It was moving, and Kate appeared from beneath it. She squinted at him as she opened her eyes, and winced as she tried to sit up.

'I owe you some wine,' she said. 'Sorry – got a bit blotto last night.'

'So I see,' Jack replied, with a smile.

Kate sat up, pulling the duvet around her. 'I don't remember going to sleep. Luke must have covered me up.'

'Quite the gentleman,' Jack remarked. 'It's his own – I recognise the cover.'

'Oh, no!' Kate looked horrified. 'He'll have been frozen!'

'I doubt it,' said Jack. 'The house is warm. Can I get you a hot drink?'

Kate shook her head. 'No thanks, I don't feel too well. Serves me right for drowning my sorrows.'

Jack thought about Sarah's concerns. Maybe now would be a good time to find out exactly what was happening between his maybe-son and his surrogate daughter. Over the years he'd shared Kate's tears and triumphs, trying his best to make up for the father who'd walked out when she was only days old. In the last year, though, their time together had become sporadic. University life had drawn Kate in, given her new interests, pushed her further along the road to independence. She'd needed him less and less.

'So, what's wrong, Freckles?' he asked. A nickname he'd given her years ago, when she was a spindly scrap of a thing hoisted high on his shoulders. She'd usually respond by calling him Mr Bigwig. But not today.

'I've moved out of home – or at least, that's what I'll be doing later today. Mum said I couldn't continue seeing Luke while I lived under her roof. So I said I wouldn't live under her roof anymore.'

Her expression was defiant, but Jack caught the slight tremor in her voice as she spoke. Sarah had jumped the gun – she should have waited until he'd tried to deal with it. Now it could be a much bigger mess.

'I'm sure you're very upset, Kate, but I think you should reconsider.'

'Why?'

Her frown should have told him to back off, but maybe this wasn't the time for caution. The horse had already bolted. 'Kate, you know how much I care about you. And it's because I care that I'd advise you not to get too involved with Luke.'

'God, you sound just like Mum!' exploded Kate. 'Have you two been comparing notes? What did she say to you? What's she got against Luke? What have *you* got against him – you're supposed to be his father!'

'I have nothing against him,' said Jack. 'But I don't want you hurt if he decides to move on. We don't really know anything about him.'

'He's your son. What else do you need to know?'

'I don't want to see you hurt.' Jack was repeating himself. A sure sign he was losing the battle. He should have left well alone. He was going to say the wrong things – might just as well contort himself and shove his foot right in his mouth and be done with it.

'But you aren't worried I might hurt Luke?'

Jack shook his head. 'I know you, Kate. I don't know him.'

'No, you don't, do you,' said Kate, her voice dripping disapproval, and she grabbed her bag. 'Tell Luke I'll call him later – I'm going to Tim's.' She stood up and dropped the duvet onto the sofa.

'Kate, please sit down – let's talk.'

'I've got nothing to say to you,' she said, storming out of the room.

As he heard the front door close, Jack sat back in his armchair and contemplated the disaster of the past couple of minutes. He'd handled things badly, and what in God's name did he think he was doing anyway? Last night with Emer had changed things – made him happier with the world and with life in general. He wanted to give Luke a chance, but he'd still had Sarah's objections fixed in his brain so had been on auto-pilot. He looked at the duvet, crumpled up on the sofa. Luke could have taken advantage of Kate, but hadn't. He'd looked after her, made her comfortable, and then gone to his own bed – minus his duvet. And he'd want to know why Kate had left so early. How the hell was he going to put things right – with Kate, with Luke, and with Emer if she got to hear of this latest mess?

'Are your parents enjoying their cruise?' Kate asked Tim over lunch, as he read a postcard that had just been delivered.

'They're loving it so much that they're moving on to the Mediterranean for another,' he said, passing her the card.

She could barely make out Lord Leighton's scrawl. The picture was of a tiny cruise ship sailing along the waters of a deep ravine. 'Risoyrenna,' she read out. 'Where's that?'

'Norway,' said Tim. 'Those fjords all look the same to me. I have a sneaking suspicion the captain just turns the ship around each night and sails back up the same one.'

Kate laughed. It had been the right decision to come to Tim's. All of Tim's friends seemed to turn to him in times of crisis, not least because he never judged and never demanded explanations.

'So, how are you feeling now, sweetie?' asked Tim, spearing a roll of ham.

'Still a bit fragile,' Kate admitted, 'but being able to stay here has taken a load off my mind. Cheers, Tim.' Sarah had thankfully been asleep when Kate had called by at the cottage earlier to pack a suitcase.

'I shall put you in the Blue Room with its enormous four-poster bed and let it work its magic,' declared Tim. 'It never fails. Although that's not strictly true. George III slept there in 1788 and began to lose his marbles not long after.'

'I know how he felt. It was such a terrible row with my mum.' Kate sighed and thought back to the previous evening, and her mother's ugly words. Words that had wounded Luke. 'Why is Mum so set against Luke? She doesn't even know him.'

'This is Baronsmere, remember? Riddled with class issues. If the background doesn't fit …'

'I hate all that,' said Kate, feeling tearful. 'And this morning, Jack was horrible about Luke, too. What should I do?'

'Bring Luke over here,' said Tim, scanning through the newspaper headlines. 'You can shag him all night, undisturbed.'

'Tim! That's not what I meant! Get your mind out of the gutter. I meant what should I do about Mum?'

'Stay here for a couple of days. Give her time to think about things and to miss you. Then call and see how the land lies. I bet she'll have changed her tune.'

'Impossible,' Kate murmured.

'Now look, Kate,' Tim said, his tone stern. 'When I told my parents, Lord and Lady Leighton, paragons of the church and stalwarts of the Conservative Party, that I was gay, my mother took to her bed for weeks in shock, and my father didn't speak to me for ten months. I thought it was impossible they'd ever come round, but they did. If my parents finally saw reason and accepted me, then you can persuade your mother to accept Luke. Just give her some time.'

'Timothy Leighton, when did you get to be so wise?' said Kate, looking at him, fondly.

'I watch Jeremy Kyle a lot,' he admitted.

Kate smiled, feeling a little better, and got up to leave.

'Right then, I'm off. Luke and I are going to Chester – take our minds off what's happened.' On impulse, she turned back and hugged Tim. 'Thanks for everything. I love you.'

Tim's voice was muffled. 'I love you too, Katie – but your boobs are in my face, and it's not pleasant.'

She giggled, and released him.

'Kate?' She was nearly at the door when he called her back.

'Yes, Tim?'

'If you decide you don't want Luke ... I'll have him.'

'Dream on!' she called as she left, feeling much happier knowing she wouldn't have to give in and go back home. And even better, she and Luke could have some privacy here. Maybe that would be some compensation for this mess.

Chapter Sixteen

Luke counted about forty people in Marsham's Community Centre. Not bad for five o'clock on a wet Thursday.

'The local paper just ran a big feature on the Woodlands development,' Kate told him. 'Painted big business in a bad light. Obviously it got a lot of people concerned.'

It meant the world to Luke that Kate had come along, that she wasn't just talk. After Sarah flying off the handle, Luke had worried Kate would call it all off, but here she was, supporting his interest in the protest against the Stewart Enterprises venture. Still, he didn't like coming between a girl and her mother, and every day he kept waiting for Sarah to come round to Jack's house and bawl him out.

A young man in faded jeans and denim jacket appeared up front and introduced himself as Duncan Gilroy. Soon everyone in the hall was listening to his passionate call for support to fight the development. When Duncan mentioned Stewart Enterprises, Luke slouched lower in his seat, uncomfortable at the mention of the Stewart name. Guilty by association.

'The residents in the riverside houses have been offered a compensation package which is at least a tenth of the profit Stewart Enterprises will ultimately recoup on each property,' Duncan informed them. 'It's proposed the residents be allowed first refusal, but the reality is they'll be unable to afford even a single-bedroom flat in the new development. Those who choose not to move will find themselves living in a messy, noisy building site, their allotments swallowed up by garages and car parks, and noise and air pollution dramatically increased. The new buildings will dwarf their houses, blocking out sunlight and any view.

'And finally,' he said, 'there are plans to build new roads to connect the riverfront properties with the rest of the Woodlands area. That will mean destroying a large portion of Cullens Wood, which is ironic given the name of the development. Those woods have been standing for hundreds of years. So,' he finished, his gaze sweeping over the audience, 'does anyone have any questions?'

There were lots of questions. Luke learned that twenty-three of the thirty households on the riverside had signed a contract, all living in a block, so Stewart Enterprises could go ahead and build, even though the other residents might protest. Social housing quotas had already been filled for that area, so the council would do nothing. It looked like those who didn't want the development were royally screwed.

An elderly woman got unsteadily to her feet. 'I'm one of the residents. I've lived at the riverfront all my life. I saw a brother go off to war and never come back. I raised two children in my home, and buried a husband from it. And now they want to push me out.' Her voice shook. 'Well, I won't let them. It's not right …' Tears spilled onto her cheeks, and Duncan moved to her side, putting a comforting hand on her shoulder. She reminded Luke of Jessie.

'Thank you, Rose,' Duncan said. 'It's for people like you we're fighting this.'

'There's a Stewart here,' said a man standing near the door. Luke recognised him as the one who'd been delivering leaflets in the pub. He pointed a finger right at Luke and heads turned. So much for anonymity. It was embarrassing. 'That's Jack Stewart's son. I'd like to know what the little rich boy's doing here, slumming it.'

If he hadn't felt so awkward, Luke would have laughed aloud at being called a little rich boy.

'Spying, probably,' someone hissed.

'He supports this protest, you idiot!' snapped Kate.

'Can't he speak for himself then?' came the response. 'Or do the Stewarts hire someone for that, too?'

Luke eased himself up. The audience looked at him, some with curiosity, some with suspicion. The room was silent except for the hum and click of the heating system. Luke swallowed hard. It was only the second time in his life that he was speaking in public, but there was no way this was worse than his mother's funeral so would surely be easier.

'I'm Luke Kiernan,' he said. 'I don't use the name Stewart. My parents separated before I was born. I grew up in Ireland – as a Traveller. Travellers get pushed round by councils and the police. Our culture is always under threat so I can understand people tryin' to hold on to what they've got. And I don't agree with this development – everythin' about it seems greedy and just plain wrong, and I'll help you fight it, if you let me.'

'What about your father, Luke?' asked Duncan. 'Won't this cause problems for you?'

'I'm an adult. I make my own decisions.'

'How do we know you won't tell him our plans?' someone asked.

'This is a public meetin', nothin' secret,' Luke said. 'And if Jack wanted to send a spy, it'd be stupid to send me.'

People nodded in agreement.

'Thank you, Luke,' said Duncan. 'We didn't mean to put you on the spot, but emotions are running high tonight.'

'No problem,' said Luke, sitting down again. Kate grabbed his hand and squeezed it like she was proud of him, but his heart was thumping and he hoped attention would move away from him. He didn't know what he could do to help, but he wasn't going to back out. Rose had decided him. One old woman bullied by men with power. It wasn't right. He was sure Annie would approve of him helping.

'Did you not like it, love?'

'It's grand, Maggie. I'm just not that hungry.'

Luke had left most of his dinner untouched. Jack had noticed him not eating, but kept quiet because the fact that they were all having dinner together was a first and he didn't want to be the one to spoil it. Usually Luke chose to eat in his room, but Matt had told Jack yesterday he wanted them all to spend more time together as a family.

'Give it here,' Matt said, and he shovelled Luke's leftovers onto his own plate. 'I've only had nuts and crisps all day. Stuck in the bowels of the pub, stocktaking. Now the builders are here, Sarah wants to know every last can and bottle we've got in case they decide to help themselves.'

Sarah was not a safe topic when Luke was around. Any mention of her usually sent him out of the room. Jack was none too keen on hearing her mentioned either. 'So, Maggie, how's the baking going for May Day?' This was surely a safe topic. 'I heard Lillian Hooper in the bank boasting her rock cakes are going to triumph.'

'That'll be a first,' declared Maggie. 'Last year the mayor almost lost a tooth. I think she uses real rocks.'

'What happens on May Day?' asked Luke.

'Oh, all sorts of things,' Matt told him. 'Drinking, feasting, wenching. Sacrifice of a virgin. Just your average village get-together.'

'There are competitions for the best home-grown produce,' Maggie added, 'and games for the children. Riding events, Morris dancing, wrestling, tug-of-war. And they choose a May Queen.'

'Our Katie was May Queen when she was sweet sixteen,' said Matt, with a sly glance at Luke, who blushed right on cue.

The front doorbell chimed. 'I'll get it,' Jack said, leaving the warm kitchen for the always slightly chilly hall. He prayed the visitor wouldn't be Sarah. She'd phoned him a few times since Kate had left home. He'd responded to her tearful concern about her daughter with the advice to be patient and not push her.

It wasn't Sarah. It was Nicholas. Looking furious. Jack wondered if a deal had fallen through. 'Dad! I wasn't expecting you. Come in …'

His father was over the threshold before the invitation had been uttered. 'We have a problem, Jack. About Woodlands. You remember that the protest meeting took place tonight?'

Jack hadn't remembered because his day had been spent out of the office on a construction site. 'Did Lynda go to the meeting as arranged?'

'She's just reported back to me. And what an eye-opener it's been. Where's the Kiernan boy?'

'Sorry?'

'He has some explaining to do.'

Jack's heart sank. He had no idea what his father was talking about, but anything involving him and Luke couldn't be good. Matt's voice floated out into the hallway and in a few strides Nicholas had entered the kitchen. Jack followed.

'Well now,' Nicholas said, surveying the room. 'I'm sorry to disturb this cosy family dinner.'

'Lamb casserole's all finished,' muttered Maggie, stacking plates.

'Granddad, is everything okay?

'No, Matt, everything is very far from okay.'

'Do you want to talk in the study?' asked Jack. He'd expected Luke to get up and walk out of the room as soon as his grandfather appeared, but no such luck tonight.

'This is something that concerns everyone,' declared Nicholas. 'Do you know what this boy has been up to?' He flung his hand in Luke's direction. 'Today, there was a protest meeting in Marsham. Agitators planning how to disrupt Stewart Enterprises' Woodlands development.'

Matt frowned. 'What does that have to do with Luke?'

'I was there,' Luke said calmly.

Jack wanted to put his head in his hands. Whatever happened next wasn't likely to help family unity. 'You were there? Why?'

'To publicly announce his opposition.' Nicholas read from a piece of paper he'd taken from his pocket. '*Everything about it seems greedy and just plain wrong, and I will help you fight it.* Is that an accurate quote?'

Luke tilted his head to the side, his finger on his chin, giving the comment blatantly mock consideration. 'Hmm, pretty much.'

Jack stared at Luke. The kid certainly had guts. But he was also insane. Nobody took on Nicholas Stewart and got away with it. It just wasn't done.

'So you did have a spy there,' Luke continued.

'Damn right!' growled Nicholas, almost shaking now, his face flushing with anger. 'And lucky we did or we'd have had no idea about the extent of your backstabbing treachery!'

There was a jangle of cutlery in the sink. Maggie had her back turned to the scene but her tensed shoulders spoke volumes.

'Granddad!' cried Matt. 'It was a public meeting, and this is a free country.'

Nicholas kept going. 'He took Kate Walker with him too. You see how it starts, Jack? Before long this – this – trash will turn everyone against us. Who's next in line, I wonder – Matt?'

'You're going to manage that without Luke's help,' Matt told him. 'My brother is not trash.'

Nicholas snorted. 'Your brother? So he claims.'

'That's enough, Dad,' Jack said, but the enormity of what Luke had done started to sink in. 'Can't you see how this could hurt the family? You're part of the Stewarts now, Luke, like it or not. We need to stick together.'

Luke shot him a venomous look. 'Oh, when it looks like I might do some damage, I'm suddenly a Stewart? Well, maybe I don't want to be part of a family that doesn't give a shit about people.'

'Come on, Luke, you don't mean that ...' Matt pleaded.

'Oh, I'm sure he does,' said Nicholas. 'Easy come, easy go. Just like his mother.'

He'd gone too far. Best if his father left now. They could continue this discussion tomorrow at the office.

'So what now, *Sir* Nicholas?' Luke spat out the title contemptuously. 'Are you goin' to try to pay me off like you did her? You'll find I can't be bought either.'

There was a terrible silence in the room as everyone absorbed what they'd just heard. Jack was first to speak. 'What the hell does that mean?'

Luke jabbed a finger in Nicholas's direction. 'He offered my mother money to leave here.'

'Dad?' asked Jack, desperate for some explanation.

'I'm not staying here to listen to baseless accusations. I've said what I came to say. Fifty years I've spent building up this business, and I'm not going to stand by while some worthless little no-mark tries to destroy it.'

Before anyone could speak, Nicholas turned and left the room. His shoes could be heard clicking in the hallway, then the front door slammed and he was gone. They were all silent for a moment. Maggie looked upset. Matt was shaken. Luke stared at the door, his expression unreadable.

'Luke, that's a very serious accusation,' said Jack, eventually.

'It's not an accusation, it's the truth. He tried to bribe her to go. She told me they never wanted her here. I saw the cheque. Fifty grand. And in case you're wonderin', Mam never cashed it. As if she would.'

'Annie told you this?' Jack asked. When the hell had that

happened? Could that have been the reason why Annie left?

'I saw it. I found it in a book of Mam's. She said she'd rather have starved than cash it. She didn't realise how hard things would get, though – by the time they did, it was too late to cash it anyway.'

'Do you still have it?'

'What's the matter, Jack? You want proof your wife wasn't a liar? Or me? More likely to be the pikeys lyin' than Sir Nicholas Stewart, right? And I suppose you'll deny you wrote to Mam telling her you didn't want her – or me.'

'That's enough, Luke!' snapped Jack. 'How could I write to your mother when I didn't know where she was? If she told you that, she lied. This isn't some sort of game, you know. Or is it? Is that what you're doing – playing us all off against one another for some sort of revenge?' That seemed much more likely than Nicholas trying to pay Annie off. His father would have known she'd tell Jack about it. Would he have risked a major argument?

Luke ran his hands through his hair, scowling. 'What's the point? I know you're lyin'. I can't prove it now – but I will.'

Jack was now feeling beyond angry. 'I said that's enough! I don't want to hear another word about cheques or letters – if you want to continue living here, you'll start treating this family with a bit of respect.'

'Dad!' Matt shot Jack a warning glance.

Luke put up his hand. 'No, Matt, let him say what he's really feelin'. Better than bein' a hypocrite like Old Nick.'

'This is my house and I won't just stand here while my family is insulted!'

'*Trash. Worthless no-mark.*' said Luke. 'Thanks for provin' your precious family doesn't include me. You never wanted me here in the first place. I'm just an embarrassment.'

'Luke ...' Matt stood up and tried to put a hand on his brother's shoulder, but it was shrugged off.

'I won't trouble you any longer,' Luke said. 'I should never have come here in the first place. My mistake.'

'Luke, please ...' Maggie was crying, and Luke's expression softened slightly.

'Maggie, it's just not workin'. I'll go in the mornin'.' He turned to Jack. 'And if you don't want to hear about the cheque and letter from me, you might just read about them in the newspapers. You'll find this trash is hard to get rid of.'

With that threat, he left the room. Maggie dropped down into a chair. 'Do you think it's true, Jack? That Nicholas tried to buy Annie off? It might explain ...'

Jack shook his head as if to wake himself from some stupor. 'His mother filled his head with God knows what. She obviously lied about me writing to her – who's to say she didn't lie to him about this, too?'

'He says he saw the cheque, though,' Matt reminded him, 'and you not believing him pushed him over the edge.'

'Come on, Matt. He can't expect to drop a bombshell like that without knowing we'd want proof.'

'It might be unreasonable, but I think he just wanted one show of unconditional support – and if what he says is true, then this has been simmering away and was bound to boil over at some point. If he takes this to the press, they'll have a field day.'

'It'll be his word against Nicholas's,' said Jack.

'Unless he's still got the cheque.'

Jack and Matt stared at each other. That was an uncomfortable thought.

Luke sat by his bedroom window, packed carrier bags at his feet. He could hear dishes clanking as Maggie prepared breakfast, then he saw Jack leave for work. Sometime later, Maggie left for the supermarket. Matt would still be sleeping. It was safe now to get some tea and wait for Kate.

Except it wasn't safe because Matt was in the kitchen. No chance of escape, either. He'd looked up the minute the door opened. 'Hey, bro – tea or coffee?'

'Tea … thanks,' mumbled Luke.

With any luck Kate would arrive soon. The last thing Luke needed was an awkward conversation with Matt. He was done talking to the Stewarts.

'You waiting for a bus or what?' asked Matt, glancing round at him. 'Take a pew.'

Luke remained standing. 'Kate's pickin' me up. We're stayin' at Tim's for a bit.'

Matt turned round, disappointment on his face. Luke felt a pang of sadness. Leaving his brother was going to be tough.

'Luke, I know Granddad was out of order last night. He always has to feel he's in control …'

'Well, he's not goin' to control me.'

Matt nodded, looking thoughtful. 'Why did you go to that meeting?'

It seemed more question than accusation. Maybe Luke could win Matt over. 'Matt, people are goin' to be forced out of their homes so's Stewart Enterprises can build high-rise eyesores for profit – *and* ruin a beautiful area in the process. I don't agree with that.'

'I understand that – really I do, but there are others ready to try and stop it. Why do you have to be one of them?'

'Why shouldn't I be?'

'Don't play dumb, Luke – you know why. Look what's happened already. A big argument, and you're moving out.'

'I didn't start the argument.'

'Well, in a way you did – by going to the meeting.'

'I have a right to choose what I do.'

'We're just going round in circles ...'

They were interrupted by a click. Saved by the electric kettle. Matt finished making the tea, then sat down at the table and pushed a cup in Luke's direction. Luke stayed where he was by the door. 'Don't go, Luke.' Matt was almost pleading. 'I know it's not been easy, but these things take time. We all need to get to know each other and learn how to live together.'

It was time for honesty. 'I don't think I *can* learn to live with Jack. I don't think I want to.'

'Could you at least give it a try for a few more days?'

Luke tutted in frustration. 'I'm sick of tryin'! Every time I do, I get accusations flung in my face – I stole a necklace, I'm not Jack's son, I'm turnin' people against the family. What's it to you, anyway? You're busy and not around much. I've had enough. I'm sorry but I'm leavin'.'

'Did you mean what you said yesterday,' asked Matt, 'about going to the press?'

'If people push me too far, I will.'

'I don't think that's a good idea ...'

Luke bristled. 'Course you don't! What you want is for everyone to bow down and do as they're told.'

'No, Luke. That isn't what I meant,' said Matt. 'If you get in the papers, your uncles might track you down.'

Fear settled at the back of Luke's neck like a cold hand. He hadn't thought about Joe much lately. Could he really find him? Especially if he was no longer staying at Jack's. He spoke with more bravado than he actually felt. 'I guess that's a risk I'll have to take.'

'Well then, it's a risk we're all taking. Including Kate. Remember, there's thirty thousand euros still in the safe in my room. If your uncles are looking for it, the trail could lead to us eventually.'

'I was tryin' to get rid of it when you stopped me, Matt! Bring it here and I'll burn it – end of problem.'

Matt shook his head. 'That's not a solution. We agreed it could be evidence. You need to keep it. And if you did burn it, your uncles wouldn't know, would they? They'd still be looking for you. I've no problem with it being in the safe – our house is secure enough – but just be careful about going to the press. Okay?'

Luke stared at his brother. 'Why do I feel you've backed me into a corner? I guess manipulation is a Stewart trait.'

'If it is, you've inherited it!' snapped Matt. 'How would you describe what you threatened to do?'

'That's not manipulation! That's tryin' to get justice – for me and my mam!'

'At any cost?'

Matt didn't get it. How could he? He was a Stewart, one of them. Luke had been fooling himself if he believed his older brother would protect and defend him. 'We're never goin' to agree. It's best if I go.'

Matt looked disappointed. 'At least think on what I've said.'

The doorbell rang. At last. Luke turned to go.

'Take care of yourself. Call if you need me – any time. I'm still your big brother.'

'Bye, Matt,' mumbled Luke. 'Thanks for everythin'.' He didn't look back. Couldn't look back. How many more losses would he have to face?

'Jack didn't believe me.'

Kate glanced from the road to Luke's troubled face. They were two orphans of the storm. Both at odds with their parents. Things seemed to be going from bad to worse.

'He wanted proof even though I told him I'd seen the cheque.'

There was frustration and hurt in Luke's voice, and no wonder. Kate was shocked to hear what Nicholas had said, but even more shocked at Jack's failure to defend his son. 'Why did your mother keep it?'

'Proof he'd done it. Proof she was no gold-digger. That she couldn't be bought.'

'I suppose you didn't bring it with you,' said Kate, 'or you'd have shown it to Jack last night.'

'Even if I *had* brought it, I wouldn't have let him see it. My word should be enough.'

And in an ideal world it would be. But this was real life. Where people attacked each other with cruel words.

'Are you okay, Kate?' Luke asked, his voice gentler now.

'I'm fine,' she lied, squeezing his hand. 'Let's hope this will all blow over.'

'You shouldn't be in this position, though. Fallin' out with your mam because of me – someone you hardly know.'

She reached out and stroked his cheek. 'I do know you. And we're a couple now.'

He caught her hand and kissed it. 'A right pair, more like. Both of us leavin' home in a cob.'

As she drove along the familiar route, Kate avoided looking at the Foresters Arms, but tears still pricked her eyes anyway and she was relieved when they arrived at Leighton Hall. She rolled down the car window and aimed a remote control at the closed iron gates. They creaked open and Kate drove through.

As she parked in front of the porticoed entrance, Tim bounded down the steps, followed by Edward, the Leighton's butler. Tim gave Kate a bony hug and Luke a reassuring slap on the back.

'Leave your stuff in the car,' he told them. 'Teddy will take it in. It's a bit of a climb.' He indicated the flight of steps leading up to the front door. 'No point in you overdoing it,

Luke, so I've had the brilliant idea of putting you both in the dower cottage near the back gates. We'll move you there this afternoon. No stairs at all, and you'll get your privacy.' He winked at Kate, and she felt herself blush.

'Teddy!' Tim called back to the butler who was emptying the car of its bags. 'Do we still have that antique sedan chair? We could carry young Luke around in that.'

Edward's face remained impassive. 'I'm afraid not, sir. The chair broke three winters ago when you tried to use it as a sled on Hartswood Hill.'

Kate failed to restrain a snort of laughter at the ridiculous vision the butler's words conjured up.

'Ah yes, so I did,' said Tim. 'Thank you, Teddy.' As they moved up the steps, Tim whispered, 'That's the thing about servants. They see and remember everything. Ma's so terrified Ted'll write a book about us that she gives him a whopping pay rise every year. I should think he earns more than your average CEO by now.'

'She's probably paying him to keep quiet about *you*, Tim,' said Kate. 'I don't think your parents have ever done anything scandalous.'

'Well, there was one shocking incident shortly after they were married ...' began Tim. By the time they entered the grand hall, Kate was relieved to see Luke was laughing. Tim's warm welcome had pushed aside the pain of rejection – for now at least.

'Thanks, Maggie. I'll be home about seven.'

Before she hung up, Maggie made a barbed comment about Jack being lucky to have a home, unlike some people – obviously a reference to Luke. She'd phoned in a huff to tell him Luke had gone to stay with Kate at Tim's.

Jack mulled over what Luke had said about the cheque. Knowing how much Grace and Nicholas had disapproved of Annie, there was a ring of truth about it, but it still seemed far-fetched. Not his father's usual style. If there was a cheque, why hadn't Annie said something? Or had this all happened while he was in Brussels?

Luke's outburst had raised a lot of questions, but the kid was unreliable. Hot-headed and grief-stricken. The businessman in Jack wouldn't let him throw baseless accusations around, particularly at Nicholas. They all needed to take a deep breath and step back from the brink. Having a timeout from Jack would probably be good for Luke.

And Jack would have his own timeout in – he glanced at his watch – twelve hours or so. A weekend with Emer in Ireland would be a welcome lull in this never-ending family battle.

Chapter Seventeen

'Shit!' muttered Kate. It hadn't been the best idea to try and lock her car and keep hold of the pile of leaflets she'd just had printed, some of which now lay strewn at her feet. At least it wasn't raining.

'Need a hand?'

Kate looked round to see Matt bent down beside her, helping. 'Where did you spring from?'

'The pub,' Matt replied. 'Saw you through the window. I came to ask Tony if we can hold the karaoke there next week. And I've just ordered myself a Ploughman's – the noise of the builders at The Foresters is doing my head in.'

'I've come to give Tony these leaflets about the next protest meeting,' Kate told him. 'He's on our side. Unlike my mum. Anyway, I've got the afternoon off now – can I join you for lunch?'

'Cool,' said Matt, holding open the door for her. 'It'll be good to catch up.'

'I'll be glad when you and your mum sort it out,' said Matt, spearing a chip from Kate's plate. 'She's unbearable at the moment. Finding fault with everything. I'm surprised the workmen haven't downed tools.'

'What do you suggest, Matt? We can't move forward unless she changes her attitude. She objects to me being with Luke and I'm sad – ashamed – to say I think she's a bigot.'

Matt nodded. 'Unfortunately, I can't disagree. And to be honest, Kate, it's made me reassess my position. Luke's my brother. I don't know how to work for someone who's so plainly against him. I'm seriously considering moving on. You know how much I've always wanted to run my own place eventually, maybe in Manchester.' He winked at her. 'Somewhere upmarket, where the girls are falling over themselves to pull the owner. And then I could give Luke a job – maybe we could even become partners.'

'I don't know if Luke would want that kind of work,' said Kate. 'He'd more likely want something outdoors, or with animals. He regrets not finishing his education.'

'He could still do that. I just want to spend more time with him – be a proper big brother. I should have been doing more for him, fitting in around him, not expecting it to be the other way round. I want him to see the Stewarts aren't as bad as he thinks.'

Kate picked up a spoon and put it in the sugar bowl, stirring the loose grains – it was something she'd done as a child, especially when stressed. 'I'm sorry, Matt – I know they're your grandparents, but Nicholas and Grace are every bit as bad as he thinks. And … and I'm having second thoughts about your dad.'

'Hello, you two. Can I tempt you with my apple crumble?'

Barbara Hayes was in her fifties but looked younger. Kate liked Barbara. Her son, Kevin, had been one of her friends at primary school and they'd sometimes piled back here for cake and lemonade after school. Barbara had been a full-time mother as well as helping Tony in the pub, but she was always there for her three kids. Not that Sarah had been a bad mother, but she always seemed to be busy with something or other, whether work or her love life. Kate had got used to being sent for 'holidays' at Jack's, where Maggie would look after her. Kate had heard it whispered more than once that her kind heart and thoughtfulness was down to Maggie, not Sarah.

'Apple crumble sounds good to me, Barb,' said Kate. 'As long as it's with that wonderful custard you make – the one you won't let my mum have the recipe for.'

Barbara tapped the side of her nose. 'Wild horses, Kate …'

'Barb,' said Matt. 'Have you got a minute?'

After calling to Tony for the two puddings, Barbara sat down next to Kate. 'It's nice to get off my feet for a bit. You should have brought Luke with you. It would have been nice to see him again. I didn't really get a chance to talk to him at the funeral. How's he doing?'

Matt sighed. 'Keep this to yourself, but Luke's moved out.'

'Ah,' she nodded, not seeming too surprised. 'Was that your grandparents' doing?'

Kate gave Matt a sidelong glance. That was too near the truth – had someone been gossiping already?

'Why do you say that?' Matt asked.

Barbara picked up a beer mat and started tapping it lightly on the table. 'Because they made his mother's life a misery. Your grandparents thought Annie was the wrong class and never let her forget it.'

'How do you mean exactly?'

Kate wanted the answer to that too, but she hoped Matt wouldn't regret asking the question.

'Maybe it's not a good idea raking over the past, Matt,' said Barbara. 'It was all such a long time ago. It's not really my place to say.'

'Annie was my stepmother, and a pretty good one from what I remember. She walked out when I was four and it was as if she'd died. No one talked about her after that – I mean *really* talked about her. Now Luke's here and I'm worried the same thing's going to happen. I don't want to lose him, too.'

Kate fought back the lump in her throat. Matt really cared about Luke, she knew that now. She reached out for his hand, squeezing it gently.

'Please tell me, Barb – what did my grandparents do?'

Kate had the feeling she was going to hear things she

wouldn't like. Maybe things even Luke didn't know. It felt a bit like she was delving, uninvited, into his background and that wasn't a comfortable feeling. How would she feel if someone did the same to her?

Kate and Matt listened in silence as Barbara told them how Grace and Nicholas refused to attend Jack and Annie's wedding, persuading others to opt out, too. How Grace stopped the long-standing tradition of Sunday family lunch, and refused to visit Matt at home, insisting Jack – and Jack alone – brought him to see her at Edenbridge once a week.

They heard about the time Jack took Annie to Grace's birthday celebration. Annie took a small gift of her own as a gesture to her mother-in-law that she wanted them to get on; it was found later, unopened, in a nearby bin, so visible it was obviously intended for her to see. Then Barbara recalled how Annie had gone with Maggie to his kindergarten play because Jack was away on business. They'd been placed right at the back of the hall, away from Grace and Nicholas seated at the front.

'If it had just been Grace on her own, I don't think it would have been so bad,' Barbara reflected, 'but many took their lead from her. Ignoring Annie in the street, even crossing the road to avoid her. She did some home baking for May Day, but it was put to one side with loud comments about it being unclean. No matter what she did, those snooty bitches froze her out. And then when Annie tried to set up reading sessions for low income children, Grace used her influence with the local magistrate to put a stop to it because she said Annie wasn't suitably qualified. I sometimes wonder if that wasn't the final straw. She told me she was going to confront Grace about it. I don't know if she did, but she left soon after.'

Matt looked shell-shocked. 'Why didn't my father do something to stop it?' he asked.

Barbara shrugged. 'Annie never told Jack about most of it. She hoped with time they'd accept her. Annie loved Jack – and you – very much. And he loved her. Was besotted with her. I think if he'd known everything that was going on, he'd have taken you both away. He'd have moved heaven and earth to make her happy. And she knew that. She talked to me but made me promise not to tell Jack for that very reason – she didn't want Jack to be at odds with the family.'

'Family is very important to Travellers,' murmured Kate. 'Luke told me that.'

'Are you okay, Matt?' asked Barbara, touching his arm. 'I'm sorry if I've upset you but you wanted to know.'

'Yes, I did,' he reassured her. 'And thanks for telling me.'

'Promise me one thing, both of you,' Barbara said as she stood up to leave. 'Take care of Luke. I wouldn't want Annie's son to have to go through the same nightmare she did.'

'We will,' said Kate, feeling anger on Luke's behalf and pity for Annie Kiernan. She was sick to her stomach thinking how a young girl had been treated by people Kate had known all her life, people she thought she knew. When Tony appeared and placed the apple crumbles in front of them, Kate pushed hers away. Her appetite had gone.

'You're right, Kate. The Stewarts *are* as bad as Luke thinks,' said Matt, taking a half-hearted bite at the pudding. 'My grandparents have always been snobs, but I believed they were still decent people at heart. How wrong I was.'

'And not only that, Matt,' said Kate, delving once more into the sugar bowl, 'we still don't know why Annie turned Luke against Jack. Was she angry with him for not doing more? What happened to make her leave without a word and never come back?'

Jack closed the front door behind him, feeling the Friday evening relief of the working week over and the weekend beckoning. It was Maggie's evening off but there'd be a plate of something in the fridge to heat up. That and a cold beer and whatever was on the TV would be just great.

Jack hung up his coat and greeted the dogs. On the way to the kitchen, he heard music coming from the living room. Matt was usually at the Foresters on a Friday evening, but of course it was closed because of the renovations for the nightclub.

He went through to say hello. Matt was sprawled on the sofa, drinking a beer, watching some reality singing show. He lowered the volume.

'What a day.' Jack collapsed into an armchair, loosening his tie. 'Stuck in a room with a bunch of finance people. How was yours?'

'Stuck in a bar with a bunch of noisy builders, though I had lunch at The Feathers, with Kate.'

A seemingly innocuous remark, but Matt looked like he had something else on his mind. Since Luke's arrival, ordinary conversations with no agenda appeared to be a thing of the past. 'How's Tony? Did you manage to get a word in?'

'Didn't see much of him. We had a long chat with Barbara, though.'

Jack was tired but supposed he should show an interest. Prepare to hear about whatever gossip was rife at The Feathers these days. 'What did Barb have to say then?'

'We talked about the old days.'

'What old days?'

'When Annie was here.'

Now Matt had Jack's full attention. 'I wish you hadn't done that.'

'Why?' Matt's tone was sharp. 'She was my mother for a while – why shouldn't I learn about her? You don't talk about her. You've never wanted to. All those years ago when she left, I thought it was my fault. Maggie was the one who persuaded me it wasn't. You always sent me to my room whenever I asked about Annie, so I learned not to.'

Jack knew there was truth in that, but putting the past behind him had been the only way he knew how to survive. He explained that now to Matt, adding, 'If you need to know something, ask me. Best if we keep it within the family. There's nothing anyone else can tell you about Annie that I can't.'

'I'm not so sure about that.'

'What do you mean?' It was Jack's turn to be sharp. 'What exactly did Barbara say?'

'She told me about the way Gran and Granddad treated her.'

Jack shook his head. 'God, that's ancient history! Everyone knows they found it difficult to accept Annie. But it's over and done with and can't be changed. What's the point of bringing it all up again?'

'Because the same thing is happening to Luke, but you don't see it. You don't *want* to see it.'

'Matt, I can't force your grandparents to accept Luke. All we can do is limit his contact with them.'

'Okay, but have you phoned Luke or gone to see him?'

'Of course not. I've been at work all day.'

'Okay then, why don't you go over to see him now?'

'No. I'm exhausted, Matt. Can we please talk about this tomorrow?'

'Dad, Luke needs to know we support him right now.' Matt was sounding impatient. 'I'll come with you.'

Jack sighed. 'Matt, Luke doesn't want to see me. He resents me – hates me even – and I haven't done anything to deserve that.'

'No?' challenged Matt. 'Hearing him called trash and saying nothing, and then having the nerve to tell him not to insult your family?'

Matt was right about that. Had things gone too far now for anything to be reclaimed? 'I'm not going to see Luke so he can use me as an emotional punchbag.'

'Dad, he's your son.'

'Maybe ...' Jack said this quietly, almost to himself, but Matt heard.

'What did you say?'

'I said he *may* be my son. I don't know that for sure.'

'I don't believe I'm hearing this!'

'Oh, come on, Matt. Don't be naïve. You know it's a possibility. Sometimes you can't just accept things on blind faith.' That's what Jack had done up till now. Never raised the issue of a DNA test with Luke because the kid had been grief-stricken and injured – and partly because Jack himself was afraid to know the truth.

'You don't want Luke to be your son, do you? You're really hoping he's not. I think you're glad he left!'

Matt's accusations were so close to the mark. Jack had been wrestling with this dilemma on and off ever since he'd learned about Luke. If a DNA test confirmed he was Jack's son, then there might be something to build on there. However, if the test revealed Jack wasn't the father, then he'd have to live with the hard evidence that Annie had betrayed him. Perhaps it would be better not to continue dwelling in uncertainty, though.

'I'm going to ask Luke to take a DNA test,' Jack announced.

Matt's expression was one of shock, incredulity. 'Luke's left home – he's upset, he's angry, he's still mourning his mother, and he's far from fit – and you want to kick him when he's down.'

'I need to know the truth, Matt. I need to know if Annie left me because she had an affair. It's eating me up inside.' It was hard for Jack to voice aloud the feelings he'd kept under wraps since he'd been hit with this whole bloody mess, but it was time for everyone to face reality. Luke might not be a Stewart.

'So you'll have a DNA test to make you feel better. Even if it turns Luke against you.'

Matt's voice was dripping with contempt, and Jack almost lost his nerve. Almost. 'Luke's already moved out. He's not talking to me. Now he's involved with this protest against Stewart Enterprises. How could things get any worse?'

'And if it turns out he's not your son – what then?' Matt was watching him closely.

'He'll still be Annie's son. I'll see he's okay.'

'Yeah – right.' Matt got up from the sofa and left the living room, slamming the door behind him. Now he'd sulk because Jack had put a question mark over the one thing he'd always wanted – a brother. A need that had made Matt blindly accept Luke as his own flesh and blood. And now Jack would be painted as the bad guy because he couldn't put on the greatest acting performance since Olivier's Hamlet and accept Luke without question. Asking for a DNA test was a hell of a risk to take. Being the only one willing to face the truth could make Jack a very lonely man. He'd postpone his decision till Monday. The weekend spent with Emer would calm him and help him see things with greater clarity.

Kate stepped out of the bathroom wearing pyjama shorts that emphasised her slim legs, and a thin top that left little to the imagination. This was the moment she'd been dreaming about since she'd met Luke. Lust at first sight had deepened into love, and she was sure he felt the same. Now they were alone in their own space, with no parents around to disapprove.

'I've got something for you,' she said. Luke was in bed, eyeing her with obvious appreciation.

'So I see,' he replied.

She giggled and threw a key to him.

'What's this?'

'The key to Betsy's heart,' she teased. 'Betsy is Tim's old car – a nice little Corsa. He said you can use it whenever you want.'

'You're kiddin'!'

'Absolutely not. And don't you go getting all hung up on charity or whatever. Tim just wants you to feel a bit independent.'

'Will I phone him now to thank him?'

Kate slipped between the sheets and took the key, placing it on the bedside table. 'No, you won't.'

For a moment, they just looked at each other. 'Hello, handsome,' she whispered, placing her hand against his cheek and leaning forward to kiss him. His response was soft, gentle, increasing in passion, and Kate pushed him back against the pillows as she kissed his neck and throat. She wasn't his first but she was determined to be his last – and best. She moved slowly down his body, caressing his arms and shoulders, and planting light, teasing kisses on his chest. Luke's breathing was becoming rapid. Her hand lingered on a circular scar on his shoulder. 'Poor baby,' she whispered. 'How did you get that?'

Luke gently pulled her hands away from his body and whispered, 'Let's just cuddle tonight, okay?'

For a moment, she thought he was teasing, playing hard to get, but once she saw the anxiety in Luke's eyes, she knew something was wrong. The atmosphere had changed abruptly from playfulness to an edgy tension. Everything had been fine until she touched the scar.

'Okay.' Kate settled in the crook of his arm. His heart was pounding. Something had really upset him. The scar looked like a burn, but he obviously didn't want to talk about it. He'd been through so much. She'd have to be patient, not pressure him. She could do that, couldn't she?

She placed her hand on his chest, a gesture of affection

and protection. And reassurance. 'I love you, Luke,' she whispered. His eyes were closed.

Luke lay on the bed, praying for sleep that wouldn't come. He was afraid to move too much in case he woke Kate. He was so embarrassed about what had happened. Kate seemed okay with it, but what if it happened again? Making love meant a commitment to emotions that were pretty new to him. Trust and self-belief, for a start. He couldn't stop loving her, but he didn't have to act on it. Didn't have to open himself to more pain and loss. And it wouldn't be fair on her either. She surely deserved someone better, who could offer her the kind of life she was used to. Which wasn't the kind he'd had. He wanted to cry …

Luke stared at the football on the table and tried to sound pleased as he thanked his mother.

'Keep practisin',' said Annie, 'and you'll be rich and famous one day.'

She was trying to make him feel better because she didn't have the money to buy him what he wanted most. In his heart, he'd known he wouldn't get the PlayStation, but he'd still hoped, especially after Danny McDonagh had got one. And he was only eight, not ten like Luke. It hadn't even cost his parents any money at all, because Danny said they'd found it when it fell off the back of a lorry or something. How come Luke's family never had that kind of luck, and what use was a football anyway? It'd just get lost or stolen or punctured. Suddenly, he was tired of always having to make do, of always going without, and he couldn't stop the tears.

'Luke!' His mother did the worst thing then and hugged him tight as she wiped the tears with her thumb.

The slam of a hand on the table made Luke jump. 'Jesus Christ, will you shut that kid up! How the fuck can I concentrate?' Joe was filling out his betting slip for the horse racing. Nothing was ever more important than that. Not even Luke's birthday.

'Stop it, Joe,' Annie said. 'You're scarin' him.'

'That's the idea, you stupid cow.' Joe slapped the back of Luke's head – hard. That just made it worse. Luke was wailing for Ireland now and couldn't stop.

Joe suddenly slapped Annie's face, his handprint red on her cheek. He scowled at Luke. 'Shut up, brat. Because that's what happens if you don't.'

Luke wanted to stop crying but couldn't just switch it off. He watched, terrified, as Joe hit Annie again, this time unbalancing her so she fell to the ground. Luke threw himself at Joe, pounding his uncle in the stomach. 'I hate you, you ugly gobshite!'

Joe pushed Luke against the wall, one hand at his throat. 'For the last time, stop your whinin'. I'm warnin' you now ... shut your mouth before I shut it for you!'

Luke couldn't breathe and his chest was hurting. He could see sparkles of light. The room was drifting away.

'Let him go!' Annie was screaming, and Joe threw Luke to the floor. It was several days before the bruises on his neck disappeared, but the memory stayed forever. Crying was off limits after that.

Finally, Luke slept, but the memories just turned into nightmares. He was running from Joe, but wherever he went, his uncle was there. Beating him. Punching him. He kicked his legs, trying to escape ...

'Luke! Wake up!'

He opened his eyes. Where was he? He scrambled upright, pain shooting through him from his ribs, which were still tender. He jerked away from a hand on his arm, expecting to see Joe. Then a light went on and he saw it was Kate, her face full of concern.

She touched his arm again, stroking gently. 'It's okay, you just had a bad dream. You're safe.'

He didn't deserve her concern. Not after the way he'd rejected her. 'I'm sorry about ... what happened, Kate. And I want to explain.'

Kate shook her head. 'You don't have to.'

'I do,' Luke insisted. 'I need you to know about my life. Mine and Mam's.'

'Did ... did they treat you badly all the time?' Kate asked when Luke had told her about those dark moments of his life that he wanted to forget. Moments he'd never wanted to share but perhaps needed to. Maybe it would free him. 'Did they give you that scar?'

Luke's hand went to it. 'Liam was angry about somethin' I said so he stubbed out his cigarette on me. It turned into one of the best days of my life.'

'What?' asked Kate. 'How come?'

'Joe went ballistic at him. He wiped my tears, put a cold flannel on the burn and gave me five euro to spend when Mam next took me shoppin'. Then he took me out and bought me an ice cream. I said I wanted to buy him one with my money ... I felt like I had a fortune ... but he said I was to keep it for myself.

'I loved him, you see, and I wanted him to love me. I guess I needed a real father figure. I went to bed feelin' really happy, and in the mornin' I couldn't wait to see him. I ran up to him – and got a slap round the head because he was listenin' to the radio. That's how it was. I never knew what mood he'd be in. I'd have preferred it if he'd given me a slap every day rather than false hope.'

'That was just cruel,' agreed Kate. She seemed near to tears.

Luke hugged her to him, kissing her hair. 'I did have a kind of relationship with my uncles, but mostly they resented me. And Mam, too.'

'But why?'

'She married outside the culture for starters, but they'd never treated her well. My grandmother died givin' birth to her, so Joe blamed her. Then she had me, and I was another mouth to feed, the son of a Brit who wasn't a Traveller, not even Catholic. Joe's just full of hate. His wife left him years ago. Took their little girl, Roisin, with her. He's never seen her since. And Liam – he used to be close to Mam until he got a head injury on a buildin' site. Then he had all these mood changes, and that made life even more difficult for us. And apart from everything else, I wasn't what they thought a good Traveller boy should be. They wanted me to do bare-knuckle fightin', like they did. But I'm not exactly built to be a fighter! Even if I was, I wouldn't want to do it.'

'Why didn't your mum take you away?' asked Kate.

'She'd tried to make it on her own once, which ended with me bein' taken into care. Maybe she should have left me there. She could have made a life for herself, and I might have had a different childhood. A proper education.'

'Without your mother?'

'At the time I wouldn't have wanted to be without her, whatever. But maybe we'd have been better off. She did what she thought was best but life was hard. She wouldn't leave my grand-da. He was a good person, but he never got over my grandma dyin'. He was sick for years. Had two strokes. Sometimes I just wanted him to die so's we could go. How bad is that? When he finally did pass on, we'd lost confidence we could make a go of it. We kept puttin' it off until they beat me up bad, then I convinced Mam it was time.'

'Finally,' muttered Kate.

'Don't think badly of her, Kate. You don't know what it's like to be penniless. She did her best.'

'I don't know if I'll ever get over her dyin'. Not when it was down to me. Mam always told me to stay calm or it would make things worse for both of us. I should have known fightin' back was stupid, but I had to be the hero. I always felt bad for not protectin' her enough, but when I did, it just got me battered. We'd never have been on that road, runnin' away, if it wasn't for me. That's why I have this guilt that won't go away. I'm sorry, Kate. For last night, and for burdenin' you with all this.'

He hadn't told her about the money. Matt's warning that he'd involved them all in this mess echoed in his head. He hoped the less Kate knew, the safer she was.

'Don't be sorry. We're a couple. We share the good and the bad. Maybe talking about it will help you deal with it. And I want to spend forever making it good for you.'

'Is that a proposal?'

'If you like,' she laughed. 'Because you're stuck with me … you're my soulmate.'

He kissed the top of her head and wound his arms tightly round her. 'Kate Kiernan has a good Irish ring to it. When I get a proper job, I'll make an honest woman out of you. I love you, Kate – and I don't want to disappoint you.'

'I love you, too,' she whispered. 'And you could never disappoint me.'

Her words were like some kind of miracle drug. He didn't know what he'd done to deserve it, but suddenly life was smiling at him. Maybe he had a guardian angel – was his mother finally helping him in a way she'd never been able to before? He and Kate were now committed to each other, and as sure as the sun would set in the west, he knew he could trust her with his dreams, his emotions – his life. Like some kind of blessing, the growing morning sunlight bathed their bodies in gold as they slowly, tenderly made love.

Chapter Eighteen

Horses were everywhere in County Wicklow, grazing placidly on rich green farmland and being exercised by riders along various side roads. Now the way was blocked by a horse trailer lumbering leisurely along the road ahead, but Jack didn't care about the delay. The slow pace of life in Ireland's countryside was so relaxing. A pale sun warmed the landscape and the car radio played mellow folk music.

'Do you ride, Jack?' asked Emer.

'I'm not that keen, but my father insisted I learn. He's Master of the Baronsmere Hunt.'

'Sounds important.'

'It is – and he's hoping when he retires, I'll take over.'

'You don't sound happy about that.'

Jack sighed. 'I'm the only son – it's expected of me.'

'Well, put your foot down,' suggested Emer. 'What's the worst that can happen?'

She had no idea. A constant stream of cutting comments from his mother and a brooding silence from his father whenever he stepped out of line. 'I work with my father, Emer. Any tension in our personal lives can spill over and that's not good for business.'

How lame that sounded. Emer must think him weak. Maybe he was. He'd left home earlier than necessary to avoid Matt, and he'd hinted to Emer during lunch that he needed a break from the subject of Luke, hoping she'd steer clear of it and he wouldn't have to tell her the kid had left. Was that weakness – or just a desire to enjoy the weekend? 'Remind me again,' he said, 'who's being christened tomorrow?'

'Gabriel. Firstborn of my cousin, Cal. Cal's the Assistant

Manager at the hotel where we're staying, so the room should be grand.'

'And the name of the place is Glenfiddich?' he joked.

Emer laughed. 'You wish! We're staying in Glen*dalough*. It means Valley of the Two Lakes. A really ancient site. Dates back to the sixth century.'

That didn't sound like much fun. Ruins weren't Jack's thing. Still, he was with Emer, which was all that mattered.

A sudden shower had just cleared when Jack caught his first glimpse of Glendalough. As they drove downhill into the wooded valley, the water on the leaves of the trees sparkled in the returning sunshine. The scene took Jack's breath away. An ancient round tower in the centre of the village pierced the vision of lakes and mountains in the distance. Houses and churches and ruins were scattered over the rich green landscape. 'It's like finding Brigadoon,' said Jack, in wonder.

'I know,' Emer agreed. 'It's an amazing place. People come from all over to visit.'

The road veered sharply to the left and soon they were in the courtyard of a large, elegant Georgian country house.

'Welcome to the Fintan House Hotel,' said Emer. 'D'you like it?'

Mansions held little charm for Jack. Too much like Edenbridge. Emer, though, was clearly delighted with the place. Not wanting to spoil her day, he said, 'It's wonderful.'

A moment later, a grizzled porter in purple uniform came to take their luggage. Jack couldn't wait to be alone with Emer. Her use of the singular *room* earlier had been music to his ears. Despite the fact they'd consummated their relationship after his birthday bash, he didn't like to take anything for granted, preferring her to take the lead – he could presume, now, that she hadn't been disappointed. During the journey, her laughter, her voice and her subtle scent had increasingly cast a spell on him, and he wanted nothing more than to hold her in his arms and make love to her again.

'We can have dinner on the terrace,' said Emer, as they booked in. 'It's cool, but they have heaters out there, and it's worth it for the view of the lake.'

'We got a grand batch of oysters fresh this morning,' the receptionist commented with a knowing smile. Hopefully by checkout time tomorrow, that knowing smile would be justified – Jack's relationship with Emer would be established and they would officially become a couple.

The room was amazing, especially the huge canopied bed, draped with heavy jacquard curtains, and Jack's imagination fast-forwarded to the many possibilities such a bed could offer. While Emer was in the shower, Jack stood at the picture window, looking at the view. The hotel's gardens sloped right down to the lake. A breeze ruffled the water, now speckled with gold, and a boat was heading to harbour at the other side. He opened the window and the sweet scent of lilies drifted into the room. Baronsmere was picturesque, but this was like something from a fairytale.

The bathroom door opened behind him, and he turned round. Emer emerged, making the towel wrapped around her look like something from Versace. At that moment, strains of classical music floated up from the terrace. Jack gently pulled Emer towards him, positioning one hand on her waist and clasping her palm with the other. Her free hand went up to his shoulder and they drifted around the room in a slow, sensual waltz.

Emer was looking into his eyes and smiling, and Jack couldn't resist leaning down and kissing her soft, willing mouth. Their tongues entwined, and she caressed his neck.

'We could always skip dinner,' breathed Jack. 'I don't need the oysters.'

He waltzed her to the bed and gently laid her down in the middle of it. Her auburn locks spread in glorious disarray on the pillows, and a light tug easily undid the knot in the towel. Emer placed her hands on his face and gently pulled him towards her. 'We'll call room service later,' she breathed, and Jack soon forgot about anything other than this woman and this moment.

Jack tried to persuade himself to get out of bed. Emer was dozing peacefully in his arms. They'd made love again a short time ago, leisurely, still drowsy from sleep. Jack wished he could stop time and defer his return to Baronsmere and all the problems there. An impossible wish, but at least he could enjoy this day to the fullest, and make sure Emer did, too. At the end of the weekend, he wanted her to think of him as fun, caring, romantic, sensitive. And to decide she needed him in her life permanently.

He gently kissed her awake, stroking curls away from her forehead. 'Time to get up,' he said, rolling over and getting out of bed.

She looked at the clock, confused. 'What? It's still early. Come back to bed.'

'I've planned a surprise for you,' he said with a smile.

'What kind of surprise?'

'Not telling. But make sure you dress warmly.'

A faint light in the sky heralded the coming dawn. Nearby, Emer could hear water, see the ghostly glimmer of it running down the nearby cliff. This was Jack's surprise. A private breakfast by Powerscourt Waterfall. An expensive breakfast because the place didn't open to the public until after ten. He'd arranged it all without her knowing – gone to a lot of trouble and expense just for her. She hugged that knowledge close as she watched him open the bag the hotel receptionist had given him.

There were smoked salmon sandwiches, some boiled eggs, Danish pastries and two bright red apples. Even better, there was a Thermos flask of hot coffee. Jack sat next to Emer and draped a blanket round their shoulders. Then they waited.

When the first gleams of sunlight hit their spot, Emer grabbed Jack's hand as they sat together watching nature's daily miracle. Neither of them spoke; neither of them needed to. She would remember this forever.

'Thank you,' she murmured, when the sun had finally cleared the horizon.

He kissed her hand. 'My pleasure, Emer. You've made me very happy, you know. Yesterday was wonderful – all of it.'

'Yes, it was,' she agreed, snuggling close.

He gently kissed the side of her head, and she heard him whisper, 'I need to have you with me, Emer. I think I'll need to have you with me always.'

Emer's pulse raced. She was falling for this man in a big way, but she was still anxious. Was her heart ready for one more great love? Losing Michael had been devastating, and Colm's betrayal still hurt. She'd not make a promise she couldn't keep, but she'd have to give Jack some kind of an answer. 'My grandmother had a saying – *What's for you will not pass by you.* If we're meant to be together, Jack, then we will be.'

He took her hand and pressed it to his mouth. They lingered on in that magical place, lulled by the music of the waterfall and the sun's gentle rays.

'Is this all yours?' asked Jack, staring at the elegant façade of the four-storey Edwardian building in the Dublin suburb where Emer lived.

'God, no! I've got the ground floor flat. It's all I need.'

Jack followed her up the steps and into the spacious hallway. The late afternoon sun was shining through the stained glass above the door, casting squares of coloured light on the polished parquet floor. A vase of lilies on a small table filled the entrance area with a heady scent.

Emer unlocked the door on the right. 'You'll have to excuse the mess,' she apologised, showing him into the living room. 'I usually attempt a clean up at weekends. Sit yourself down and I'll make us some tea.'

She headed for the kitchen, leaving Jack free to explore the spacious room. The walls were a soft buttery yellow and two large paintings commanded attention: a wild seascape, and an unusual canvas of a smiling young man casting his arms wide as if to gather the whole world to him. A bookcase near the window was filled with a mix of psychology textbooks, classics and popular novels. Framed photographs of freckled, red-haired children crowded the top of the bookshelf: Emer's nieces, nephews, and godchildren, some of whom he'd met earlier at the christening. He'd liked Emer's relatives. They'd easily accepted Jack and Emer as a couple and given him a warm welcome.

Jack sat down on a comfortable blue sofa and gazed through the tall windows at the massing clouds. He let his mind drift, hearing the clanking of china in the kitchen and voices followed by beeps – Emer checking her answering machine. A sudden tiredness washed over him. The early morning start was catching up with him. He dozed off.

Jack woke with a start, not sure where he was at first, stretched out on a sofa, still in his clothes. A table lamp gave out a soft light to combat the dusk. He sat up and saw Emer, resting in an armchair, watching him.

He smiled but she didn't speak. She looked grim.

'Sorry I drifted off ... I didn't mean to be rude ...'

'There was a message on my answering machine from Matt. You'd left my phone numbers with Maggie in case of emergency. Your mobile's been switched off the whole time.'

'Matt? What did the message say?'

'I phoned him back in case it was urgent. He asked me to tell you he's left home. He's staying at Tony's pub for now.'

'What!' Jack's mind was racing. He was an idiot. Sneaking out of the house early so he wouldn't have to face Matt after their argument. Now it had all gone belly up.

'Why didn't you tell me Luke had left home as well? Matt said he left because Luke did, and you didn't seem to be in much of a hurry to persuade him to come back.' Emer's voice was cool, her expression disapproving.

'Now wait a minute!' This was injustice on a grand scale. He was being blamed for something he hadn't done. 'That's not true. I *was* going to speak to Luke.'

'When?'

'Tomorrow. I thought I'd give him time to calm down first.'

'You must see how it looks, Jack. You come to spend the weekend with me while your sons are in crisis. And you leave your mobile switched off so no one can contact you.'

Jack stood up, paced in front of the windows. 'A crisis that Luke caused. He's supporting a protest against Stewart Enterprises. My father was furious. He saw it as a betrayal. That Luke was doing it for revenge.'

'And you believe that, too?'

'I don't know. Maybe. My father thinks so.'

'Never mind your father. What do *you* think? Be your own man, Jack. At least Luke has the courage of his convictions.'

'So you're siding with him?'

Emer threw up her hands in frustration. 'Your *parents*

are the ones wanting you to take sides, and that's not good. Can't you see that?'

'All I see is you're blaming me, and that's not fair.'

'You know what really bothers me about all this, Jack? That you never told me any of it.'

'But why spoil our weekend? What would it have achieved? Anyway, I was—'

'—going to tell me?' Emer finished his sentence. 'Like you were going to speak to Luke? Everything has to happen to your timetable.' She shook her head, and his heart sank. 'I thought we got so close this weekend – now I find you're keeping things from me. That's not what a relationship should be about.'

'I'm sorry …'

'Me too.'

Her words had a ring of finality, which startled Jack. 'Emer, I understand what you're saying – really I do, and I can see why you're angry. But right now, it's because of you – even just the thought of you – that I'm keeping everything together. Please – please – don't pull away from me. Not now.'

Emer's expression softened, but her look was pitying, not loving. 'Jack, you need to sort out your life. And you need to think what kind of relationship you want. I want a partner who shares things with me, who doesn't keep me in the dark. Right now, I can't trust you, and that's not something I can build on.'

Jack wasn't angry now. Just sorry. He'd had something good within his grasp, and he'd screwed it up. He'd lost Matt and now Emer. Luke had never really been his to lose. 'Do you want me to leave now? I could try to get a flight …'

'Of course not. You can sleep on the sofa. I can order some food …'

'I'm not hungry,' said Jack.

'Me neither,' said Emer sadly.

They looked at each other like two survivors on separate life rafts, drifting slowly and inexorably away from each other.

Jack's car inched through Manchester's morning traffic. His flight from Dublin had been delayed, so he'd be late to work, but right now that seemed the least of his worries. All he could think about was Emer. How could they have got so close then ended up poles apart?

Rounding a corner, Jack saw a large crowd of people blocking the pavement in front of Stewart Enterprises. He scanned the placards, which read 'Hands Off Woodlands' and 'Stewart Enterprises: Bullies 'R' Us'. Shit! This was all Richard's fault.

As he drove slowly forward, Jack caught sight of Luke. And Kate was there too. His father had been right. Luke was pushing things too far. Jack's car screeched past the security booth. He didn't so much park it as abandon it in the reserved space. He marched toward the lift, stabbing angrily at a button once inside, and then fumed his way to the executive floor. He wasn't looking forward to this. Nicholas would be raging, and the blame for everything would be laid at Jack's door.

'Better late than never,' Nicholas snapped as Jack strode into his father's office.

'I suppose you've just run the gauntlet outside, as we all did,' said Richard, clucking in mock sympathy.

Jack ignored him, focusing on his father. 'So – what are we going to do?'

Richard spoke again. 'You tell us, Jack, since your son appears to be one of the ringleaders.'

'Richard, let me remind you, the Woodlands development was *your* idea. You pursued it against my advice ...'

Now Nicholas cut Jack off. 'And I gave the project final approval. I stand by that decision. Finger pointing isn't going to solve this. I'm having lunch with Lou Jacobson from Redgate ... Richard, you'd better talk to Keith Torr in Construction and set his mind at rest – he's probably foaming at the mouth right now at the prospect of a delay. Circulate the press release as soon as it's good to go. Heads of departments give out the message it's business as usual, and if anyone so much as breathes near the press, they'll be fired on the spot.'

Nicholas Stewart during a crisis was an impressive sight. Levelheaded and focused. Nerves of steel. Jack felt like a foot soldier in the shadow of a four-star general.

'And I want regular updates from Legal and PR,' instructed Nicholas. 'Well, what are you waiting for, man? Get to it.'

It seemed like Richard just stopped short of saluting. He pushed past Jack with a face like thunder. When they were alone, Jack said to his father, 'Seems like you've got everything under control. What do you want me to do?'

'Talk to that boy, for God's sake!' snapped Nicholas, pushing abruptly up and out of his chair and glaring at Jack. 'He's out of control – a loose cannon. If the press get to know there's one of our own fighting against us ...'

'One of our own?' queried Jack. 'You've changed your tune.'

'That's how the media will perceive it, Jack. Do something about him.'

'He's a grown man. And this is a free country. What exactly do you suggest?'

Nicholas leaned forward, his hands flat against the smooth wooden surface of the table. 'I don't care how you do it. Just sort this mess out. Lock him up, if you have to!'

'That'd be a little difficult since he's no longer living with me. You managed to achieve that with your appearance on Thursday.'

'I said what needed to be said, Jack. I'm not going to apologise for that.'

His arrogance irritated Jack. Nicholas was the one who'd blown everything wide open. 'For your information, Matt's moved out, too.' There was some satisfaction in seeing the shock on Nicholas's face. 'He's staying at the Fox and Feathers for now. He's angry at the way Luke is being treated.'

'I don't understand any of this,' said Nicholas, throwing his hands up in exasperation. 'Suddenly everything is in chaos. You should never have brought that boy here. He's caused nothing but trouble. Have you talked to Matt?'

'I haven't had a chance yet. I was away this weekend.' Jack felt a twinge of guilt. He really *should* have stayed home and sorted things out. 'He just needs some time alone. He'll come round.'

'That sounds a bit cavalier. We need family unity at a time like this.'

'Don't preach to me about family unity, Dad,' warned Jack. 'You're on thin ice there. I'll deal with Matt in my own way.'

'And Luke?'

'We've got our planning permission. Enough of the Woodlands residents have signed. Construction starts in a couple of weeks. What can Luke do?'

As he spoke, Jack remembered the threat to tell the press that Nicholas Stewart tried to buy off Annie. He was about to raise the issue of the cheque when Nicholas spoke. 'Why don't you take the bull by the horns? Tell him you don't want anything else to do with him. That you'll run him out of town if he doesn't stop this nonsense right now. Face up to your responsibilities, Jack.'

Jack stared at his father, this burly, aggressive bear of a man who had dominated his life, and felt intense dislike. Emer had told him to be his own man. Perhaps he should try that. 'Making Luke a martyr is the worst thing we could do. You're not thinking straight and that's not like you.'

Nicholas seemed flustered. 'Just get rid of him.'

'I feel I don't know you anymore, Dad. Maybe I never did.'

Nicholas shook his head and passed a hand over his face. 'You just don't want to hear what I'm saying – or admit you've made a big mistake.'

'You need to deal with your own mistake, Dad. A mistake called Richard. If you don't keep a tighter rein on him, he'll sink us all. I warned you about that before.'

Jack turned away. It was something no one should do to Nicholas. Like not turning your back on royalty. A small protest, but a protest nonetheless. There was absolute silence behind him as Jack walked out of the office.

When Jack approached the driveway of his house, he saw a black Range Rover at the entrance, two men leaning casually against its side. At the sight of Jack's car, one of the men started snapping pictures. The other tried to flag him down, but Jack veered the car and roared up to the house, where he swung the front door open with such force it banged against the wall.

'Who is it?' shouted Maggie, appearing in the kitchen doorway wielding a broom, which she lowered when she saw Jack. 'I thought you might have been one of those reporters.'

'Yes, I saw some at the gate,' said Jack, taking off his coat. 'What were you planning to do, Maggie – give them the brush off?'

Maggie didn't respond. Not even the hint of a smile.

'It's going to get worse before it gets better,' Jack told her. 'Thanks to Luke …'

'Yes, blame Luke,' she muttered.

A large suitcase was in the hall. Louis Vuitton, still in immaculate condition, though it had been a present from Jack to Maggie more than five years ago.

'Going somewhere, Maggie?' he asked.

She sniffed. 'Yes. I'm going over to Baronswood to stay with my sister.'

'How long for?' asked Jack.

'Not sure,' she said evasively.

'Is everything okay?'

She shook her head. 'Of course it's not okay. Both your sons have left home, and who knows if they'll ever come back. You've made a right mess of things.'

'*I* have? I've tried my best, Maggie, and it's not been easy, let me tell you. A little support wouldn't go amiss … and shouldn't you be giving me notice of time off?' He was just trying to make a point. They'd never had a typical employer–employee relationship.

Maggie's jaw set, never a good sign. 'I have to get ready – Maisie's expecting me. There's plenty of food in the fridge and freezer, and I believe you know how to operate the washing machine.'

'Maggie, I'm sorry,' said Jack, not wanting to part on bad terms.

'It's not me you need to apologise to, is it?'

She disappeared into the kitchen, leaving him alone in the hallway. Now he was truly at odds with everyone who was important to him.

A weak late-afternoon sun came out as Kate approached The Fox and Feathers pub. Perhaps a good omen for her mission.

Matt had been her best friend for as long as she could remember, but for the first time in her life Kate felt awkward at the prospect of seeing him. She loved him like a brother, but if she had to choose a side, it would be Luke's. It was terrible that there was so much division between people who should be close, not wounding each other. Matt had been so thrilled to learn he had a brother, and it was obvious from Luke's expression whenever Matt was mentioned that he longed for a reconciliation.

He was stubborn, though – so lacking in self-belief that he needed Matt to make the first move. Kate could sense that Luke thought being needy was a weakness. If she could just talk Matt round, then Luke would think it was all his brother's idea. Matt would go along with it for sure, and anyway he should have been more understanding and supportive. He'd said so himself during their lunch last Friday in the pub. Taking a determined breath, she knocked on the door to the small flat Matt was renting from Tony Hayes.

'Kate!' Matt's arms immediately encircled her in a brotherly bear hug.

'You look tired,' said Kate, kissing his cheek and following him into the flat.

'Lousy night,' Matt explained. 'Too much going on in my head.'

Kate held up a box. 'I've brought your favourite jam doughnuts. From the bakery – not the crap supermarket ones. Won't spoil your dinner, I hope.'

'I've always room for doughnuts.'

Five minutes later, they were settled at the kitchen table, eating the sugary treats. Almost like old times except Matt's face was troubled. 'What a bloody mess this all is,' he said. 'Me and Luke, me and Dad, Dad and Luke, you and your mum … he's quite the provocateur, my little brother.'

Kate was immediately defensive. 'It's not just down to Luke.'

'Well, to be fair – it's *all* down to Luke. But not his actual fault, if that makes any sense. By the way, your mum was beside herself when she saw you on the news at the protest. She asked me to try and persuade you to go home but I've no intention of doing that. I'm not into banging my head on brick walls.'

Sarah would use anyone she could to get to Kate. She'd already been texting Abbie. It was more sad than irritating. 'Stewart Enterprises are wrong, Matt. Ruining land, forcing people to give up their homes. Life shouldn't be all about profit and power. That's why I'm involved in this protest.'

'But why does Luke have to get so involved, Kate? He's a newcomer here – why can't he just settle in and get to know people, especially family, before alienating himself in this way ... You don't think he came here deliberately to wreck the Stewarts for treating his mother badly, do you?'

Kate thought about that for a moment. It would be naïve to dismiss the idea out of hand, but she didn't believe Luke was a malicious person. 'No, Matt, I don't. He doesn't like to see people bullied. It's something he's lived with all his life. He's been a victim of bullying at home and because he's part of the Traveller community.'

Matt nodded, his face grim. 'I know – he told me a bit about that. If I ever meet his uncles ...'

Luke had shared that information with Matt before he'd even told her, which proved Luke trusted his brother. That had to be something she could build on. 'Will you go and see him tomorrow, have a chat with him? Let him see you support him?'

Matt nodded. 'I'm glad he's got you, Kate. I don't want him to feel alone.'

That was reassuring. Other people, notably her mother

and Jack, were concerned Luke was going to hurt her in some way, but Matt was worried about Luke.

'You've got jam on your chin,' said Matt, licking sugar off his lips and trying to stop his own jam escaping.

Kate swore under her breath. 'Not just my chin. Look – it's all down my top and my jeans. What a waste!'

There was a knock at the door and Kate jumped. 'Who's that?'

Matt peered through the curtains into the parking lot. 'It's my grandfather's car!' exclaimed Matt.

'I don't want to see him,' said Kate. 'I'm sure I'll say something *he'll* regret. I'll go into the bathroom and clean this mess off my clothes. I look like a Wes Craven victim.'

Through the paper-thin walls of the bathroom, Kate heard Nicholas say, 'I thought maybe you weren't in.' The arrogance of the man irritated her. So used to never being kept waiting. She attacked the jam on her clothes with even more vigour, imagining she was pounding Nicholas's arrogant face. She'd never like him much, but now she hated him for the way he'd treated Luke.

'What do you want, Granddad?' Matt asked.

'Do we need a reason to talk, Matt? We are family, after all.'

Matt snorted. 'I'd say our days of cosy Sunday lunches are over.' Kate wanted to kiss him for that.

'Why?'

'Why! You need to ask after your performance the other night? I've left home, Dad spent the weekend playing ostrich with a piece of skirt in Ireland, and Luke's been treated like *shit*!' He flung out the last word aggressively, but Nicholas took the outburst calmly.

'Jack needs a break right now,' he said. 'The past few weeks have been a terrible strain on him. But let's talk about you, Matt. I sense you're restless. Hardly surprising, given your talents are not being fully utilised …'

'I'm not going to join Stewart Enterprises, so don't even suggest it,' interrupted Matt.

'I wasn't going to. I know the business isn't what you want. I have another proposal I'd like you to consider. I've just had a chat with Dylan Weston. He's considering selling The Swan over in Hadleigh. As you know, his wife's a London girl at heart, so they're thinking about moving down there.'

That was big news. The Swan was a popular pub. Sarah's nearest rival. Part of the reason she'd decided on the nightclub was to try to tempt away some of Dylan's regulars.

'My proposal is, Matt, that I buy The Swan for you. It would be in your name – you'd be the sole owner. I'll support you for the first year until your profits kick in. I plan on buying it anyway, so if it's not for you, it'll still be in the family. Maybe Gavin …'

Matt's dream was to have his own pub to run and local ones were few and far between, especially of The Swan's quality. Seeing Gavin reach that pinnacle first would kill Matt.

'I'm too young, too inexperienced,' he said.

'I know someone on the Licensing Commission,' said Nicholas. 'He owes me a favour. There would be only one condition. All I ask is that you don't do anything to disgrace the Stewart name. You need to establish good contacts, not just in business, but socially.'

That set alarm bells ringing. Kate could guess where Nicholas was heading.

'Life can be tough,' Nicholas continued. 'Sometimes we have to make difficult choices. We need to be driven by what's best for ourselves. Our futures. This could be the making of you, Matt. A chance to show everyone what you can do.

However unfair it might seem, Travellers are undesirable. If you're associated with one, you'll get the cold shoulder from people who could otherwise help you up the ladder. Do it right, and you could have one of the most successful pubs in the country.'

Kate was outraged. It was all she could do to stop herself rushing out of the bathroom and slapping Nicholas's face. If Matt needed any more convincing, this was proof of just how little his grandparents thought of Luke.

'Let me get this straight, Granddad. You'll set me up in my own business, as long as Luke isn't in my life?'

Nicholas nodded. 'Can you blame me, after that performance today? The boy is like a virus. Infecting everyone he comes into contact with. Why else would Kate Walker have been protesting – and Timothy Leighton, of all people. Don't throw away an opportunity like this for a virtual stranger who may not even be your brother. Take some time to think it over.'

Kate waited for Matt to tell his grandfather to shove his offer, but he said, 'I'll think about what you've said, Granddad. You'll have my answer tomorrow.'

As soon as Kate heard Nicholas leave, she confronted Matt. 'You have got to be kidding! Please tell me you're not seriously considering that disgusting offer.'

'Whoa!' said Matt. 'Give me a break here. I said I'd think about it. There's no harm in that.'

Kate wanted to cry. This wasn't Matt speaking. Not her precious Matt, her big brother, her best friend as long as she could remember. 'No harm? Accepting means cutting Luke out of your life.' Kate couldn't recall a time when she'd ever felt so angry. 'What will he say when he hears you've traded him in for a pub?'

'It wouldn't have to be forever ... just until I'd made a name for myself. Then I'd be in a position to help Luke

– offer him a job. Maybe we could be partners. I could refurbish The Swan, get good reviews in magazines and guidebooks ... if I made a success of it, I could go anywhere and kiss Granddad's conditions goodbye. I'd be doing it as much for Luke as for me ...'

Kate pulled on her jacket and picked up her bag. 'You keep telling yourself that, Matt.' At the door, she paused and went back to the kitchen table to take the remaining doughnuts. Let Matt buy his own. 'And you can think of those as our last supper.'

Chapter Nineteen

Waiting for their coffees in the café close to Stewart Enterprises, Luke and Tim paid little attention at first to the man sitting in the corner. He was wearing sunglasses and a baseball cap, and appeared to be using a newspaper as a shield. When he lowered the newspaper, however, Luke realised with some shock it was Matt. And he was waving Luke over to his table.

'I'll take these on out,' said Tim, handing Luke a polystyrene cup of coffee and putting the rest on a tray. 'You take all the time you need.' Luke watched him go and felt a rush of affection for his new friend, who pretended to be the world's worst gossip but was really the soul of tact and discretion.

'All right, bro?' asked Matt when Luke went over to his table and sat down.

Luke nodded. 'You?'

'I am now,' said Matt. 'Got a few things sorted in my head. You know how it is – everything can be a fog and then it lifts.'

Luke wasn't sure he did know how it was but he murmured agreement anyway. 'So what are you doin' here, Matt?'

'Got to see Granddad. He came to see me and made me an offer I'd be stupid to refuse.'

'The pub at Hadleigh.' Luke knew all about the offer. An angry Kate had told him about it when she arrived home yesterday. It had taken a massage, a footrub and a whole tub of ice cream to calm her down.

'I promised him an answer today. Did Kate tell you the conditions?'

Luke nodded. 'Yes. She also told me why you were considerin' it.'

Kate had been more than a little surprised when Luke had said he understood where Matt was coming from. A year out of their lives might not be so bad if the end result meant some kind of security for both Matt and Luke. It wasn't Luke's idea of a career move but obviously Matt had good intentions. 'You'd be mad to turn it down,' he said.

Matt opened his eyes in surprise then reached out and tugged at Luke's protest T-shirt. 'Have you got a spare one of these?'

'Why?'

'Because I am mad … and stupid. I'm here to join you. I want to go and tell Granddad what to do with his offer, and I want to be wearing one of these when I do.'

Matt gave him a hug and it was the best feeling in the world. Things were right again between them. Soon Jack and Nicholas would find out The Good Ship Stewart had just sprung an almighty leak.

Jack slammed down the phone. How much worse would this all get? Canalside Leisure had just put final negotiations on hold, nervous about the adverse publicity the protest was bringing. A year Jack had spent setting that deal up. All wasted.

The door opened and Richard barged in. The man who'd created this whole nightmare. The last person Jack wanted to see. He flicked open his laptop and snapped, 'I'm busy, Richard. Make an appointment.'

Richard marched up to the desk and set his phone down in front of Jack. 'You'd better take a look at this photo.'

Jack took the phone and saw what had obviously made Richard's day: Matt wearing a protest T-shirt and carrying a placard, Luke beside him. Jack shouldn't have been surprised, but still he felt the sharp stab of betrayal. He handed the phone back.

'Sir Nicholas knows,' smirked Richard. 'Apparently Matt

paid him a visit earlier. Perhaps you should lie low for a while.'

'Cowering in corners may be your style, Richard – it's not mine.'

Nicholas was in the middle of a phone call. He didn't look that upset, but then he was the master of the poker face. Jack wandered over to the window and peered out. Perhaps he should go out and confront Matt? The media would have a field day with that, though. Best if he called him when he got home.

Nicholas ended the call. 'Have a seat, Jack. I just heard about Canalside Leisure. I'll go over there this afternoon.'

Jack sat down, feeling puzzled. If Nicholas knew Matt had joined the protest, why wasn't it the main topic of conversation?

'Dad, about Matt …'

To Jack's amazement, Nicholas shrugged. 'I'm disappointed, of course. I saw it coming. Did my best. Some you win, some you lose.'

'Did your best. What do you mean?'

Nicholas was reading his phone messages as he spoke. 'I offered to buy The Swan pub for Matt if he stayed away from Luke.'

Jack shot up from the chair as if it had burned him. 'You did what!'

Nicholas assessed him critically. 'I did what you should have done, Jack. Tried to sort out this Luke situation before it went too far.'

Inside, Jack was shaking with rage. 'How dare you, Dad! I told you not to interfere, that I'd deal with Matt.'

'So I jumped the gun a bit – what's wrong with that?'

'He probably thought I put you up to it. You've just made things worse.'

Nicholas stood up, looking angry. 'How could things be any worse than they are already? You botched things badly, bringing that trailer trash back here. He's got Kate Walker and Tim Leighton onside. Now we're losing Matt.'

'*You* lost us Matt by your interference. He probably thought he was being manipulated – which he was.'

'Well, someone had to do something. You've been worse than useless. Where's the son I raised? You've never been spineless before ...'

Before he knew what he was doing, Jack had pulled his fist back, ready to punch his father's face. He was so close to doing it and shocked by how much he wanted to. It took all of his willpower to lower his fist. What was happening to him? He was losing it, badly.

Nicholas shook his head. 'We both love this company, Jack,' he sighed. 'That's why we get so overwrought when someone attacks it. You should use some of that fight in you to protect it, not the opposite.'

Was that grudging admiration in his father's eyes? God, how twisted was that? 'Dad ... I'm going home ...'

'Maybe that's best. Give yourself some time to cool off.'

'No ... I want to take a leave of absence ... a couple of weeks ...'

'We're in the middle of a crisis here!'

'I know. I just ... can't deal with it right now. Sorry.'

'Jack!'

He turned and left. Walked right out of the building, into his car, and once through the protestors, drove home at speed. After downing over half a bottle of whisky, he was finally able to drift into oblivion on the living room sofa.

Jack was dreaming about Ireland. He was near the Powerscourt Waterfall, trying to find Emer. She'd said something about skinny-dipping and then disappeared.

Suddenly, Sarah was there, telling him Emer had made a fool of him. 'Get lost!' he told her.

'I beg your pardon!'

That was his mother's voice. Why in God's name was she there? Jack jerked awake. He was lying on the living room sofa and Grace was standing over him, frowning. He sat up and groaned. His head throbbed. The nearly empty bottle on the coffee table was the culprit. Of course, Grace had seen it.

'Now I see why you didn't answer any of my calls yesterday.'

Yesterday? He must have slept right through. He looked at his watch. Just turned ten. He rubbed his aching neck and sighed. 'Good morning, Mother.'

'Is it?' she responded. 'Forgive me if I think otherwise since I can no longer hold my head up in Baronsmere.'

The real reason for her visit. Not genuine concern for him, just for what the world would think about the Stewarts. 'I apologise for ruining your social life, Mother,' he drawled.

'It's not just my life you're ruining – you seem intent on destroying your own as well.'

'I'm hardly on the slippery slope to oblivion.'

She looked pointedly at the whisky bottle. 'Really?'

Jack felt wrong-footed and irritable. 'I need to freshen up. How about some coffee? Maggie's away, so would you mind making it?'

While Grace went into the kitchen, Jack trudged upstairs and into his bathroom. Showering and shaving helped him feel more focused, but it did little to improve his mood. Only his mother's exit would help with that. He downed two painkillers and prayed they'd work quickly.

When he entered the kitchen, Grace pushed a mug of instant across the table. She probably had no idea how to work a coffee machine. 'Thanks,' he said, taking a welcome gulp. There was an uncomfortable silence, punctuated only by the lilac bush blowing against the window and Honey's restless skulking around the kitchen.

'That dog isn't getting enough exercise,' stated Grace. 'She'll run to fat.'

Jack sighed at this interference. 'She's fine.'

Grace was watching him like a hawk. Probably waiting for an apology. Best to get it over with. 'I assume Dad told you I nearly hit him. I'm sorry. I was out of control. That's why I came home. I need a break.'

'Your father's very concerned. He wanted to come over to see you this morning, but …'

'He's got a business to run, profits to make, people to crush.'

'Jack! It's not like you to be so cynical. The business is what supports us all, keeps us comfortable. And you know it means everything to your father.'

'But it no longer means everything to me,' Jack said, and he meant it.

'Perhaps you just need a holiday …' suggested Grace.

'I think it's going to take more than a fortnight in Barbados to fix this.'

'Talk to Matt. He loves you. You'll work it out.'

'Matt's very angry, not just with me, but with you and Dad – because of the way you treated Luke. And Annie.'

Grace looked shocked. 'What have you been saying to him?'

'Nothing. He heard about it from someone else.'

'Village gossip,' said Grace dismissively. 'Matt should know better than to listen to that.'

'I don't think it was all gossip. Annie was made to feel she could never belong. And you were one of the people who made her feel that way.'

'I tried, Jack – Lord knows, I tried, but we had nothing in common.'

Jack shook his head. 'You didn't try. I saw that with my own eyes but didn't want to rock the boat by pointing it out. And I'll never forgive myself for that. I should have had more guts. And you should have had more compassion. Been less of a snob.'

Grace stood up. 'I'm *not* going to stay here and be insulted ...'

Jack cut her short. 'No, I'm sure you can go elsewhere for it – I'm realising exactly what the people in this village think of us.'

'I'll put your rudeness down to the drink, Jack, and I just hope when you're fully sober, you come to your senses ...'

Grace marched away, her heels clacking angrily on the wooden floor. Jack remained where he was at the table. 'That's already happened, Mother,' he called after her. 'I'll leave you to see yourself out.'

At the resounding slam of the front door, Honey whined and hid beneath Jack's chair. He patted her head and wondered how long it would be until he managed to upset her as well. When he picked up the coffee mug, his hand was shaking.

Friday morning, and another solitary breakfast. The house seemed to echo around Jack. Usually Matt had music thumping somewhere in the background and Maggie would be roving the rooms, cleaning and scolding as she went. Now there was nothing. They had gone, taking their life and their laughter with them. He missed them. But he was coping. Adjusting. That's what he was known for, after all.

As for Luke – well, maybe he was his son, maybe he wasn't. There was no way Jack could have broached the subject of the DNA test since he'd got back from Ireland. Not if he'd wanted to avoid another scene even worse than the one after Nicholas's visit. It just wasn't worth it. Maybe

Luke himself might suggest it in the future. Until then, it just didn't seem to matter any more. He was too tired to care.

Jack hadn't left the house for three days. He didn't need to. The fridge and freezer were stacked with enough food to last out weeks of a siege. He'd told Emer everything when she called in response to his e-mail. She'd approved of his taking a break from work but felt he shouldn't be alone too much. It had been on the tip of his tongue to ask – no, beg – her to come to the May Day festival. He'd have to go, to fulfill his charity commitments, but he was dreading the sly looks and whispers. The gossip grapevine would be in full swing. He hadn't wanted to expose Emer to that. So he'd told her he was taking a vacation and would be in touch on his return.

And that's exactly what he was planning to do when May Day was over. He'd take a hire car down to France – to Antibes, to visit Caroline's parents, the Ingrams. Then he'd move on to Italy, island hop in Greece, take a boat over to Turkey and sip coffee with the Bosphorus spread before him. He'd travel as far as he wanted, as far as he needed, until the painful memories faded. He was loosening the bonds, backing away, withdrawing. Some would say he was running away. Perhaps he was, but he needed to get away from Baronsmere, from everyone – especially Luke. The time was ripe for change. He would view it all as the Chinese philosophers had done – not as a crisis, but as an opportunity. Perhaps he wouldn't come back to Baronsmere at all.

When Luke arrived with Kate at The Fox and Feathers, the pub was packed.

Abbie waved to them from the far corner. 'Wotcha!' she said, as Kate and Luke joined her. 'Where've you been? We got here ages ago to get these seats. The karaoke's just about to start.'

'Okay,' said Matt, standing at the microphone on the pub's small stage. 'Those fortunate enough to have hearing aids, turn them down now. It's Al and Tim, with sincere apologies to The Proclaimers!'

When Al and Tim turned around to face the audience, everyone laughed at their thick-rimmed specs. Faking Scottish accents, they began to sing 'I'm Gonna Be'. Luke knew the song, otherwise he wouldn't have understood a word.

'I'd walk five hundred miles to get away from that God-awful racket,' said Abbie, swigging from a pint glass.

Kate laughed and caught hold of Luke's hand. He smiled at her. Everything suddenly felt so right. And this was the pub where his mother had worked. It was a comforting thought.

Abbie was staring. 'So – you've done it now.'

'Done what?' asked Kate.

'Appeared in public. Now everyone'll know you're an item.'

'That's the idea,' said Kate, and she kissed Luke full on the mouth.

'Oh, get a room!' said Abbie. 'Gavin looks fit to burst a blood vessel.'

Luke followed Abbie's gaze and saw his cousin seated at the bar, scowling back at them. 'Guess I'll always be a pikey to him,' he said.

'No, it's Katie he'll be pissed about,' Abbie told him. 'She was his girlfriend once – for all of one date.'

'Really?'

Kate sighed. 'Alas, yes – last year. I was young and very foolish. But all Gavin ever talked about was money and cars … and himself. Unbearable.' She touched Luke's arm. 'It meant nothing. Believe me.'

He did believe her but couldn't help wondering if she'd

slept with Gavin. Stupid male jealousy. The git was still staring at them. Luke couldn't resist – he smiled and winked. Gone were the days he'd be made to feel inferior.

Still wearing their glasses, Tim and Al crammed into the space left by Abbie as she ran to the stage.

'Luke, my man!' screeched Tim. 'That song was in your honour.'

'Luke's Irish, not Scottish, you drunken dimwit!' said Al.

'Well, they're all Celts, aren't they?' insisted Tim. 'Oops ... time for the ear plugs.' He pointed to the stage, where Abbie was singing 'I will survive'.

'More than we will then,' called her brother, thumping the table. 'Right, I need beer! This performer's thirsty!'

'I'll get us a round,' volunteered Kate. When she reached the bar, Luke watched as Gavin slipped from his stool and put his arm around her. Kate immediately shrugged it off, but the cocky git just grinned and whispered something in her ear before moving towards the stage. Luke was vaguely aware of Abbie returning to the table, declaring, 'I don't know why I put myself through that every week.'

'Put *us* through it, you mean,' said Al.

Abbie gave him an exaggerated smile and poked her tongue out.

A moment later, Gavin took the mic and started to sing 'Never Gonna Give You Up'.

'Oh God,' said Abbie, pretending to throw up. 'And tonight, Matthew, I'm going to be ... a complete tosser.'

It was obvious the song was aimed at Kate. The prat was looking across at her as he sang.

'Alcohol!' cried Al, grabbing a bottle from the tray as Kate returned to the table. 'Thank God! Need something to dull the senses when he's on!'

When Gavin finished singing, there was muted applause, mainly from his friends and some young girls who must have been out on day release. He bowed. 'Thank you, fans. Now we all know that karaoke night is a big part of our social week, and to really enjoy it – to belong – you have to sing.' Gavin switched his attention to Luke. 'If he's going to be a regular, then he's got to give us a song. Ladies and gentlemen, I give you – Luke Kiernan – or Stewart – or whatever.'

There was silence, and Luke felt everyone in the room was watching, waiting to see how he would respond.

'Shut up!' hissed Matt. 'No one *has* to sing.'

Luke got up, though, and made his way to the stage. He'd show them.

Gavin handed him the mic. 'How about 'Gypsies, Tramps and Thieves'?' he said. His friends laughed and banged their table.

Luke ignored them. He'd found the song he was looking for and smiled reassuringly at Kate. He knew he had an appealing voice. It ran in the family. Gavin had no idea Luke was used to singing in public. He enjoyed it. He'd done it in bars, or on evenings when he and other Travellers would make their own entertainment. He tried to imagine he was back there, with his mother and their friends.

'Go on, son!' shouted Tony. 'Your mother stood in that very spot and sang for us – and bloody good she was, too.'

Luke focused on Kate. Gavin had purposely directed a love song at her. Two could play that game. Chatter in the bar died away and the smile disappeared from Gavin's face as Luke sang his mother's favourite song, 'You Light Up My Life.' He didn't take his eyes off Kate, and not just for Gavin's benefit – the lyrics summed up his feelings so well that he became lost in them. He wanted Kate, wanted everyone, to know exactly how he felt.

When he'd finished, there was silence at first, then applause. Matt was grinning, and Tim and Al were whooping and banging the table. Kate came onto the stage and threw her arms around him. 'That was wonderful!'

'Stay here,' said Luke. 'This one's for you as well.' He quickly showed Matt the song he wanted, and then launched into 'Uptown Girl'. Al and Tim jumped up and joined in as Kate strutted across the stage, acting the role perfectly. Luke had achieved exactly what he wanted. Let people throw his background at him. This song would show them he didn't care. He wasn't ashamed of who he was, and anyone who had a problem with it could take a hike.

The music ended to more applause, and Tim and Al bowed several times, saying with false modesty 'It was nothing – really.'

Back at the table, Tim said, 'Shall we say ten per cent?'

'What?' asked Luke, puzzled.

'Stick with me, kid – I can make you a star. Or … I've just had this *great* idea! We could start our own band! You can be lead vocal – you look like you've just stepped out of a boy band anyway. I can play guitar and so can Matt. Al can learn the drums. We'll be a tribute band! Call ourselves *Vestlife* and promote my T-shirts at the same time! What do you say?'

'I'll think about it.' Luke was laughing so hard his ribs ached, but the pain was worth it. At that moment, he felt he belonged.

'Your little scheme backfired there,' Al challenged Gavin, who was heading for the door. 'Luke beat you hands down!'

Gavin shrugged. 'Amateur night crap.'

'That includes you then,' said Abbie.

'Shut your mouth, slag!'

Before he could think about it, Luke grabbed a pint of beer and threw the remains at his cousin. Gavin looked startled but then grabbed Luke's T-shirt and yanked him to his feet. Christ, the pain in his ribs! For a second he was back in Ennis facing Joe, and he headbutted Gavin, who fell backwards, blood streaming from his nose.

Matt was on the scene in seconds. He didn't seem to care Gavin was hurt because he jerked him to his feet and thrust him into the arms of his approaching friends. 'Get him out of here – now!'

Gavin's face was a bloody mess, and he glared at Luke. 'You'll regret that, pikey,' he spat. 'I'll bring your world crashing down.'

'Fuck off, Gavin!' said Matt.

'You can't order me around!' Gavin was wiping his nose with a handful of paper napkins he'd grabbed from a nearby table. 'This isn't your pub.'

'No, but it is mine and I want you out of it,' said Tony Hayes. 'You're barred.'

'But it was that gypo who hit Gavin!' said one of Gavin's mates.

'He's been begging for a fight and he got one,' said Matt. 'Now, piss off!'

Glaring at Matt and Luke, Gavin spat on the floor. 'Let's go before the Chuckle Brothers make me throw up.'

When they'd gone, Luke slumped back into his seat. He felt sick.

'All right, bro?' asked Matt, sitting down in the seat opposite. 'What happened? First Richard, now Gavin. It's becoming a habit. Great targets, though.'

'Luke defended me!' said Abbie. 'That bastard Gavin insulted me!'

'Luke, you're a regular knight in shining armour,' murmured Al, looking impressed.

Luke was no hero. What he'd just done – getting into a fight – was everything he despised. Why had he allowed Gavin to get to him?

'Gavin grabbed him,' said Kate. 'It was hit or be hit.'

Kate was wrong. If he hadn't thrown the drink at Gavin, it was likely nothing would have happened. He'd lost his temper, and not because Gavin had insulted Abbie, but because he'd been flirting with Kate.

The others smiled, but the evening had ended badly and it was Luke's fault. He turned to Kate. 'Can we go?'

As Luke headed out, several hands patted him on the shoulder. People were saying 'Well done' and 'Good lad'. He'd never felt such a fraud.

'Luke,' called Matt from the door, just as they got outside. 'That first song, 'You Light Up My Life' …'

'Mam's favourite,' Luke told him. 'Though it made her cry.'

'Just wondered,' said Matt. 'Last time someone sang it, Dad was here and walked out. He was in a foul mood for days.'

Proof that Jack loved Annie – or hated her? Luke was too upset to try and fathom things out. He followed Kate to the car, thinking about what Gavin had said. *I'll bring your world crashing down.* He'd need to watch his back.

Chapter Twenty

Ten o'clock on the village green and May Day was about to kick off. Luke was with Tim in front of a makeshift stage. The Baronsmere brass band started to play.

'That sounds like 'Thriller',' said Luke. 'Not very May Day, is it?'

'Totally May Day.' Tim was swigging vodka from a lemonade bottle. 'Because this place is full of the living dead. All prone to acts of reckless violence.'

'Bet she's the worst,' joked Luke, as an old biddy with a blue rinse tottered past.

'Sadie Nelson,' observed Tim. 'Definitely. Last year, her dahlias were passed over so she whacked the judge with her handbag. I thought she was barred this year.'

Luke grinned. He didn't always take Tim seriously but his entertainment value was priceless. May Day looked like it would be fun. Clowns, jugglers and merry-go-rounds, just like the big horse fairs. Tony Hayes waved to Luke then turned back to the sign he was hammering up over a stall that read 'Madame Zelda: Fortune Teller'.

'Madame Zelda's really Babs Hayes,' Tim told Luke. 'She wears a headscarf and hooped earrings. Last year, she told me a temperamental woman would come into my life.'

'And did she?'

'Well, I was hoping it might be Lady Gaga. That she'd somehow become my New Best Friend. But it never happened. Ma did get Suki, the Pekingese, last year, though. And that's one bitch with serious attitude problems. The dog, not my ma. So maybe it did come true.'

Following a drum roll, an announcement from the stage told people to take their seats.

'Show time!' cried Tim, as people started to climb the side stairs to the stage. 'That's the May Day organising committee. The parents wanted me up there to represent them in their absence. Told them I'd rather stick my head in boiling chip fat.'

Luke scowled when he saw Grace Stewart in the middle of the front row, her hat so big it should have had its own seat. And there was Old Nick, smiling down at the common folk. Patronising git.

Another drum roll, and a short, stocky man with an obvious hairpiece stepped up to the microphone.

Tim offered the lemonade bottle to Luke. 'Want some?'

Luke shook his head.

'You might regret it,' Tim warned. 'The speeches have been known to turn the normally sane into gibbering wrecks.'

Hairpiece started talking. 'Welcome one and all to Baronsmere's May Day Festival. A tradition that has graced this green – this jewel of a corner of England – for well over a hundred years. Times may change but May Day in Baronsmere is timeless. A chance for our community to come together and celebrate its most cherished values – compassion, decency, good sportsmanship.'

'Who is he?' asked Luke.

'Our mayor,' Tim told him. 'Horace Henderson. "Hungry Horace" we call him. Short on height, big on ambition. Napoleon complex.'

'This great day would not have been possible without generous contributions from ...' Horace then started giving out more names than the phone book. Luke glanced across at Tim. The vodka was taking effect. As the speech continued, Tim dozed off and then jerked awake at each round of clapping.

Ten minutes later, Luke poked Tim in the ribs. 'He's windin' up now.'

Tim looked at his watch. 'God is merciful. Horace's speeches can rival *War and Peace*.'

The mayor apologised for his wife's non-attendance, saying she was indisposed. Tim nudged Luke. 'Dipso, he means. She's currently drying out in a Swiss clinic.'

'In her absence,' droned Horace, 'Lady Grace Stewart has kindly offered to speak on behalf of the organising committee.'

'Oooh!' said Tim, straightening up in his chair. 'Old Grace must have pulled some fast moves. According to rank, it should have been Lady Middleton. In fact, Lady M looks a bit puce – she must be furious.'

'Well, the Stewarts are experts at shafting people,' Luke commented bitterly as Grace stepped up to the microphone.

'Oooh!' exclaimed Tim again. 'Perhaps Grace actually shafted the mayor!'

When Grace started speaking, Luke had to go. 'I can't sit through this, Tim. I'm going for a walk.'

Tim stood up, too. 'No problem, mate. I'll come with you. We'll go raid the cake stalls, then get smashed.'

The showjumping event was over. Kate smiled for the cameras, nudging Petruchio's head round so the blue rosette showed. Second place. A knock-down on the last fence. Last year, she would have been inconsolable. This year, losing didn't matter. All she cared about was Luke, standing by the paddock fence, clapping madly.

'You were wonderful, both of you,' he told her as he caught her up in a close embrace. She clasped her hands around his neck and savoured a long, sweet kiss.

'I'll take Petruchio back to the stables,' said Kate, 'then I'll get changed. Don't want to spend the rest of the day in jodhpurs.'

Luke nodded. 'I'll wait near The Great Oak in about an hour.'

At that moment, Gavin appeared, face like thunder, and bearing the evidence of Luke's headbutt the night before. If he tried to spoil this day, she'd swing for him.

'Piece of shit!' he called, staring directly at Luke. Then he added, 'On the ground, I mean. Watch your step.'

'Something certainly smells around here!' snapped Kate, pushing past Gavin, hoping Petruchio would give him a crippling backward kick.

She felt Luke's arm slide round her waist. 'Ignore him. We'll not let him spoil our day.'

'You're right,' Kate agreed, and kissed him goodbye. Missing him already, she set about boxing Petruchio. She'd just finished when she smelled a familiar perfume behind her.

'Hello, Kate.'

She turned round to face her mother, who was glam as ever in red silk, but her eyes were sad. Kate tried to push away a stab of guilt. 'Hi, Mum.'

Sarah smiled. 'Congratulations on your rosette.'

'Thanks.'

The silence swelled and filled the space between them. They'd once shared everything; now they were struggling with small talk. 'Well, I'd better get Petruchio back to the stables ...'

'Come home, Kate – please!' Sarah's voice was desperate. 'This is all wrong. We shouldn't let things come between us.'

'I don't *want* anything to come between us, Mum, but you'll have to accept Luke.'

Sarah shook her head. 'I can't. Don't ask me to do that. It's not possible. He's wrong for you ...'

Now Kate shook her head. 'You expect me to do what you want, but you haven't given me one good reason. Why are you so against Luke? He's a *good* person. Give him a chance!' She willed her mother to understand.

'Kate, he doesn't fit in here. He never will. They won't accept him. You're being selfish, making him stay …'

Kate backed away, not wanting to hear any more. Sarah reached out but Kate dodged her grasp and ran to the truck door. Kate's last vision before she drove away was of her mother, head down, and shoulders quivering. Kate couldn't remember when she'd last seen Sarah cry.

Luke climbed the slope to The Great Oak, Baronsmere's oldest tree. Kate wasn't there yet and the big showpiece was about to begin. He called her number but it went straight to message. Hopefully she was driving back. He leaned against the tree, looking at the fancy VIP tent. Only snobs allowed in there. No champagne for the plebs. Still, their perfect little world was about to be disrupted thanks to Duncan Gilroy – and Tim, who'd covered the costs of this part of the protest. He was a bit of a rebel on the quiet.

Luke glanced at his watch. Three o'clock. Right on time, he heard a dull roar in the distance. It grew louder. He stood up and a rush of cold air blasted over him as a helicopter passed over and circled the village green. There were shrieks as paper cups and food wrappers swirled crazily in the updraught, marquees flapping dangerously. Leaflets scattered down over the green. Luke picked one up and read the impassioned plea for people to stand against the Woodlands development, to care about the affected residents and their rights.

Glancing across the green, Luke saw the bigwigs come out of their marquee to see what was happening. Grace was among them, looking fit to spit. She was having to clamp her stupid great hat to her head to keep it from blowing away in the wind from the circling helicopter. Luke caught her eye and couldn't resist giving her a smile and a little wave. He was determined to stare her down, and felt great satisfaction when she eventually turned away.

'Kiernans, one, Stewarts, nil,' he muttered, then turned as he heard footsteps behind him scrunching through the scattered leaflets. He'd expected to see Kate but it was Gavin. Luke clenched his fists, remembering his cousin's words from yesterday.

'Waiting for Kate?' Gavin asked. 'Probably having a quick shag somewhere. She's a bit of a slapper. High class one, though.'

Luke wasn't going to rise to that one. This time he'd not give in to his temper, but Gavin seemed set on trouble. 'I don't know how you have the nerve, pikey. Regular people wouldn't do what you lot do. Still, it must make finding a date easier.'

'Meaning?' asked Luke.

Gavin smiled. 'In the civilised world, we don't shag our sisters.'

Luke's mind replayed the words in shocked silence.

'Did you hear me, pikey?' asked Gavin. 'Jack-is-Kate's-*dad*.'

Luke couldn't speak. His knees felt weak.

'Course it might not matter – I've heard your mother spread it around a bit so you're probably not even a Stewart ... thank God.'

Gavin winked and walked away, whistling. Luke felt giddy and sank slowly to the ground, where he sat against The Great Oak in shock, the protest leaflets drifting around him.

Sarah wanted to be alone. Had snapped at a couple who'd tried to join her. Misery didn't want company in this case. It didn't even want a drink. Her glass of wine was untouched. She'd tried disappearing into the bottom of a bottle when Jack split up with her, but it hadn't helped. Only postponed the inevitable. Baronsmere was a small place and she couldn't avoid Jack forever. She was now trying to desensitise herself by watching him – from a discreet distance so she didn't look like some sad stalker. He was queuing at the hot-dog stall. Trying to be your average Joe.

'Sarah …'

God, why couldn't people leave her in peace! She looked up, ready to snap at the intruder. It was Luke. Deathly pale and gripping the table for support. There was no sign of Kate. God, had there been an accident …?

'Is it true?' Luke's voice was little more than a whisper.

'What?' she asked. There was a desperation in his eyes that scared her.

'Is Kate Jack's daughter? Gavin just told me that. Is it true?'

Sarah felt a brief flare of anger at Richard for breaking his word and telling the secret to Gavin, but then she realised this might be part of his plan to get rid of Luke. She also wanted Luke gone. This was a God-given opportunity.

'Luke, I'm sorry …' She saw the light of hope flicker and die from his eyes. The guilt was crushing. She'd have to live with it always. 'Kate doesn't know,' she continued. 'I don't want her to. I— I don't know how Gavin found out.'

'For Christ's sake, Sarah! Why didn't you tell *me*, before—'

'I tried to warn Kate,' Sarah protested, 'but she thought I was prejudiced. I'm not, believe me. I have nothing against you, Luke, but I couldn't tell Kate the truth. Or Jack. I didn't want him to be with me out of obligation. If you love Kate, you won't tell her either, Luke. Please.' That was low but might ensure his silence.

His shoulders were slumped, his head down. It was obvious how much he cared for Kate, and Sarah felt a lump in her throat. Luke was still grieving for his mother, and now this. For a moment, she wavered. But it was too late.

Luke glanced up again and now there was bitterness in his

eyes. 'Kate's two months older than me. You were screwin' Jack when he was with my mam. Is that why she left?'

'I-I don't know, Luke. I don't know why Annie left.'

She glanced across at the hot-dog stall. Jack was still there. Luke followed her gaze, and then he abruptly left the table and walked across the green. Sarah watched, mortified, as Luke's fist connected with his father's jaw. Jack staggered backwards but was caught by two bystanders. Luke shouted something, turned on his heel, and marched away, his expression part anger, part misery. Sarah was full of self-loathing. 'Oh, God,' she thought, as the enormity of what she'd done hit her. She grabbed the wine glass and drained it. 'Bitch,' she cursed herself.

It took every ounce of willpower to concentrate on driving. Living didn't figure very highly on Luke's list of priorities, but he didn't want to kill anyone. Or smash up Tim's car. He'd surely broken the speed limit leaving the village green after hitting Jack. Not that being arrested for assault bothered him. He just wanted to get away quickly, to put distance between himself and the Stewarts.

It all fitted. Sarah had been apologetic, seemed guilty. Genuine guilt surely, because she'd been almost nice to him. Maybe Kate's fair hair and green eyes should have given him a clue. Jack had deserved that punch, the bastard, though Luke had probably ruined any relationship with Matt and he *was* sorry about that.

Luckily, Luke still had a key to Jack's house. Expecting someone to turn up any minute, he moved fast, taking the thirty thousand euro from the safe and stashing it in one of Matt's sports bags. The dogs were barking and he wanted to go and fuss them one last time but couldn't risk it.

Twenty minutes later he was back at the Leighton's, shoving his few belongings into the sports bag. He tried not to look at the unmade bed, tried not to think of Kate and what he couldn't have. He didn't leave a note. He'd text her to say goodbye when he was well clear. He couldn't just disappear from her life without a word. He'd text Tim, too, to tell him where the car was. He paused for a moment and looked around sadly, before finally closing the door on his brief stay in Baronsmere, and his even briefer life with Kate.

And now what? His long-term future had little meaning. He wasn't even sure he'd have one, but he had something to do first. He'd wondered how to do some good with the money and had suddenly thought of Jessie. Thinking about that kept him focused, able to reach his destination in one piece.

He stopped the car and stared ahead. He was tired and overwhelmingly homesick. He couldn't – wouldn't – run any more. The sign in front of him was strangely comforting. *Welcome to the Port of Holyhead.*

Matt entered the First Aid tent, looking anxious. Maggie had insisted he be called over the tannoy, and Jack had been too shocked by the incident to protest.

'Jesus, Dad! What the hell happened?'

'I was assaulted,' mumbled Jack, slumped in a chair, holding an ice pack to his jaw.

'Who did it?' demanded Matt.

'Luke.'

'Come again?'

Jack wasn't in the mood for going into a lot of detail. It hurt to speak. 'Luke punched me – for no reason,' he managed to say.

'Actually, he punched you because of Annie,' Maggie chimed in. 'Apparently he was heard to say "That's for my Mam".'

Jack glowered at her and she shrugged. 'All I'm saying is, that was his reason.'

Matt looked confused. And disbelieving. He most likely had Luke earmarked for sainthood, such was the relationship between the two of them. 'But why now?' he asked. 'Luke's been here a while and you've given him plenty cause to clock you before ...'

'Oh, *thank* you!' snapped Jack. '*I'm* the injured party here, Matt. Literally.'

'Nonsense. It was just a tap.' Maggie pulled Jack's hand with the ice pack away from his jaw and peered at the damage. 'Hardly a mark. It's your pride that's been hurt most. That boy weighs next to nothing. He just caught you unawares.'

'The nurse said I was lucky not to lose a tooth,' declared Jack, but no one seemed interested.

'Matt, find Luke,' said Maggie. 'Check he's okay ... Something happened to set him off. Something to do with his mother. The lad's still grieving, you know ...'

Jack hoped Maggie was being overcautious – Luke was touchy and hot-tempered but he'd not do something stupid.

Matt pulled out his mobile. 'I'll call Kate. She's the first person Luke will go to.'

Five hours later there was still no sign of Luke and Kate was beside herself with worry. At first, everyone had been convinced he would contact her, but there'd been no word, no message. Driving round and round Baronsmere, she'd started to feel dizzy. Luke seemed to have vanished. Now it was getting dark and chilly and she hoped he had shelter, wherever he was.

At the village green parking area, Kate met as arranged with Tim, Matt and Al. The night sky was alight with fireworks, the May Day finale, and their worried faces glowed a ghostly green. None of them had found Luke.

'Dad's driving round Hadleigh and Marsham, just in

case,' Matt told them. 'He insisted he was fit enough to do it.'

That was a long shot – Luke didn't know either of those villages – but Kate appreciated Jack's efforts.

'Shall we stay here and scan the crowds as they leave after the fireworks?' Tim suggested.

Kate gave a half-hearted nod. Luke had been so wound up that he'd punched his father. He was unlikely to be watching a firework display.

'Do you want to go home, Kate?' asked Matt. 'You look done in. And Luke may go back there when he's cooled down.'

Kate shook her head. 'I need to be doing something, Matt. Let's have just one last look round and then decide what to do next.'

The village green looked unfamiliar in the murky evening light. They did a quick check of the marquees where volunteers were stacking chairs and packing things in boxes. Tony Hayes waved them over. 'Afraid the food's all gone. How's Jack? Reckon he'll have quite the bruise tomorrow.'

Matt sighed. 'That's the least of our worries, Tony. We can't find Luke.'

'Sorry to hear that. I suppose he's keeping his head down for a bit.' Tony looked genuinely concerned. 'Have you asked Sarah why he was so upset?'

'My mum?' asked Kate, startled.

'Babs said she saw Luke talking to Sarah a few minutes before he went over and decked Jack.'

Had her mother provoked Luke into hitting Jack? At least it was something new to follow up, but the answer might be the final nail in the coffin for Sarah and Kate's relationship.

Kate quickly roamed the rooms, but the cottage was empty.

'I'll make us some coffee,' said Matt. 'Then we'll work out what to do next.'

Kate tried her mother's mobile again but she still had it switched off. Sarah had left messages and texts every day since Kate had left home, but they'd gone unanswered. Perhaps Kate should have got in touch. Her mother's tears today had seemed genuine. And Kate's rejection had pushed Sarah into saying something upsetting to Luke – something about Jack. *That's for my Mam.*

Kate's mind kept raking over the pieces of the puzzle as she and Matt drank their coffee.

'I feel there's something we're missing,' she said. 'Let's look at the facts. Luke was talking to my mum, and then he went straight over to Jack and punched him, saying it was for Annie.'

'So?' Matt rubbed his eyes, obviously fighting to stay awake.

Kate was exhausted, too, but the thought of Luke being out there alone forced her to focus.

'My mum must have said something that implied Jack had hurt Annie in some way.'

'Dad wouldn't have hurt Annie. He loved her.'

As much as Kate didn't want to believe it, her mother would have said anything if she thought it would cause trouble for Luke. Matt said Jack loved Annie, and everything other people said – Maggie, Barbara – seemed to bear that out. Did it mean, though, that Jack was totally innocent?

'My mum's filing cabinet,' she said, thoughtfully.

'What?'

'The filing cabinet in the study. It's always locked.'

'I don't see …'

'Neither do I, Matt! I'm clutching at straws here, but if my mum knew something about Jack, or Annie, or whatever, then maybe – just maybe – there's a clue.' She put down her coffee and stood up. 'If nothing else, it'll pass some bloody time.'

Ten minutes later, Kate still hadn't found the keys to the filing cabinet. Only one thing for it …

'Matt – can you force it open? Mum must have the key with her.'

He looked horrified. 'Kate, I can't do that …'

'Please! I'll take responsibility. The more I think about it, the more I'm convinced she's hiding something, Matt. Last time she was in here, I came in to talk to her and she slammed the filing cabinet shut. Looked guilty as hell. I didn't think about it at the time, but it's not my imagination, I know it's not.'

'What makes you think I can get it open?' said Matt.

'You can do anything.' She gave him her best smile.

He sighed. 'And so begins my life of crime. Where's your tool box?'

Kate's eyes were beginning to blur. She'd gone through the contents of the top two filing cabinet drawers and found only information about the business: invoices, bank statements, insurance files.

'I'm very uncomfortable with this, Kate,' called Matt from the living room, where he was keeping an eye on the driveway in case Sarah returned. If she did, Kate would just say they thought they'd heard an intruder. Sarah could believe that or not. Kate was past caring.

'I'm on the last drawer,' she called to him.

The bottom drawer looked more promising. Letters from Kate's grandmother in Spain, some holiday snaps, Kate's school reports – she'd like to look at those but now wasn't the time. Close to the back of the drawer, she pulled out a file with 'Jackson' written on the cover, not a name that meant anything to her. She opened it and something fluttered to the floor. A photo of a young boy. Picking it up, Kate's heart – and time – seemed to stop. She held the picture, staring at it in disbelief, until suddenly Matt was there. Had she called out? She didn't know. All she knew was that her world had just collapsed. The file lay where she'd dropped it. Jackson. Jack-son.

It was the early hours of Sunday morning and the ferry was packed with Bank Holiday travellers. There wasn't a seat to be had so Luke sat on the floor, leaning against the side of the walkway between one of the lounges and the cafeteria. He picked up a magazine from the floor and rested it against his knees but couldn't concentrate on reading. What a cock-up. He'd left the car in Holyhead because the ferry was fully booked, except for foot-passengers. So were the ferries for the next day. Maybe flying would have been the best option, but airport security was probably tighter. He didn't want to have to try and explain why he was carrying thirty thousand euro in cash. Not to mention a valuable necklace.

He thought about Kate and the love they'd shared. So brief but so strong. He didn't want to forget, but it hurt too much to remember: her smile, the affectionate way she would be watching him when he woke in the morning, the habit she had of gently pushing his hair away from his face. He took out his mobile and switched it on. God, so many texts. From Kate, from Matt, from Tim. None from Jack, of course. Why did that bother him? His fingers hovered over Kate's number. It was so tempting, but what would he say? 'Hi Kate, sorry I took off, but I just found out you're my sister.'

He felt sick when he thought of how they'd made love, and he wanted to spare her that. He switched the phone off again and drew his knees up tight to his chest, putting his head down and using his folded arms as a pillow. He felt wretched. Damp seeped into his sleeve, and instinctively his hand went to his face to wipe away tears. Finally, after ten years, he was crying.

It was nearly nine and the bloody church bells were ringing when Sarah arrived home. Did the vicar really expect people to turn up when they'd spent all yesterday gorging and boozing? Most of them would feel like she did – wrecked. All she wanted was to shower and sleep.

She'd spent the night with Justin Somerville, local entrepreneur. He'd found her on the village green before she'd had a chance to completely disappear into her bottle of wine. He'd called himself her white knight and said she shouldn't be alone on May Day. It had been so easy through the haze of alcohol to let him take charge, but back at his house, she'd not been able to block out thoughts of what she'd said to Luke so romance hadn't exactly sparked between her and Justin.

She thought about what had happened yesterday. Surely Luke would have to leave now? But what about Kate? Would she get over Luke, or had Sarah ruined her daughter's life? She leaned her forehead on the steering wheel, the tears close. Crying wasn't going to help, though. She should think about the positive. Kate might not thank her now but Luke being out of her life would be best in the long run. Sarah got out of the car, looking forward to a long soak in the bath and then bed.

Walking into the kitchen, she almost fainted with fright to find Matt sitting large as life at the table. He was unshaven and looked exhausted. His expression was grim and Sarah's stomach lurched. Dear God, don't let something have happened to Kate. She sank into the chair opposite him. 'What's wrong, Matt?'

He looked at her as if she'd just crawled out from under a stone. 'What's wrong is what you said to Luke yesterday.'

So Luke had talked. The cat was out of the bag. How was she going to get out of this?

'Yesterday? Did I speak to Luke? Can't really remember. I'd had quite a lot to drink ...'

'Don't try to kid me you don't remember.' Matt's voice was cold, hard. 'You were talking to Luke just before he punched Dad. Why did you do it, Sarah?'

Her heart was pounding. The last thing she needed was to be harassed like this in the morning. 'It wasn't my fault. Gavin was the one who told Luke that Kate was Jack's daughter.'

The shocked expression on Matt's face told her she'd just made a huge mistake. 'You didn't know, did you? You tricked me, you bastard. Get out.' And he could kiss his job at the Foresters goodbye, too. She was done with the Stewarts.

Matt didn't leave. 'Luke's gone, you know,' he said quietly.

'Well, I'm not sorry. He didn't belong here. And he didn't belong with Kate.' He would think her a bitch but she didn't care. She'd only been protecting her daughter.

'Kate's gone, too,' Matt said.

'What?' Sarah's stomach flipped.

'Gone,' Matt repeated. 'If I were her, I'd never want to see you or speak to you again. You've ruined her life. She said she couldn't live without Luke.'

Sarah felt faint. 'Matt, what are you saying? Kate wouldn't do anything stupid – she wouldn't!'

'Who knows what was going through her mind? She loves Luke. He's gone. She'll be very emotional right now.'

Sarah started to panic. Her baby girl was gone. 'Get her back, Matt, get her back!' she heard herself saying. 'It's not true. Jack isn't her dad ... but I told Luke he was. I didn't want them to be together. I'm so sorry.'

'And what about this? Are you sorry for this, too?' Matt reached inside his jacket and pulled out a photo, which he pushed across the table to her. Oh dear God, no …

'How … how did you get this?' she asked.

'More to the point, how did you get it?' Matt asked. The way he was looking at her was more than she could bear. Like she was the scum of the earth, which maybe she was.

'It's Luke, isn't it?' said Matt.

Sarah looked at the photo in front of her, at the boy with a mass of dark curls and huge, haunted eyes, who looked remarkably similar to the man he'd grown into. Sarah opened her mouth to lie but then Matt reached into his pocket once more and put a sheet of paper on the table.

'And this,' he said. 'A letter Annie sent, ten years ago, begging Claire to act on her behalf and ask my dad for help. He never saw this, and I'm guessing Claire didn't either. How did you get it, Sarah?'

'Has Kate seen it?' she whispered.

'Why do you think she's gone?'

'Oh, God!'

'Tell me, dammit! How did you get hold of it?'

Sarah was shaking with nerves. Such a long time to keep this secret, it was hard to give it up.

'Of course, I could take it to the police,' said Matt. 'Let them handle it. Maybe they can't make anything stick but you'll be ruined by the end of it all. Tell me the truth about this and it stays in the family, I promise.'

It was probably the best deal Sarah was going to get. She'd lost Jack so it didn't really matter what he thought. But if Kate knew she'd come clean, it might help. 'Could I have a coffee? Then I'll tell you what happened.'

'Annie sent the letter to Claire,' said Sarah, nursing her coffee. 'But Richard … intercepted it.'

'Why?'

'He said he had to stop her ever coming back here. Your grandparents didn't want it. Jack had been so upset when Annie left …'

'Spare me the altruistic motives,' sneered Matt. 'I'm not buying that. Annie was writing to Jack about Luke – wanting him to take care of their son. And he would have done that, if he'd seen the letter.'

Sarah nodded. 'I know. Richard told me he was going to Ireland, and that he'd tell Annie Jack was in a relationship with me. That he didn't want to take Luke.'

'Why did he involve you in all this?'

Sarah looked out of the window to escape Matt's critical gaze. It was painful to dredge up those memories from so long ago. 'Twenty years ago, Richard and I … got close …'

'Were you shagging him?' demanded Matt, the distaste evident in his expression.

The coarse word shocked her into a nod. 'It was over almost as soon as it began. But when the letter came, Richard showed it to me … He wanted me to give him Annie's necklace …'

'The sapphire and diamond one?' asked Matt.

'How did you know that?'

'Luke still has it. Dad couldn't figure out how Annie got it. Did you steal it from him?'

'No!' But Richard had and she'd accepted it, so Matt was right. She was kidding herself if she thought otherwise. 'Jack gave them to your grandmother to be auctioned. Richard "rescued" the necklace before she sorted through the pieces. He knew I'd always liked it. They're Ceylon sapphires, you know. Best quality.' Richard had wanted her to wear it when she was in bed with him. Probably gave him some kind of thrill to know he'd tricked both Jack and Grace. 'He wanted to give Annie the necklace and say Jack had sent it for her to

329

sell or do whatever she wanted with it. So she would know Jack had drawn a line under their marriage and moved on.'

'Did Richard organise all this on his own?'

'Well …'

Half an hour later, Matt knew everything she did. 'Does Richard know why Annie left?' he asked.

'He told me he didn't know. Now please, will you help me look for Kate, Matt? Where do you think she's gone?'

'Kate's fine. She's at Tim's.'

Sarah felt weak with relief, then angry. 'You lied to me!'

'Doesn't feel good to be on the receiving end, does it? Maybe you should have thought of that before you kept this from Dad – before you betrayed Claire. How could you do that to her?'

Matt was hardly ever with the same girl twice. What could he possibly understand about unrequited love? 'I know it doesn't make it right, but she was never meant to know. She'd had several miscarriages. I thought Richard reached out to me to help him through his own suffering. I was weak, and vulnerable – and lonely. Martin and I had been husband and wife in name only for months.'

Matt looked like he might be physically sick. She wondered if she'd ever see again the smiling, joking Matt she knew so well. 'What are you going to do?' she asked him.

'Get some justice for Luke. And Annie. I think they deserve that, don't you?'

She nodded, closing her eyes. She didn't care much about the Stewarts anymore. All she could think about was Kate.

'Sarah – Sarah?' Matt sounded agitated. 'What you said about you and Martin – who *is* Kate's dad?'

Oh God. This was a step too far. 'Martin is her dad,' she said. But it was too late. She'd already admitted they weren't living as man and wife.

'It's Richard – isn't it?'

'Matt – please don't say anything. For Kate's sake. I don't want her to know who her father is, ever. She'd hate me. Richard doesn't even know she's his. He asked once, but I panicked and told him I'd had a fling with Jack and that Kate was his daughter. Richard accepted that. He knew I'd always had a thing for your dad. He must have told that idiot son of his, yesterday or before. Probably had a good laugh over it.'

'So that's why you didn't want Luke and Kate to be together! If you hadn't tried to break them up, Richard would have guessed Jack wasn't the father – and would probably have guessed *he* was.'

Sarah nodded. 'He had asked me to burn this letter and photo – and of course now I see that I should have – but I kept them as insurance in case Richard ever found out and tried to be a part of Kate's life.'

'You let Kate go out with Gavin!'

'She had one date with him – I was away at the time and knew nothing about it. Thankfully, it was over almost as soon as it began. Matt – you won't tell anyone?'

'My dad has the right to know,' said Matt, 'and if we keep it quiet, it'll be a burden we bear for the sake of the people we love.'

He left the kitchen without another word.

Jack was drinking his third cup of coffee when Matt arrived. It was a week since his son had left home and Honey was all over him like a thing demented. 'Any news?' asked Jack.

'Plenty. But no sign of Luke yet.' Matt sat down and poured himself some coffee. He looked rough. Worse than Jack, whose jaw was bruised and still hurt like hell. 'I do know why he hit you, though.'

'Insanity?' suggested Jack.

'Yesterday, Sarah told Luke you're Kate's dad.'

'What! Jesus Christ! Matt, I swear to you—'

'Relax, Dad. I know it's not true. Sarah only said it to split Luke and Kate up. But Luke doesn't know this. I've texted him and tried calling, but his phone's been switched off. We're going to head out again today to look for him, but there's something else …'

Matt took a photo from his jacket pocket and pushed it across the table.

Jack stared at it. 'This is Luke.'

Matt nodded.

'God, he looks so like Annie. Where did you get this?'

'Sarah's had it – for ten years.'

Jack frowned. 'I don't understand.'

'This photo was sent to Claire along with a letter. She never got it. Richard found it, opened it, kept it from her.' He passed Jack a yellowed piece of paper. 'Prepare yourself, Dad.'

Jack recognised Annie's small, neat handwriting straight away. There was a growing sensation of pain and anger as he read the words his wife had written.

Dear Claire,

You will be surprised to hear from me after all this time, and I know you must have been shocked when I left. I'm sorry that I went without saying goodbye. Although it was heartbreaking, especially leaving Matt, I had no choice but to go.

I'm writing to you now because I'm desperate and don't know what else to do. When I left Jack, I didn't know I was pregnant. My son, Luke, is now 10. I enclose a photo of him. He is a good boy – very bright, and he loves football.

Life is very difficult. I've tried to make a home for

the two of us, but it's hard for unqualified people to find work, especially if you are a Traveller. I don't want to go into much detail now, but I hope you will just trust me when I say that I fear for Luke's safety.

Because of this I think that although it will break my heart, he should live with his father. I know this is a shock for you, and will be for Jack, too. I should have told him about Luke before now, but I worried he might take him away from me. The courts would likely have said Jack could give him a better life. Now I know that Jack can give Luke the protection I can't. I'm sure Matt and Luke will get along well together. Matt always said he wanted a brother.

Please, Claire, will you talk to Jack for me? Try to persuade him. I'm afraid he might hate me for leaving and not listen to me.

I have a friend, Jessie, who lives at a Traveller halting site, and you can write back to me care of her at the site address at the top of this letter. I hope you can write back to me soon and let me know if Jack will take Luke. Please trust me, Claire, and treat this as urgent. You're my best hope.

Your loving friend,

Annie

'Oh, my God,' moaned Jack when he finished reading the letter. 'She wanted me to take Luke. And I didn't know.'

'I'm so sorry, Dad.'

As Matt started to share with Jack what Sarah had told him, anger didn't cover what Jack felt at that moment. If Richard had been within striking distance, Jack doubted whether he'd have been able to prevent himself committing a serious crime. Beneath the anger, though, there was also a deep sense of loss, of grief. Of sheer disbelief, and even more confusion. The letter raised more questions than it answered.

'Richard made arrangements for Annie – a monthly payment,' continued Matt. 'Enough for her to rent somewhere decent in Ireland and to provide for Luke. Richard said she was happy with that because she didn't want to come back to Baronsmere – she just needed money. I think he was lying, and I doubt she got any of the money. Luke told me Joe and Liam always seemed to have cash but never shared it. We can guess where they got it.'

Jack got up and started pacing the kitchen. 'Annie must have been desperate if she was prepared to give up Luke. But where did Richard get the money? I can't believe he paid it out of his own pocket. If he's been embezzling from the company, I'll have him ...'

Matt shook his head. 'He didn't do anything illegal. Richard was just the monkey.'

'Who was the organ grinder?' Jack asked the question, but he already knew the answer.

'Gran. Richard told her about the letter. She didn't want to get involved, and told him to deal with it in whatever way he saw fit. Just so long as Annie didn't come back here to Baronsmere.'

Jack sat down again. He felt sick to his stomach.

'Dad, she must have really hated Annie to go to so much trouble.'

'Grace Stewart is a shallow snob who'd sell out anyone to keep her reputation. Annie was worth ten of her.'

Matt's mobile rang. 'Tim,' he mouthed, and relayed the conversation in bursts. 'Luke's just texted Kate. Text says "sorry" ... He's also texted Tim ... Fuck! Fuck! Tim – I'm at my Dad's. You and Kate get over here right now!'

He switched off the phone and ran out of the kitchen. Jack called after him as Matt pounded up the stairs. When he didn't respond, Jack followed him to his bedroom, where Matt was standing by the open safe.

'What is it, Matt? What's wrong?'

'Dad, we've got to get after Luke. I know where he is. Luke texted Tim that he left Betsy – Tim's car – at Holyhead.'

'Sounds like he's gone home. What's the problem?'

Matt gripped the edge of a table. 'Dad, your son is alone, depressed, and has two psychopaths looking for him, because he's walking around with thirty thousand euros he took from them.'

How much more could Jack take? They were back at the kitchen table, having been joined by Tim and Kate. Matt was telling them about Luke's stash of money. That certainly explained why he'd been so jumpy about the suitcase.

'So is he planning to give the money back to his uncles?' asked Tim, munching his way through some toast. He was the only one with an appetite.

'Oh God, he can't go near them!' wailed Kate. It was the first time she'd spoken in ages. She'd looked shell-shocked when Matt told her about Sarah's lies. 'Luke's uncles nearly killed him,' sobbed Kate. 'That's why he and Annie were running away.'

'What?' Jack was feeling something close to panic. All his neat little assumptions about Luke – about Annie – were slowly being peeled away. He'd suspected Joe and Liam but hadn't really wanted it confirmed. Facts could soon lead to involvement. It was hardly surprising that everyone else knew so much more than he did, though. Jack was the last person Luke would trust.

'They – they beat him so badly … he ended up in hospital …' Kate said, struggling through tears.

'As Emer suspected then,' muttered Jack.

'They abused Luke for *years*, Jack.' Kate's expression seemed part appeal for belief, part accusation for Jack's sins of omission. He listened, feeling increasingly sick, as she related the catalogue of abuse Luke had shared with her. His eyes were closed, but the images Kate had conjured up played in his mind with sickening brutality. And these were the men Luke might be going back to? Had Jack treated him so badly he would rather return to Ennis? Was he that desperate for a family – or did he have a death wish?

'So what do we do now?' asked Matt.

Jack opened his eyes. Everyone was watching him. Waiting. All his doubts and indecision suddenly crystallised into a hardness like a fist. 'We go to Ireland. Bring him home.'

Matt nodded. The approval in his eyes made Jack feel better than he had in weeks.

'Tim, see if you can book Matt and I on a flight to Ireland this afternoon ...'

'I'm coming, too!' Kate insisted.

She might slow them down, be too emotional, yet she was probably the one person Luke would trust. He'd listen to Kate. 'Okay, get ready. I'll be back in an hour. I think my mother owes me answers.'

'I'm coming with you,' said Matt. 'Don't argue, Dad. Luke is my brother. They're my grandparents. This is family business and I have a right to know what's going on.'

Grace might clam up if Matt was there. Or lie. He'd have to risk it, though. There wasn't time to argue.

As he got up from the table, Kate came and hugged him. 'Thank you, Jack,' she whispered. 'For caring about Luke ...'

Her words touched a place in Jack's heart he didn't know existed. If Luke was his son – as now seemed likely – he'd been deprived of everything that was rightfully his. Not just material things, but love and security, a decent chance in life. The extent of his ill-treatment was gut-wrenching. Was it any surprise the kid was so bitter? Jack wasn't suddenly filled with love for his maybe-son. But he had finally found compassion and understanding. And guilt.

Chapter Twenty-One

Jack was barely able to keep his anger in check on the drive to Edenbridge. The pieces of the puzzle were fitting into place and the resulting picture was ugly. Shocking. The people closest to him had conspired against him and changed the course of his life. Wild horses couldn't drag him into Edenbridge after today. Just walking into the chilly hall with its oppressive portraits was enough to set his teeth on edge.

'We'll keep our coats, Henderson,' he told the butler. 'We're not staying.'

'Sir Nicholas is not home today, but her ladyship is in the morning room, sir. Shall I announce …?'

'Let's make it a surprise, shall we? Richard's here – yes? Tell him to join us.'

Jack and Matt made their way up the grand staircase with its dark wood banisters polished to perfection. As a child, Jack had loved to slide down them until one day he was caught by his father and punished. At the top, before the turn, was a vast family portrait of privileged Victorian ancestors taking tea in the estate gardens; he'd once used crayon to black out the teeth of the youngest boy – it was months before it was discovered, and the pleasure this small act of rebellion gave him was worth the thrashing he received. How he hated this museum of a house, where all his natural childish urges had been suppressed. As a childhood, it didn't compare with the nightmare Luke had endured, but he was thankful his son had known a mother's love. Jack hadn't.

He opened the door without knocking and entered the morning room where the usual tableau greeted him: country gentlewoman busy at her writing desk, soothed by the fragrance from vases of hothouse roses, secure in the

338

knowledge her word was law for all who were fortunate enough to dwell in her home.

'Morning, Mother.'

Grace looked up, startled. A second later, she switched on a smile. 'Jack! I wasn't expecting you. Your father's playing golf and Claire's watching Gavin play rugby ... but they'll all be back for lunch – will you stay, too? It will be so nice to have the family together.'

'I don't think so,' said Matt.

'Matt – darling!' Grace stood up and moved to give Matt a kiss on the cheek but he drew back. She frowned. 'What's wrong?'

'You're what's wrong, Gran.'

Grace stared at him in amazement. 'I beg your pardon.'

'Yes, you really should,' Jack told her. If this situation hadn't been so serious, he'd have enjoyed seeing her discomfited.

Matt stepped forward. 'The balloon's gone up, Gran. We know you paid the Kiernan brothers to keep Annie and Luke away. Sarah told me everything.'

Grace grabbed the chair arm and lowered herself into the seat. It looked like her defences were about to crumble but she rallied. Grace Stewart was nothing if not a fighter. 'I haven't the faintest idea what you're talking about!' she protested. 'Sarah's obviously unhinged!'

Matt shook his head. 'I don't think so. The evidence is quite conclusive.'

He pulled out the image of young Luke and thrust it in front of Grace, who recoiled in her chair as if she'd been struck, but then her mouth set defiantly in a firm line and she said nothing.

Jack sighed. 'Well, I sent Henderson to fetch Richard. Perhaps he'll be more communicative. I particularly want to hear about his affair with Sarah twenty years ago.'

'What!'

'Ah – didn't you know? That one went under the radar, eh? You must be slipping, Mother. Foiled by an unhinged woman.'

'I think you should leave,' said Grace, coldly.

Jack sat down on the sofa near the window. 'Not till we've got some answers.'

'This is *my* house – I say what happens here.'

'And Luke is *my* son!' Jack snapped, increasingly convinced now that he was. 'Denied to me for twenty years. So – let's hear the details.'

At that moment, the door opened and Richard came in. 'Details about what?' He glared at Jack with his usual disdain. 'Grace, is everything all right?'

'No, Richard,' she said. 'Everything is far from all right. Jack is making all kinds of accusations.'

Jack had been waiting years to finally get something concrete on his brother-in-law. This, at least, would be satisfying. 'See, here's the thing, Richard – ten years ago, you found—'

'Stole,' Matt interrupted.

'Ten years ago, you *stole* a letter from Annie to Claire,' Jack continued.

Richard glanced at Grace before saying in a flat voice, 'I don't know what you're talking about.'

'That's exactly what Mother said. I daresay the two of you have got your cover stories planned.'

'Careful, Jack,' Richard warned him. 'There are laws against slander …'

'And there are also laws against theft,' Jack replied. 'Not just of a letter that wasn't addressed to you, but of Annie's necklace which you gave to Sarah. So *you* be careful, Richard.'

'What is it you want, Jack?' asked Grace.

'A confession. I deserve that, don't you think? So does Luke.'

'That little shit deserves nothing!' raged Richard.

Matt sprang forward, grabbed Richard by the lapels, and shoved him down into the nearest chair. 'Luke is my brother and worth ten of you.'

'Tell me everything, Mother.'

'Grace, you don't have to say anything!' said Richard. 'Let me call Nicholas ...'

'Yes, you do that,' Jack retaliated. 'And I'll call Claire – it'll be hard to tell her about you and Sarah, but it's time she knew.'

Grace glared at Richard, whose shocked and embarrassed expression told Jack he was now on the ropes and would likely give no further trouble.

'No one's calling Nicholas,' asserted Grace. 'He wasn't involved.'

According to Luke, though, Nicholas had tried to bribe Annie to leave, so that was small consolation. However, Jack had found the gap in his mother's defences. She would want this matter dealt with, hushed up, before Nicholas came home.

'So, Mother – Richard showed you Annie's letter. Then what?'

When Grace spoke, her eyes were downcast. Like she was defeated. 'Richard went to Ireland, but he didn't see Annie. He dealt with her brothers – they said that was the Traveller way. Men dealt with finances. They said Annie would use the money to get herself a small house – she didn't want to come back here, and obviously it was better for the child to remain with its mother.'

Jack felt sick. Grace was so cold and detached, referring to Luke as though he was an object, or at best, an animal. He turned to Richard. 'You sent Annie her necklace, knowing she'd take that as a sign we were truly over. So why did you then go to Ireland?'

Richard shrugged. 'Joe Kiernan got in touch. Said it wasn't enough. That there should be regular payments. Maintenance.'

'The money was enough to ensure their comfort until the boy was twenty-one,' Grace added, as though she'd done Annie a favour. She was seemingly oblivious to the fact that she'd denied her own grandchild his rights as a son. Jack's rights as a father.

'And what then, Gran?' Matt demanded. 'You washed your hands of them? Luke and Annie never saw a penny of that money. The brothers kept it all.'

Grace tutted and threw up her hands. 'What was I supposed to do, Matt? Check receipts? Play social worker? I did my best to ensure they were provided for.'

'Not good enough, Gran!' said Matt savagely. 'The whole thing stinks!'

Grace had always adored Matt, so his reproach must have been wounding. She stood up and walked over to the window, keeping her back to them. 'I'm sorry you feel that way, Matt. Perhaps when you have children of your own, you'll understand how strong the need is to protect them.'

'Protect!' exploded Jack, rocketing up from the sofa and moving swiftly over to his mother. 'You didn't protect me! You ruined my life. And Annie's. You were just protecting yourself and your precious status. And what about the protection I should have given *my* child? Protection from two thugs who made his life hell. Your own grandson, Mother!'

Grace didn't move or speak, and Jack felt an overwhelming urge to wrench her round, to shake her. She'd given her confession and obviously planned to brazen it out, hoping it would all blow over. Jack turned away from her in disgust.

'Okay,' he said, 'But none of this explains why Annie left. She wasn't always a victim. She had a spark, could stand up for herself.'

'Who knows?' said Richard, casually. 'Maybe she thought you and Sarah were at it in Brussels. It's what everyone else thought.'

Could that be true? Jack dismissed the idea even as he contemplated it. Annie would only ever have believed that story if it had come from Jack's own mouth.

'I never ...' he began, then noticed Matt shaking his head anxiously, and he stopped short. They'd agreed not to tell Richard he was Kate's father. No good could come of it – she loathed the man. Not to mention the hurt it would cause Claire. If Grace had a brain in her head, she'd come to the same conclusion about Kate's parentage, but at some point Jack would warn her not to tell Kate. Then he'd probably never speak to her again.

'The letter from Annie wasn't even about money,' said Jack, changing tack. 'She wanted me to take Luke because her brothers were being abusive.'

'The letter never said anything about abuse.' Grace's voice was cold and controlled.

'She was worried for Luke's safety. What did you think that meant? That they lived near a busy road?' How could he make his mother see her actions had been callous in the extreme. Negligent.

'I thought that was her ploy to get you back.'

'Jesus!' Grace had judged Annie by her own manipulative standards. 'I'd have you both behind bars if I could. Let me ask you one thing – was it worth it?'

Grace avoided his gaze and instead walked over to the fireplace, her back to them once again, as she rearranged ornaments. 'At the time I thought it was,' she said. 'I didn't want Annie back here, I admit it. I never wanted you to marry her in the first place. When I heard she had a son, I knew you'd be too weak to resist and you'd bring them both here. Then all the bitchy remarks about my gypsy daughter-in-law would start up again. My family's name has been respected in this part of the country for nearly a thousand years and I didn't want it tarnished. Reputation matters to me and I won't apologise for that.'

So that was it. This whole mess was down to snobbery, Grace's relentless quest to always be at the top of the social tree. 'You're a disgrace to all your noble ancestors,' Jack told her. 'And your gypsy grandson has more decency in his little finger than you have in your whole body. You're no mother of mine.'

Grace whirled round. 'Well, I certainly hope he's happy. He finally got his revenge!'

'Happy?' cried Matt. 'How can he be *happy*? His mother's dead at forty but would probably still be alive if it wasn't for you. And I'm sickened because you don't even care. You're just upset you've been found out.'

Grace finally showed some emotion, some sadness and regret at Matt's angry tone. 'I was trying to protect this family, Matt. To protect your future. Stewart Enterprises will be Jack's one day, and then yours.'

'Stuff it!' said Matt, and Grace flinched. 'Offer the business to Gavin. He's your only grandson now. My brother is more important to me than your money. C'mon, Dad – don't let them take up another minute of our time.'

'You don't know he's your brother,' said Grace. 'Just because *he* says so.'

'*I* say so!' snapped Jack. 'Because there never was another man, was there? And you never hired a detective. You fabricated it all.'

For a few telling seconds, there was silence before Grace reacted. 'Nonsense! Now you're becoming ridiculous.'

'Nice try, Mother,' said Jack. 'But your eyes just confirmed it.'

He and Matt moved towards the door, and then Jack turned back. 'One more thing – have the Kiernan brothers been in touch with you since Luke got here?'

Richard stood up, shrugged his shoulders. 'Why would they? Your ex is dead. They aren't likely to expect the payments to continue even if the kid isn't twenty-one yet.'

'Luke's gone back to Ireland,' said Jack. 'If he comes to any harm, I'll hold you both responsible. Like I hold you responsible for his mother.'

Richard smirked. 'So much misplaced emotion for your slut of a wife …'

Jack couldn't hold back any longer and swung a punch into Richard's smug face, watching with satisfaction as his brother-in-law stumbled backwards, blood spurting from his nose. He fell onto the table, smashing Grace's favourite Lalique bowl.

'That's for my wife and son – and for my sister,' Jack snarled. 'Start planning a future elsewhere, Richard. I don't want Claire contaminated by you any longer.'

Jack left the morning room and went down the stairs so quickly that Matt couldn't keep up with him. His breathing only returned to normal once the car had put some distance between himself and the lies and deceit of Edenbridge.

Jack saw signs for Ennis not long after they left Galway Airport in their hire car. The journey to Ireland had taken almost nine hours. Flights had been fully booked because of the Bank Holiday so they'd roughed it as foot-passengers on the ferry – the holiday also meant there was no room to take their car. It was the worst possible time for Luke to do a runner.

Once the ferry reached Dublin, they took a taxi to the airport, where Emer met them for the next leg of their journey, a flight cross-country to Galway. She'd also booked hotel rooms and hired the car she was now driving along Ennis's narrow streets. Definitely the kind of woman you wanted with you in a crisis. Definitely the kind of woman Jack wanted, full stop. Despite their recent problems, she'd come up trumps after he'd phoned to tell her the latest developments. It was obviously because she was concerned about Luke, but Jack didn't care. It was enough to have her with him, even if it was only temporary.

Jack looked out of the car window. Annie had spent many years in this town and he'd be walking in her footsteps. Was this going to be the final chapter in her sad tale? Doyle had suggested they talk first to Annie's friend, Jessie Reilly – the detective had texted Jack details and her whereabouts. She'd been the woman Annie had shared a caravan with when she went back on the road with two-year-old Luke. Later, when Annie had moved with her family into a house, she'd found a place for Jessie in a nearby halting site. The woman might be able to give some clues as to where they could find Luke. Or perhaps he might even be staying with her. The last thing Jack wanted to do was to question the Kiernan brothers. He was sure he wouldn't be able to control himself and didn't want to end up in an Irish police cell.

While they were waiting in the car at a red light, Emer spoke. 'I know you won't like this, Jack, but I don't think it's a good idea for you to go and see Jessie … no, hear me out. She may well have been told the same thing about you as Luke was. Travellers are very loyal to their friends, passionately so. If Jessie sees you, she might clam up completely …'

Or throw him out on his ear. What Emer said made sense but Jack had wanted to talk to the woman who'd been so close to Annie for much of the last twenty years. She might have a lot of answers.

'Emer's right, Jack,' said Kate, from the back seat. 'Why don't you and Matt ring round the hotels tomorrow morning in case Luke's checked in somewhere. He has the money if he wants to do that. I'll go with Emer. Jessie might open up more easily if she knows I'm Luke's girlfriend.'

Jack didn't like that he'd be out of the loop, but Kate's feelings for Luke were so positive that they'd surely shine through. She stood a better chance than he did of getting Jessie to help them.

He glanced round at Kate. Matt was snoring gently on her shoulder. 'Okay, Detective Freckles.'

She smiled but her face was pale and strained. Like him, she probably wasn't going to get much sleep tonight.

Next morning, Kate went with Emer to the Traveller halting site, where they'd arranged to meet with Jessie, the one sure person Luke would consider a friendly face.

'We'll pull in here,' said Emer, as she spied a parking space in front of a boarded-up shop.

'Why here?' asked Kate. 'It's the next street, and it's raining.'

'Best be discreet,' Emer told her. 'Travellers are tight-knit. We don't want to stick out like a sore thumb. I once turned up at a Traveller site wearing a suit, asking questions about a patient's family. Met a wall of silence. Someone who looks official is often associated with prying authorities.'

They got out of the car and shared an umbrella on the short walk. Kate hoped Jessie wouldn't clam up on them. Surely not, once she knew Kate was Luke's girlfriend. She had to make the Traveller woman trust her. She was the only lead they had in their search for Luke. Kate felt her mouth go dry, her hands grow clammy. She tried to quell her anxiety, her desperation. She summoned up an image of Luke in her mind and willed him not to do anything foolish before she found him.

The halting site was made up of rows of bays, each one surrounded on three sides by low boundary walls. Jessie's caravan was white with an orange trim, raised on blocks. There was a garden bench out front, surrounded by pots of flowers.

'Could the council not provide a house for Jessie?' Emer asked John, the site supervisor.

'Doesn't want one,' he replied. 'Been most of her life on the road. Traveller, through and through. Said she'd not be comfortable in a house.'

He knocked on the door and stepped back in view of the windows. A net curtain twitched and a small wrinkled face appeared. John gave a wave. A few moments later, the caravan door was pushed open.

'I'll get back to the office now,' John told them. 'Hope you find Luke. If you do, tell him I was askin'. He came here a lot – helped out where he could. Nothin' was too much trouble, especially if it was for the older folk. He's a good kid.'

Kate felt a surge of pride – and love. Hearing someone from Luke's other life confirming he was a special person meant so much. Her mother, and even Abbie, had suggested Luke was only a novelty with a pretty face, and that romantic notions of Travellers had brought some excitement into Kate's sheltered, privileged life. Maybe all that was true but Kate had also chosen Luke because he was a man who was decent and honourable.

'C'mon, Kate,' murmured Emer, putting a reassuring hand on her arm.

It was cramped inside Jessie's caravan, and there was a powerful smell of lavender. The old woman was seated on

348

a fold-down bed, stroking a cat with gleaming eyes. She indicated a bench settee, and Kate and Emer sat down, briefly introducing themselves.

'Can't offer any tea,' said Jessie, in a voice cracked with age. 'Electricity's off. So – ye've come about Luke.'

Emer nodded. 'That's right. We haven't seen him since Saturday. Thought he might have come back to Ennis. Back to you.'

Jessie shook her head. 'Wish he had. My home's his – he knows that. I've been prayin' for him ever since I heard about … the accident.' She stared into a corner, where there was a little grotto of porcelain saints. 'John says ye're from Dublin. From the hospital where they took Luke.'

'I was Luke's counsellor there,' confirmed Emer. 'I spent quite a bit of time with him.'

'Was he stoppin' with ye, then? After the hospital.'

'No. Luke's been in England, staying with his father.'

'His father!'

Jessie's expression was so angry, Kate wondered if Emer should have mentioned Jack at all. Maybe it would have been better to explain the circumstances first, and tell her how Jack's family had been so manipulative.

'A lot has come to light about what happened all those years ago,' said Emer. 'Jack didn't know about Luke – he didn't know why Annie left him, or that she asked him for help.'

'And what about the letter?' Jessie shook her finger at Emer.

'Jack never received that letter,' Emer told her, but Jessie looked even angrier.

'I don't want to hear your lies,' she said, her voice emotional. 'He got that letter – because he wrote back tellin' her he didn't want her, or the boy. Said their marriage was a mistake – that he couldn't be connected to a 'gypo'. He sent her a fancy necklace and told her to sell it. As if she could be bought off. And I know all this because the package was brought direct to me.'

Kate looked at Emer, who seemed uncertain how to deal with what, to her, was new information. She bit her lip – Luke had told her about that letter, and he'd told Jack who hadn't believed him. But there obviously was a letter – had Jack been lying all the time? She didn't know if she should mention it to Emer now or wait until they were back at the hotel.

'That letter broke Annie,' Jessie continued, and Kate could see the gleam of tears on her cheeks. 'Made her feel like nothin'. How could anyone be so cruel? I hope Luke got a chance to tell Jack Stewart exactly what he thought of him. All those years of sufferin' he caused.'

The cat jumped from Jessie's arms and hid under the bed. The old lady was breathing heavily now. God help them if her heart gave way. Kate got up and knelt in front of Jessie, staring into eyes that seemed as old as the world. 'Jessie, I'm Kate. Luke is my boyfriend.' She pulled out her mobile phone and showed Jessie a photo of her and Luke, arms entwined, as proof of what she said. 'I'm so worried about him. We all are. Please help us find him, if you can.'

Her eyes filled with tears but she maintained eye contact with the old woman, who suddenly took hold of one of Kate's hands, turning it palm up, tracing the lines with her gnarled fingers.

'Are ye a Traveller, lass?' Jessie asked, still staring at the hand she held.

'No, I'm not,' Kate admitted. 'But that makes no difference to how I feel about Luke. We love each other.'

'I can see that,' murmured the old woman. 'And he's easy to love, is my Luke. But it's a hard road for Travellers and country folk to walk together. Annie found that out. And, ye know, a Traveller man needs respect more than anythin'. Can ye respect who Luke is and not want to change him?'

'I can.' Kate was already at odds with her mother over Luke. If that wasn't proof of her love, what was? 'I wouldn't ever want him to change.'

'Ye say he's disappeared. Is that down to the Stewart man?'

'There was a misunderstanding,' Emer told her. 'Jack is here with us – he's come to Ireland to find Luke. To sort things out. I don't know about the letter he's supposed to have written, and I will ask him about it – but the important thing is that we find Luke.'

'Luke's not been here,' said Jessie. 'His uncles came by, though, askin' if I'd heard from him, but they didn't get anythin' out of me.'

'Oh God!' Kate felt sick to her stomach. 'They mustn't find him. He told me what they did to him. If he goes near them, they might hurt him again.'

Jessie nodded, pulling out a set of rosary beads from her pocket and passing them one by one through her fingers. 'He must have trusted ye to tell ye about that. Sit up here beside me, lass.'

Kate did so. It seemed like she'd gained some of Jessie's trust. 'He did trust me. He also told me about you – how you were like a grandmother to him, a mother to Annie. He loves you very much.'

'And they were my family,' whispered Jessie. 'Gave me somethin' to go on for after I lost my man and my two babies.'

Luke had told Kate about that tragedy. How a faulty gas canister had exploded in Jessie's caravan while Jessie was taking tea with a friend on the same site – Jessie had had to be held back by other Travellers as her caravan burned out of control.

351

'I'm so sorry about that,' whispered Kate.

The old woman didn't appear to hear. Her eyes were distant, replaying some memory. 'And now my poor Annie's cold in the ground. I told her not to drive them roads at night. I wanted her to stop with me and go in the mornin'. But she was so scared. That accident – it was all Joe and Liam's fault really. They made her life a misery. Treated her like a slave. Bullied that poor child. Sometimes, when we were all on the road together, I could hear Luke at night in his grand-da's caravan, cryin'. I told Annie I could have him with me. Keep him out of Joe's way. But Luke wanted to be with his mammy.' Jessie sighed. 'The damage Joe Kiernan's done to his own folk, I wonder he can sleep at night.'

'Annie wrote to Claire, Jack's sister. Is that right?' Emer asked Jessie.

'That was my idea,' confirmed Jessie. 'They got close over there in England. A woman's touch can soften things at times, right? Annie was so desperate, the poor wee lass.'

Kate knew Jessie had been well-meaning yet if the letter had gone to Jack, not Claire, Annie and Luke's life would have turned out very differently. There was no point in saying that, though, and hurting this old woman.

'Truthfully, Jack never got Annie's letter,' said Emer. 'Neither did his sister.'

Jessie stared at Emer, shock written large all over her face, as she heard how Grace and Richard had conspired to keep Annie away from Jack. Eventually, she managed to croak a question: 'Does Luke know this?'

'No, he doesn't. We only found out after he left. Jack's mother confessed, although we didn't know there was a fake reply letter until you said. I assume they did that, too. I know it's a long time ago but do you know what happened to the letter? Did Annie keep it?'

'I don't know,' said Jessie. 'I never learned how to read,

so she told me what was in it. Said he didn't want her or Luke. She was so upset. Walked away and left it on my table. I thought of burnin' it – and Jack Stewart's soul with it – but I gave it back to her later when she was calmer. Said she might need it one day … when she'd made it by herself and could wave it under the noses of them Stewarts. But, of course, that never happened …' Jessie's voice tapered off into sadness.

'Why didn't Annie leave Joe and Liam long ago?' Emer asked.

'That's easy enough for country folk. Much harder for a Traveller. Besides … Annie took sick not long after gettin' the letter. She had a kind of … breakdown, I guess they call it. Nerves and that. She was lookin' after the boy all right but she wasn't eatin' enough herself and got run down. Kept sayin' she was tired and just wanted to sleep for a long time and wake up when the memories had all gone. She was cryin' a lot, too.'

'Did she get help?' asked Emer.

Jessie nodded. 'One of them Traveller activists got her a bed some place and Luke stayed with me. About four weeks later, Annie came home. She took pills for quite a bit after that. And then of course her daddy had a couple of strokes. Needed her to look after him.'

Kate sighed. 'So sad …'

'What makes ye think Luke's comin' back here?' asked Jessie.

'He left his car at Holyhead,' Emer replied. 'So he must have been making his way back to Ireland. It's somewhere he knows, and he might want answers about what happened all those years ago.'

'If he goes to talk to Joe and Liam, he'll not risk goin' to the house, I'm sure of it. They're always drinkin' in The Green Man of an evenin'. He'd talk to them there.'

'Like Jack, he still doesn't know why Annie left England,' said Emer. 'Do you know? Did she ever tell you?'

Kate held her breath, hoping they'd finally get the answer to the last part of the mystery.

Irritatingly, John chose that moment to knock on the door and enter the caravan. 'Just to tell you the electricity is back on, Jessie,' he said. 'In case you wanted to make your visitors some tea.'

'No, they're leavin',' Jessie told him.

Kate wondered if what appeared to be a sudden change of attitude was because of Emer's last question. Maybe she was just being suspicious but Kate was sure she'd seen a knowing look on Jessie's face. It was a dead end for now, though. She stood up. 'Thanks for your help, Jessie. If Luke does come to see you, please ask him to call one of us. Tell him – tell him that the information he was given on May Day was incorrect. It's really important he knows that. We've tried calling him but his phone is switched off.'

'Happen he doesn't want to talk to ye.'

'He would if he heard that message,' said Kate. 'I promise you.'

Jessie nodded. 'And if ye find him first, tell him to keep away from Joe and Liam.'

Kate prayed Luke *would* visit Jessie first. He could hardly expect a welcome from his uncles. Surely he knew that? Perhaps he no longer cared about himself or his safety. Or maybe he just wanted a family of any description.

Jack and Matt arrived at the small backstreet pub in Ennis after a fruitless morning spent tramping round hotels and guesthouses in search of Luke. Emer and Kate were already there, and they shared the details of the meeting with Jessie. The biggest revelation was the answer letter Annie had received, supposedly from Jack.

So many things were starting to fall into place now. 'It makes sense, Luke resenting me so much,' said Jack.

'But why would Richard forge a reply from you, Dad?' asked Matt. 'Grace agreed to send money.'

Emer sighed. 'Annie had to hear it from Jack, not a go-between. Otherwise she might have tried again.'

Jessie had said Annie was devastated when she got the letter. No wonder. She must have thought the very worst of Jack. That he was a hypocrite through and through, just like his mother. 'I wish I had that letter. It's evidence. Then I'd make Richard pay for doing what he did.'

'Luke still has it,' said Kate, and they all looked at her in surprise. 'His uncle showed it to him and when Annie threw it in the bin, Luke took it out without her knowing. He said one day he planned to confront Jack with it, but he and Annie were in such a rush when they left Ennis that he didn't think to take it with him.'

'Pity …' said Matt.

When the barman brought their meals, Jack could only make a half-hearted attempt at tackling the lamb shank he'd normally have devoured. A silence settled on their table. Even small talk didn't appear to be an option, apart from a whispered 'Pass the pepper, please,' from Kate. Eventually, Jack reached a decision. 'I want that letter. I want proof of what Richard did. Then I'll make him confess in front of Luke, before I kick him out of my life and out of Claire's.'

'Nice idea, Dad,' said Matt. 'But what do you suggest? We knock politely on the door and ask the Brothers Grimm for it? We'd probably get a fist in the face first.'

'We wait until they're out of the house,' Jack said.

Matt's shocked face as he gasped 'Come again?' would have made Jack smile in different circumstances.

'If what Jessie told you is right, they'll be at that pub this evening,' Jack continued.

'Do you know,' said Emer, 'for a minute there, I thought you were planning to break in to the Kiernans' house.' Jack didn't reply. 'My God, you are! Jack, you can't be serious!'

Jack went on as though she hadn't spoken. 'First, we'll have to check out the house. Maybe I can get in round the back ...'

'And if there's an alarm – or a guard dog?' Emer interrupted.

'Then I'll give it up as a bad idea,' Jack conceded – but he was going to get into the Kiernan house, come hell or high water.

'It *is* a bad idea!' Emer protested. 'For God's sake, someone could see you, hear you – call the police!'

'Maybe,' said Jack. 'But maybe the Kiernan brothers are so unpopular the neighbours won't give a damn.'

'I'm coming with you,' said Matt. 'You'll need backup.'

'Matt!'

'Emer, we've come this far. We can't walk away from a chance to find out why Annie left us.'

'You're mad, the pair of you!' Emer declared. 'We came here for Luke – how will it help him if you both end up in a police cell?'

'We'll be careful,' Matt promised.

Jack was still planning. 'I'll need a screwdriver,' he said.

'And we'll need to wait until it's dark,' said Emer.

'We?' asked Jack.

'If your mind's made up, I'm coming with you,' she told him.

'Like hell you are!'

'I have an idea,' Emer continued. 'I doubt The Green Man is the kind of place two women would go together, but Matt and Kate could go as a couple and phone you if the brothers leave. And I can keep an eye out from the car.'

'Good idea,' said Kate, smiling for the first time since

she'd arrived at the pub. 'I'm impressed, Emer. Have you done this sort of thing before?'

'I used to read Nancy Drew,' Emer laughed. 'Never thought I'd get the chance to be her for real.'

'Life with the Stewarts is never dull,' said Matt, and they all managed nervous smiles.

The sound of a siren woke Luke and he peered with bleary eyes at the time. Half past three. Monday afternoon. He'd slept on and off for a whole day. Time to drag himself out of bed. A shower revived him a bit and reawakened his appetite. He'd had nothing since a cheeseburger at the May Day hooley, and some crisps on the ferry.

He took some money from the safe. Not too much. No point inviting temptation. Just enough to get himself a hoodie, a beanie hat and some sunglasses in Penney's. He wanted to look anonymous when he went to Ennis. Tomorrow he'd contact a private clinic to arrange a hip replacement for Jessie, then stay here in Limerick for a while. Relax and try to get his head round everything. Come to terms with it before taking off somewhere. Having money was giving him a freedom he'd never known – able to stay in a decent hotel, buy anything that took his fancy. It would be easy to lose sight of the fact he'd nearly burnt it because he thought it brought him bad luck. Well, he surely couldn't have any more bad luck, so he might as well put it to good use. Maybe buy a caravan, or even better, a motorhome. Get a dog for company and take to the road again.

Luke sat alone in the pub, watching the evening crowd enjoying themselves. Families. Friends. Even the words brought a lump to his throat. He'd just smoked a cigarette, which he hadn't done since he was sixteen, and polished off a huge plate of sausages and colcannon. Now he had a vodka and coke in front of him. If anyone offered him a joint, he'd probably have that too. Anything to stop him feeling the gaping hole where his heart had once been.

A scruffy band was singing 'The Rocky Road to Dublin', and the accents around him were Irish. He was Irish. He was washing away the Brit. This was home. A woman across the pub smiled at him. Would she have smiled if she'd known Luke was a Traveller? But no one here knew who he was and despite everything, it was good to feel accepted.

After his all-day sleep, Luke wondered if he'd end up awake all night. He didn't want that. Didn't want to lie in the dark, thinking about Kate. Wishing she was there. He went to the bar and ordered another vodka and coke. When he got back to his table, Smiling Woman was there.

'Hi,' she said, giving him a look that was more than friendly. 'You're staying at the same hotel as me. I saw you earlier. I'm Fionnula.'

Half an hour later, Luke was in her room, standing nervously by the door. He was already having second thoughts. She'd disappeared to the bathroom, probably to change into something more comfortable. She was older than him, maybe twenty-five or more. Not unattractive but definitely pushy. When she'd suggested they go back to her room, he'd just thought *Why not?* and downed his drink for courage. Now he wondered what the hell he was doing. He'd been propositioned by a woman who obviously spread it about a lot …

Spread it about a lot. Gavin's words came back to him like a punch. Jesus! When would he learn? As usual his temper had got the better of him, the red mist robbing him of common sense and logic. What if it *was* true, that his mam had had an affair? If he'd a brain in his head, he wouldn't have hit Jack with his fist – just with a demand for a DNA. If he wasn't Jack's son, then he wasn't related to Kate. There'd be a chance for them to be together.

Clinging to the hope his mother had left Jack because she was pregnant by someone else, Luke left Fionnula's room and returned to his own, but there was no peace there. As much as he wanted to think maybe he wasn't Jack's son, he couldn't really believe Annie had been playing around. She wasn't that kind of woman, he'd stake his life on that. And why would she have lied to him and said Jack was his father, with all that went with it – the pain of rejection?

Luke helped himself to wine from the fridge then got into bed still wearing his clothes, and pulled the covers over him. He wanted Kate; his arm went round the pillow, hugging it tightly, so he could pretend. He'd been devastated by his mother's death, but Jack had been there, a parent of sorts, and then there'd been Matt and Maggie and Kate. He'd still felt alone at times, but nothing compared to this. He felt like he was five years old again, and he wanted his mam to make everything right, but she was gone and now he had no one to turn to. He'd lost Kate, his soulmate. And his brother. Was he always going to lose everyone he cared about? It scared him to think he was now truly alone. He curled up, tears close once more. Years with none, and now he couldn't get rid of them.

Emer jumped as a ginger cat suddenly appeared, stalking across the bonnet of the car as though to remind her this was his territory. Thankfully, the cat was the only sign of life as she sat parked a short distance from the Kiernan house, waiting for Jack.

It was after eight and dark now. They'd had to wait an hour before the brothers left their house. Joe and Liam had headed down the street on foot, thankfully in the opposite direction from Jack and Emer in their car. The Green Man was three streets away, and Matt and Kate phoned when the brothers arrived. They'd phone again when Joe and Liam left, so there'd be time enough for Jack to get out safely.

Emer sighed with relief as Jack reappeared, shifting his attention from one end of the street to the other. He looked suspicious, but maybe that was because she knew his intentions.

He got into the car beside her. 'No burglar alarm and no dog. The back door looks very basic. I should be able to jimmy it with the screwdriver. Don't want to risk breaking a window.'

'It's not too late to change your mind, Jack,' said Emer. She wished he would, but he had the look of a determined man.

It was as if he hadn't heard her. 'There's access to the house from the rear but to get there you have to approach it from one of two pathways. This is a good vantage point – you've got a view of both directions. You can clearly see if anyone's going round the back.'

He opened the glove compartment, taking out a torch and screwdriver from a small tool kit they'd bought earlier. 'I'll check the upstairs first. Hopefully, this won't take long.'

'Jesus, Mary and Joseph!' exclaimed Emer. 'I never thought this trip could end with us being arrested.'

'That's a risk I'm prepared to take,' said Jack. 'There's still time for you to back out.'

'I'm in for the duration, Jack.'

Breaking in was easier than Jack imagined. No wonder people turned to crime. The lack of real security was either down to the fact people knew there was nothing worth stealing or, even more likely, no one would knowingly mess with the Kiernan brothers. Thankfully, the windows had curtains, and Jack closed them and switched on his torch, keeping the beam low in the hopes that no one would see it from outside.

Upstairs, he started trying doors. The first led to a bathroom which looked like it hadn't been cleaned for weeks. The next door revealed a room which was neat and feminine. Annie's room. A picture of the Virgin Mary on the sparse white walls. A small portable TV on the dressing table, along with various jars of skin products. His stomach turned over as he looked at the single bed with its pretty lilac quilt. Annie had lain here, her long black hair splayed against the pillow ...

Jack's mind had now taken him to the one place he didn't want to go. To memories of Annie's lithe, sensual body and of her passionate delight in lovemaking. She was a virgin on their wedding night, ever mindful of her Catholic upbringing, but once married, she was a natural and exciting lover. When he'd told her so, she'd simply replied, 'That's because I love you so much.'

Almost trance-like, Jack sat on the bed and caressed the pillow gently before taking it in his arms and hugging it to his chest. Luke *had* to be his son, created from the passion he and Annie had shared. All that nonsense his parents had spouted about her seeing someone else was just that ... nonsense. Annie was a devout Catholic and would never have broken their marriage vows. His chest felt tight and he closed his eyes, willing her to be there when he opened them.

Eventually, Jack shook himself from his depressing nostalgia and went back out into the hallway. One of the remaining two rooms had a few car posters, and Jack guessed that belonged to Joe. As the older brother, he'd likely have his own space. Traveller culture wouldn't approve of a woman sharing with an adult male who wasn't her husband, so that would explain the two single beds in the last room Jack entered. Luke had shared with Liam.

It was definitely a room of two halves, one half a mess of clothing and little else, the other half with Manchester United posters on the wall, and strewn with personal items: a radio/CD player, a handful of CDs and some dog-eared paperbacks on the floor. Luke had been drawn to the bookcase back home and had obviously inherited his mother's love of reading. Emer had told him Luke was articulate and intelligent, and he'd virtually laughed that off. It seemed he was as guilty of prejudice as the next.

On the bed in Luke's half of the room was a tatty blue towelling dressing gown, which was sure to have been needed. The house felt cold. God knows what it must be like in winter. Jack slid back the door of the built-in wardrobe. There wasn't much in there, just jeans, T-shirts, a woollen jumper and a suit. He remembered the new clothes he'd bought for Luke, who clearly needed them yet had resented what felt like charity. And wouldn't anyone? Designer label clothes bought for you by a father who didn't really want you. Jack felt the sting of shame.

Five minutes later, Jack found what he was looking for, at the back of a drawer. He sat on Luke's bed, his hands trembling. Emer would be frantic with worry, but he wanted privacy for this.

Emer drummed her fingers on the steering wheel, agitated and more than a bit scared. Jack had been gone for at least twenty minutes, and during every one of them she'd expected to see Joe and Liam Kiernan. What if Matt and Kate couldn't call for some reason?

When people passed, she'd pretended to be reading a map, convinced she looked as guilty as she felt. She jumped as a torchlight shone through the window, and a near heart attack followed when she saw a Guard. Swallowing hard, she rolled down the window. 'Good evening, Officer.'

'Can I ask what you're doing here?' said the policeman.

'I'm waiting for my … my boyfriend. He has business with one of the tenants. He should be back soon.'

'What business does your boyfriend have?'

'He's a debt collector,' Emer replied, thinking on her feet and wondering when she became such a proficient liar.

'He'll be lucky round here,' said the Guard, tipping his cap. 'Good night, then. I'll be around for a while if you need me. You really shouldn't be here by yourself.'

'Yes,' smiled Emer, trying to look calmer than she felt. 'It is getting quite dark.'

'Dark or broad daylight makes no difference here,' he replied.

Hopefully, her relief at the policeman's leaving wasn't too obvious. When Jack appeared ten minutes later, Emer hardly gave him time to close the door before she started the car and drove as fast as was legal away from Carnlough Street.

Jack was deathly quiet and Emer could sense the tension in his body as he sat beside her in the car. She resisted pushing him for information, and when they picked up Kate and Matt, she shook her head, indicating they shouldn't ask questions yet.

Once back at Jack's hotel room, he went into the bathroom, and moments later Emer heard the shower start up. She couldn't be certain, but she thought Jack might be crying. Although exhausted, Emer wouldn't be able to go to her own room until she knew he was okay. Finally, the shower stopped and a few moments later Jack emerged from the bathroom, towelling his hair. He gave her a weary smile then headed to the minibar, taking out two small bottles of brandy, the contents of which he poured with absolute concentration and precision. He handed her a glass and downed his own in one gulp. She watched as he rummaged in the pocket of his jacket on the chair. He took out a paper and handed it to her. There was the slightest tremor in his hand.

Setting down her glass, Emer gingerly took the paper and unfolded it. It had worn away slightly at the creases but the words were legible. She glanced up at Jack. 'It's typed.'

He nodded. 'Richard only needed to forge my signature, and that was easy enough.' He sat down heavily on a chair. 'Read it, Emer.'

So she did.

Annie

Years ago, you left Baronsmere without warning or reason. Matt cried for you for months, and I had to pick up the pieces of my shattered life and find a way to move on. Now you suddenly tell me you have a son – that we have a son. You expect me to accept responsibility and take you both back into my life. Well, I'm sorry, but that's just not possible. How can I not have doubts, given the way you left?

When we married, I ignored the warnings that eventually your background would come between us. I should have listened to that advice, but I think I was too grief-stricken after Caroline's death to think straight.

When you left, I was considered by many a fool for having married you, and it's taken years for me to build up that lost trust and respect again. My position in both the business and the village would be less respected if I was known to all as 'the man with the gypo kid'. Sadly, prejudice still exists. Also, I am in a relationship now – a happy one – and don't see why I should jeopardise that. Haven't you made me suffer enough already?

I'm sorry if you're having problems, but this is the

risk you took when you walked out on me and a lifetime
of security. It might have been better if you had taken
the necessary steps to ensure you didn't have to be a
single mother. Getting rid of it would have released you
from the burden. Released you from me.

Do as you please with my wedding gift to you. The
symbol of the start of our marriage now symbolises
the end of it. Please consider this letter as the last
communication there will ever be between us.

Jack

A chill settled over Emer despite the warmth of the hotel
room. She took a quick gulp of the brandy. The letter
was nasty, mean, intended to hurt, to wound. Intended to
make certain Annie never returned to Baronsmere. 'That's
vile,' she said. 'The person who wrote this ... is sick,
twisted ...'

Jack nodded, anger and pain evident in his eyes. He went
to his jacket once more. 'I found this, too.'

Emer took what he handed to her, and opened it. It was
a cheque for fifty thousand pounds, made payable to Annie
Stewart, and signed by Nicholas Stewart.

Jack took the letter and the cheque back, putting them in
his wallet. 'I tell you this – they'll wish they'd never crossed
me,' he promised, his tone dark, threatening. 'No wonder
Luke hates me. He thinks I wanted him *aborted*. That I told
his mother she should have got rid of it – *it!*'

'The letter doesn't explain why Annie actually left
Baronsmere, though,' said Emer.

'I know. Looks like I'll have to talk to Joe and Liam, after
all. Beat it out of them, if I have to.'

His anger was understandable but still alarming. Emer
could see he was very much on the edge right now, capable

of anything. 'Perhaps we'll never know the reason,' she cautioned. 'Perhaps she never told anyone.'

Jack thumped the desk in frustration. 'I have to know! It's eating me up inside!'

'I understand, Jack – but surely the most important thing now is Luke. Rebuilding your relationship with your and Annie's son.'

Jack sighed. 'I don't know what to do for the best. I don't know anything any more. I'm dog-tired. Emer, could you hold me – just hold me – tonight? Nothing more than that, I promise. Please.'

Emer had already decided that even if she and Jack were a couple again, it wouldn't be in the true sense until he'd worked through his feelings. There would be no making love tonight, not even for comfort. Everything had changed, because now Jack was truly a bereaved man. The woman he had loved was dead, and the knowledge she hadn't just abandoned him meant he could now properly grieve. The man was in deep crisis. She curled into him, her hand on his chest. He was staring at the ceiling, lost in his own thoughts. Emer felt drained, close to tears, and wondered what tomorrow would bring.

Chapter Twenty-Two

So far, so good. Nearly ten-thirty in the morning but few people around. Not even John, who seemed to have built-in radar when it came to visitors or intruders. Luke knocked on the door of Jessie's caravan. He saw her peering from the window, no sign of recognition. The dark glasses, the hoodie and the beanie were obviously a successful disguise. He must look a bit suspicious, though. He removed his sunglasses and her face broke into a smile. A moment later, she'd pushed open the caravan door.

'Hello, Jessie.'

'Luke! My darlin' boy.' She stood aside to let him in, and once inside, he hugged her tight. This woman was like a grandmother to him. What a grandmother should be, totally unlike Grace. She stroked his cheek, tears in her eyes. 'I heard what happened. Your poor Mammy, God rest her. Are ye all right, son?'

'I am now, but it took a few weeks,' Luke said. No point letting Jessie know he didn't think he'd ever be all right again.

'Ye look tired,' she said. 'I'll make some tea.'

Luke sat down on the bench sofa. 'Mam's buried in England, Jessie. My da' turned up at the hospital and brought me home with him. He sorted the funeral.'

Jessie sat down next to him. 'I know. A lass called Emer was here yesterday. She told me.'

'What!'

'Lookin' for ye. Worried like.'

Luke was touched Emer cared enough to come looking for him.

'Worried? Or mad?' Luke asked. 'I hit Jack before I left, Jessie.'

367

Jessie frowned. 'Well, happen he deserved it. But they didn't seem mad. Just anxious to find ye.'

'They?'

'Another lass was with her. Kate. Said she was your girlfriend. Do ye think it's wise to get with country folk after what happened to your mammy?'

Kate! That wasn't good. He wanted her to forget him not follow him – he didn't want to have to tell her they were brother and sister, but there was no way he'd be able to look at her and say he didn't care.

'They left a message for ye,' said Jessie. 'Thought ye might come to see me. Now, let me remember it right. They said it was important – that ye'd want to know. Let me think on it while I make that tea.'

'Did they say why they're here, Jessie?' He hoped nothing bad had happened, maybe to Matt or Maggie.

'The Irish lass told me they were worried about Joe and Liam catchin' up with ye. After what they did before.'

Matt would know he'd taken the money. Maybe he thought Luke was going to give it back to Joe and Liam. As if.

'Ye weren't happy in England then, darlin'? Even though ye had a lass?'

'For a bit,' Luke told her, not keen to go into details, not even to Jessie. 'It wasn't all bad. But it wasn't home. I didn't fit in there.'

'Then they're fools.' Jessie was emphatic. 'And it's their loss. Anyone should be proud to have ye in their family.'

'We didn't get on, Jack and me,' Luke told her.

'Well, the lasses said he was here in Ennis with them. Him and your brother.'

Christ! Should he be pleased about that? It would depend on Jack's reasons for coming, but if Emer, Kate and Matt were with him, then it seemed he'd come to help.

Jessie handed him a mug of tea and sat down on the bed. 'Luke, the lasses told me somethin' you need to know. It's about the letter your mammy sent to the Stewart one's sister.'

It took a few seconds before Luke realised the implication of what Jessie had just said. 'What? Mam wrote to *Claire*? No, that can't be right. The reply was from Jack.'

Jessie explained she'd advised Annie to write to Claire in the hopes that she could talk Jack round into taking Luke away from Joe and Liam.

Luke's thoughts were all over the place. 'Jessie, Claire never knew about me, and I'm sure of that. She *did* like Mam, and she was great to me in England.'

'It seems one of those Stewarts at the big house took the letter before Claire could see it.' Jessie's voice was trembling with emotion now. 'Sent her a fake letter back with the necklace.'

Luke's mind was in turmoil. He thought back to the time when Joe had forced the letter in front of him, made him read the cruel words. 'That letter wasn't written, Jessie. It was printed. Anyone could have sent it. Jesus! Maybe Jack's been tellin' the truth.' Luke now had a gut feeling. 'Jack, Maggie, Matt, Claire – they all said Jack didn't know about me. Said he and Mam had a good marriage and wanted a kid. I need to get that letter. I'd have taken it with me if we hadn't left so quick. I've got to show it to Jack so he can find out who wrote it. It's the only way to get justice for Mam.'

'No Luke,' Jessie said, shaking a warning finger at him. 'Ye can't let that pair know ye're here. Ye aren't goin' back to that house.'

'Not when they're there, I'm not,' Luke reassured her. 'Don't worry, Jessie. I'll be careful. But listen to me now … it's why I'm back in Ireland. This mornin' I phoned a doctor in Limerick. You're goin' to get that hip replacement you need …'

It wasn't until after Luke left he realised Jessie had forgotten to give him the message from Emer and Kate. It couldn't be more important than the news about the letter. He'd phone Emer tomorrow when he'd achieved what he was planning to do.

Luke thought his heart would leap from his mouth when he saw Joe and Liam. He was seated on a bench next to a bus stop between his old house and his uncles' local pub. True to form, they were heading off for their nightly binge, following the usual route.

Luke had his head down, pretending to read a newspaper, but despite his attempt at anonymity, he felt conspicuous. Probably looked it, too. How many people sat around on benches reading newspapers in the fading light? Hopefully, Joe and Liam weren't paying attention. He prayed they wouldn't break the habit of a lifetime and cross the road.

As soon as they turned the corner and were out of sight, Luke ran to what was once his home, hoping his key would still fit. Ten minutes was all he needed. At least, that was what he'd thought before he realised someone had been in his room. He knew exactly where the letter and the cheque had been, and both were gone. Had Annie taken them? He closed the drawers and cupboards and hurried to her room, where he was hit immediately by the pain of her loss as he looked around at the familiar reminders. 'Sorry, Mam,' he said aloud. It seemed wrong to be going through her private things.

Despite the light from the street lamp filtering through the window, it was getting difficult to see. Luke was rifling through the dressing-table drawers, feeling for paper, but there was none. Joe or Liam must have taken the letter, for whatever reason. He would have to look in their rooms. But before he could, the sound of a key in the front door put paid to that idea. Luke felt as though he was going to throw up. They were back.

As he heard footsteps on the stairs, Luke was sure the sound of his heart would give him away. He lay pressed against the side of Annie's bed, his legs slightly bent so they didn't stick out past the foot of the single divan.

'Everything okay?' he heard Joe call out, and light from the landing came into the room as Liam pushed the bedroom door open. The wardrobe was just behind where Luke lay, and for a moment he was convinced his uncle was going to come right into the room and look inside it. What the hell was going on? It was almost as if Joe and Liam were expecting intruders.

'Seems to be,' Liam replied to Joe, but he didn't come right in, and Luke heard him move along the landing, probably looking into their shared room now.

Luke closed his eyes and sighed in relief when Liam went back downstairs. The immediate danger was over, but he still had to get out. And he hadn't found the letter. He could hear the television in the living room and he weighed up the chances of getting downstairs and out the front door without being seen. Possible of course, but the stairs tended to creak and the door to the living room was almost certainly open. Could he risk it? As he lay there, his mind drifted ...

Annie checked her watch for the tenth time in as many minutes.

'Mam, will you stop doin' that. It won't make us move any quicker.'

'Luke, they're going to be so mad when they get home. We should have taken the old car.'

Luke shrugged. 'They're always mad about somethin'. They'll get over it.'

In truth, Luke wasn't feeling that confident, but his

mother didn't need to know that. It had been hard enough to persuade her to come out with him in the first place. But he'd passed his driving test that day and wanted to drive her to the Shannon in Joe's Espace to celebrate. An hour, there and back again, he'd told Annie. Joe and Liam had gone off to a bare-knuckle fighting contest earlier in the day, in a mini-bus that had been laid on for those who planned to drink themselves senseless after the fight. The Espace had been just sitting there in front of the house, almost begging Luke to take her for a spin. Unfortunately, a brewery truck flipped over on the main road between Limerick and Ennis, causing an almighty tailback on their way home.

Annie checked her watch again. 'I should never have let you talk me into this.'

'Mam, come on, don't ruin the day! We can't change it now ... and you enjoyed it, didn't you?' His mother just gave him a weak smile in reply, looking so worried that Luke reached out and gave her a hug. 'So they'll mouth off a bit – what's new? I promise I won't give them any lip to make things worse, okay?'

When Luke and Annie finally arrived home, the brothers were waiting outside the house, swigging from beer cans. Joe walked to the driver's side and wrenched the door open, snarling, 'Where the fuck have you been with my car?' and dragging Luke out by his hair. Luke tried to protect himself with his arms as he was thrown to the ground and a heavy boot hit his ribs. Dazed, he heard Annie pleading, 'Leave him alone, Joe. He didn't mean any harm ... he passed his test today.'

'Did he now? And that gives him the right to take my fuckin' car, does it?'

'Don't touch her, you bullyin' bastard!' Luke had managed to stand and saw Joe push Annie against the garden's wooden fence. He grabbed a piece of wood and hit

372

out at Joe, a jutting nail catching his uncle on the forehead, immediately drawing blood.

Luke held the wood defensively, breathing hard, waiting for Joe to react. A dog started barking a few gardens down, and Joe glanced out to the street. He wiped the trickle of blood away with his sleeve and raised his hands in a conciliatory gesture. 'Okay, let's get inside and calm down a bit. We'll have a jar and you can tell us about your test.'

Luke wondered why Joe had backed off and would have taken the piece of wood into the house with him, but Annie signalled him to drop it. He was about to follow her into the kitchen when Liam pulled him into the living room and kicked the door shut before throwing Luke to the floor, where he was subjected to a vicious kick from Joe. Luke tried to roll into a ball, but both brothers kicked him repeatedly, in his chest and his side, before Joe dragged him to his feet and slammed his fist into Luke's cheek. Luke fell back into Liam's arms, and his uncle gripped him tightly as Joe punched him hard in the gut twice. When Liam released his hold, Luke sank to the floor, gasping for air, but Joe wasn't finished.

The beating was brutal. Worse than anything to date. With each punch, Luke became more dazed, more desperate. He was sure he was going to die. Somewhere far off, Annie was shouting and hammering at the door. Why didn't she come in? Finally, Luke was hauled up from the floor after another kicking, and his head was forced back painfully by a rough hand grabbing his hair while another tightly gripped his throat. Through a fog of pain and panic, Luke could feel hot breath in his face as Joe spoke. 'Don't you ever cross me again, you filthy little half-breed.'

Luke was fading now. Couldn't breathe. The last thing he knew was the sensation of something connecting again with *his chest and his side, and then he drifted away from the pain and knew no more.*

He woke up hours later in hospital, with Annie pale-faced beside him. She kept saying how sorry she was, how guilty she felt for not being able to stop them, but Liam had blocked the door with the armchair. Luke stayed there just long enough to know dying was more a possibility than a probability then discharged himself. It took him half an hour to walk out of the hospital. The doctor had asked him what happened, but Luke – and Annie – knew better than to tell him. No point in making things worse ....

As the memory ended, Luke found himself dry-retching. The terror that had been at bay for the last few weeks was back in force. He'd have to get out of here. They might kill him this time. He took out his phone. He could call the Guards, but how long before they showed up? Joe could make them get a warrant, and then he'd find Luke. Make sure no one ever found his body ...

Call if you need me – any time. Luke suddenly remembered Matt's words. Big brother to little brother. He buried the phone under the duvet to muffle its musical welcome tone and texted Matt his whereabouts, with a warning not to call or text him back. He couldn't think straight – couldn't remember how to put the phone on silent. If he played around with it, he might trigger off an alarm or something.

He was getting cramp – and panicking. What if the text hadn't gone through? He had to try and get out. What was there to lose? Maybe they wouldn't hurt him. Well not much, because they'd want their money back. That would be a good bargainer. He carefully eased himself up and went out onto the landing. The door to Joe's room was open, and for a moment he was tempted to carry on looking for the letter, but that was just asking for trouble. Heart in mouth, he crept downstairs.

Luke slowly opened the front door. Almost there. Then Joe's voice yelled 'Gotcha!' and his uncle grabbed for him. Luke was yanked back inside, but Joe looked shocked when he saw him and his grip loosened for a split second. It was enough to allow Luke to wriggle free and run outside. He just needed to get down the road to where it was busier, but he hadn't bargained on his injured knee. It was obviously still weak, choosing that time to give out, and the sudden pain pulled him up. Joe was there instantly. They struggled, Luke finding strength he didn't know he had and resisting his uncle's attempts to drag him back to the house. Suddenly, though, he was pulled roughly around and a fist connected with his face. The last thing he heard as he fell back and cracked his head on the kerb was the voice of his uncle Liam. 'Feel the force, Luke.'

When Luke regained consciousness, he was sprawled on the living room floor. There was a killing pain in his cheek and jaw.

'He's awake,' called Liam. Joe ambled into the room, swigging from a can. Luke's heart pounded as he remembered the last time he'd seen him. But this time he had something they wanted. He carefully got himself up, half expecting to be knocked back to the floor. Liam moved towards him, but Joe checked his brother with a raised hand.

'Go on then – hit me again,' Luke said, trying to sound braver than he felt. 'It won't get you anywhere. Not if you want your money back.'

'Might be worth it,' said Joe. 'You think we're just goin' to forget what you did?'

Despite his fear, Luke managed a laugh. 'But I should forget what *you* did?'

'So – you didn't find what you wanted last night?'

'I wasn't here last night.'

'Someone was,' said Joe. 'Forced the back door and closed all the curtains. Obviously wanted something in particular because nothin' was taken. Seemed a bit weird. Then tonight, someone sittin' at the bus stop, readin' a paper when it's nearly dark ... well, that was suspicious.'

So they had seen him. Luke was annoyed with himself but shrugged as though he didn't care. 'You're not as stupid as you look. Anyway, last night was nothin' to do with me.'

'I want that thirty grand.'

'Can't,' shrugged Luke. 'It's gone. I burnt it after Mam's funeral.'

Jesus, why did he say that? If they thought the money was gone, they might just dump him in the Shannon. It was good, though, to see Joe was shaken. His uncle knew the old Traveller tradition of burning a dead person's possessions. Luke had had a taste of living life without having to worry about how to pay for stuff, and he liked it. He had no intention of giving the money back.

'You'd better be lyin',' Joe said.

'I'm not lyin',' Luke replied, which technically, he wasn't.

'Well in that case, you'd better find it elsewhere,' said Joe. 'Because if you don't ...'

'You'll do what?' mocked Luke, determined not to show fear, although inside he was shaking with it. 'If anythin' happens to me, they'll know it was you.'

He felt in his pocket for his mobile. Maybe he'd get the chance to call someone. It was gone, and then he saw Joe holding the phone. Must have taken it from his pocket after Liam knocked him senseless. Joe sat down, slid open the phone. 'Well, you're a popular boy. Look at all these texts.' He read aloud.

'Come back, bro. We can work it out.'
'Luke, please phone me. Emer.'

Luke sighed. 'So?'

'This is the one I like best,' said Joe, grinning. *'Jack's not my dad. I love you.'* That one from 'Kate' sounds a bit juicy. So little Lukey has a girlfriend ...'

Luke hardly heard him. Kate wasn't his sister! That must have been the message they left with Jessie. He didn't know whether to laugh or cry.

'I take it you wouldn't like anythin' to happen to her.'

Joe's words were a heart-stopper. Surely he was bluffing? Considering the thug he was, he'd never been in real trouble with the law. But could Luke take that risk with Kate's safety? He decided to test the water. 'Okay, I didn't burn the money – though I nearly did – but you'll have to give me some time. I haven't got it all.'

'Why not?' Joe asked, quietly. 'Been on a spendin' spree?'

'I paid for Jessie to have a hip replacement.' He hadn't, yet. But there was no way he was going back on his promise.

Joe nearly dropped his can. 'You did what? What kind of idiot are you? She's on her last legs as it is ...'

Luke was defiant. 'At least she'll be able to use them, then.'

To his surprise, Joe started to laugh. 'I've missed you, Luke. You belong here, you know that, don't you? More than you do with the Stewarts. We're all the family you've got.'

'Jesus!' Luke exclaimed. 'You're somethin' else. You've *never* treated me like family.'

'No,' Joe conceded. 'Not often. But there were good times too, weren't there? I know I've got a temper after a jar or two.'

'You weren't drunk when you nearly killed me,' accused Luke. He wasn't stupid. Joe was just messing with his head again, playing the family angle to try and confuse him. Luke had always been hurt as much by Joe's mood changes as by anything physical, and Joe knew that – Luke had made the mistake of telling him, believing he could reach his uncle's heart. That was at a time when he thought Joe actually had one.

'We can start again,' suggested Joe. 'You're a Traveller, Luke. You'll always be a Traveller.'

'You're right – I will – but you can fuck off!' spat Luke. 'You're just sayin' what you think I want to hear, but you're a scumbag. It's no wonder you'll never see Roisin again.'

Afraid he'd gone too far, Luke instinctively pulled back, but the blow he expected didn't happen.

'Why d'you think your mam lied to you about Jack Stewart?'

So Mam *had* lied. Luke swallowed nervously, suddenly feeling more afraid than when he was goading his uncle to hit him.

'Why did she never tell Jack she was pregnant?' Joe asked. 'I'll tell you, shall I? It was because she didn't want him to know the truth.'

Luke gave a sardonic laugh. 'You wouldn't know truth if it introduced itself.'

'She was raped.'

Nothing his uncle had ever done compared to the pain Luke felt right then. 'That's a lie,' he said, his voice little more than a whisper. But somehow, he knew it wasn't.

'You're the son of a rapist, Lukey-boy,' said Joe.

A loud hammering on the front door disturbed Luke's thoughts. In a flash, Liam had him in a stranglehold, with one hand clasped tightly over his mouth. Joe went to the hallway, calling out 'Who is it?' and Luke's heart leapt when he heard the reply.

'Jack Stewart.'

'Sod off,' was Joe's response.

'I'm not leaving,' shouted Jack.

'Suit yourself,' Joe replied. 'I've been workin' all day and I'm off to bed. Night, Jack.'

With that he put the lights out and returned to the living room, where he cautiously peered round the curtain.

Luke was struggling to free himself, but Liam was a strong man, and if he struggled too much, he was likely to be choked. Please God, don't let Jack just walk away.

'Shall we kick the door in?' asked Matt.

Jack shook his head. 'Only as a last resort. If Luke isn't there, we could get ourselves arrested.' He didn't actually believe it would come to that as the Kiernans were unlikely to call the police, but he didn't want anything to get in the way of their search. He wondered if the brothers had fixed the back door after he broke in yesterday.

'Dad – put your ear here.' Matt indicated first the letterbox, which he was holding open, and then his mobile phone.

Jack caught on instantly. The text had suggested Luke was here but couldn't speak. It was possible he'd put the phone into silent mode, but they couldn't risk calling him before. Now it didn't matter. Within seconds, he could hear Luke's phone ringing inside. He stood up. '*Now* we kick the door in!'

Both Matt and Jack assaulted the front door until it burst free of the lock. They were faced by Joe Kiernan, his face ugly, distorted with rage.

'Get the fuck out of my house!' he snarled, but Jack ducked the swing of his fist and pushed him aside as he and Matt went into the living room and turned the light on. Liam was still restraining Luke. 'I'll break his neck,' he threatened.

Jack sat down on the sofa. 'No, you won't. Even you aren't that stupid. Now, let him go. We're going to all sit down and have a nice chat.'

Inwardly, Jack was raging. As he looked at Luke's pale, bruised face, he could see first-hand the kind of brutality he'd been subjected to for half his life. All Jack wanted to do was punch Liam in the face, and then do the same to Joe. To make them pay for what they'd done to his wife and son.

'I want some answers,' said Jack. 'And be grateful I'm not tearing you apart.'

Joe laughed. 'You could try. So – ask away then, Jack.'

'I know all about your sordid deal with my mother,' said Jack. 'I know she paid money to you that was intended for Annie and Luke.'

'So it's not your money!' Luke exclaimed, now free from Liam's grip. 'It was mine and Mam's all along.'

'Well,' said Joe, 'that's as good a cover story as any. But that money was paid to *me and Liam*, fair and square, and it wasn't nearly enough to have to put up with this brat and his lunatic mother.'

Jack had to fight to stay calm. 'Why did Annie leave me?'

Joe waggled his finger at Jack. 'It was *you* who broke in, last night. You sad bastard – twenty years on and you're still in the dark. Maybe you should be thankful – it's better not to know some things.'

'It was you who went through my stuff?' Luke was staring at Jack, shocked. His son had always been more than a bit cagey about his home life. He probably saw this as another case of Jack sticking his nose where it wasn't wanted.

'Sorry,' said Jack. It sounded lame and he waited for the usual angry rant.

Luke just gave a weak smile. 'If I'd known, I'd have got you to get some of my stuff.'

Jack smiled back. He'd just cleared a major hurdle, but then Luke's expression changed. He stared straight at Jack. 'I know why Mam left.'

Jack's stomach lurched. This was the first time they'd

made proper eye contact since Jack had come to believe Luke was indeed his son. He looked different, maybe because Jack was seeing him with different eyes. His face, so like his mother's, seemed open and honest, kind and gentle – everything she'd been.

'She … she was raped,' Luke whispered, and Jack felt as though he'd died inside.

'Well, that's what she said,' said Joe. 'But who knows? Maybe she just couldn't live with the guilt of cheatin' on ya, Jack. Of bein' a slag.'

It had been an effort for Jack to keep his cool ever since he'd forced his way into the house, and this pushed him over the edge. He launched himself at Joe, who fell back into the television set, knocking it to the floor.

Taking advantage of Joe's fall, Jack hauled him up and smashed a fist into his face, watching with satisfaction as Joe fell back to the ground, blood gushing from his nose. The man seemed stunned, and Jack allowed himself a quick glance around the room.

Liam was grappling with Matt and Luke, but Matt took a blow to the stomach and fell back onto the sofa, winded. Jack had no time to help because Joe was getting to his feet again. 'Jack!' shouted Luke. He turned to see Liam advancing on him, clutching a flick knife, but Luke sprang between them. Before Jack could react, Joe gripped his shoulders from behind and threw him backwards. As he fell against the corner of the table, he heard Joe shout 'Liam, you fuckin' idiot!' before they both ran from the house.

Gritting his teeth from pain in his bruised side, Jack saw Luke just standing there. He appeared to be in shock. 'Thanks,' said Jack, smiling as he got up. Luke didn't answer. Jack moved towards him, wanting to hug him for what he'd done, until he noticed the spreading red mass on Luke's stomach. 'Jesus, Luke!'

Luke's face was ashen and his expression one of fear as he sank to the floor. It had all gone horribly wrong, and Jack was beside himself with guilt.

'Matt, get some towels from somewhere,' he instructed. He needed to try and stem the flow of blood. Moments later Matt returned with two hand towels. 'Found the airing cupboard,' he told Jack. 'So at least they're clean.' Jack folded one of the towels into several thicknesses, and applied it firmly to the wound.

'Is it 999 here, Dad?' Matt asked, his mobile in his hand.

'I don't know,' Jack replied, 'But we'll take him – I don't think we can wait.'

Between them, Jack and Matt lifted Luke's slight frame into the back seat of the hire car.

'I need something to keep him warm,' said Jack, and Matt ran back into the house, reappearing soon afterwards with a duvet. While Matt drove, Jack held Luke tightly in the duvet, still exerting as much pressure as he could on the source of the bleeding.

'Sorry,' came a whispered voice. At least Luke was still conscious.

'What for?' asked Jack, verging on tears. He strained his ears to listen to the weak response.

'Bringin' you nothin' but trouble.'

Jack's arms instinctively tightened around his son's bleeding body, and he felt both shame and grief as Luke struggled to speak. 'I want a DNA ...'

'You are *my* son!' Jack told him fiercely. 'Don't imagine anything else.' He squeezed his eyes shut as tears welled up inside. He opened them to see a faint hint of a smile on Luke's face, but he seemed to be falling into unconsciousness.

'Luke – stay with me,' pleaded Jack. 'Keep talking ... about Kate, about Manchester United ... anything.'

'Cold …' whispered Luke, who was shivering.

Blood was seeping through the duvet and Jack hugged Luke tightly, trying to warm him. Tears flowed freely as he kissed Luke's dark head. All the parental feelings he'd been denying for weeks overwhelmed him now. This was his son. His and Annie's longed-for child. He'd known him for a couple of months, and apart from Luke's collapse at the funeral, this was the first time he'd held him. His thoughts flashed back to the hospital in Dublin, when Luke was recovering from serious injury, bereft and in shock. Any human being would deserve the comfort of a hug at such a time, but Jack had made no such gesture. Even if Luke had resisted, which he may well have done given his frame of mind at the time, Jack should have made the effort. And now he might never get the chance because Luke had put himself in the way of a knife meant for Jack. He'd let his son down badly. And his wife. 'Forgive me, Annie – forgive me,' he whispered.

Chapter Twenty-Three

'He'll be okay, Dad. He's tougher than he looks.'

Jack nodded at Matt's reassurance, but wishful thinking wasn't going to pull Luke through the emergency surgery he was having at that moment. A little blood could go a long way, but it was obvious Luke had lost a lot of it. The pool on the floor of the car and Jack's own sodden clothes were testament to that.

'It was my fault,' he said, as he and Matt waited in the Relatives' Room. 'I lost control. I let him down – and I let Annie down. I should have been looking out for him.'

There had been a few low points in Jack's life but nothing compared to this. The guilt was overwhelming as he thought about Luke. Abused physically and emotionally, and seeing the same thing happen to his mother; believing his father had wanted him aborted; and finally, losing the one constant in his life in the most traumatic of circumstances.

It was no wonder his attitude had been hostile and vengeful. Jack had shown no understanding or compassion, no love or support, just impatience, irritation and anger. He rubbed his forehead, wearily. 'I'll never forget it, Matt. Holding him on the way here, wondering how much blood he could lose and survive. Wishing I'd treated him like a father should. Christ, Matt – he'd just lost his mother and I gave him *nothing*.'

He turned in nervous anticipation as the door opened, expecting to see a surgeon, but it was Kate and Emer who walked in.

'We took a taxi as soon as you called,' said Emer.

Kate was white-faced and tearful. 'They said he's still in surgery. It's really serious, isn't it?'

'He's in good hands, Kate,' Jack told her. It sounded lame, for he was far too worried to be convincing. Kate turned towards him as though she was going to hug him but her expression changed to horror as she reached out and touched his bloodstained shirt.

'Oh my God, Jack! Is that …?' She swayed and Emer put an arm round her, guiding her to a chair. Kate sat down, head in hands. After a while she took her mobile from her bag, gazing at it through the tears. 'I took this a few days ago.'

Jack held out his hand. 'May I?'

It was a photo of Luke, happy and relaxed, smiling into the camera. A Luke Jack had never known. As always, he had the features of his mother, but he was a person in his own right. Why hadn't Jack seen past the likeness to Annie? Why had he punished her son for what he'd believed were her sins? He returned the photo to Kate just as one of the medical staff came in and informed them Luke's condition was critical and the following twenty-four hours would be crucial.

Eventually, Kate fell asleep on Matt's shoulder, exhausted from tears and worry. Emer looked worn out, too, but Jack needed to speak to her and motioned her to follow him outside into the corridor, where he told her Luke's revelation.

'Raped?' Emer looked shocked to the core.

Saying it aloud meant finally facing it, and Jack wanted to be sick. 'Sorry. I need to be by myself for a bit,' he said, as he walked away.

The hospital chapel was open but empty. Jack sat near the small altar, his head in his hands. Concern for Luke had suppressed all other emotions, but here, alone with his thoughts, he was able to focus on what he'd learned.

Annie had been raped. The horror of that fact was now

hitting him like an actual body blow, and he had to fight waves of nausea. His mind would take him so far – Annie distressed, fighting an attacker – but then it would cut off. He couldn't bear to imagine her in pain, perhaps in fear for her life.

Why hadn't she told him? The question tormented him. Had she thought he would reject her? Was the shame too much for a devout Catholic? Or was it that Annie didn't know who the father of her child was – Jack or the rapist? She'd been strongly against abortion so that would never have been an option, but the thought of carrying a rapist's child would have been traumatic.

And so the possibility again presented itself that Luke was not his son. Despite their difficult history, this didn't make Jack feel any kind of relief. He now had more positive feelings for Luke than at any time since he'd known about him. What had happened was neither Luke's nor Annie's fault. They had all, Jack included, been the victims of a crime. One of the worst crimes possible.

Jack's mind was reeling with so many thoughts and possibilities as he stared at the row of flickering candles near a statue of the Virgin Mary. Annie's face appeared in his mind – the beautiful girl of all those years ago, not the broken figure in the hospital morgue.

'I'm sorry, Annie,' he whispered. 'For everything.'

He felt a rush of love for her, a love he'd thought had gone forever but which had been reignited when he'd sat on her bed. He hoped wherever she was now, she'd found peace. His torment would continue, but perhaps he deserved that for doubting her. He'd been weak for just accepting that non-existent detective's report – shouldn't have trusted his mother. Should have been man enough to make his own decisions. And he should have swallowed his pride and looked everywhere for her.

When he finally left the chapel, Emer was waiting outside and took his hand. He could feel the tightness in his face, caused by the stickiness of dried tears. Emer's expression was one of compassion and sympathy. She understood. That was why he loved her. He squeezed her hand. 'When Ollie was a puppy, his mother was hit by a car. She died on the roadside. Ollie just sat by her, whimpering. Lost. I picked him up and held him close to me for most of the day – to be there for him. I could feel his pain. His confusion. I offered him love and security.'

There was no need to explain the analogy to Emer. No need to reiterate that he'd failed Luke. That he'd never afforded him the same compassion he'd given his dog.

'I need some air,' he said, and together they went to the hospital's main entrance. A heavy rain was falling so they stood by the doorway.

'Annie loved the rain,' he said. 'She'd often run down to the lake to watch the drops falling into the water.'

'She was a good person, Jack,' Emer said. 'And she loved you. I doubt she ever stopped. Even after ...'

Even after the letter. Jack put an arm round her shoulder, pulling her closer to him.

'How do you feel about Luke now?' she asked.

'How do you mean?'

'Well ... you know there's a chance he ... may not be your son. A lot of men might—'

'I've *always* thought there was that chance. The difference now is it wouldn't have been any fault of Annie's. In one way, it's easier because I know now why she left, but part of me wishes I didn't. How can I go back to Baronsmere and behave as if nothing's happened? I'll be looking at everybody with suspicion.'

'I don't suppose you have any idea who it was?'

'I've been thinking, of course, but it was over twenty

years ago. It's hard for me to be objective. These are people I've lived with all my life. Of course, it could have been some stranger passing through ...'

'I don't think Annie's rapist was a stranger.'

'Why not?' Jack's voice was sharper than he intended.

'There'd be no reason for her not to tell you what had happened if it was a stranger – and the majority of rape victims know their attackers. That could have made things much more complicated for her ...'

Jack was silent, his imagination in overdrive.

'Jack, are you okay?' Emer asked, putting her hand gently on his shoulder.

'I can't do this,' he said. 'I can't rake through everyone I know, wondering if they raped my wife.'

'Then let's stop talking about it ...'

'I can't!' Jack cried. 'You've put it in my head now and it won't go away!'

'I'm sorry ...'

'It's too bloody late for that!' He walked out into the rain and just stood for a moment, welcoming the freshness and the purity of the cool drops. Part of him wanted to continue walking, away from everything. From everyone. Finally, though, he returned to the doorway, dripping and miserable. He clutched Emer's hand, and whispered, 'I feel like I'm going crazy. I don't know what to do.'

'Let's go and get a coffee and warm up a bit,' she suggested. 'Being cold and wet won't help you.'

They walked to the near empty cafeteria, where they sat down, grateful for the presence of a coffee machine. For once, the coffee tasted like nectar.

'Luke wants a DNA test,' said Jack. 'Even semi-conscious it was the first thing on his mind.'

'I'm not surprised.'

'I just keep going over and over that moment when I

realised he'd been stabbed, like a bloody nightmare video on a loop.' Jack felt wearier than he'd ever felt in his life, but another thought occurred to him. 'When Matt and I were at Edenbridge, Richard called Annie a slut. Why would he do that? My mother gave him one of her looks and he clammed up. I always thought Richard detested Annie, but Tony Hayes said he once made a pass at her. It was Richard who took Annie's letter. Maybe there was more to him not wanting her to come back to Baronsmere than I thought.'

'Are you thinking *Richard* raped Annie?'

'It makes sense,' said Jack, increasingly convinced he was right. 'And if my mother knew, she wouldn't want it to come out, not if she was protecting Claire … Jesus Christ!'

'What is it, Jack?'

'The money my mother was paying, supposedly for Annie. Joe Kiernan said it was "a good cover story" …'

'And?'

'What if it was hush money? Because my parents knew what Richard did, and the Kiernans were blackmailing them.'

'But Luke and Annie knew nothing about the money,' Emer reminded him.

'If Annie told her brothers, or her father, about the rape, Joe and Liam would have seen an opportunity to profit from it …'

'Or they wanted revenge for what happened to their sister.'

Jack shook his head. 'If they wanted justice for Annie, they'd have shared any money with her and Luke.'

Emer bit down on her thumbnail. 'Well, it's a theory. You know what you're implying, though? If Richard is Luke's father …'

It took a moment for the penny to drop, and it was sickening. Like bloody Groundhog Day. If Richard had raped Annie, and Luke was the result, Kate really was his half-sister. Jack sighed. 'What a mess. Sarah doesn't want Kate to know Richard is her father, but what the hell do we do if he does turn out to be Luke's, too?'

'I don't know. Let's just wait and see. As soon as Luke is conscious, we can sort out the DNA.'

Jack had wanted the test done right away. After all, it was Luke who requested it. 'The hospital can't just take your word for it,' Emer had told him, and he'd had to reluctantly agree.

'Shall we go back?' Emer suggested. 'Kate and Matt will be wondering where we are. And it might be a while before Luke is coherent, but he should wake up quite soon.'

'The first hurdle,' said Jack. 'I know he's not out of the woods yet.'

As Jack and Emer returned to the Intensive Care Unit, the nurse-in-charge called to him. 'Mr Stewart, could you come into my office, please?' Her expression was grim.

Five minutes later, Jack was at the hospital entrance again, feeling the rain stinging his face. It was hard to breathe, but he forced enough air into his lungs to give a howl of pain and anguish. His despair was complete.

When Jack marched into Stewart Enterprises the following morning, he was a man driven by love, anger ... and hate. He headed first for Richard's office but there was no sign of him. His father wasn't at his desk so Jack grabbed Nicholas's appointment book and scanned the day's events. Then he hurried out and down the corridor, entering the boardroom without knocking.

Nicholas was seated at the head of the conference table, surrounded by the delegation from Redgate. He showed a moment's surprise at Jack's entrance. Then the usual cool control took over. 'Jack, our discussions are rather finely balanced at the moment. Could we meet for lunch in an hour?'

'No,' said Jack. 'I need to talk to you now. I suggest everyone take a coffee break.'

His father glared, but then backed down. 'I ask for the indulgence of our friends from Redgate. A fifteen-minute break. Please avail yourself of refreshments.' He stalked from the boardroom, Jack following in his wake.

'Hold all calls!' Nicholas snapped at his secretary. Closeted in the privacy of his office, Nicholas sat at his desk, whilst Jack paced the floor. 'So what is this about, Jack? The Woodlands deal is on the verge of collapse because of all the adverse publicity. What is it that couldn't wait until later?'

'Where's Richard?' asked Jack. 'The man who deliberately kept Luke's existence from me. Who has ritually humiliated and degraded your daughter, both by his attitude towards her, and by cheating on her. I didn't see him at the board meeting.'

'I've made arrangements,' Nicholas replied. 'I realise it's impossible for him to remain here with Claire ... I'm sending him to Hong Kong.'

'You're rewarding him ...'

'He's still my son-in-law. The father of my grandson. And we don't want bad publicity.'

'God forbid!' Jack exclaimed. 'Let's not worry about the crimes as long as we can sweep it all under the Axminster, eh? Well that may be your way, Dad ... but not mine. Since Luke arrived, I started to question things which I should have questioned much earlier – like twenty-one years ago. Why did my wife just up and leave? Why did she tell Luke I'd rejected them? Nothing made sense, so I started piecing together little snippets of evidence. I found out about the letter Richard forged to Annie. Then I found out why Annie left, and it wasn't because of anything I did at all … my wife was raped.'

'Jack, I really don't …' Nicholas began.

'Shut up!' snapped Jack. 'Don't open your mouth until I've finished or I won't be responsible for my actions. So – I find out my wife was raped and, of course, my next question was, who by? Over the past few hours, I've been facing up to something I didn't want to acknowledge. That it probably wasn't some stranger but someone much closer to home.

'I remembered what Tony Hayes said at the funeral. That Richard obviously fancied Annie. And it was Richard who was involved with the forged letter, with making payments to the Kiernans. Payments that Mother claimed were to help Annie and Luke. I never liked Richard, but I was shocked at what I was beginning to suspect. Although what shocked me even more was the realisation that if I was right, my parents – or my mother at least – knew what he'd done and helped him cover it up. That rather than incriminate Richard, they would allow me to stay in blissful ignorance, even to the point of not telling me I had a son. My fine, upstanding parents were allowing a rapist to share their home. Not just a rapist, but a man who had betrayed their daughter with at least one affair, maybe more.'

'We didn't know about Sarah,' protested Nicholas.

'Whether you did or not is irrelevant,' Jack continued. 'But I gave you the benefit of the doubt – I thought that, however misguided, you were protecting Claire, and then I convinced myself that all I had was circumstantial evidence – that I didn't know for sure.'

'And now?'

'And now I do know for sure. I know everything. The Kiernans were arrested in Ireland last night, after stabbing Luke. The knife was meant for me, but the *trashy no-mark* put himself in front of it.'

'You've been to Ireland?'

'Did you hear what I said, Dad? Luke was stabbed. Have you not got one grain of feeling? No, don't answer that. Anyway, when the Kiernans were questioned, it all came out.'

Nicholas snorted. 'Those two are thugs and liars, you've said so yourself.'

Jack nodded. 'They are, but not particularly clever thugs and liars, and Liam Kiernan could never have held up under questioning and maintained the same story as his brother unless it was the truth. And now ... *now* it all makes sense. What was it you said about a DNA test, Dad? That it wouldn't do for a scandal to come out? I thought it was just because you didn't want it proved that Luke was mine. That if that happened, you'd have to either accept him or face a lot of bad publicity for not doing so. But I was barking up the wrong tree there, wasn't I? You weren't afraid a DNA would prove I was Luke's father. You were afraid of just the opposite – that it would prove I wasn't.'

Nicholas faced his son squarely, but said nothing.

'You didn't hate Luke because he was Annie's son, did you?' Jack continued. 'You hated him because you thought he could be the result of a rape.'

'Jack, will you listen to yourself! This is just wild speculation,' protested Nicholas.

'Give it up, Dad! I told you – the Kiernans have blown the whistle. I know why you and Mother couldn't bear to look at Luke, why you've treated him with such contempt. He was an unpleasant reminder, wasn't he? All that crap you spewed about him not being my son ... you really *did* believe that, didn't you?'

Jack was raging inwardly as he moved towards his father. 'You bastard – you hypocritical bastard. You didn't think Luke was my son. You thought he was my *brother*.'

The look in Nicholas's eyes confirmed the truth for Jack. It felt like a death. Maybe worse than a death.

'What was it, Dad? Was she the lowly Traveller girl, just like a serving girl of old, for her master to take whenever he wanted? Someone not worthy of respect or courtesy – or common decency?'

Nicholas seemed rooted to the spot, unsure how to respond, and Jack finally lost control, pulling his father out of the chair by the lapels. 'Why? She was my *wife!* What kind of man are you? Tell me, Dad, or so help me, I'll beat it out of you!'

'I thought she wanted it,' said Nicholas finally, his voice low and uncertain, so unlike the father Jack had always feared as a child. 'I thought she was only with you for the money ... I thought ...'

Nicholas faltered and Jack tightened his grip and shook his father. 'Go on ... I want to know it all. You owe me that.'

'She came to Edenbridge. It was when you were in Brussels. Annie had received a letter from the council, rejecting her request to hold reading classes at the library, and she obviously blamed us.'

'I wonder why.' Jack finally let go of his father. Resisted the urge to beat him to a pulp.

'She stormed in, waving the letter and yelling abuse,' Nicholas continued. 'Your mother wasn't at home. She and Claire had gone away for a couple of days – to the Lakes, if I recall. Claire was recovering from a miscarriage. Annie was ranting and calling me names and ... and I just thought how beautiful she was ... how passionate. It was a long time since I'd seen such passion. She was right in my face and before I realised what I was doing, I kissed her. After that, there was no going back. I don't even know if she resisted or not – all I could think was how much I wanted her. It had been a long time for me ...

'Afterwards she cried, and I knew I'd made a mistake. I'm not trying to excuse myself, Jack, but I really did convince myself that we were sharing a moment of mutual lust. I thought she wanted it as much as I did. That it was all part of the excitement, one Stewart as good as another.

'I told her it might be best if she left – and I said you had long since realised the marriage was a mistake. I believe Richard told her later that you were in love with Sarah and were together in Brussels. I don't know if Annie believed it. Anyway, I wrote a cheque there and then, and told her to go and make a life for herself somewhere – to maybe get her teaching qualifications so she could do some good for her people.

'She took the cheque but didn't speak to me at all, and I knew she was in shock. She was just leaving when Richard arrived, and it didn't take much for him to guess what had happened. She was still crying and her clothes were torn. I told Richard she'd come on to me and had then regretted it. He never questioned it. I asked him to take her home because she wasn't in a fit state to drive.'

'How considerate,' said Jack, feeling sick to his stomach.

'I suppose she felt no one would believe her so she didn't tell anyone. I never saw her again, and it wasn't until Luke arrived that I realised she never cashed the cheque. I just assumed she would.'

'So where did the Kiernan brothers come into it?' asked Jack.

'You know about the letter Annie sent. Richard tried to deal with it himself, sending her a reply letter along with her necklace, but a few months later, the Kiernans contacted your mother. Annie had told them about ... what happened. Maybe they thought Grace would be easier to deal with than me. It must have been a huge shock for her, but she never mentioned it. I knew nothing until the day we came to see you after you'd brought Luke home. When we arrived back home that night, she told me everything, and that she knew … what I'd done. The Kiernans told her Richard had helped me deal with Annie, so she enlisted his help as a go-between when they demanded money to keep quiet.'

'No wonder you were so keen for me not to get a DNA,' said Jack.

Nicholas looked at him levelly, as though still trying to maintain some authority, some semblance of righteousness. 'I wanted the boy gone before you had the chance to arrange that. If a DNA test showed you weren't the father, it would still have shown Stewart genes and you'd have guessed. Richard told me he'd find a way to get rid of Luke – I only wish he hadn't manipulated Gavin into setting things in motion with that nonsense about Kate's parentage.'

'You've surprised me, Dad. I didn't think you'd admit to everything quite so easily.'

'I'm weary of it all, Jack. I know you won't believe me, but it's weighed on my conscience.'

'I believe you,' said Jack. 'But we're over. Finished.' He took an envelope from his pocket and handed it to Nicholas. 'This is my letter of resignation. Effective immediately. And as if you couldn't sink any lower in my estimation, you haven't even asked about Luke, who could be your son!'

He turned on his heel and walked out of Stewart Enterprises forever.

Jack was back in Ireland by mid-afternoon. Less than twenty-four hours since Luke had been admitted to hospital. He should have been exhausted, but adrenalin and anger were powerful stimulants.

'How is he?' he asked Matt, who jumped up as soon as Jack entered the Relatives' Room.

'Hanging in there,' Matt replied. 'He came round a few

hours ago, but drifted off again almost immediately – he's full of painkillers on top of the anaesthetic. They're moving him to High Dependency tomorrow, if all goes well.'

'Emer and Kate?'

'Gone for coffee. Dad, Emer told me – about Granddad. She said that after you spent some time in the chapel last night, the police showed up here, that they'd caught Joe and Liam, and Liam came clean about everything. I wish you hadn't taken off on your own, Dad.' Matt took a shuddering breath. 'I never thought …'

Jack's voice was grim. 'Who would have? I'll talk to you about it later, Matt. Not now if you don't mind. I'd like to sit with Luke. To be there when he wakes up. For it to be the beginning. I can't explain …'

'You don't need to, Dad. I'll go and find the girls.'

Luke opened his eyes and tried to focus on what appeared to be a tiger and a blue donkey hovering in front of him. It took a while to realise he was in hospital, and he was looking at Tigger and Eeyore balloons tied to the end of his bed.

He swallowed and his throat hurt. There was a weird kind of pain just above his waist. Not excruciating but not normal. He tried to move and sucked in air as the pain became infinitely worse. He turned his head to see a dozing Jack sitting beside him, looking uncomfortable, his head flopping forward.

It was all a bit vague. Jack had fought with Joe … and then? That was it. Liam was going for Jack with a knife and he'd got in the way of it. Couldn't remember if it had hurt or not. He supposed it must have. This was all too much like Dublin. He'd had more than his fair share of hospitals, for sure.

There was a jug of water on the locker and he tried to reach it but the pain was now intense and he was hampered by wires. He caught his breath, moaning slightly.

Jack woke up instantly, concern on his face. 'Luke!'

'Tryin' to get the jug ...' It hurt to speak.

'I'd rather you didn't ...' Jack was smiling as he spoke and Luke managed a weak one too, remembering the scene in St Aidan's some weeks earlier.

Jack poured some water and held it to Luke's mouth, helping him to drink. It hurt as he swallowed and he pulled a face. 'Why does my throat hurt?'

'You've had surgery,' Jack explained. 'You had to be intubated.'

Luke listened silently as Jack reminded him of the events that led up to the fight, and what had happened after Luke lost consciousness.

'Do you reckon I'm part cat?' asked Luke. 'I seem to have nine lives.'

'Thank God for that,' said Jack. 'I ... I couldn't bear it if I lost you.'

Luke felt a surge of pleasure, then frowned. 'I'd still like the DNA test.'

'If you're sure. It's not necessary as far as I'm concerned, but it's up to you.' Jack reached out and placed his hand gently on Luke's head. 'Whether or not you're biologically mine, you're Annie's son, and that makes you *my* son, Luke, the son your mother and I wanted, and I thank God there's a part of her left.'

Luke felt moved but years of disappointment weren't going to miraculously disappear. 'I can't promise it'll be easy,' he said, his voice husky. 'I don't know if I can settle down and toe the Stewart line.'

Jack smiled. 'I'm sure you can't, and I can guarantee you and I will have more clashes. Like fathers and sons do. Luke, I'm sorry. About everything. It's no excuse, but every time I saw you, I saw your mother. I couldn't handle it. You brought it all back. Everything I'd tried to forget.

Now we know the truth, I hope this will be a fresh start for us.'

Tears pricked Luke's eyes as he thought about everything he and Annie had missed. She'd died never knowing Jack hadn't rejected her. He didn't know how he'd ever get over the tragedy of that. It was all too much at the moment.

'I'll go and tell the others you're okay,' said Jack, standing up. 'Kate's been waiting very impatiently.'

Kate! Suddenly everything seemed brighter again. And as Jack smiled at him, a father's smile, he knew that it was.

Luke had been awake most of the night and had only managed to catnap during the day. His mind wouldn't give him peace. Although it had been useful before, he'd refused medication to help him sleep. He had to get used to doing without it. Couldn't spend the rest of his life relying on drugs to blot out the fact that his mother had been raped by his grandfather.

When Jack had first broken that news to him a few days ago, Luke was glad he was confined to a hospital bed. He'd wanted to go to Baronsmere and confront Nicholas – hear what he had to say and then smash him to pieces. But violence was never an answer and it was himself who would end up paying the price. Better to give the courts a chance, for revenge to be legal. To Luke's surprise, Jack had promised him that neither Nicholas nor Richard would get away with it. Even if it meant destroying the Stewart reputation, Nicholas and Richard would be prosecuted. Jack was okay. One of the good guys. A victim, like Luke. Like Annie.

This was Nicholas Stewart, though – rich enough and important enough to buy himself and his son-in-law out of trouble. It wasn't going to be easy hearing Annie's name blackened. As sure as eggs were eggs, that's what Nicholas would do. He'd paint her as the seducer. Hopefully, Grace would have to testify – God, one look at her frosty face would convince any jury that Nicholas would have been starved of sex. And if he got away with it – well, then Luke would need to think again. Old Nick would find that Travellers always defended their own. And at least the Woodlands deal had collapsed. Matt had told Luke that. A piece of good news. One victory at least for the little people – and one in the eye for Sir Nicholas.

The thought that he could be Nicholas's son made Luke feel physically ill. He'd missed out on a lot as a child – having a da' to look up to, a da' to take him to the park and play football, and everything else that having two parents should mean, but he couldn't let himself dwell on all that. It wouldn't change anything and the future was what mattered, the good times to come. It was Annie who'd had the roughest deal – living without the love of her life, believing he'd rejected her, then dying without ever knowing the truth. Luke's faith had been badly shaken, but if there was an afterlife, then at least Annie could rest content. He nodded off, clinging to that thought.

A gentle kiss on his cheek woke him. He smiled sleepily at Kate as he looked into her lovely green eyes. 'Sleepyhead,' she whispered. 'You've got a visitor.'

Luke stared in disbelief at Jessie, sitting beside his bed in a wheelchair, wearing what she always called her 'church clothes'. Coming into the city was a big event for Jessie.

'John brought me,' she said, as though she'd guessed what Luke was thinking. Maybe she really did have the gift of sight. 'I wanted to see ye before ye go back to England. With your da'.'

'He's a good man, Jessie,' Luke told her. 'Mam and me – we were told so many lies. And so was he.'

'The others will be here in a minute,' said Kate. 'They're finishing lunch. I just got here and found Jessie.'

'She's a good lass,' said Jessie. 'I looked at her palm. And I know folk. Can see what they're like. Ye won't find anyone who'll love ye more.'

Luke smiled. 'I know that, Jessie.'

Jessie looked sad. 'But ye won't be a Traveller anymore.'

'I'll always be me, Jessie. I won't change. Bein' a Traveller will always be part of me.'

'Like I promised you, Jessie,' said Kate, 'he'll never need to change for me.'

Jessie reached out and squeezed her hand. 'As long as ye make him happy, nothin' else matters.'

'Jessie!' Emer looked shocked as she entered the room, followed by Jack and Matt. 'Jack, Matt – this is Jessie Reilly, Annie's friend.'

Jack must have been aware of what Jessie's opinion of him had been, but he seemed undaunted by it as he thrust out his hand. 'Mrs Reilly,' he said, 'I want to thank you for everything you did for my wife and son. Without you, their lives would have been … even worse than they were.'

Jessie said nothing, but looked directly at Jack. She was weighing him up. Luke had seen her do this before. It was like she could tap into someone's soul. Eventually, she took his still outstretched hand, and spoke. 'She loved ye. Ye were the only man for her. The first, and the only.'

'And I loved her,' said Jack, his voice breaking. 'I loved her so much. If only she'd been able to tell me … if only she'd come back, long before she had to write that letter.'

Jessie still had hold of Jack's hand. It looked like he'd passed the test.

'There was too much stoppin' her. Family is important to us Travellers. She didn't want to break yours – or for ye to suffer knowin' what your own da' had done. She loved ye too much for that. And she didn't want to have to face the man who did it to her. She didn't know if ye'd blame her –

some men do. She didn't know if the child was his – that maybe he would have taken him away from her. She thought ye were likely his da' but couldn't be sure. It wasn't her fault. She was just so shocked and confused. And ashamed.'

'I'd have supported her,' said Jack. 'I'd have done what I'm doing now – my father committed a crime, and should pay the same penalty anyone else does.'

'And she knew that was somethin' else that might happen,' said Jessie, 'and she didn't want that either – to have to talk about it to people, stand up in a court of law and say what happened. A Traveller girl takin' on a man as rich and powerful as him? It was hard enough for her to tell me, let alone go through all that.'

'But she told her brothers,' said Jack, his head down.

'She told Liam. They'd been close before he had that accident. When she got that letter, well it finished her. He found her cryin' and got it all out of her.'

Jessie let go of Jack's hand then, but not before she'd patted it. The room was silent for a while, as everyone thought about what had been said. When Jack lifted his head, his face was wet with tears. 'Finally,' he said. 'Finally, we know it all.'

Epilogue

It was the beginning of July and summer had come to Baronsmere. Fields of ripening barley shimmered silver in the sunlight, and the gardens were a riot of colour. Emer drove slowly along the country lanes, drinking in the tranquillity. Memories of her childhood in rural Mayo filled her thoughts. What a long way she'd come since then. So much passion, so much grief, so much *life*.

Now here she was in this little English village, about to be reunited with the two men she'd met barely three months ago but who'd woven themselves tightly into the fabric of her life. She'd suffered through their traumas with them, shared the pain and frustration of their discord, but was now visiting them in better times.

After Luke had been discharged from hospital, Jack took his sons to Antibes for a month. The Ingrams, Caroline's parents, had invited them, wanting to meet their new grandson. It was gratifying to hear how they had welcomed Luke into their lives. Maggie told Emer they'd appreciated the love Annie had given Matt, and there was no question they would have treated Luke as their own grandchild had Annie remained in Baronsmere.

Emer rounded the corner and caught a glimpse of the familiar house through the trees. It wasn't a given she'd end up with Jack Stewart, but they'd both had their share of sorrow. Perhaps they'd earned this final chance at love.

'Another four hot dogs, please,' requested Tim, holding out his plate. He had ketchup on his T-shirt, today's slogan suggesting 'Try my buns.'

'Bloody hell, Leighton!' exclaimed Jack, as he served

up the food. 'Where do you put it all? You're thin as a rake.'

'It goes straight to the brain,' Tim told him. 'It's hard work being a genius.'

'Tell me about it,' agreed Al as he moved next to Tim. 'Two more veggie burgers, please, Jack.'

'Since when did you start eating that crap?' asked Tim. 'A man needs real meat.'

'They're for Abbie,' explained Al. 'The new love of her life doesn't eat meat. Odd that, for a farmer's son.'

They looked over in the direction of the bench near the lake, where Abbie was resting her head on the shoulder of a stocky young man with tattoos decorating his muscly arms.

'Where did she find *him*?' asked Tim.

'Hadleigh Fayre. He won a prize.'

'What for? Tossing the caber?'

'Biggest turnip, I think.'

'Sounds about right.'

They wandered off, giving Jack a chance to restock the barbecue. He was running low on drumsticks.

'I'll take over for a bit if you like, Jack,' said Barbara Hayes.

'Thanks, Barb,' he said. 'I'll just get more supplies.'

'Lovely barbecue,' she said, as she took his place at the grill. 'So nice to see everyone together. Thanks for inviting us.'

'It was all Maggie and Claire's doing,' he told her. 'We knew nothing about it till the doorbell started ringing.'

'He looks well.'

Jack followed Barbara's gaze. Luke was seated on the grass, Ollie splayed at his feet. He was laughing with Kate, their happiness evident. He was recovering well, physically and mentally, after the shock of learning what Nicholas had done. Despite his own pain, though, Luke recognised Jack had lost his parents, maybe even in worse circumstances than he'd lost Annie. At least Luke had his memories. It had fallen to Matt to try and raise their spirits, even though he too was still suffering from the shock of it all.

However, the slow pace of the summer sun and the kindness of the Ingrams had helped to cushion the blow for all of them. Luke had spent many hours on the phone to Kate, who had been invaluable to his recovery, but he was still extremely vulnerable and Jack had frequent moments of protectiveness towards him. He'd have felt like that even if the DNA test hadn't confirmed that Luke was indeed his son. It did seem, though, that the worst was over – for all of them.

Kate looked up at that moment and smiled at Jack. She'd been through a lot, too. She was still living at Tim's, blaming her mother for much of what had happened, both now and in the past. Lord and Lady Leighton, back from their cruise and likely to turn up at the barbecue, had told her their home was her's for as long as she needed. Luke wanted her to move in with him, but taking a leaf from Emer's book, Kate was giving the Stewart men some time together.

Jack's progress to the kitchen suddenly halted. Walking towards him was Emer, carrying a plate of chicken, a smile lighting up her face. The afternoon was truly complete.

'I come bearing gifts,' she said. 'More drumsticks, Chef?'

'Well,' Jack said, as she stopped in front of him, 'you kept this quiet.'

'I'm not one to spoil a surprise. Maggie called me a few days ago, but I wasn't sure I could make it.'

'So glad you did,' said Jack, pulling her close. Without breaking their kiss, he took the plate she was clutching and held it out to the side so their bodies touched. Someone took the plate from his hand and Jack heard Matt murmur, 'Get a room, you two.'

Eventually Jack and Emer had to come up for air but still stood there, eyes locked on each other. The sounds of the barbecue around them seemed distant. They could have been on the moon for all Jack cared.

'How was the holiday?' Emer asked.

'It was good. It was … healing.' He stroked her cheek. 'I've missed you. That ban you imposed on us seeing each other …'

'Was essential. You had to focus on Luke.'

'I know,' he said. 'And you were right … as usual. And right about Luke. He's a great kid.'

She smiled and they were about to move in for another kiss when they heard the tinkle of cutlery against glass. Jack looked round as Matt called, 'Can I have everyone's attention, please. We've an announcement to make … Dad?'

An hour or so earlier, Jack and his boys had agreed this afternoon was as good a time as any to announce their plans. Everyone they cared about was there, and Tony Hayes' presence ensured that the news would be broadcast around the rest of Baronsmere and the neighbouring villages in no time.

Jack walked over to Matt and motioned to Luke to join them. It felt good to stand there with his sons beside him, Emer close at hand, and the sun shining down on their celebration.

'Thanks to everyone for coming,' he began. 'And thanks to Maggie and Claire for organising everything.'

'Hear, hear!' shouted Tim, putting an arm around Maggie and planting a kiss on her cheek.

'The boys and I have something to tell you,' Jack continued, 'and it might come as a bit of a shock.' He hesitated. 'We're leaving Baronsmere. Leaving England, in fact.'

'When?'

'Why?'

'Where are you going?'

'For good?'

'What about the house?'

That last question came from Barbara, and Jack decided to answer it first. 'The house is going to be in good hands – Claire is taking it over. She has some great plans for making it a short-term foster home, and Maggie will stay and help her – although the offer is there for them to come with us, whenever they want.'

'What a great idea!' said Barbara, giving Claire a hug. Claire flushed with all the sudden attention and Jack watched her anxiously. She should ultimately flourish without Richard, but the news that Gavin had decided to go with his father to Hong Kong had hit her hard. He hoped her new project would distract her until she was emotionally stronger.

'Where are you going, Jack?' asked Dave, who looked more than a little sad. They'd been friends since they were kids and Jack would miss him.

'I've bought a small hotel in Ireland – about ten miles from Glendalough in Wicklow,' Jack said. 'Before we went to France, we checked it out. Matt's going to help me run it, and Luke'—he put his arm round his younger son's shoulders—'well, Luke is going to study with the aim of eventually qualifying as a vet. So, those are our plans. And we hope you'll all visit us … at special rates of course.'

'Bags first visit!' cried Tim. 'You'll need help with the décor.'

'Not a chance!' responded Matt. 'I don't think the locals are ready for gold lamé seats and strobe lights yet.'

'What about you, Kate?' asked Barbara. 'Are you going, too?'

Kate nodded, and smiled at Luke. 'Yes, of course. Not right away, though. I'll finish my degree, and Abbie and I are going to share a flat in Manchester for a while. I'll miss him, but I want Luke to spend time with Jack and Matt and I don't want to distract him from his studies.'

'So,' said Jack, 'that's it really, except to say a big thank you to everyone for supporting us these last few months. We couldn't have got through them without you. Now – please – eat, drink, and be merry!'

Luke eased himself discreetly out of the circle of people surrounding Jack and clamouring for more details about the hotel. He preferred to let his father do the talking – he was still trying to come to terms with the dramatic changes in his life. He'd been stunned when Jack first suggested they move to Ireland – it seemed too good to be true. Perhaps things wouldn't work out, but he was determined to give it his best shot. A future was opening out before him and it felt good.

'Hello, you.'

Emer was holding a plate stacked with three hot dogs. 'Please tell me those aren't for me,' he said with a grin.

'Oh yes, they are. You've got to eat them – Maggie's orders.'

Luke gave a mock groan. 'She's always tryin' to feed me up. Matt says I should wear three T-shirts at once so she'll think I've put weight on.'

'You're looking well,' Emer told him.

'I feel well, Emer. The break was good.' The holiday had given him some much-needed time to sort out his feelings about Jack, and to come to terms with the nightmare his mother's life had been. Despair had loomed frighteningly close at times, but he'd eventually realised there was nothing else for him to do but soldier on and make something of himself, for her sake. This resolve, hard won, had finally brought him some sort of closure.

'So – how does it feel to be going home – this time, with your family?'

'Grand,' he said, looking across at his father and Matt

who were posing together for a photograph. 'It'll be good. You'll come to visit – soon – won't you?'

Luke had been touched by the way she had distanced herself from Jack for the past weeks – such a selfless gesture. He wanted nothing more than for her and Jack to become a permanent couple.

'For sure I'll visit,' Emer said. 'Once you're all settled in.'

Luke suddenly felt a surge of anxiety. 'We're doin' the right thing, aren't we, Emer? I feel bad that we'll be in Ireland and Mam'll be here … but Maggie and Claire have promised to look after her – well, you know, the grave.'

Emer's expression softened and he felt her deep affection for him. 'Luke, your mam would want you to do whatever makes you happy,' she said. 'She'll be with you anyway, wherever you go.'

Her words comforted him. Luke reached forward and gave her a hug. 'Thank you, Emer – for everything.'

She'd been there for him in the hospital when he'd needed reassurance, and she'd helped Jack piece together the past. She'd done her very best to make them both whole again. That father and son were now getting along was largely due to her. She was wonderful, and Luke loved her.

Emer held his shoulders gently, tears in her eyes. 'You did most of it yourself, Luke. And it took great courage. I'm so proud of you. You've come such a long way.'

Luke smiled and glanced over at Kate, who was bouncing Tony Hayes' toddler granddaughter on her lap. 'And the best is yet to come.'

He wished he could bottle this moment, keep it fresh forever. The warmth of the afternoon sun, the chatter of friends and family, the welcome future that beckoned. He silently absorbed it all then offered it up with love and gratitude to Annie Kiernan.

* * *

409

The afternoon slowly merged into evening at Jack's house by the lake. Emer watched the man she loved as he chatted and laughed. He seemed in his element, freed at last from the heavy weight of the Stewart family's obligations. They met up later by the drinks table on the patio, and Jack poured them both some wine.

'What a great day!' he said, his enthusiasm making him seem touchingly boyish.

'For sure,' Emer said. 'And you are going to be so missed when you go.'

'I'll miss them, too. But I'm looking forward to Ireland ... especially since you and I will finally be living in the same country.'

His words touched the chords of her passion, but she tried hard to stay focused. 'True, but – don't take this the wrong way, Jack – we need to wait. It's still on ice – for now.'

'Ice has a habit of melting,' said Jack, moving closer so that she could feel the warmth of his body.

'Just be patient.' Her advice was directed as much to herself as to Jack. 'You've got so much catching up to do with Luke. And you're still grieving for Annie.'

He sighed. 'I loved her, Emer, but she's gone and I did most of my grieving twenty years ago. I know what you're saying, but I'll never fully get over what happened and the circumstances of her leaving, even if we wait another twenty years.'

'It won't be that long, I promise. And it's more about Luke than it is about Annie. I just don't want you to have any distractions. Let him see he's a priority. Really get to know him ... Jack, what's going to happen to your father?'

'I'm taking legal advice. If I had my way, he'd be treated just like any other rapist, but it was more than twenty years ago and the key witness is dead. I don't know what's going to happen, but it could get messy when the Kiernans go to trial.

They're almost certain to talk. I'll try to go after Richard, too – for theft and forgery. Claire wants me to do that.' Jack sighed. 'I'm just going to take each day as it comes.'

Emer nodded. 'It's all you can do, I suppose.'

'I don't want to think about it, to be honest. It's bad enough that we're going to have to testify at the Kiernan's trial. It's going to be hard for Luke, especially. It's not something he wants to do at all.'

'Travellers are generally very loyal,' said Emer. 'It's a pity Luke's uncles weren't more typical.'

'Perhaps because of that, other Travellers will understand him testifying against them,' suggested Jack.

Emer nodded her agreement. 'How's Matt doing?'

'He's a good lad,' Jack told her. 'Grown up a lot in the past couple of months.'

Emer looked towards the lake where the young people were singing. Luke and Kate were holding hands while perched on Matt and Tim's shoulders. They were all punching the air as they sang the chorus of 'Hi Ho Silver Lining', and she watched as Luke launched into an impressive air guitar. It was a scene of friendship, happiness and love, and was a joy to witness. It was sobering to think they came so close to losing Luke.

'It was hard for Matt to learn what my father did,' continued Jack, 'but he knows Luke has suffered more, and he stays strong because of that. Once he'd only have thought about himself, but now he takes on board that it's been hard for me, too. I feel like we're a team again, which is great.'

He turned to face her. 'But about us, Emer – we're okay, aren't we?'

The anxiety in his voice was almost more than Emer could bear, and she had to reassure him. 'I love you, Jack Stewart. And if you still want me in a few months, I'll join you.'

'Oh, I don't think there's any doubt I'll still want you,' murmured Jack, leaning forward and kissing her tenderly on the mouth. For a moment, she felt the world around her spin. This man was in her blood now, a part of her that she couldn't – and didn't want to – resist.

'It's been a roller coaster, hasn't it?' commented Jack. 'But some good has come out of it. I may have lost my parents, but I've got another son, Matt's got a brother, and I've got you – the chance to be a real family unit.'

Emer held up her glass. 'To the future.'

'To the future,' echoed Jack, and their glasses came together like an omen of good fortune.

When Jack and Luke arrived at Baronswood churchyard that evening, the sun was still shining, but the yew trees cast patches of shadow on the grass and the graves.

Jack shivered despite his jacket. He remembered the day they'd lowered Annie's coffin into the cold, dark ground – he'd had to keep his emotions tightly in check, but still the misery of knowing Annie was gone, and the pain of the lost years, had threatened to overwhelm him. Now he was visiting her again, the sadness still there, but the circumstances so very different.

'Look, Jack,' said Luke. 'The stone's up now.' He moved forward quickly to Annie's grave and Jack followed. Luke knelt down and read out the words carved into the black marble stone.

In memory of
ANNIE KIERNAN STEWART
Beloved wife of Jack,
Loving mother of Luke and Matthew.
Taken too soon and greatly missed.
Never to be forgotten.

Jack had expected Luke to protest at the use of the Stewart name, but he'd said it was fine, and that, after all, Annie had been Jack's wife right to the end.

'It looks good,' said Luke, standing up.

'It does,' Jack agreed. Maybe one day when they too were dead and gone, when the Stewart name was not even a distant memory, somebody would read the words on the gravestone and wonder about this woman who had inspired such devotion.

Jack moved round the side, knelt down, and gently placed a bunch of lilies on the grave. They'd been Annie's favourite flower and Jack had carefully selected the mix of white, peach, pink and yellow. He trailed his fingers along the cool marble stone, choking with emotion, not trusting himself to speak. He turned to look at his son. The resemblance to Annie was so striking that it made his heart skip a beat. Tears welled in his eyes. 'I don't know how to … what to …' he murmured.

'It's okay, Jack,' said Luke. 'You don't have to say anything. Mam knows.'

Jack hoped that was true. That somewhere beyond the grave Annie finally understood the whole sad story, and was at peace. He slowly stood up, still feeling a little shaken.

'Can I have a few minutes alone with her?' Luke requested. 'To say goodbye.'

If anything, Luke was in a much better state than Jack. He looked centred, balanced somehow, as if he'd accepted that this was how things were. That you had to live with sad partings and farewells. Jack moved away from the grave and wandered around the side of the church to give his son some privacy.

Luke knelt down in front of the grave, gathering up some of the soil. It wasn't Irish earth, but it still came from a place that had known his mother. He looked around at the centuries-old church, the strong and steady trees, the sheltering wall. She would rest easy here. A blackbird trilled, as if reminding Luke he had things to say.

'I know everything now, Mam,' Luke began. 'Why you left. What you tried to keep from me.'

A gentle breeze plucked at the edges of the lily petals and they shimmered.

'Things are good now, Mam. There's Jack – and Matt and Kate and Emer. They'll help me. They'll take care of me so you don't have to worry.'

He could see Annie's face so clearly in his mind's eye, and she was smiling.

'I'm going home soon – to Ireland. But I'll be back to visit. And I'll make you proud of me, I promise.'

He gently replaced the soil. 'I'll miss you always, Mam. I'd swap everything in a heartbeat to have you back.' There were tears in his eyes but despite his grief, he would survive. It was all he could do for his mother now – be happy, make others happy, live a rich and full life.

Luke stayed a while longer among the lengthening shadows, and then stood up as he heard Jack's footsteps on the gravel. A moment later, he felt his father's hand on his shoulder. They didn't speak. There was no need for words. Father and son were going home, united in the love they both felt for Annie Stewart.

As they left, the silence settled slowly back, broken only by a lone blackbird singing its heart out in the peace of Baronswood churchyard.

About the Author

Isabella Connor is the pen name for
Liv Thomas and Val Olteanu.

www.facebook.com/isabella.connor.hartswood.hill
Website: www.blog.isabellaconnor.com

Liv Thomas was born and raised in the South of England.
She always had the dream of becoming a writer, but never
had the confidence to pursue it completely. After positive
responses to Lord of the Rings fan-fiction, she decided it
was time to make the dream a reality.

Wife and mum, Liv works for the NHS, and is employed
at the hospital which first featured in Channel 4's One
Born Every Minute. Liv has travelled extensively, and as
far afield as the United States and the Caribbean, without
setting foot on an aeroplane as she has a fear of flying.

Reading tastes vary from contemporary women's fiction to
works by Dean Koontz and Terry Pratchett, with Lord of
the Rings and Harry Potter thrown in for good measure.
Anything with an Irish theme will find itself on the bookshelf. (Or on the Kindle).

www.twitter.com/Livbet

Valerie Olteanu grew up in Scotland, and her childhood ambitions were to travel and to be a writer. After studying English and Art History at the University of Glasgow, she moved to London where she worked in the Literature Department of the Arts Council England.

Some years later, she decided to teach English and see the world. She lived and worked in Croatia, the West Bank, and Mexico, before settling with her husband in Canada. She is currently an adult educator in Burnaby, British Columbia.

More from Choc Lit

If you enjoyed Isabella's story, you'll enjoy the rest of
our selection. Here's a sample:

A Stitch in Time
Amanda James

**A stitch in time saves nine …
or does it?**

Sarah Yates is a thirty-
something history teacher,
divorced, disillusioned and
desperate to have more
excitement in her life. Making
all her dreams come true seems
about as likely as climbing
Everest in stilettos.

Then one evening the doorbell rings and the handsome and
mysterious John Needler brings more excitement than Sarah
could ever have imagined. John wants Sarah to go back in
time …

Sarah is whisked from the Sheffield Blitz to the suffragette
movement in London to the Old American West, trying
to make sure people find their happy endings. The only
question is, will she ever be able to find hers?

Visit www.choc-lit.com for more details
including the first two chapters and
reviews, or simply scan barcode using
your mobile phone QR reader.

The Silent Touch of Shadows

Christina Courtenay

Festival of Romance

Winner of the 2012 Best Historical Read from the Festival of Romance

What will it take to put the past to rest?

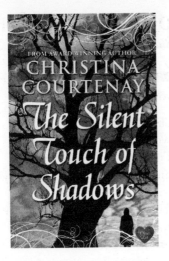

Professional genealogist Melissa Grantham receives an invitation to visit her family's ancestral home, Ashleigh Manor. From the moment she arrives, life-like dreams and visions haunt her. The spiritual connection to a medieval young woman and her forbidden lover have her questioning her sanity, but Melissa is determined to solve the mystery.

Jake Precy, owner of a nearby cottage, has disturbing dreams too, but it's not until he meets Melissa that they begin to make sense. He hires her to research his family's history, unaware their lives are already entwined. Is the mutual attraction real or the result of ghostly interference?

A haunting love story set partly in the present and partly in fifteenth century Kent.

Visit www.choc-lit.com for more details including the first two chapters and reviews, or simply scan barcode using your mobile phone QR reader.

Dream a Little Dream
Sue Moorcroft

What would you give to make your dreams come true?

Liza Reece has a dream. Working as a reflexologist for a troubled holistic centre isn't enough. When the opportunity arises to take over the Centre she jumps at it. Problem is, she needs funds, and fast, as she's not the only one interested.

Dominic Christy has dreams of his own. Diagnosed as suffering from a rare sleep disorder, dumped by his live-in girlfriend and discharged from the job he adored as an Air Traffic Controller, he's single-minded in his aims. He has money, and plans for the Centre that don't include Liza and her team.

But dreams have a way of shifting and changing and Dominic's growing fascination with Liza threatens to reshape his. And then it's time to wake up to the truth ...

Visit www.choc-lit.com for more details including the first two chapters and reviews, or simply scan barcode using your mobile phone QR reader.

Move Over Darling
Christine Stovell

When is it time to stop running?

Coralie Casey is haunted by her past. Deciding it's time for a fresh start, she sets up 'Sweet Cleans', a range of natural beauty and cleaning products, and escapes to Penmorfa, a quiet coastal village in west Wales.

Gethin Lewis thinks he's about to put his home village Penmorfa behind him for good. Now an internationally-acclaimed artist living in New York, he just has to return one last time to wind up his father's estate.

But the village soon disrupts their carefully laid plans. As truths are uncovered which threaten to split the community apart, Gethin is forced to question his real reasons for abandoning Penmorfa, and Coralie is made to face the fact that some stains just won't go away.

Visit www.choc-lit.com for more details including the first two chapters and reviews, or simply scan barcode using your mobile phone QR reader.

Up Close
Henriette Gyland

Too close for comfort …

When Dr Lia Thompson's grandmother dies unexpectedly, Lia is horrified to have to leave her life in America and return to a cold and creaky house in Norfolk. But as events unfold, she can't help feeling that there is more to her grandmother's death than meets the eye.

Aidan Morrell is surprised to see Lia, his teenage crush, back in town. But Aidan's accident when serving in the navy has scarred him in more ways than one, and he has other secrets which must stay hidden at all costs, even from Lia.

As Lia comes closer to uncovering the truth, she is forced to question everything she thought she knew. In a world of increasing danger, is Aidan someone she can trust?

Visit www.choc-lit.com for more details including the first two chapters and reviews, or simply scan barcode using your mobile phone QR reader.

Out of Sight Out of Mind

Evonne Wareham

Everyone has secrets. Some are stranger than others.

Madison Albi is a scientist with a very special talent – for reading minds. When she stumbles across a homeless man with whom she feels an inexplicable connection, she can't resist the dangerous impulse to use her skills to help him.

J is a non-person – a vagrant who can't even remember his own name. He's got no hope, until he meets Madison. Is she the one woman who can restore his past?

Madison agrees to help J recover his memory, but as she delves deeper into his mind, it soon becomes clear that some secrets are better off staying hidden.

Is J really the man Madison believes him to be?